The Furies

By: Corey Croft

FLY PELICAN PRESS

Published by: Fly Pelican Press

Vancouver BC, Canada V6E 1N9

www.flypelicanpress.com

Registration number: 1157856

ISBN E-BOOK: 978-1-9990730-3-9

ISBN PAPERBACK: 978-1-9990730-4-6

First edition

Cover illustrations: Spencer Croft

Photograph: Winston Fong

Interior design: Indie Publishing Group

Editing: Syndey Triggs

Dedicated to Blair Mercer.

AKA Mr. Merc. AKA Mercakahn. AKA Plair E. Dercer. AKA One of the strongest motherfuckers that I ever met and will ever know.

The fact that we're still alive means they haven't killed us yet. Let them try.

It's love always, Brother.

Suckers I clobber, because my town is full of cops and robbers

You're not promised tomorrow in this little shop of horrors

...You lose, cause I got the ill street blues

-Kool G Rap

CONTENTS

ST. VINCE

"WAKE UP, HOMIE!" A playful, heavily French-accented voice stirred Cava from his deep slumber; he didn't have to open his eyes to recognize his best friend, his brother-in-arms: Luc Kalou.

"Jesus, Luc. What time is it?" He rolled into an obstruction on his left, then another on his right. His eyes still closed, he stretched his legs and rubbed his dry lids, feeling the welcome ache of his still-growing limbs.

"It's time for you to get ready, Cava. You know what day it is. You better get ready!"

Cava opened his eyes to find Luc standing astride him. "Are you standing on my bed with your nasty-ass kicks on, man? Get your skinny punk-ass off my blanket! My own gramma would break your ankles."

Luc closed the basement window he'd just crawled through.

"I took them off," Luc retorted, hopping off Cava's futon and collecting his pristine, white basketball shoes. "I'm not a punk, man. I'm not Rat-Fink."

"Yeah, right." Cava sat up and looked at his alarm. 9am. "Man, I just left you, like, six hours ago. Wasted. How are you awake? Why are you so... up?"

"It's Saint Vince, yo! I could hardly sleep at all last night! All of Fury will be in New Am! We own that city today!"

Saint Vincent's Day was the official end of summer holiday for the citizens of the Quad-Cities, or, as the locals called them, the Four Fingers. The people of all four boroughs (New Amsterdam, Vincennes, Figaro, and Fury) descended on the centre of New Am for a day-long celebration capped off with a 'world famous' fireworks display. Held on the first Sunday of September, it was the swan song of summer break for high school kids, who, almost as a rite of passage, attended the spectacle and then showed up for the first day of school as disheveled as possible. Of course, showing up at all was the hardest part.

"You were makin' out with *La Rosee*, hmm?" Luc leered at Cava, his shoes still held in his folded arms. "You take her home? I don't see her little blonde head and snaggle-tooth up in here."

"Nah," Cava grunted. "The usual, the same old shit, man. She said that I was nice and that she thought of me more as a friend than a... a bang. Goddamn."

"*Mon frère*, let me say that... she's not right for you. She's like a snake. And you, you're like a little hamster. You'd do better to meet a girl at the fireworks, or school, or somewhere. Anywhere."

"I mean... maybe?" Cava answered slowly. "But, I've been crushing on her for like, ever, man." His eyes floated skyward. "She's... just such a babe."

"She's okay. Great body... great damned body. That ass is *sick*. But she isn't a... trustable broad. And *franchement*? Not a great lay, man."

"Well, I need to get laid at least once before I can decide what a great lay is and what a great lay isn't. Besides, if she's not so great, why do you always sleep with her?"

Cava asked the last question with irritation. Since they'd met four years before, Cava had been drawn to Rosee. He couldn't explain it, but he pined for her. She would seem interested, but then reject him. They'd hang out, just the two of them, have a brown bottle and some herb, and talk and laugh and flirt, but when he thought that the time was right, she'd shoot him down. Sometimes, like last night, she'd come on strong, make all the advances, and then change like the wind. Only hours earlier, they'd ventured to Cava's window and kissed and touched each other for tantalizing minutes before she'd asked to go into his room. Cava had climbed in first, but when he turned to take Rosee's hand to help her through, he saw that she'd she slipped away.

Despite Cava's feelings, it was Luc who seemed destined to maintain a passionate, antagonistic relationship with Rosee. Cava tried hard not to blame him. He was who he was, after all. Nor could he blame Rosee. Cava knew that he couldn't trick, or will, or persuade Rosee to grant him her affections. When she and Luc got tender in front of him, most often from booze, Cava would leave to hang out with someone else. Cava had learned to hide his emotions and take council from his other best friend, Sally. He was unable to fully appreciate Sally's wisdom; he'd learned to shield his emotions but not defeat them.

"I dunno, man... She just... she just irritates me. She pisses me off. She gets under my skin... And I love it." Luc snapped his fingers. "That's it, man. You have to be an asshole to her. Like her old man and psycho brother. She wants a guy that might slap her or call her a bitch. You're so nice to her. I worry that when she's had a run through all the other guys, she'll come crawling to you, and you'll take her in like a stray kitten."

"I might..."

"I know." Luc sighed, then brightened. "Also, I do just love sex. You'll see, we'll give that V-card of yours to someone this year. It's way overdue!"

Cava's cheeks reddened. He wasn't the *only* virgin he knew, but his best friend was almost out of fingers with which to count his conquests. That included Cava's crush. He hated being teased about it, but what could he do? There was a surgery to fix it, but the doctor didn't follow him through the window. He was hostage to Luc's endless stories, brandished about with the cocky pride that was part of his charm. Cava wanted to be able to throw in a story of his own, too.

"I smell it, it's happening soon." Luc sniffed Cava's still uncovered chest.

"Fuck off, man," Cava laughed. *Goddamn Luc*, he thought. *I can't stay mad at this guy for a second.*

"Okay... I actually smell coffee and bacon in Mrs. Cavanaugh's kitchen. Get ready fast and I'll save you half your breakfast."

Cava was alone. As he stood up to pick out his clothes, he thought about Rosee and why he was so smitten with someone who pummeled his self-esteem so regularly. She'd always reminded him of a fox: pretty and gritty, small and combative, and the shape of her mouth and sharp chin, which seemed to smile and snarl simultaneously. Could it just be that she was *there*? That by being a hot girl in the crew, she attracted him for reasons he couldn't explain? Were they reasons he made up to justify his attraction? He thought for a second that he might not be the only one, that maybe other boys longed for her the way he did.

"Aww man... When does Sally get home?" Cava muttered to himself before leaving his basement room and trudging up the three flights to the shower awaiting him.

* * *

The Cavanaugh house was the same as the Kalou house, which was the same as the Doktor house, which was the same as everyone else's house in the Oxford Projects, one of many late 70s attempts to escape rising rents in the cities. The houses were clumsy stacks rising from the basements (traditionally occupied by the eldest kids and laundry) with four narrow floors up to the master bedrooms, where the adults were found. Each had a plinth of concrete as a backyard, which abutted the neighbouring lots and barely had space for a small table and a chair or two. A spindly row of hedges pretended to provide privacy from the path behind.

The Oxford projects were infested with the children of young, blue-collar and immigrant families. Cava's family had come from the Maritimes and the Kalous from the Haitian community in Montreal. Ivan Doktor and his wife were gypsies, originally from Romania, or Bulgaria, or Hungary, or wherever the patriarch felt a glimmer of attachment to on any given day. Rat-Fink's parents, the Kosh clan, had moved from Crimea in the 80s.

* * *

Cava slid down staircases in socked feet, dressed but still moist from the shower. The conversation between Luc and the Cavanaughs paused abruptly. "You pay for the water around here, Quinn?" Nora growled.

"No, Ma. You and Dad do."

"What takes you so long? You're not that tall or that wide, are you?"

Luc and Cava's father, Joe, exchange playful smirks as Cava seated himself on the same chair as Luc. Half the bacon, half the toast, half the hash browns and one egg were pushed to one side along with a whole cooked tomato and a full cup of black coffee.

"You Irish and your cooked tomatoes," Luc said mockingly. "You know that's pretty gross, right?"

"Pipe down, young fella," Joe responded. "I don't want to hear about your plantains again."

"Yeah, but they're sweet, easy to cook, and don't look like a stab wound," Luc insisted.

"Your mouth will get your nose broken, Lucky Luc," Nora said. "Quinny, you'll be up for school tomorrow, won't you?"

Cava was trying to fit all the remaining items onto his slice of bread to eat as a sandwich, slowly and methodically. "Why do you even have to ask?"

She tilted her eyes towards Luc, who was grinning dopily with cloudy eyes and tapping his fingers against the kitchen table.

Joe, Nora, Cava, and Luc shared the table with Henry, nervous and excited about his first day of Grade 8.

"Why can't I come with you, Quinn? I'm going to Bendis this year, too!" Henry's summer-long pestering to Cava about high school life hadn't even started to abate.

"Well, I can't watch out for you there… There's too many people, and I don't want you to get hurt. It gets pretty rough." Sensing his mother's worried gaze, Cava quickly added, "not rough, just… It's pandemonium."

"We can go on a family outing; you, me, and your mother," Joe said calmly.

"No way, man! Only nerds go with their mommies and daddies!" Henry rolled his eyes.

"Listen," Luc said. "Mr. and Mrs. Cava, no one is embarrassed to be seen with you. All the homies love you guys. Especially you, Nora. You make those bomb-ass cookies, and this breakfast, *magnifique*." He then turned to Henry. "Young Cavs, you ain't ready. There's a lot of craziness and, if you go, it should be with'dem," he pointed to the elders. "My brothers didn't take me until I was old enough, and when you're old enough, Cava and I will take you."

"Young Cavs? Dope! Alright, deal," Henry said, pacified.

Luc looked at the clock on the oven. "Oh shi-shoot! We gotta get to the Bench. You know Sally's home, right? She's coming."

"Really? She's back from Europe? I figured…" Cava trailed off.

"Quinn Padraig Cavanaugh! You didn't even know that Sally, who might as well be your sister, was home? What kind of boy did I raise to ignore the people closest to him?"

"Well, I guess I'll get to see her now, okay? But don't call her my sister, Ma. It's weird."

"He's right, those two might get married one day," Joe said, half-jokingly. "If you see Dok, tell him to bring the Dobro and some moonshine, boys."

The boys slid on their shoes—Jordans for Luc and skateboard sneakers for Cava—and hurried down the steps, leaving Nora to berate Joe for wanting to drink and strum guitars on a Sunday.

"Dude," Cava said, "your brothers took you to St. Vince when you were like, eight."

"Seven," Luc said as he threw his backpack over his shoulder. "Young Cavs don't need to know that." A smile crept over Luc's face. "Your parents still want you to be with Sally, huh? That's cute. And… what's that word? A-stute?"

"Yeah, whatever, man. You got your stuff?" Cava tried to shake it off as the boys neared the Bench.

"Ink pens, eighth of bud, two micks of brown," he slid one into Cava's sack to polite acknowledgement. "Long-sleeve, and the spiked-knuckles… the *snukts,* I calls 'em, that Fabi made me. You?"

Cava shuffled his contents. "My pipe, a hoodie, a white sharpie, two bottles of clear," one of which he handed to Luc, to a nod of acceptance, "pack of darts, papers…"

"No weapon?" Luc stopped him.

"Nah man, I hate that shit," Cava started, "can't we just have a good time?"

"Of course, but you know this thing. Shit pops off, son. Cliff or Finkie will have something, I'm sure. Hell, even that little hood-mouse Rosee will have a cutter or something. She's always got a blade on her."

* * *

Cava and Luc could see the familiar figures of their friends as they approached the Bench: a simple wooden table and two benches bolted to the ground. It was the traditional meeting point for the Ox kids. Even kids from other projects knew its name and location at the nexus of all the little paths and lanes of Ox. Thick conifers blocked any casual peeping from nosey neighbours, while the central location offered a vantage point to all the entrances of the Ox, which made it easy to stash contraband or steal over a fence when necessary.

The boys were first spotted by the giant Cliff, seated on the table with his feet on a bench. He raised a tall can of malt liquor above his head and bellowed, "Fury-Us!"

Rat-Fink, or Marek Kosh according to the attendance sheet, looked up briefly, then continued to write his tag, *Krshr*, on dozens of name-tag stickers. Rosee looked up and smiled, a cigarette dangling between her lips, then continued rolling a pile of joints. The last to look up was Salomea Doktor, standing with her hands on the straps of her backpack underneath a low-hanging, chartreuse tree limb. The boys slowed down, their eyes growing wider as Sally came into focus. "Dude, what happened to Sally?" whispered Luc in astonishment.

Sally had left Fury before the second semester of Grade 11 as an honour roll student, volunteer, superior volleyball and soccer player, and fluent speaker of several languages. Despite her accomplishments, she'd always been ridiculed for her appearance. An early growth spurt had left her far taller than all the other girls, and puberty had only made her difference worse by endowing her with a thick unibrow, greasy skin with dreadful acne, hair with untameable curls, gangly limbs, and a nose that jutted from her face like an isosceles triangle. She looked like a cross between Olive Oyl and a starving coyote, smelling a bit more like the latter. Cava had always been protective of Sally, and the only fights he'd ever started had been in her defense. Such heroism, of course, only provoked the kids to turn on him, too, taunting him about his 'love' for the ugly girl. He hated it, but he tried never to let it show as he dried Sally's tears with his sleeve.

Now, the boys barely recognized the young woman that was standing under the tree. Her pale green eyes shone like jade against her smooth bronzed skin. Her masses of wild curls had been tamed into a gleaming black ponytail, pulled back tight to reveal the now-fuller contours of her cheekbones. Her nose seemed graceful and somehow noble, like an impala.

Luc raced towards her. "Damn, damn, damn! You look fine as a motherfucker, girl. *Shit*!" Holding his arm against hers, he continued. "Damn girl, you almost as dark as me!"

"Luc wit da C," Sally began while accepting a hug. "I missed you! Have you been staying out of trouble?"

"Nah!" Luc said, "ha! I been having fun, baby!"

Cava came up and noticed Sally's gaze shift to him. The two friends stood still, momentarily unable to maintain eye contact.

"Well," Luc pushed Cava into Sally. "Give her a hug!"

The two hugged each other lightly, then sunk into one another's arms, pressing their entire bodies together. "I missed you," they said at the same time.

"Jinx," said Cliff, burping and already bleary eyed, taking another swig of his beer.

"Damn man, you drunk already?" Luc started. "Ain't even noon!"

"Goddamn right. I got my aunt watching the kids and today is *my* summer vacation," Cliff said with a broad smile on his round face.

Sally and Cava were still locked in an embrace, quietly sniffing each other, appreciating both the familiarity of old scents and gestures and the changes in their newly matured frames.

"All done," Rosee said as she lit one of the joints, brushing the stems and crumbs off her thin, white thigh. "Jesus, you two need a room? Fags."

Cava and Sally silently released each other, both slightly flushed.

"Alright, everybody got their bags? Booze? Loot? We good?" Luc asked.

"Yeah, I got my stuff," Cliff said.

Rat-Fink nodded with his head still down, and Rosee mumbled her assent as she puffed the herb, sealing a tear in the joint with a finger of saliva.

"Every fucking time!" Luc said as he was passed the joint and the lighter. "You roll too tight, girl. *Way* too tight for a Fury girl!"

As Rosee went to punch Luc below the belt, he shifted his hips back, taking a big pull.

"I got my some of my dad's moonshine, but we'll need a chaser," Sally said, waving her hand to refuse the joint.

"Ooh, Dok's special reserve!" Luc laughed, "you got a pillow for when that shit sleeps the crew, Sal?"

They passed the joint, leaving Sally out, and headed to board the Quad-City Express at the infamous Fury Exchange, now rebranded as River City Central. Passing the Doktor house, they weren't surprised to see Sally's father Ivan and Joe peering under the hood of one of Ivan's many 'projects,' drinking glasses of moonshine and orange juice.

"Hey, hey, Salomea! You kids be good, hey?" Ivan shouted as they all waved. "Quinny, you take care of my baby bird! But, no babies of your own yet! I'm a doctor, remember. I'll know!"

Ivan was no doctor, though he claimed medical expertise, experience, and talent passed down from a long line of healers and surgeons. His wife, Danuta, who shot down all of his tall tales except the one about having kidnapped her to be his bride, maintained that he'd changed his name to make people believe that he was a doctor when he emigrated.

As the kids continued their way down Eckersley towards O'Connor (X and O, as they called the intersection), Cava walked beside Cliff Paul, who was two years his senior and massive. Having been held back two years, Cliff had left high school early to care for his much younger twin siblings after his father was incarcerated and his mother succumbed to the bottle. Aware of his family's troubled history and his responsibility to the twins, Cliff rarely drank these days.

"So, you got the day off, Cliff?" Cava asked.

"Yup, my aunt has the kids for the night. Be nice for them to get away from our damned window. They see too much shit. I really gotta fix the goddamned TV."

As the boys passed Cliff's apartment, he peered up at the darkened window. "It's hard, man. I can't even leave them kids alone with Mom, and my auntie has enough shit going on. But I love them, you know? The only reason I didn't end up like my old man is because I don't want the same for Lightning and Thunder." Cliff took a sip from his tall can and offered it to Cava.

"Nah," Cava waved it off, "I'm good. Those *are* some badass names though. Yours, right?"

"Yup. You know what's really fucked up? Mom named them Misty and Cliff. She forgot that she already had a kid named Cliff. So, I had to step in and celebrate the culture a little bit."

"How long have you guys been in that apartment?"

"Three years, maybe? Crackheads and fiends everywhere. It's a full-time job making sure no one kicks the door in. You can smell the meth cooking, you can hear the hookers bringing dudes in all night… It's not cool. I mean, the trailer park was no heaven, but at least you had your own walls and roof. At least when a lab exploded there, you didn't share a wall."

"Word, man. So… you bring any weapons?"

"Ha!" Cliff crushed his tall boy like a tissue. "You think I need a weapon? Weapons are for pussies. What do I look like? Rat-Fink?"

Fink glanced up quickly, spat, and slapped one of his stickers on a lamppost.

Fink and Rosee walked along, not saying much. Rosee was fairly new to the crew, but Luc and Cava had been trying to ditch Fink for years. He seemed oblivious to their growing dislike for him and continued to hang around like a virus.

"Stinks like piss around here," Fink remarked.

"Smells like this every summer, especially when it doesn't rain," Rosee replied.

Rosee and Fink attempted to join the other conversations, but Rosee found Cliff boring and couldn't bring herself to compete with Sally for Luc's attention. Meanwhile, Fink was above the flirty chatter between Luc and Sally and couldn't stand Cliff. So, the pairs stayed as they were.

"Look at all those damned gooks," Rosee said. "Trading shitty darts for a VCR. Screaming at the top of their lungs. My daddy says that they aren't even here legally."

Rat-Fink nodded. "My pops says that the Flips, the Chinks, and the Nammers are taking all the jobs at the docks, taking money under the table, and totally fucking up the game."

Luc walked with his arm around Sally's shoulder as the two laughed about their summer adventures.

"It was crazy," Luc began. "I had community service for tagging, but instead of making me scrub walls, they sent me to an animal shelter. I did nothing but play with dogs. They even gave me a key! So I did what anyone would do: stole a shit ton of K, sold it to Tic-Tax, and bought me some new Jordans and a dope lid!"

"K?" asked Sally.

"Ketamine, baby doll! I think he gypped me, but whatever. Found mon-ay! I meant jewed, not gypped, sorry."

"Oh, Luc. Would you please stop looking for trouble?"

"Bah, I'd already be with JJ right now if I weren't so slick. Don't worry, *chérie*. I'm straight."

"Hmm. When does JJ come home anyway? Soon?"

"Oh, yeah! He *and* Fabi are both coming home!" Luc squeezed Sally's shoulders tight and she pushed him off. "The fabulous Kalou brothers will be reunited!"

Janjak, Luc's oldest brother, was serving a sentence out East for his part in a criminal network. Fabienne, the middle brother, had been sent up North by the Singh family to try to carve out an operation in Gainsborough. Luc was eager for their return, especially now that he felt he was old enough to contribute and make them as proud of him as he was of them.

"You're excited, eh?"

"Are you kidding?" Luc picked up the sunglasses that had fallen off his head from his outburst. "I've got you back, Sal! I've got brand new, all-white Js on my feet and Scotty Summas on my face! We have the fireworks and the beach! And soon, I'll have my brothers! We could run this town! Man, I miss them…"

"I bet they're looking forward to seeing their young brother just as much!"

"So, how was Europe, baby doll?" Luc asked. "I can't believe you ain't said nothing about that yet."

"It was good. I got to play sports, practice different languages, and see so many beautiful towns and monuments. I traveled. It was great."

"So, you got a boyfriend?"

Cava looked back at them from the front of the crew.

"Umm…" Sally dropped her head, put her hands in her pockets, and went silent.

As the kids approached the station, they joined a clamorous swarm of teenagers, adults, and families shoving their way onto the platform. Conversations stopped as the kids grew more serious about pushing their way through the crowd. The police formed several strong lines in an effort to limit the number of passengers pouring onto the trains, all running in a non-stop flow from the station. Those foolish enough to wear bandanas over their faces or even just pull their hoods too far forward were plucked from the mob and had their bags searched.

The group moved as a unit and the pairs dissolved. Cava now stuck close to Sally, their forearms touching. Cliff shoved the crowds aside easily to follow Rosee's mercurial zigzagging through small openings in the mob. Fink was on his own as Luc's popularity drew him to different clusters of friends.

"Yo, Luc wit da C! What's goodie?" a voice called from the top of the stairs.

"Yo, Apache! What up, son? Good look with them dunks, Martian!" Luc hollered to the platform. "Fury!"

"Us!" The well-known call and response began and was quickly taken up by the rest of Luc's crew, as well as nearly everyone else from 12-to-20-something. It was a calling card for Fury's younger population. In the dark setting of parks, at the New Am Hammers games, and anywhere else that the Furians might turn up together, one side would yell "Fury" and the others would roar "Us" back.

The line moved surprisingly quickly. People were hustled aboard the trains and the crew was shoved on by the teeming crowd behind them.

Fink grabbed a seat in the back, throwing his backpack beside him. Cava and Sally had linked arms and took the seats in front of Fink.

"Watch it, asshole!" Cliff warned a bleary-eyed man who'd shoved Rosee a little too violently for his liking.

"Fuck you, chug."

Cliff threw his closed fist into the man's chest and his shoulders nearly touched. The crew backed up, allowing him to land, crumpled and fetus-like, on the floor. Cliff moved Fink's bag and took the seat next to him, while Rosee stood and moved coquettishly in front of Cava. Luc eased himself through the crowd, handing out high-fives and greetings to friends and strangers alike.

As the train pulled out, the smell of weed became pervasive and the cacophony continued with chatter, laughter, and friendly cursing. Cans cracked and bottles popped open to the hiss of carbonation, and the scratching of lighter flints added a hint of regular percussion. The young Furians had packed the last car instinctively, knowing that no one would complain about the sounds and smells.

Cava peered back at the River City Tower project. It was a massive undertaking known as the Singh-scraper, after Jack Singh: Fury businessman, entrepreneur, investor, and father of one of the most infamous drug lords in the city. He'd always thought that it looked like a giant middle-finger, a big 'fuck you' to the Quad Cities, which needed shelters and social programs, not ostentatious displays of wealth. But, also, a 'fuck you' to the locals returning from their jobs or visits to the city.

"Fuck you for trying to leave, you'll always be back! Welcome to Fury, bitches!"

Cava loved his city and had the pride of a people who found an *esprit de corps* within a fraternity of fellow outcasts who chose hubris over humiliation. People who left Fury and never returned were vilified with the reflexive solidarity of an isolated tribe. Cava, who'd never been outside the Quad, was torn between his loyalty to Fury and his fascination with everywhere else. He wanted to nibble at Sally's ear and ask about her trip, but he was made shy by her magnificent blossoming and ashamed by his envy of her experiences. He secretly wanted to give the 'fuck you' finger back to the Towers and explore the world, returning with his mind and imagination quenched by visions of London, Cairo, Montevideo, or wherever else the winds carried him.

"What are you thinking, Quinn?" Sally asked.

"Ah, nothing much." Cava's gaze remained fixed on the window as the skyscraper began to shrink. "Just that…"

"Fury!" Luc yelled, cupping his mouth with one hand and hanging from the upper hand rail with the other.

"Us!" the entire train responded, so loud that the windows shook.

THE QUAD CITY EXPRESS

LUC WAS UNABLE to stay seated on any ride he could avoid being buckled into. He was a spitfire, as the teachers called him; his restless energy, lack of self-restraint, and contempt for rules sparked into constant creativity; his fierce loyalty, wild humour, and dark good looks gave him an almost supernatural charm. He created new slang just by talking, and had created a line of clothing after accidentally spilling paint on a white shirt. He could make a propeller hat look cool if he wanted to.

Luc swung from the handrails and bounced around the car, hitting on girls and joking with guys.

"Yo, Luc, you dropping your line this year?" asked one.

"Maybe. Depends how much math those fuckers give me. I've got a new way to sew pockets into jeans and shoe tongues. Add that to the shirts and socks, and all I need to do is find a printing company that won't stick me. When I get that, I'll put you on."

Prolific with a needle and thread, Luc had quickly branched out from a line of colourful shirts—starting when he'd worn the painted accident to school—to designing clothes with secret pockets for weed and weapons. He silkscreened shirts celebrating his city and took ink pens to plain white shoes to create elaborate, custom motifs. His art was evident on massive murals throughout the city, and he planned to make a line of graffiti artist apparel. He also sold weed disguised in empty cigarette tubes, mainly to smoke the profits.

"Yo, Cliff, how fucked up you getting today, son?"

"Man, I'm good. I know how to hit my stride. When you guys are all puking and seeing stars, Imma look the same way at midnight as I do now. Ain't gotta worry about no kids, no nothing." Cliff cracked another beer.

"Finkie, what you got in that heavy ass bag?"

"The goods," Fink responded unenthusiastically as he scrawled his text onto a window with a lava rock. "Some paint pens, sand gloves, bear spray…"

"What?!" Cliff grabbed the bag. "Look at this little fucker. Motherfucking bear-scare! He's got a lead pipe, and what's this? A bent fork made into a punching spike? A Rambo… and the lunch his mommy packed."

The kids laughed as Fink shrugged off Cliff's rifling of his bag's contents. "Whatever man, I'm ready… And I won't be hungry."

"Man, you're a scared little white boy, hmm?"

"I got spray, too, and a couple knives," Rosee said. "I'll fuck whoever tries some punk shit up… I ain't going down like that."

"Yeah, I got a couple things… Damn… you're a goddamn hoodmouse," Luc said. "Sal, you got anything?"

Sally shook her head and huddled closer to Cava. The others continued to heckle Fink, who simply shrugged. Sally was telling Cava about the old architecture in Europe, how it made Vincennes seem so new, and how the people and food were so different. Cava listened, asking questions to avoid talking about his own comparatively lacklustre year. "Have you been working out?" Sally asked, and almost under her breath, added, "you look… bigger."

Cava flushed. Sally's own transformation had changed their previous dynamic. "Just the usual rugby and soccer… I dunno. Maybe a little?"

Rosee, alarmed at the flirtation, sat herself on Cava's lap and threw her arm around his neck. "Oh, he's *much* bigger than the last time you saw him. Way stronger, too."

"There she goes," Luc said to Cliff quietly as they tittered.

"He's more *fine* every day," Rosee locked eyes with Sally until she sunk and pressed herself tightly against the window. Satisfied with Sally's diffidence, Rosee leapt off Cava and straightened herself out. Perturbed, Cava still admired Rosee's petite, voluptuous frame dressed in tiny black denim shorts and a bikini-top under a white camisole. He wondered yet again, *why*? Why did he not see the danger Luc and Sally warned him about? And why could they not see the vulnerable girl beneath her tough bravado?

Rosee had already been embroiled in things that most people, even in Fury, go their entire lives without having to endure. The stories she'd told Cava when they were alone moved him to deep sympathy and anger. The assaults on her tiny body incensed him, and those feelings were heightened by the laconic, aloof manner in which she described them. Before being sent to jail, her brother had made her walk the street, using her as a foil to loot the Johns that took her around the corner. Eventually, she was used to lure a rival who ended up being kidnapped. The finger he lost wound up in a box in her room; she'd kept it until the smell became too much.

Many times, Cava had offered to help her; to be her boyfriend and to let her stay with him, safe and protected. She refused his kindness, however, saying that she already had Cliff, who annoyed her with his guardianship, and just wanted the freedom to do whatever she pleased. Usually, Cava's attempts at chivalry were followed by one of her self-destructive disappearances from school and the crew to sleep with someone, anyone, else.

Still, Cava both yearned for and pitied Rosee. He wished that he could share his healthier family life with her, and show her what safety and love were. But, Nora thought Rosee was an irreformable tramp, and Joe thought she would be more problems than peaches for his eldest son.

* * *

The train continued its raucous jaunt through the Four Fingers; through the gentrifying, brownstone Vincennes, the sleepier, seaside Figaro, onto the final stops in the cosmopolitan New Amsterdam. Each stop in these cities produced a similar episode. The cars were packed like cigarettes in a factory-fresh seal as they left the Fury station, with little room to pick up any passengers by the second stop. Furians knew to board at the first station, River City Central, as the resulting chaos increased station by station.

Residents of the other, more prosperous Fingers referred to the less privileged, less educated Furians as riffraff, hood-rats, and most disparagingly, 'Furies.' Like tornadoes tearing through the platforms, train after train wreaked the same anarchy each time the doors slid open and allowed the free-riding Furians to insult and threaten the awaiting crowd. Security and police forces tried to ensnare the most menacing actors who let their guard down. But, mostly, they just aimed to calm the crowd, fizzing with agitation as each train passed, and assure them that, eventually, the Furies would taper out.

* * *

By the time the trains rolled into New Amsterdam, the passengers' initial excitement had melted into the general irritability that presages explosive hostility. A previously forgivable bump on the arm was exacerbated by claustrophobia and the growing ache to stretch, urinate, and escape from the smoky car. Adding to the danger, people who were already in a beef were as likely as not to have been sitting near each other on the train, and past feuds were set to reignite with the faintest spark.

Three stops away from their usual jump-off, Fink finished a beer and unthinkingly lobbed the empty aluminium can towards the *hoi polloi* crammed into the centre of the train. In a discussion about the correct way to roll, Luc and Rosee were discovering that Cava rolled joints 'backwards,' with the glue on the thumb-side. Cliff, in a happy stupor as welcome as a warm bath, was grinning and peering over Fink out the window.

"Who the fuck threw that?!" a voice boomed through the train. It was less a question than a war cry. Most passengers fell silent, though the debate about rolling carried on. The can had struck a man—not a youth, but a grown man who looked to be in his 50s. "I said, who the fuck domed me with this cheap fucking beer can? Who's drinking this Commie-looking fucking beer?"

The joint-rolling debate trailed off and the group shot sideways glances at Fink, who was staring blankly towards the sound of the anger. The man began to push and shove the mob aside, who shook and trembled in the aisle as he strode down the line like a titan. Glances turned into glares at the silent Fink, and the group shook their heads in disgust and dismay.

"Someone in the back, I seen it fly over my head," said a panicked voice. Further commotion vibrated through the mob in the aisle, now grabbing onto the handrails to avoid being cast aside.

Behind the man, more pushing and shoving began, followed by spitting, punching, kicking, and head-butting. The boiling point had been reached, and melees were now germinating from the slightest nudge or memory of what someone had done last winter.

As the man approached, the crew gazed upwards, lifting their eyes to the limit and craning their necks. The man towered over them, even over Cliff; a giant with salt and pepper hair and a beard, he resembled a mastodon cut from marble. He wore the patches and colours of the Dead Souls biker gang, and was flanked by equally patched associates. The man stepped close to Luc who, at nearly six feet, barely reached the top of the man's shoulder. Rosee had squeezed her way out of a potential sandwiching as the biker confronted Luc and the group.

"Which one of you little bitches hit me with the goddamn can?"

Keeping his composure, Luc stared back up at the biker. "Didn't come from over here, man, sorry."

Cliff was dragged back from his hazy sojourn as he eyed the Ukrainian beer can in the biker's hand and the vacant, unmoving Ukrainian boy beside him.

"Got something to say, big boy?" The biker looked down at the only one close to his stature.

Cliff, remembering his little ones at home, replied, "no, sir."

Sally was holding onto Cava's arm, shocked and afraid. She abhorred confrontation, but especially the violent and always the needless. Cava was torn between remaining seated, hoping that silver-tongued Luc could talk them out of this, and rising to his feet in solidarity with his friend.

"No?" the biker growled. "One of you little punk motherfuckers better step up. I want a face to crack before we get to the stop."

Cava and Luc exchanged brief glances as they tried to communicate telepathically to find an answer. They knew who raided his father's fridge for beer cans with Cyrillic lettering. They also knew that no matter the immediate peril, no one would snitch.

The biker advanced even closer to Luc and grabbed the strap of his tank top, eyeing him like snack. Luc shrugged the first grab off, and the biker cackled. There was no lack of fight in the kid. Cliff stared up at the massive figure, squinting his eyes under his shades. When Rosee slapped at the man's second attempt, he moved slowly and deliberately, like someone enjoying their supper, to place another hand on Luc. Cava shot up from his seat with a bewildered and panic-stricken expression.

"Fucking Furies. Always gotta learn things the hard way," the biker said as he nodded to the big men on his left and right.

"Uncle Damian, wait, stop! I know these guys!" a voice piped up from behind. "Yo, Luc with da C!"

"Yo, Bertie... You made it on our train," Luc said cautiously.

"Word up, we been on the other side chilling, but some dummy threw a can at my uncle," Bertie said.

"Lil Bertie... Uncle Damian... We apologize, but it wasn't us," Luc said.

"Yeah, some other bitch-ass chucked it," Rosee added for good measure.

"Hmm..." The uncle squinted down on the blank, wide-eyed Fink, who began shifting nervously.

"Yeah, Uncle. That's Cava, that's Sally, over there is Rat-Fink and the big one is Cliff," Bertie said cheerfully. "They know Alistair, too."

"And the black?" Uncle Damian asked. "He looks like that Kill'em."

"I'm Luc, spelled with a C... and Kill'em is my brother," he said, regaining his confidence. "Yo, Bertie! Sick sleeve, bro. And yeah, we know Tic-Tax, too."

"Thanks man. I got it for my dad, to remember him," Bertie responded, rubbing his arm, freshly inked with skulls and flames.

The group caught up with Lil Bertie. Bertrand Levesque III had moved to Vincennes with his mother after his father's murder, but he still hung out with his uncles and cousins at their clubhouses in Fury. Bertie Jr. looked like a young Scandinavian god with his icy blonde hair and blue eyes. His impeccable manners and gracious pleasantries ingratiated him with teachers and parents. He was a biker gang prince, and as untouchable as they came.

"Tic-Tax? You mean Alistair? That little waste of sperm? Jesus H. Christ… You guys have a nickname for everybody."

"We call him that because he has those nasty little teeth, probably from meth or jib or something. He's one *ugly* motherfucker," Rosee poked in, gleefully.

The uncle laughed hoarsely. "That hang-around piece of shit is as useless as a busted condom."

They all laughed, some more nervously than others. Rat-Fink remained motionless, breathing steadily and occasionally staring out the window. As the uncle lit a joint, Bertie started talking about Luc's clandestine pockets, and the conversation quickly turned to smuggling.

"What the fuck?!"

Amidst the disorder and madness on the train, a teen in the front row vomited the entire contents of his stomach all over himself and the floor. A river of stinking bile flowed down the car. Everyone fought to clamber up onto seats, away from the flow and towards the windows. As the doors opened at the penultimate stop, the Furians stormed out of the car, some getting knocked down into the reeking mess. The few people waiting on the platform avoided the car and looked on with confusion.

* * *

The kids said goodbye to Bertie and his Leviathan uncle. Luc had promised to think of ways to conceal contraband in cars and motorcycles for the gang. The kids hitched their bags and scraped their dripping soles on the platform.

"All those weapons, and like I said, still a fucking pussy," Cliff muttered.

"Yeah, man, you fuckin' snake, Rat-Fink, pinko-Commie fuck boy," Luc said as he popped Fink on the shoulder.

"You always do this shit. Quit starting fights for the others," Sally chimed in with disdain.

"I wish my brother was free so he could mash you," said Rosee.

Cava simply shook his head and spat on the ground in front of Fink before walking away, leaving him alone momentarily. He pulled up his sagging pants and jogged to catch up with the crew.

The train rolled into the terminus where the rest of the Furians disembarked to storm the streets of downtown New Amsterdam *en masse*. People poured out of every packed carriage except one, where a kid, covered in vomit from his white t-shirt to his white tennis shoes, sat with his eyes closed and chin slumped to his chest, an empty bottle of gin soon to fall from his weak grip.

FIREWORKS

NEW AMSTERDAM WAS often ranked in the world's top five most liveable cities, with its beautiful views, proximity to the Pacific Ocean, and year-long, snow-capped mountain ranges. Its rapid expansion from a sleepy capital city into a high-priced condominium metropolis over just two decades had altered the entire landscape of the Four Fingers.

The Furians' descended on the sparkling beaches and stainless streets of New Am three times a year in full force, with 40 or so mini-assaults during various sports seasons. The residents kept to their patios and apartment decks if they could, sensing the swarming of their 'city on the hill' by armed groups of legal miscreants, like Visigoth mercenaries permitted to wander the streets of fortified Rome.

* * *

The crew emerged from the station with Fink still trailing like a wounded hound. They stopped by their normal haunts: the New Am Hammers pro store, St. Vincennes Park to smoke a little herb, a cheap Persian food cart for a shawarma, and the pristine buildings and facades where Fink and Luc could get their *ups* by slapping stickers and spraying their tags while the rest kept six.

Their final destination was a spot on the beach at the mouth of Huxley Bay. There was a vast coastline to choose from, but their usual spot had an optimal view of the fireworks launched from a barge a mile out from the shore. This was where Luc's brothers had always taken him, close enough to the train and just a couple of minutes from the corner stores, should they run out of cigarettes or mix. Of course, they weren't alone. The space was already a mosaic of towels and chairs belonging to spectators who'd camped out for as long as twelve hours to secure their prime positions.

"Over there! I see a spot!" Luc raced off half a football field away from the group to claim it. They heard his periodic shouts of "sorry!" as he jumped and juked his way through men and women sunning themselves, returning a few kickballs, spraying sand everywhere, and eventually arriving at a rare, unoccupied central spot that was high enough to avoid the approaching tide.

"Great spot, Luc!" said Sally. Luc stood almost still, beaming and pleased with himself, his dark skin glistening with sweat.

"You still here?" Luc joked to Fink as he sidled up behind the crew, also kicking grains of sand onto their neighbours, but with no apology. Fink shrugged and set his pack on the sand. No one in the crew had remembered to pack a beach towel, except for Sally. Such trivia could not diminish their high spirits, however.

Before the others could drop their bags, Luc was stripped down to his boxers and leaping over a snoozing couple as he raced to dive-bomb into the water. The others laughed while Sally picked up his clothes, shook out the sand she knew he would regret later, and folded them neatly on his bag.

"Where's Cliff?" Whoever asked it first was immediately echoed by the others. How had he slipped away from them? He was nowhere to be seen. Fink, shrugging, uncharacteristically volunteered to try to find him. They watched Fink leave, still in his baggy pants with his hoodie pulled up, almost masking his eyes, heading in the opposite direction they'd come from.

"Worst decision, ever," Rosee muttered bitterly as she put down her bag and unzipped her shorts.

Cava and Sally exchanged looks, wondering if they should take the bait.

"What was?" Sally asked.

"I fucked him." Rosee rolled her eyes. "I mean, ew. I know, right?"

Sally looked as Cava, who was going through his bag, stopped and raised his entire face, ears dragged along for the ride.

"Last night, we were all hanging out and after I left you, Cava, I was walking home, and he was sitting on the Bench. He asked me if I wanted to smoke before bed, and I said yes. Then, he asked me if I wanted some plum brandy shit his dad makes, and I said yes. Next thing I know, we were banging by the Bench against some dumpster. Ugh, right? I mean, how could I?" Rosee said as she slid her shorts down and removed her top, awaiting their reaction.

"That's... Well..." Cava struggled to form a sentence, gripped by a tightness in his throat and around his eyes.

"I know," Rosee started, tucking her breasts into her bikini top and fanning her bottoms out with her thumbs. "I'm *such* a slut. I'll never meet a *nice* guy." Then, perhaps noticing Cava's creased expression, Rosee finished, "didn't mean nothing, I was just lit up a bit."

Sally folded her arms and looked at the two of them. Cava groaned, tilting his face towards the sky. Rosee tucked her clothes into her bag and frolicked down to the water, apparently carefree.

"Quinn," Sally said as Cava finally dropped his head and remained motionless. "You *are* over her, *right?*" Her tone was authoritative, but it carried a faint plea.

"I... uh, guess I am now," Cava returned, glumly.

"For your own sake, you should be."

Cava laughed dejectedly. "The same thing, the whole time you were gone. I thought, you know, I'd made some ground. Last night! I thought for sure, but she just slipped away. Again. To *Fink*! *Brutal*."

"Brutal," Sally repeated somberly. "You wanna share my towel?"

"Okay." Cava sighed.

Left with only the bags and each other's company, the two friends sat close to one another and talked. Cava told Sally about his year, ashamed at his lack of noteworthy accomplishments or events, given her recent adventures. Sally suggested that they travel Europe together after they finish high school. She knew that he enjoyed studying history and geography, but seeing it all outside of books and videos was another experience altogether. A better one. She continued on about how it was such a relief to leave Fury behind, even for a spell, and that the travel bug was real.

"Well, I don't like being sick," Cava joked.

Sally snort-laughed and covered her mouth. "Silly, it's what I know you've always dreamed about."

"Going to Europe?"

"Leaving Fury."

Cava though for a moment. "Yeah, but who will take care of Luc? He ain't going nowhere. He loves that city."

"Well, he's a big boy. His brothers will be back, and you know he can take care of himself."

They sat in silence, occasionally looking up at the two playing in the water. They were wrestling, playing volleyball with some others, laughing, and chanting "Fury-Us!" with other Furians. Cava and Sally sat and looked at each other, enjoying the silence and the comfort of being around each other again.

"Sal?"

"Yes, Quinn?"

"Did you... did you, um, see someone while you were gone?" The question had been on his mind since their reunion at the bench.

Sally paused for half an eternity.

Cava continued. "Did you have sex?"

Sally's dark bronze skin flushed a deep vermillion as she turned her face away.

"Sal?"

"...Yes, Quinn?"

"You know... You really look..."

"I bought chairs!" yelled Cliff, obviously wasted, as he stomped around onlookers towards the awkward duo. "Five bucks apiece! I broke one. But, I stole two! We got chairs!"

Cliff planted his fold-out chair behind Cava and Sally and stretched his feet out onto their towel. "So! What're we talking about?"

Luc and Rosee returned from the water while Cliff wavered in and out of siesta. Fink, meanwhile, was nowhere to be seen. Luc shook the water off his boxers and Rosee squeezed the brine out of her hair.

"You got any rolled ones left?" Luc asked. "I seen a couple homies in the water, and we were going to match them."

"Yeah," Cava answered. "We haven't touched anything."

A group of soaking wet boys and a couple of girls made their appearance, unzipping their backpacks and chatting noisily as they approached. Groups of people to the left and right made room for the loud, swearing teens who sat themselves promptly in a circle and began to light herb, passing and receiving.

After some catching up and a few rotations between the young Furians, Cliff rose, stretched his long limbs and said: "I can't take this heat. Cavs, Sal, wanna take a dip?"

The crew laughed, having been seated for almost a half hour. Cava and Sally chose to follow Cliff, still fully clothed, as he lumbered towards the reflective blue waters.

Cava tucked his socks into his shoes and stripped down to his boxers, his pallid Irish skin earning him some jokes about the sun reflecting off his whiteness.

Sally slid her coveralls down and removed her shirt as the boys bit their breath. Luc gnawed his fist, and even the girls raised their eyebrows.

"What?" she giggled at Cava's dumbstruck expression.

"Uh, nothing."

The group sniggered.

"Too bad they didn't teach you how to wax, Salomea!" Rosee taunted, pointing to a small curl peeking out from Sally's bikini bottom. She froze, worried about what would happen if she pulled too hard.

"Pipe down, you raggedy hood-mouse," Cava said as he guided Sally by the small of her back towards the water. Rosee cursed Cava, loud and shrill, but he tuned her out by talking to Sally. "She's just bent because you... you look a lot different than the last time she saw you."

"You really think so?"

"Dude... you serious? You're a dime... plus five! I mean, I've always thought you were cute. You gotta know that. To me, you've always been that nerdy, cool, girl-next-door. Literally. But you *do* look a lot different. I can see you getting a lot of attention this year."

"Like my sister?"

They entered the water slowly, letting the lukewarm waves splash their knees and thighs.

"Sort of?" Cava responded while thinking. "But, you're so much smarter than she could ever be. She was always kind of..."

"Crazy."

"A bit, I guess... Kami-Kasia. But, she was always very nice to me. You know... what do you do when all the boys, *and men*, in the whole city have a crush on you? Want to take advantage of you? I think she was kind of cursed, in a way."

They spotted Cliff, floating, treading, and waving at them.

"Look, maybe it's just that your looks have caught up with your brains. You've always been the smartest, and now you're the most beautiful person I know."

Sally blushed and looked at Cava. He was looking straight ahead, too timid to make eye contact after what he'd just said.

"Just... don't change on me, is all. I missed you a lot. Something felt incomplete the whole time you were gone. I know that you can't hold a moment like a picture, but I don't want to have to miss something that's right beside me."

"I couldn't change who I am, even if I wanted to."

"I know. You're the daughter of a Doktor!" Cava joked. "I guess what I'm trying to say is... I'm there for you. Don't let people walk on you or use you or treat you differently."

Sally rubbed Cava's shoulder, greasy from sunscreen. "Thank you, Quinn. You know, I thought about you the whole time I was gone. I..."

"Stop!" Cliff shouted. "I been pissing here, you might want to play over there for a couple minutes."

All the people bathing, Sally and Cava included, gave Cliff a generous circle.

Cliff, Cava, and Sally returned, water-logged and rejuvenated, ready to tag in whoever wanted to hop back into the water. Various conversations were happening among the now twenty or so Furians, many partially sitting on Sally's towel, much to her dismay.

Fink was back, seated on Cliff's chair, still clothed like it was November. He was comparing the contents of his armory with those of his peers.

"It's going to be a bloodbath tonight," said one kid.

"I been waiting for this night! It's like Hallowe'en, but for big kids," another teen broke in.

"Check this," said a tall, gaunt, older-looking kid. "I got this from the gang." He was flicking and twirling a balisong, showing how easily it went from concealed in his palm to open, thrusting a stab straight in front of him.

"Ah, man," said Fink. "Ali, you so cool."

"Butterfly knife, man. Super illegal. I could probably score you one, Crusher." Tic-Tax called Fink by his tag name, returning Fink's favour of using his real name. A little gesture of respect between the disrespected.

"Shut the fuck up, Tic-Tax," Cliff said, staunchly pointing a fat finger at him.

"Watch your mouth, Cl…" The consonants showed the entire wreckage of Alistair's tiny, pitted teeth, slicing out at all angles from his gums.

Cliff stepped towards Fink and Tic-Tax. "He's *Fink*, not *Crusher*. And you're motherfucking *Tic-Tax*, not *Ali*. Don't diss the Greatest like that. Fink, get off my chair. Tic-Tax, careful what you say. You want to keep those little-ass teeth in your head, right?"

"Whatever, man," Tic-Tax grumbled. "Yo, Crusher, I'll catch up with you later. Good haul. Peace." He hitched up his heavy bag and marched towards the pavement, his pants sagging to the very bottom of his buttocks.

"Good haul?" Sally inquired.

"Yeah," Fink said. "I did a little scavenger hunt."

Fink showed them some of the radios, beepers, shoes, and other random articles swiped from trusting beachgoers. The crew shook their heads but resisted jeering at Fink. Almost all of them had done, or had thought of doing, the same thing.

"Man, that's why these rich cats say 'Furies' with such hate," Luc said, without anger. "We can't help our hood-asses. It's worse and more embarrassing than Cliff leaving his shirt on to go in the water. Don't be the fat kid at the pool, Fink."

Cliff grinned, removed his white shirt and then wrung it over Luc, who was lying on his stomach.

Luc piped up. "My brother said that Tic-Tax was selling an ounce to some random kid from Vince. No name, no cred, no nothing. Just some kid who wanted a bag and got Tic-Tax's number. He got out of his busted-ass Olds with a lead pipe and asked the kid for the loot. The kid asked why he had a pipe, and if it wasn't a shakedown, to let him hold it for a second, you know, for trust or something. *Tic-Tax fucking gave the pipe to the kid!* Then, he told the kid to give him the loot or he'd smash his brains in. Kid says, 'with what?' Tax says with his lead pipe, and the kid cracks him on the dome with it, puts him on the mat, and bounces with the ounce *and* the dough. *And,* the bitch ass had pinched it from, I dunno, the Souls, maybe? Somebody real. Fucking guy had to try and vick some random dude for the loot he was gonna owe, but he couldn't even do that. So, he asked his damn grandma for the loot to pay off his debt. I bet that bitch is still in hot water. You heard what Bertie's uncle said, he was a waste of sperm or some shit." Luc was laughing so hard he couldn't sit up. "He got beat with his own pipe, ha-ha."

"I bet Lil Bertie told them not to mash him out. Bert's got a heart. He's a stand up dude," a boy said.

"Truth, but why keep a dude like that around?" a girl added. "He's that creep who puts shit in girls' drinks and sells Tylenols with the letters scratched off, or weed that's sprayed with Windex."

"Maybe he just does whatever they say? Like *he* goes to prison if shit hits the fan, a fall-guy like..." the speaker threw the brakes on hard and checked for Luc's reaction.

"That's not what happened to my brother, motherfucker," Luc corrected him.

"My bad, my bad." The kid reached out to bump fists with Luc.

"It's okay, lots of stories out there about what happened… Anyways, Tic-Tax *would* be the trigger man. He stabbed up some kids because they dissed him about the pipe shit."

"Well, he's putting in work. He's been doing grimy shit for a minute now. Still, wouldn't trust him further than I could throw a cement truck," a voice added.

"Word… Yeah, Fink, why do you like that guy?" Luc asked. "And why does he like you? No one likes you."

"He's Eastern European, like me," Fink answered, bluntly. "My family knows his family. He likes to paint, and we've bombed a few times together. I bet he's gonna be a name in the city. I'm telling you, he's gully as fuck and don't give a shit about nothing. And he doesn't call me Rat or Fink or Rat-Fink or Russian. He's a *real* cat. Y'all should probably watch all them little comments."

The group sucked their teeth at Fink, but quickly let it drop. Fink stayed quiet and sipped his father's homemade brandy out of a plastic pop bottle.

The sun eventually snuffed itself out on the liquid metal horizon of the Pacific. Gradually, all of the add on group members disbanded to grab more booze, get food, or find other friends to watch the spectacle with. The six-person core was left as they were at the beginning. Cliff had sobered up a bit and was maintaining a responsibly scaled-down level of inebriation. Fink was scrawling his tag in the sand over and over again, starting conversations and then exiting them, feeling the drink and the drugs. The other four were gingerly putting their clothes back on, shivering in the nocturnal air, the grit of the sand sticking to their bodies, and feeling dazed after a long day of sun exposure.

A single flare shot into the air, warning that the sky dancing light show would begin immediately.

The 20-minute display—the curtain call of summer break and flawless summer weather—was underway. The crew stretched their necks and watched as the heroic anthems of gunpowder and giant loudspeakers playing classical music created an integrated, captivating symphony. The spectators marveled at the intertwining of the music, the explosions, and the brilliant colours. Luc was particularly arrested by each magnificent display and moved with the sounds and the dancing lights, completely absorbed. Cava and Sally inched closer and closer to each other until their shoulders touched. Each inch closer to Sally moved Cava an inch further away from Rosee.

Rosee was determined, however. As Cava continued to shift slowly and steadily away from her and towards his old friend, Rosee, frustrated and without fully understanding why, lengthened her body and lay face up, with her head on Cava's lap. "Do you mind?" Rosee said seductively, rubbing her head into Cava's crotch, arousing him against his will.

Sally moved towards the edge of the towel as the fireworks blasted on, her knees tucked into her chest.

The fireworks advanced towards their lavish, final salvo. Local attendees and parents with children had already gathered up their property and progeny before the conclusion. As during Hammers home games, they'd wisely learned to skip the last exciting moments to avoid the hassle and congestion of the throngs of rowdy carousers all struggling towards the train station through New Am's narrow maze of bottleneck streets.

"Man, it gets better every year," Luc said, wiping away tears that he claimed came from barely blinking for 20 minutes.

"Yup, I'm good. Time to go home," Cliff said, stretching his arms. "I'll leave the chair, unless one of you guys…"

"No," the crew answered.

"Mmm, thank you for the pillow," Rosee cooed. "A little hard, but I liked it." she winked, rolled to her side, and pushed herself up off his inner-thigh.

Sally was already standing. "Up!" she said. Cava turned to conceal himself and waited gratefully while she fanned the towel out and rolled its immense dimensions down until it was small enough to fit in her bag.

The group made their way up towards the station alongside the hundreds of other spectators in Huxley Bay. The streets were instantly jammed with people entering from the various connecting streets that fed from the multitudinous shorelines where people had set up camp for the fireworks.

"I never seen it this busy," said Cliff. "We'll never make it home."

The crew trudged up the street, bumping and colliding with people heading up the road to the station.

"The whole goddamn city is here. All the other cities, too," remarked Rosee.

Amidst the shuffling of feet, music from stereos, and loud, drunken wailing were the distant whines of police and ambulance sirens. Police in full riot gear lined the sidewalks, holding shields and truncheons. Intoxicated citizens winged middle fingers at them, spat on the shields, and chanted "fuck the police!"

"Fucking Furies." One of the cops shook his head.

Halfway up the street, not even fifteen minutes after the concluding blast of light and sound, the first melee broke out. One man insulted another, and the two squared off. It started in the middle of the street and the cops couldn't see or push their way through. They didn't try.

The media routinely lamented the booze and drugs as key contributors to the yearly episodes of violence. An op-ed piece by a tenured journalist would predictably decry the lack of discipline of 'today's' parents.

The two men began boxing poorly, each trying to get a grip on the other, jersey his opponent, and feed him a series of uppercuts. Neither were able to land any decisive blows, and the crowd began to chide the contestants.

"Come on, you pussies!"

"Throw a fucking slug!"

The Furians, like the two liquored-up combatants and the majority of those circling the standoff, were unaware of their stereotypical behaviour, but played their role sublimely.

"You Fury or Figaro? Fuck boys!" Luc's clarion taunt drew laughter from the onlookers, showing where most of them were from. "Chuck a fist already."

A loud, hollow *shlock* came from the back. The group turned and saw that Cliff had taken a bludgeon to the head and was leaking a trail of red down his large, square face. At the same moment, a man emerged from the circle around the two combatants, stuck one of them with a pocket knife between the ribs, and darted through the crowd, slicing at any Samaritan who tried to block him.

Luc took out his spiked brass knuckles and began punching wildly at the people who'd attacked Cliff. Cava dragged Sally out of the main fighting crowd and rushed back in, tackling a man with a black metal club before he could strike Luc from behind.

"What are you doing?" Rosee asked Fink. "Get your fucking weapons out!" She took out a knife, held it blade to the bottom, and ran in yelling.

Luc, Cliff, and Cava were joined by some of the kids from the beach and a few onlookers who'd watched before choosing a side. The other group had also received reinforcements. Punches, kicks, bats, knives, razors, and brass knuckles were being rained on whoever was closest.

One kid emerged with a blade under his tongue, something he'd probably heard about in a song or had seen in a film. As he went to spit out the razor, he sliced his tongue and palm open, falling to the ground in agony, and leaving himself defenseless to a steel-toed boot. He lay there as blood poured onto the street from numerous openings. The fighting around him continued, unbroken.

Cliff had two men in headlocks, and ground their heads under his arms until he heard their jaws crack, unfazed by the kidney shots and tap-out attempts that had struck his sides. Cava moved to back up Luc, who was winding intrepidly through the crowd, punching ribs with his spiked device to shore up his crew's offence.

Cava took a potent right hook to the nose, which stunned him and caused his steps to falter as though he were walking on an iced-over pond. Cliff came in for the save, bringing his fist down on the assailant's head like a mallet.

"You okay?" Cliff asked Cava, who nodded and trailed further into the skirmish. He tried to follow the blazing trail that Luc had set, but everything was moving around him in blurs. The sounds of war were muffled, and quicker movements were abstract gestural brushstrokes.

Luc broke his brass knuckles on the motorcycle helmet of a man who was swinging a yard of chain at the knees and torsos of people at random. He tore the knuckles off, settled into a classic, pugilistic stance, and turfed the man, knocking him out beneath the helmet. He raised his bloodied, torn fists and screamed "I love this shit!"

Cava was trembling, still following his friend, and taking a couple of errant blows to the head while Cliff followed him and returned heavy ones-and-twos on his behalf.

"Ok, buddy," Cliff said, concerned. "You're done."

"No, I'm not... I need to protect Luc..." Cava said, shakily.

Luc had teamed up with a dozen schoolmates, and they were now engaged in a large brawl with an equal sized force. The ferocity was evident by the heels stomping on the faces and ribs of fallen fighters. One such looked up at Cava with raccoon eyes and a mouth half-full of broken teeth.

With his shirt now off and wrapped around his writing hand, Luc picked one opponent at a time to box to the floor, deliver a kick to the liver for good measure, and move on.

Rosee was fighting a girl three times her size, pulling her hair and swinging around her, driving palm shots and knees to the fallen.

Cava felt his feet lift out from under him as he looked around confusedly, expecting to hit the ground. To his surprise, he'd been thrown over one of Cliff's shoulders and was moving like a scythe through wheat.

He found Sally standing on a raised step and placed Cava on his feet shakily. "Can you take him? I have to get Rosee out now."

"What about your head?" Sally asked, concerned.

Cliff touched it and licked his face. A long trail of blood had entered his mouth. "Wasn't sure if that was my blood. Just a goose egg."

"Is he okay?" Sally asked, inspecting Cava's inflamed nose.

"He took a massive slug. I mean, anyone would've ate shit after that duffing. Might as well try to head home. We'll catch up with you or see you back on the other side."

"What about Luc?"

They turned and heard his distinct laughter and trash talking.

"He'll be fine... Can't see the pigs letting this go on for much longer."

Cliff headed back into the mayhem out of obligation, with all the enthusiasm he would bring to cleaning vomit from a bathroom stall, wondering, *why it always ended with this kind of shit.*

Sally grabbed Cava by the arm. "Quinn, are you okay?"

Cava grumbled and nodded, spitting out a wad of blood and snot. "I got my teeth?"

He gave her an exaggerated, open-mouthed smile that forced his swollen, purpled eyes even more closed. She nodded and giggled at the way he asked the question, smiling like a child on picture day with jam on his teeth. Sally then led him down the quieter back street.

"What were you thinking, just running in there?"

"I followed Luc. He might've needed me. I know I saved him from one bad one."

"Maybe, but you could've gotten yourself killed. Every damn year. I thought you hated this?"

"I do, but Luc is family. I'd do the same thing for you."

Cava's answers were slurred by the sun, alcohol, weed, and now, head trauma. Sally led him two blocks along the dead beachfront streets. They occasionally passed teenagers having sex, as well as scornful dog-walking locals.

"Where are we going? I feel like you know."

"Hold on," Sally replied, sitting Cava on a ledge in front of a large condo building. Loud *thunks* could still be heard the short distance away.

"Must be the gas," Cava said to himself, noticing that Sally was operating an intercom a few feet away. He lit a smoke and sat there, coming out of his haze and shaking his head, trying to clear the cobwebs. He played with his nose. It was sensitive to the touch, but probably not broken. That was a plus.

"Okay," Sally said triumphantly. "I was hoping she'd be here. I visited them at their downtown condo once, and luckily, they came to watch the show tonight."

"Huh?"

"Oh, right." Sally brought Cava to the door and waited for the buzzer. "My sister said that if we were ever downtown and needed a place or a ride, she'd help out."

Buzz. The glass front door clicked as Sally opened it and ushered Cava inside.

"Kasia?"

"Yeah, she said she could give us a lift home. She and her husband have a little pad out here for concerts and whatnot. Thank God she has herself together nowadays. She's actually doing... really well."

Kasia Papanicolas met the two in the lobby and invited them into the elevator to retrieve the car.

"Quinn, Jesus, you took a punch, eh? You okay? Let me guess… Luc got you guys into a scrap."

"Nice to see you, too. You should see the other guy. I didn't."

"Always a pleasure, Cavanaugh. Other than the nose, you look good."

"We'll see tomorrow. I might win the contest for worst shape on first day."

Sally shook her head and lowered her chin to conceal a faint smirk.

Cava took off his dirty, white shirt and wrapped his nose with it to avoid spilling blood on the pristine interior of Kasia's brand new Mercedes E-Class.

"Look at you two back there. So cute." Kasia remarked.

"I hope it's not a concussion," Sally said, grabbing Cava's hand and tilting his head back. He turned with a smile, followed by a grimace from the pain.

Tap. Tap. Tap.

"Fink?" Cava asked, muffled by his shirt.

Kasia unlocked the doors and Fink hopped in the car. "Jesus," he said. "It's wild out there."

"You get in on it, too, Marek?" Kasia asked, fond of neither of Fink nor of having him in her car.

"Nah. I'm too pretty." He then huffed a breath onto the window and began to draw his tag, his fingers making subdued squeaks as they traced the letters.

"Your greasy little fingers leave any marks and I'll chop them off myself. Got it?"

He sunk down into his seat and pulled the strings of his hood, closing it tight around his face.

BACK AGAIN

THE ALARM SOUNDED far too early for Quinn Cavanagh, signalling the beginning of the end. He'd never thought about post-secondary academia, let alone any basic survival strategy, after bursting from his juvenile cocoon.

He allowed the dissonant twang from his alarm clock and the welling of liquid in his bladder to reach their obnoxious crescendos; the symbiosis finally driving him to a seated position on the side of his mattress.

"Jesus H." Cava felt a swirl of fluids rush from the back of his head to the front, nausea rising behind his sinuses. He prodded the tight, turgid skin on his shiner lightly. It was hot and tender under his fingertips. *Ma's gonna have some questions*, he thought, unsure of what bumps and burgundies were marring his complexion. He grimaced at the thought, sending a twinge of pain to his nose and upper gums. He touched the bridge; swollen, but thankfully not broken. He then used a fingernail to scrape his nostrils and rubbed the flakes of dried blood off onto his nightstand.

Cava bundled up a set of fresh clothes so that he could dart up to the bathroom and get a better look at himself before seeing his family. He would assess the damage and work out an alibi that fit his appearance.

He ran up to the bathroom, heavy heels pounding the loosely spiralled stairs. He yelled a passing "good morning," noticing that his younger brother was already up and showered for his first day of high school. Once safe in the bathroom, still balmy from the others' bathing rituals, he scrutinized his face.

"Not *too* bad," he murmured to himself. His nose was banged up and puffy, but was no more crooked than it'd been the day before. He had a minor cut on the bridge, some purpling beneath his eyes, a yellowed bruise on his left cheek, and a small slice on his bottom lip. The cut, luckily, was mostly buried inside his mouth, and appeared superficially as nothing more than a minor split. His body seemed to bear no injury, contusion or otherwise, since he'd luckily taken all the abuse in just one easily hidden spot. *Bright side,* he thought. As he entered the hot shower, his head began to throb. He saw the water run red from his head down into the tub. How many slugs had he ended up taking?

Cava lurched down the stairs on soft-padded heels and pondered bypassing the kitchen to grab a ball cap before showing his face. He squeezed his cheek muscles, thinking that he might be able to hide the swelling, but grimaced from the discomfort.

"Now, Quinn, you'll walk your brother to school and get him all set up," Nora demanded. "I want him to know where everything is so he's not walking around with his head in a fish bowl."

Cava, his back to the table as he reached into the cupboard for a coffee cup and bowl, answered in the affirmative without turning around.

"Look at me so I know you understand. Your father had to leave early, but he wanted me to wish you both luck."

Cava turned to acknowledge his mother and was rewarded with a caustic reprimand. "Quinn Padraig Cavanaugh, what have you done to your handsome face?! See, Henry, this is why you don't go to the stupid fireworks. Even bright fellas act like complete imbeciles! Is this Luc's fault? Was it that drunk, Cliff? That snake-boy, Marek? That hussy, Rosee? I'd hoped that Salomea would've had a better influence on you."

"No… Ma. It was a random punch-up. Just a free-for-all that kicked off and I took a few slugs getting the girls out of harm's way!" He backed himself further into the tiered drawers behind. "I didn't want Sal to get hurt, I…"

"Quinn, you're no brawler. You're a smart boy who's nearly a man. Soon, you and your little friends won't be able to get away with this reckless behaviour. You'll be adults, and your troubles will get the best of ye. You could've called us for a ride. You have a good head on your shoulders. I can't wait until this year is over and you can do better things. Which reminds me, have you looked into any colleges yet?"

"Ma, come on. It's only the first day."

"Don't you 'it's only the first day' me, boyo. I bet Salomea's already picked out her school."

Cava tried to deflect the question and defend his friends, but Nora wouldn't let him wriggle out of a yet another conversation about his future.

"Did I raise a thicko? A coward? Are you too scared to figure it out? Too lazy? Because I know you're not too stupid. Too much arsin' around? What? Tell me."

"No, it's none of those things! I just need better grades, and an idea of what I want to do. I don't want to waste time and loot just taking classes and doing whatever."

They carried on in the same fashion over a cup of coffee and a bowl of porridge. It had become the trademark topic of conversation whenever Cava came home late, smelling of weed or booze, or slept in. It bothered him, but he knew that it was the smart move. What irked him was accepting his own laziness about deciding what to do and his fear of moving forward. Though he earned decent grades—and much better since Luc had been shuffled to the remedial classes—Cava wasn't passionate about any subject. His mother often suggested that he should be a teacher, but he found the pedestrian nature of the profession, and the absence of any of the rugged masculinity that he attached to his own identity, ultimately to lie beneath him.

The unavoidability of having to make a choice on his own, and commit to it, was what worried him even further. Cava was notoriously fickle, not indifferent, but unable to pick one idea and run with it. With

Luc, for better or worse, Cava was rarely forced to think critically about his actions. Though Luc had more often than not led him into trouble, legal and personal, his angst over his own indecisiveness was soothed by his friend's bright impulsivity.

"Oh, jeez, ma!" Cava cut into his mother's persistent homilies, checking his watch. "Me and Hank better get a move on. I still gotta make sure that Luc's up."

"You know, he'll be fine without you," Nora said. "He *does* have a mother, too."

Cava gave his mother a patronizing look. "Have a great first day, my baby boy," she said, squeezing her youngest like a mama gorilla. "And Quinn? Start the year off right, please."

The boys slid on their shoes, grabbed their backpacks, and headed out the door. The faint sound of their mother sending her love faded as they made their way from the porch.

"Hey, hey, Henry boy! Good luck! Quinny, Sally left a while ago! Take care of the babies!" Ivan Doktor yelled, sitting on his stoop in his reflective vest with a travel mug in one hand and a burning cigarette in the other, also preparing to shove off for the day. The boys waved and thanked him, continuing down the path towards the Kalou house.

"What happened to you last night?" Henry asked his older brother, his voice cracking with the arrival of adulthood.

"Uh, just the usual St. Vince bullshit, little brother," Cava returned. "Just the train, that was a headache as usual. Then the beach, which wasn't the worst. The fireworks get better all the time. Then there was the stupid mess at the end. I took a couple slugs, but I'm a little worried about Luc."

"How'd you get home? What time?"

"Kasia drove me, Sal, and Fink home. No idea what time."

The boys stopped at the Bench. Henry had overheard stories of the Bench so many times while he'd been cooped up in his little room or the shrub-divided, concrete square behind their house. The meeting point for so many occasions was also the *rendez-vous* for the walk to school, with a cut-off of quarter to eight to be on time. Sally usually got to school much earlier for sports or studying, Cliff had been out of school for years, and

Fink would join whenever he felt like it. Everyone else tried to get there in time to walk with their friends.

The brothers waited a little longer than usual, as school started late and finished early on the first day. Cava proposed they make the short trip to the Kalou house to ensure that Luc was coming to school—or had even made it home. He would never get to school on time were it not for Cava.

Cava climbed the steps to bang on the Kalou's glass-paneled door. The inner wooden door was already open, and the smell of Caribbean and Italian spices, marijuana, and coffee were wafting around the house. Luc's mother, Apollonia, a short woman of Sicilian descent, came to the door with a joint in her hand.

"What you want, Quinn?"

"Hi Mrs. Kalou… Just seeing if Luc's ready for school?" Cava was nervous. Dealing with Mrs. Kalou was always a gamble with her caginess and quick-pivot mood swings.

She seemed stunned that school was beginning and fired off towards the basement to rouse her youngest child. Screaming, banging, and clattering echoed up the dark staircase. French, English, Italian, and a unique hybrid of the three rose, slightly muffled, from the lower level. The only definite, well-formed sound was Luc's cry of "*Maman! Maman!*" as he tried to quell his mother's hurricane.

Moments later, a smiling Mrs. Kalou stepped lightly up the stairs. "Luc will be two minutes more," she said with a warm smile. "Is this your first day, *Henri*?"

Henry nodded shakily from the bottom of the entrance-level stairs, where he'd descended to upon hearing the uproar.

"Ah, *bien, c'est magnifique!* Would you boys like some coffee, or a pastry?"

Henry shook his head, mouth agape. Cava, accustomed to Mrs. Kalou's free-spirited ways, said, "No thanks, Mrs. Kalou. Next time, I promise."

She winked at the boys. She was petite and wiry, five feet tall, with dark features and deep brown eyes. Full of fun and contradiction, she was also a passionate battler. She cuffed her son on the head as he walked by, saying something in Kalou-specific Creole that sounded like *kochon*. As Luc bent down to kiss his mother on the cheek, he had to squint in the morning sun.

"Wow, that's bright!" Luc rubbed his eyes as he took the lead on the walk to school. Cava remarked that he'd be in considerable pain if he massaged his face the same way.

"What happened to you? No wounds?"

"Not where you're looking," Luc responded. He pulled his hands out of his pockets to show his battle scars. His left hand was bruised and discolored, but he showed that he could move it. "This one, though…" He tried in vain to fully close or open his right fist, pocked all over with abrasions.

"That looks rough," Henry said, looking at his own fluidly clenching and unclenching paws, healthy as a puppy's.

"Oh, shit, Lil Cavs. I didn't even notice you there! First day, my boy!" Luc said, a bit too jovially, still under the influence from the night before. "Look at that hair! You gonna be a little lady-killer. A miniature pussy-magnet from hanging with the big boys."

Henry smiled.

"Yo!" Luc belted out, placing his palm on his wide-eyed face. "You remember Rosee telling us that she banged Finkie? That's *fucked* up, *man*."

Cava most definitely recalled the disbelief that he'd felt when he heard that story. He'd since forgotten about the revelation, until Luc mentioned it. He felt slightly ill. "Yeah…" Cava said shakily, "she's something else, man."

"Word up, she is!" Luc returned. "So, after you guys were gone, she was mangling this chick, twice her size. Just laying a beat-down on her ass. So, the girl's friend pulls R off by the hair, gets a little clump out, and just stands there with the blond hair in her hand. Rosee whips out her goddamn blade and starts slicing at the bitch. Cliff comes in and says 'nope,' picks Rosee up, slings her over his shoulder, grabs me by the collar as I was bashing some dude with my bloody knuckles, and drags us both towards the train."

The Cavanaugh boys, listening intently, waited for Luc to continue.

"So, we got all this adrenaline going through us, and we start making out. I'm pretty gooned, and R's probably fucked up, too. A fight breaks out on the platform, and all the cops rush in to break it up. Dunno who that was, but Cliff grabs us both and pushes us onto the train. People are yelling shit, but we don't care, we on the motherfucking train, son! Quick-fast, like that!"

"Then what happened?" Henry asked.

"Well, we get back to Central, and we're walking through that mutant factory, everyone's eyes glowing like cats'. We get in front of Cliff's shithole crib, and he asks me to take Rosee the rest of the way, you know, to make sure her wandering ass gets back to the trailer park in one piece. So, I get her to her place, and she don't wanna go in. She wants to come to my place, but *maman* thinks she's a little ho and slaps me whenever she finds R in my bed. I was still pretty lit from all the brawling and shit."

"So…?" Henry asked, as Cava braced himself for what he knew always happened.

"So, we pop her dad's tailgate down, crawl into the canopy, and bang. We go at it for a while, shaking that busted-ass Ford's shit-ass suspension. Then, I guess I finished and fell asleep. When I wake up, she ain't there. I guess she was smart enough to crawl into her bed after. I only woke up because her old man was heading to work at like 5am or something. Suddenly, I'm getting tossed around cause that drunk motherfucker drives like he stole the bitch. Takes me a bit to figure out where in Jesus' name I am. I realize that I might be heading to the docks, or wherever that guy works. I might be in for the long haul! He bent a left onto X, stopped at a red light by the Swan Market, and I rolled my dizzy ass out. He opened the door and yelled some shit, and I almost got drilled by another car. Then, I ducked into the bushes and slid home. Next thing I know, you motherfuckers come knocking. *Maman* whooped me till I got up, and here we are."

Henry was entranced. Once in a while, he would find himself exposed to the boisterous recollections of debauchery ladled out by Cava and his cohorts—especially Luc—but now, he'd be hearing the stories all the time.

Cava nodded and forced a laugh. "Crazy French bastard." In his own

mind, he was trying to force the coffin-nails quicker, with more prejudice, towards his feelings for Rosee. No matter what words he used for
her in his inner monologue, though, he didn't truly believe them.

"You *do* have some nice shiners there, brother," Luc said, snapping
Cava back to reality. "Thanks for having my back."

The boys made sure to get Henry to his homeroom, with Luc osten-
tatiously presenting 'Lil Cavs' to the classroom, finding him a seat next
to a cute girl, and finessing an introduction. Cava stood at the door and
observed, happily, that Luc had the audacity and charm to ingratiate his
baby brother to the class with such élan.

Luc then accompanied Cava to his homeroom, knowing that he
could find Sally and wish her a good first day, too. The Cs and Ds formed
their own large classroom, and every year since Grade 8, Cava had taken
his seat next to Sally Doktor at their adjoined desks in the front row.
Sally's choice.

"What up, Sal?" Luc said, executing an overhand-five. "Every year,
you make this kid sit in the front row. He don't need glasses, nerd."

Sally laughed and moved her backpack from the chair beside her.
Cava took his seat, rubbing Sally's shoulder and thanking her for getting
him home. Luc was quickly chased out of the class by the teacher and
he set off down the corridor noisily, banging lockers and stopping by
virtually every classroom to shout out his friends and teachers.

"Are you okay, Quinn?" Sally looked at his bruised face and was immediately concerned, "You might have gotten a concussion. I tried not to let
you sleep, but eventually I passed out, too. When I woke up, I had to go. I
saw Luc coming home at the same time. It was already getting light out."

"Yeah, I'm okay," Cava said sullenly. "He was coming back from
Rosee's."

Sally glanced at Cava with pitiful irritation, trying unsuccessfully to
modify her expression into one of consolation.

"Nah, it's cool," Cava insisted. "I'm way over her, like I said. Ain't no
coming back from a Fink-fucking."

Sally laughed with a disgusted grimace. She'd wondered if Cava
would remember, and was relieved, knowing how much time, emotion,
and stress he'd devoted to a girl she considered to be beneath him.

"Hi guys!" a girl's nasally voice broke Sally and Cava's shared silence.
"Hey, Sam," Sally said amicably.

"Hi Sam," Cava replied with mild irritation.

"Woah, Sally! What happened to you? You got hit with the sexy stick! And Cava, you must've had a good time in New Am yesterday." Sam's tone belied the enthusiasm of her words and was almost bitter.

They both acknowledged the girl's comments civilly as she took her seat beside them. Cava looked at the girl, Samantha Suggs, Slug, or Sluggo, as she was called by the kids since elementary school.

Cava had no problem with the girl, though he found her annoying. She was an acquaintance of Sally who lived in the Honeyview Trailer Park with her mother and father. The Honeyview was the last barely liveable area before the marshlands and the flats, and no one but the residents ever went there. Even the mail was delivered to post boxes located outside of the potholed dirt roads of the once arable land.

Cava, even more than Sally, pitied the girl. His soul stung when he looked at her and listened to her muddy, unrefined speech. He refused to make fun of her, and hearing the cannonballs slung at her many weaknesses made his intestines feel knotted.

Slug, or Sam, continued to heap praise on Sally and her newfound beauty as Cava rested his head on his desk, waiting for the bell to start the pointless first day introductions. He heard Slug talking about her summer, but her adenoidal voice, and the boring, sullen tone she was using, were beginning to test his empathy.

Luc, unsurprisingly, was late for his first class of the year. He'd popped into—and been kicked out of—all the classrooms on the way to his own. "Yo, Luc wit da C!" shouted several male students as he shuffled down the hallway, unhurried.

He explained to his unsurprised homeroom teacher that it was important to maintain character and set proper expectations for the year on the first day of school. As in all the previous years, she told him that he smelled of alcohol and to shut up and sit down.

He took his usual seat beside Kosh, Marek. Fink was sketching in his notebook, practising hand-styles and one-lines, while Luc chatted with everyone around him. Some shushed him, but more succumbed to his amiability.

Schedules were finally passed around to the students, in what felt like the longest hour of Luc's life. His courses were largely electives that revolved around physical education, sewing, cooking, French, and a litany of remedial courses. Intelligent in his own way, Luc would probably never need chemistry, biology, or any knowledge of literary devices.

Fink looked up, received his schedule without reply, and continued sketching *KRSHR* over and over, until his page was filled entirely with pencil lead.

* * *

The four met in the hall after their respective classes and discussed their plans for the day.

"I have a volleyball meeting and then a basketball meeting. Then, I have to go to the lab and talk to Professor Hui about being the assistant for younger grades. Then…" Sally was cut off by Luc as she rolled her eyes upward to try to remember what other tasks she had to complete.

"And… Sal's obviously out," Luc summarized. "I want to get some fucking sleep, to be honest. I'm fading bad. I didn't even shower… My goddamn balls are so itchy. But I do gotta get some thread and look at some fabrics, get an idea of what I wanna make this year. I made it so half of my classes are just sitting at a machine!"

Slug sidled up to the group, hoping to join the little circle.

"Fuck off, Slug, you blob," Fink said with enmity.

"Hey, take it easy," Cava said.

"Whoa, whoa, whoa." Luc put his hands up to slow Cava down.

"No, it's cool," Slug said in her lackadaisical tone. "Just wondering if you guys were going to the party this weekend at Drew's."

"Maybe," Sally said. "I'm starting baccalaureate work and prep for uni."

"Yeah! Party?" Luc replied. "We'll see you there, girl!"

Slug didn't alter her expression at all as she walked away.

"Come on, man. You gotta feel bad for the girl," Cava said.

"Nah man, that's out," Fink responded. "She's annoying, and

heinous, and she ratted on me in the third grade. A Kosh don't forget. My momma gave me a bad-ass belting. Fuck that bitch. You feel so bad, let her suck your dick."

The group went silent and frowned at Fink.

"I'm gonna get some paint and hit the walls," Fink said, unbothered.

"I'm gonna meet my little brother… Maybe I'll find you later, and we'll smoke some," Cava replied.

Fink turned and marched in the other direction as the rest set off towards the front of the building.

"That guy…" Sally frowned.

"He ain't *that* bad," Luc began. "I mean, he's a piece of shit, but he's *our* piece of shit. Every team needs one."

Sally turned left up the stairs. Luc and Cava paused before continuing, watching her climb the steps.

"Alright man, seriously!" Luc grabbed Cava's collar as Henry joined them. "You 'ave to get on that. Man, if you don't, I will. That girl is *fine*. Mint. I dunno what happened, but my god, she is fire!"

Henry laughed and thanked Luc for helping him get his first number scrawled onto the back of his hand. "Serious, man, be like your baby brother. 'ave some balls."

"It's not like that," Cava said thoughtfully as the boys exited the school. "I mean, yeah, she's hot… but I've *always* been attracted to her. I don't want her to think that I'm trying to flip her skirt because she came back looking like a model. And, she had a boyfriend, I'm 99% sure, out there. I…" he paused, not wanting to talk about his virginity in front of his brother. "Safe to say, she might've moved on."

They hit the sidewalk, saying their hellos, throwing high fives, and intermittently returning to the conversation. "I'm not saying I wouldn't, but I don't think she's the kind to make the first move. And if I did? What if she shot me down? There goes my friend, a best friend who spends holidays with her family and mine. I mean, what would happen to the Doktors and the Cavanaughs at Christmas? At Easter? All that weirdness while we're trying to eat delicious lamb and potatoes? *And,* we go to school together. And, she probably knows how much of a babe she is now. She's a head-turner, fully. She could have all those douche bags, bros, and whoever. What chance do I have? She'll probably have a dude by the time Drew's party rolls around, and three more after…"

Luc and Henry exchanged worried glances. "Yo, Cava, baby," Luc began. "Are you okay? You catch a bad head-knock or something?"

"Well, yeah, I'm fine," Cava said, as if he believed it.

"Then, you gotta get out of your head, brother. You sound insane. You sound like you been thinking about dis for two life sentences and a day. Be easy, just relax. No pressure. I was kidding about fucking Sally, alright? You sound like you don't even know her… She still a nerd, man. She still that goofy, gypsy doll that only *you* ever thought was cute. Just breathe, okay? Forget I brought it up." Luc soothed his friend, recognizing that this was not a new thought for his pal. He was also aware of the crazy way that Cava could turn a pebble into a meteorite with his incessant rumination and self-tormenting obsession.

"So, Young Cavs," Luc switched it up. "How was your first day?"

RAGER

THE FIRST WEEK of school passed as it usually did; hastened by its lack of magnitude and concluding without ceremony. For Sally, the days whistled past her like a bottle rocket, investing herself in advanced placement classes and extracurricular activities that consumed any time that wasn't spent studying. The opposite proved itself true for Luc, whose days were rife with tedium whenever his hands weren't occupied with a spool and thread.

Cliff walked his little brother and sister to school, handed a carton of Native cigarettes off to Luc to sell, and returned later to collect both the profits and his cubs. His days were boring, but in his view, necessarily and functionally so. The stipend he received paid for their food, and his apartment was rent free. He had an old clunker, a 20-year-old Ford Fairmont forged of equal parts metal, rust, and bondo, which he was itching to get back on the road. He attended the 'work and learn' adult education centre every second day to shore up the requirements for his diploma. The other days, he worked at the canary, smelling of oysters, herring, and sprat. Cliff resigned himself to a hermit lifestyle, built on protecting his young and setting a positive example through work and education.

* * *

"I'm sorry, I can't come!" Sally shouted down to Cava from her upstairs window. Her hair was in a disarray, proving too much to handle for the elastic that she was using to keep it out of her face. It resembled a wedge tornado.

"Well, come down and say hi?!" Cava shouted back, cupping his mouth to concentrate the sound.

"No," Sally pleaded. "I'm ugly!" She lifted her sweater collar over her mouth and nose.

"Impossible!" Cava hollered.

"I have to read half of this text tonight, because I have a tournament all weekend." She dropped a leaden hardcover text, shaking the window frame and nearby lattice.

Cava realized that he was fighting a losing battle. He was having fun prodding his friend, but he deeply respected her work ethic. "Okay, fine. If you don't get an 'A,' I'm going to climb up this bitch like King Kong and punch a helicopter out."

"Hey, hey! No one's breaking my lattice," Ivan's voice came from up the stairs.

"Sorry, Doktor!" Cava shouted.

"Quinny, is your dad home?"

"Yeah, he said to tell you to bring over the harmonica and some shine, or something!"

"Ha! That delightful bitch-bastard," Doktor said, accompanied by a clap. "Danuta, I'm going to go make music and get drunk! Have you seen my Jew's harp?"

"Don't go out drinking and come home stinking and looking for love, you buffoon!" Danuta yelled from another part of the house.

"You don't tell me not to have a good time! I pay the bills, I work all week, I make the bread, and I can eat it with olive oil and vinegar if

I buy them, too!" Shuffling and stomping could now be heard from the outside. A full-scale yelling match was now in progress.

* * *

Cava approached the bench to see Luc and Fink passing a joint back and forth, sitting on the tabletop with their bags in between their feet on the seat.

"You guys got booze?" Cava asked as he walked up and slapped hands with his friends.

"Yeah, I got some beers and some brandy... Mostly *percy*, though," Fink replied as he hit the joint, choking out the final words.

"Ha!" Luc contrived a laugh as he accepted the pass, "as per usual. Yeah, I got some brown and made these little vials of moonshine that Sally didn't want. To sell. I really don't want to get into the shine tonight, though, and I had some vials leftover from the batch of oil. You?"

"I still got that clear shit and I pinched a couple beers from the old man," Cava responded. "Hoof or bus?"

"Bus, yo! That kid lives in the nice part of town. Almost fucking Vincennes."

"I'll hoof it," added Fink. "It's not *that* far, and I wanna bomb down X. One side the way there, the other on the way back."

After the joint was smoked, until the sticky resin burnt their fingertips, the boys went their separate ways. Fink pinched the ember and put the roach into an Altoids tin. Cava and Luc went left to grab Rosee from the Orch, while their counterpart could be heard sloshing a magnum paint pen behind them.

* * *

Luc dinged the pull-cord as they hopped off the bus on the far west-side of Eckersley, before it passed over the river and bifurcated into the two main thoroughfares of Vincennes. The long avenue transformed incrementally as one moved westerly from its intersection with O'Connor Street, the location of the central train station. With the distance the kids had traversed, the slight changes amounted to a dramatically different, almost unrecognizable portion of Fury when compared to the centre, where they lived.

Luc and Cava were somewhat familiar with the area, well-traveled for sports and hang outs, but Rosee was seeing the docile suburbs for the first time in her decade and a half. "Holy fuck. These are goddamn mansions. Is this where the newsmen and the Hammers live?"

The boys chuckled at her naivety and the way she stared at the houses in awe, not unlike Luc's salivating maw at the fireworks. She was enchanted by the grandeur of the stucco, the number of respectable-looking cars parked in the driveways, and even the freestanding basketball hoops and trampolines that seemed to dot every other yard.

"Yeah, the kings and queens of Fury, R." Luc joked. "Mostly Indians and whites. Not whites like you guys, but, you know, normal whites. Not Irish. Hah."

Cava chuckled, but Rosee remained silent, perhaps pensive. Her head cocked towards the satellite antennas bolted to the roofs and television screens that were visible through sprawling rectangular living room windows.

"It's so quiet," she said. Cava caught himself staring at her. He resisted the falling sensation he sometimes felt when he looked at her; the endearing rawness of her youth and inexperience, the vulnerabilities that drew his care, the animalism of his physical attraction.

"Stop," Luc said as he placed his hand on Cava's chest, snapping him out of his contemplation.

"What?" Cava responded, astounded that Luc had noticed.

"I just realized that I'm wearing a brown belt," Luc said, distraught.

"So?"

"So? I'm wearing a black shirt, tucked in, with black jeans and black Chucks. And a brown belt."

"I don't see the problem, man."

"Yo, the shit clashes, man. Bad. Shit's mega unflattering. I look mad dopey."

"Well, we aren't going back. We're like two doors away. Untuck your shirt."

"I know, I know… Look, switch me shirts."

"Why?"

"Because your shirt is white, and I really wanna try this whole tuck thing. I think it'll be a good look. Plus, my shirt is hella baggy on me, so it will fit you fine."

"Okay, man. Whatever."

The boys veered off the light sidewalk and removed their shirts for the exchange. Passersby turned their heads and Rosee watched, giggling, but appreciative of the display. Luc tucked Cava's white shirt in and rubbed his chin.

"Now what?"

"I like those shoes better…"

* * *

The party was well underway by the time Cava, Luc, and Rosee arrived. Fink was nowhere to be seen. He was most likely taking his sweet time sipping brandy and dropping tags wherever he could find space. Still fairly early, the group maintained its three-person core, conversing with others. The vibe was friendly, relaxed, and with good energy. Drew Smith, a well-liked and charming athlete, was hosting the festivities with his parents' permission. He was something of a big man, whose name regularly appeared in rumours about students sleeping with faculty. *His parents must be professionals*, Cava thought. It was a genuine house, with both a front and back yard, multiple levels, and bathrooms.

"Yo, the Ox's in the house," Drew cheered with the refined, corny tone of a well-bred white boy as he slapped hands with the two lads, scoffing at the young lady.

"What up, D?!" Luc pulled the host in, feeling friendliness stemming from the brown liquor he'd slugged on the bus ride.

"Luc wit da C! Hey, Cava, what's up my man? Where's Sally? I thought she'd come, I asked her personally. She's looking fine as hell these days."

"She's, uh, studying, brother. Sorry." Cava was taken aback.

"Yeah, yeah, next time, D, next time," Luc said thoughtlessly as he slid his shoes off at Drew's request. "Yo, let everybody know, I got booze and weed if motherfuckers got the loot and the need."

* * *

As the night rolled, the music got louder, the kids got drunker, and the host's tone—when asking people to take their cigarettes and weed outside—became more truculent. He was flustered despite his own consumption, which made him seem panicked.

Rosee was quiet, attached to Cava's side, and staring at all the faces untrustingly, even those she was familiar with. As the alcohol began to take her over, she started bouncing from arm to arm, asking kids if they lived nearby, and what their parents did for work.

Luc was in his element. He could be found at any moment chanting, yelling, and lifting his shirt to let girls touch his abs. He was also making a few ducats here and there selling his supplies to underprepared kids whose supply of drugs and drink had dried up.

Cava, though occasionally treated with an arm around his shoulder or bear hug from wandering Luc, played the wall. He chatted with his various classmates, sometimes stepping outside for a cigarette, but mainly observing the various microcosms of drunken behaviour. The foolish ones who placed their drinks in the fridge, only to have them pilfered. The attempted pairing off of two kids, trying to find a spare bedroom or an empty bathroom. Heated arguments that required valiant diffusion from comrades, not unlike the restless atmosphere of the train.

Rosee, rubbing the biceps and accepting sips from the bottles of older guys, made Cava wonder if he actually felt jealousy or just a Cliff-like sense of protection for her. He wondered how Sally was getting on with her trig or bio or whatever, probably bothered by the hillbilly Romani-Irish sing-a-long happening beneath the carport next door. She was likely making a point of slamming her window, with gusto, but would more than likely be unheard.

"Yeah, man… I knew one of you threw that can at my uncle. He was pissed. I figured it was probably Rat-Fink… He seems to always do messed up stuff like that, dragging you guys in. Where is he?" Lil Bertie asked as the two leaned against the wall amidst the furor of drunken youth.

"He was taking the long way, on foot, down X," Cava replied. "Thanks for saving our asses, man. Your uncle is scary as fuck."

"Hah, yeah… He's a sweetheart if he likes you," Bertie responded. "He was a big fan of Kill 'Em Kalou. I think he won him some loot more than once, not too sure. Speaking of which, where's Luc? He have any ganja?"

The boys stopped momentarily. Cava raised his eyes skyward and placed a finger to his ear; a clamorous noise was heard from the living room behind them. The boys peered around the corner and saw Luc jumping off a couch while drinking from a green bottle and being caught by members of the football team.

Bertie laughed. "Mad, that one. Think my beer is safe in the fridge if I leave for a toke?"

"I do not," Cava replied, matter-of-factly.

"Yeah, me neither. I don't wanna have to start a fight for something dumb. Watch it for me? 10 minutes, max."

"Yeah, take your time. I ain't going nowhere anyways."

Bertie started towards the living room, then paused. "Yo, *your* Sally was looking good, by the way." He winked and continued through the mass of kids.

Cava remained at the same spot, watching over Bertie's beer, some girl's handbag as she entered the bathroom for a long spell with two girl-friends, someone else's backpack, and a mickey he'd slid into his back pocket. A one-man coat check. Scanning the room with no intent, his hawkeyed surveillance caught a sight that stilled him.

He spotted a short girl, not quite thick but by no means skinny. He couldn't remember seeing her at school, parties, or anywhere before. She was overdressed for the occasion in a black dress, tight, that cut midway up her heavyset thighs, with little black Nikes. She turned her head and he squinted at her side profile. She had a long, graceful nose, a plump, friendly countenance with high cheekbones, and full, ruby lips that made her wheat skin look less dusky. Her eyes were large and round, almost sitting outside of her face; ivory orbs with big ink blots that reflected no light. Cava was enamoured with her face and her deeply wholesome smile that exposed big, white, and perfectly straight teeth. The final product made her appear, in his mind, a sincere and affable person.

She turned in his direction, momentarily making eye contact with her depthless iris, causing him to seize internally, darting his head away. He remained downcast for a moment, then looked up to see her whip her head away from him. *Interesting*, he thought. He noticed his breath-ing had become sharp and weak.

All the kids had reclaimed their belongings, and Cava was no longer bound to his location. Feeling his introversion begin to militarize against its leader, he took a big swig of booze, turning his cheeks up after the burning drink ripped through his throat. That ought to quell the junta.

He entered the foyer to slide on his shoes, only to find them missing. Looking out the open front door, he saw Luc, passing a blunt and wearing his sneakers. He demanded his shoes from Luc, who gladly tossed them over and remained outside, barefoot.

"Here's the guy, this is the guy! Step on out and join us," Luc hooted like a midway operator. Cava declined and motioned Luc to join him a step away from the oblong of smokers.

"Yo… I need a favour," Cava whispered.

"A favour!" Luc yelled as he took the bottle out of his back pocket and unscrewed it. Cava tried to silence his friend and brought him closer.

"There's this girl," he began, quietly. "And I need you to do whatever it is that you do and introduce me to her."

"Why you need me?"

"Because… you're *that* guy," Cava reasoned to his friend, who'd already loosened the rope of his third sail. He lowered the bottle from Luc's mouth and made earnest visual contact, silently imploring a few moments of his time.

"Okay, then. Let's go!"

* * *

Cava kept his shoes on while they entered the house, feeling that the Asian custom had been eschewed at this stage. Luc strode in beside his friend, barefoot. They made their way to the kitchen; the girl was still there. *That one.* Cava pointed so that only Luc could catch his gesture. She was standing with some girls, some of whom they recognized from school. Seeing Luc in the light, Cava was plunged into second thoughts, thinking about retooling or abandoning the plot altogether. Luc had, meanwhile, slogged his way up to the cluster of girls, bumping into one of them.

"Hey… Oh, hey Luc wit da C," a brown girl said to him. "Where are your shoes? Why are you barefoot?"

The girls giggled. Another tipsy lout may have precipitated an adverse reaction, but such was the Quebecois' gift. He made small talk with the girls he recognized, said they all looked lovely, that the summer had done them right, and asked if they were excited about the coming year.

"And, you!" He focused on the unknown girl as Cava finally limped up, fearing the worst. "You look new. My name is Luc, spelled with a C—the right way. And you are?"

"I'm in your homeroom, silly. On my first day, I knew who you were. The teacher hates to love you." She laughed. "My name is Anjuli. I *am* new. I moved here with my mom and dad a couple weeks ago. From Rockford."

"Well, you came to the right place, I guess. Are there lots of Indians where you come from? There are here," Luc blurted out. Cava made a shocked expression.

Anjuli remained pleasant. "There are some, but true, not as many as in your city. Especially Sikhs."

"*Our* city," Luc said as he put his arm around her shoulder. Cava wondered for a second if Luc's consumption had taken over, beguiling the stratagem. "Now, I know you, and we'll have all year to get to know each other in homeroom. Have you met this fine Irishman?"

"I don't think I have," she said as her rotund cheeks lifted and reddened, her eyes locking with Cava's. He felt as though someone had removed the ground beneath him.

"This is Cava," he said. "Shake his hand. He's my bestest, oldest, and closest friend."

Cava took her small, supple hand in his, still unsure of what to say.

Luc made a point to distract the three girls in the vicinity, two brown and one white, with questions about fashion and clothing design. Whether he'd intended to draw attention away from the other two, or genuinely wanted to speak about couture, was questionable.

Cava and Anjuli kept their hands locked for a few moments more. When they finally released them, Anjuli said: "Cava? Like Spanish champagne? You don't look like a Spaniard."

"Racism? How *dare* you?" Cava joked. "I could be straight from the streets of Barcelona for all you know."

"Maybe…" Anjuli grinned. "But something tells me an *Irishman* with no Spanish accent is probably not from Iberia."

Cava was intrigued by her word choice of 'Iberia.' It was something he knew, but he doubted that any friend beyond Sally would have picked it up. "Fair play." He grinned in return. "It's just a nickname... Well, half of my last name. I'm Quinn Cavanaugh, and it's nice to meet you."

"Anjuli Mann," she returned. "Quinn Cavanaugh?" She paused contemplatively. "That's like a super hero's real name... Like Peter Parker, or..."

"Stephen Strange? Bruce Banner? Bucky Barnes?" Cava returned, smitten by her geeky response. He cut himself off before he rattled off any more signs that excavated his possible deal-breaking love for comic books.

"Yes," she agreed with a laugh. "But I love Spiderman the most, Quinn Cavanaugh."

Cava couldn't hold back a cheek depleting smile as he noted hers. "Nice dimples."

"Back at you."

He felt the indent on his right cheek. "Oh, that's an old injury."

"Like your nose?" she noted, remarking the still-swollen nasal bridge. "Are you one of those fighting Furies?" She moved her hand to softly touch the cut.

"No, not by choice. Never by choice."

* * *

Cava and Anjuli carried on with their small talk in what felt like the eye of a hurricane. Debris, in the form of other people, periodically threw their arm around Cava, remarked that little other than simple conversation was happening, and then moved on. Cava hadn't touched his bottle for over an hour. He noticed that the girl was maintaining a cutesy, hands-behind-her-back timidity, twisting her foot into the ground while explaining her travels and lucrative family business that resulted in their relocation to Fury.

"Where do you live?" she asked.

"The Ox," Cava responded. Noticing her confusion, he elaborated: "The Oxford Houses."

"What's that?" she asked. "It sounds fancy."

"Ha!" Cava squawked. "It's really not. Luc's my neighbour. It's fine. It's a melting pot of families and stuff. It's a block of X and a few down from O."

"X and O?" she puzzled.

"Yeah… Eckersley and O'Connor. Where Central is. The train station?"

"Hmm, I'm not too familiar with that area. I don't think, at least."

"It's… central." Cava laughed nervously. "Where they're building the new towers…"

"Oh! The Singh Tower!"

"That's the big one, yeah."

"My uncle says that area is being revitalized! They're putting a university campus there, and a bunch of businesses. They're developing the area and cleaning it up."

"That's the goal, I hear. Couldn't happen any sooner."

The two continued their introductions, talking about movies, video games, school, travel, and whatever else they could pull from the air. Cava was becoming more comfortable. He surmised that she was intelligent and that her interests were similar to his—albeit his tamer, less risk-taking pursuits. She seemed like a nerd, which he liked. He wagered that she probably came from wealth, or at least some kind of money, but noted that her style of dress and makeup wasn't as ornate and carbon-copied as the rich girls normally styled themselves with. He was taken by her quick wit and seemingly open mind, not overtly judging or making faces at the details relating to where he lived, the appearance of drunken friends asking him if he wanted any drugs, or even Rosee approaching and trying to squirm her way between them.

"Cava, I'm so drunk. I need you to take care of me." Rosee approached, conspicuously grabbing at his collar and whispering flagrantly into his ear. "Can you take me home, baby? I really need to lay down on something hard… I mean soft."

Cava gave Anjuli a look of disgust and surprise. Rosee didn't seem to expect the way he batted her hand from his collar and looked down at her. "Then you better ask Drew if you can use the phone and call your ass a cab, Ghetto Rose."

He knew she hated that name. "Fuck you, bitch-ass, you ain't shit," she said as she punched him in the chest and walked away, discarding the saccharine looks she'd given him a moment ago.

"Your ex?" Anjuli asked.

"Just a… someone who likes to… I dunno, man. But *definitely* not my ex."

"Boyfriend?" He pointed at Anjuli with a raised eyebrow.

"Nope. Girlfriend?"

"Neither."

* * *

Luc was bobbing around the party, still being trailed by the three girls he'd swooned away from Cava and Anjuli. He returned to the spot where he'd left them for a moment. "Still here? That's cute! Girls, follow me, we'll smoke the sacred herb of La Maria."

"Oh my god, I've never gotten high before," one of the girls said as they left.

"Your friend is quite the… spark plug," Anjuli said.

"Very much so," Cava agreed. "He might get your friends into trouble tonight."

"Well, one is my cousin and she could use it. The others I've only just met." Anjuli laughed.

"Don't know many folk yet?"

"Just moved here… But now I know you."

"Yo, Cavs… Who's that with Fink?" Drew tapped his shoulder, concernedly.

Fink was slowly making his way through the entrance, taking in his surroundings, with a group of several other older-looking cats. Cava immediately noticed Tic-Tax skulking behind Fink, hoodie up. The others he knew in varying capacities. Cava tried to cut his eye through the crowd, and mentioned that the others were some guys from his area. When asked if they were previous grads, Cava responded: "Really doubtful. Just some dudes from around the way. Fink probably saw them while he was painting."

Anjuli and Cava watched as Drew tapped on a couple of his friends' arms, bigger types with stocky frames, also multi-sport athletes at school. Their eyes followed as the jocks approached Fink, who gave a shallow nod to the host. Drew prevented one lad from immediately darting up the stairs and pointed him to the bathroom queue through the kitchen.

Cava discerned tentative greetings from the hesitant host and a series of provisional handshakes exchanged between Drew and the unmoved, stone-faced newcomers.

"You know them, Quinn?" Anjuli asked as she gripped Cava's arm. His chin and neck remained elevated to inspect the proceedings.

"Some more than others," Cava responded, mildly distracted. "This is usually the time of night where shit goes down in Fury."

Anjuli remarked that, aside form Fink—whom she also identified from her homeroom—the others looked older and rougher. Cava validated her statement and watched from the corner of his eye as one guy, with his hood still covering his head, went for the stereo and flipped through the CD booklet. Another, with a shaved head and a pencil-thin goatee, was standing in line for the bathroom, bobbing his head and tapping his fingers against his thumb rapidly, failing to galvanize conversation with the girls nearby. Fink and the other two men moved in a unit, as a dark, heavy cloud, tenebrous and brooding, through the otherwise Halcyon atmosphere.

Fink nodded through the crowd at Cava and signalled his cohorts to follow him. Once inside the kitchen, two of the other members veered towards the fridge. One kept six while the other rooted through plastic bags and beer cases. As Fink went to make his greetings to Cava, Tic-Tax stepped in front, and said: "Where's Frenchie?"

Cava poked his head up, shrugging and said that he was around— maybe outside, maybe pissing. Tic-Tax smacked his teeth, noticing Anjuli squinting at his mouth. "Fuck you looking at, Hindu?"

She instantly dropped her head as Fink simpered. Cava twisted his face up at Tic-Tax. "Watch your dolphin-ass mouth."

"Fuck you just say?" Tic-Tax needled his beady eyes down from above. Cava stared back into them, noticing their bloodshot, stretched-corner fogginess. He glanced at Fink's eyes, also coloured a firetruck red, but more sloped and tired.

The two held their ground silently, each maintaining a look of unimpressed disregard. Tic-Tax asked Cava what he wanted to do, indicating something in his jeans with his finger and revealing the outline of a rectangular object. Cava resisted the urge to move his insensate gaze towards whatever it was.

After a minute of action unfolding in a vacuum around them, Cava scoffed and shook his head. "Nothing, man. Just enjoy the party." Tic-Tax let out a sharp exhale through his conical teeth and turned his head.

While the two were standing off, the two characters at the fridge had been accused of thievery and, though culpable, were inclined to fight for their innocence. In the living room, the goon hovering around the stereo ignited a beef over switching a disc and putting on music that was immediately disputed by a few people; he turned the volume up to a crackling peal, pocketed the CD book, and threw a girl by her hair. The guy with the goatee returned from the bathroom with powder clumped to his facial hair and kept mumbling, "someone about to get bottled up in this bitch."

"Uh… Why you have to go and say shit, Cava?" Fink demanded. "You know that guy has a few screws loose."

"He disrespected Anjuli, here. There ain't no Hindus in Fury. All the brown people here are Sikhs. You don't like it when cats call you Russian, right? Besides, you shouldn't bring, or even hang around with, people who you don't trust in the first place."

Cava was unable to appreciate the irony of explaining this to Fink, but asked if Anjuli was okay. She insisted that she was fine. Fink anxiously backed away without a sound.

* * *

Tic-Tax approached Luc with his hand out and pulled the happy drunk in close to him. "You got the loot?"

"Yeah, man, yeah!" Luc responded nonchalantly. "I got it all at home. Meet me tomorrow and I'll pick up some more! Shit went fast, we got some good business at the school."

Tic-Tax grinned, exposing his teeth and pointing his sharp, Luciferian chin. The two discussed Fabi, Luc's middle brother, scheduled to return home from his 'trip' any day, and how they would make even more loot. Luc mentioned that he was just happy to see Fabi after his time away. Fink approached the two of them, was pat on the shoulder by Tic-Tax, who mentioned that he wanted to get *Crusher* on board with the *crew* as well. Luc was silent for a moment, but responded with languid affirmation.

The jittery guy from the bathroom, crystals still caked under his nose, approached the three and said, "yo man, we can stick this place, man. These are all just *kids* man. Most of them look like pussies." Tic-Tax laughed as Fink and Luc looked at each other with slight concern. The two fridge thieves started to fling bystanders out of the way as they encroached on the circle of four.

"Yo man, we gonna have to slug our way out. They saying we stole their booze. Lucky for them, we didn't stick them for their riches," said one of the guys.

"Word, you guys got our back?" The other, with diverse colours of spray paint dried thickly on his pointer, gesticulated towards Luc and Fink.

They were distracted for a moment as they noticed the girls hanging out behind Luc. The three stepped to the girls, and within seconds, dispersed them to another corner of the house.

"Whores," said the one with the paint-crusted index finger. The entire sleeve of his hoodie was equally paint-spattered.

A mixture of shouting and furniture displacement suddenly came from the living room; one of the figures noticed that their last member was absent. As Tic-Tax led the group towards the living room, Luc tailed them in time to see the missing guy, his paint-splashed hoodie still drawn, push Drew into the glass stereo cabinet. One of Drew's friends grabbed the troublemaker's arms, while the four outsiders jumped in, leaving Fink standing still and Luc holding himself on people's shoulders to survey the dustup.

The gritty underground New York rap that had induced the original scuffle was elevated to an even higher decibel as the skirmish became more heated. *Shook Ones* was the next track, the crackle of the vinyl sample, the sinister keys, and the ominously orotund bass-drum kicks sibilated with confounding distortion.

Rosee appeared and kicked a guy's groin, coming behind Tic-Tax, who turned around and fish-hooked the hunched student's cheek, ripping it open. He smiled at her as he grabbed the butterfly knife from his pocket, opened it, and twisted it down into the trapezius of another kid, all in one motion. The blood was mud-coloured as it dripped onto the powder blue carpet. The host was bleeding from the glass shards that had torn through his back, and one of the nameless assailants screamed "Fury-Us" as he back swung a fire poker at another kid's face, laying him facedown on the floor.

Luc was flung out of the way as someone rampaged towards the one-sided fight. Lil Bertie, shirtless with lipstick marks on his neck, had heard the commotion, popped out of the upstairs bedroom to catch a glimpse, and recognized at least one of the fire-starters immediately.

Bertie grabbed Tic-Tax by his sweatshirt and raised him to his feet. As he was lifted, Tic-Tax raised his boody blade, but pulled back at the last second. "Oh, fuck."

Police sirens and red-strobed cruiser lights filled the room through the bay window. In a panic, kids began to flee from the exits, knocking over pictures, portraits, tables, and each other. Luc ran to the kitchen to find Cava, but found his spot for the night vacated. The brawlers rose and grabbed what they could as they left. One of them kicked a hole in one of the speakers, tripped over a plug, and jetted out the back. The attendees who'd taken their shoes off discovered that many were missing, some seen on the fleeing older cats, having been replaced with grubby, mud and paint covered skateboard shoes.

Fink and Rosee waited and watched as Bertie continued to hold Tic-Tax in place, as if he'd caught him, weighed him, and was now waiting to have their photo taken on the pier. He pierced the quavering Tic-Tax with a steely glare, a snarl, and snapped a punch to his jaw with the same hand that was gripping his jersey. Tic-Tax's blood-covered hand dropped his knife and grabbed his jaw.

"You're lucky we don't mess with pigs," Bertie said, throwing him into a wall and turning to watch him run out the back, followed by Fink and Rosee.

The post-cyclonic scene had produced six teenagers with various battle wounds lying prone on the ground. The walls were full of divots, spattered with red and brown stains. Some people were still hanging around, either unaware of the incoming patrolmen or unworried by their lack of involvement in the violent episode. The carpets had tiny burn scars, like welder's clothes, and the empty drinking vessels were crunched and shattered all over the carpet and hardwood flooring.

Cops stormed through the doorway and looked at Lil Bertie, shirtless with his arms folded. "This your place?" they asked.

* * *

Cava and Anjuli heard the commotion and saw a horde of kids rushing towards the living room. Confrontational shouting and ghastly screaming began as Cava leaned into Anjuli. "You live nearby?" She mentioned that her place was probably half an hour by foot, five by car. Cava mused about that being Fury in a nutshell, the sprawling nature of constant development where yards and space between houses became larger and larger as one moved westward on Eckersley.

"I feel like the 5-0 is going to show up pretty quick here," Cava replied. He thought about what might come of Luc, if he'd be inclined to jump in, but decided that he'd rather Luc take a slug than protect one jagged tooth in Tic-Tax's snout.

"It's not too chilly, and you can borrow my hoodie. Here." Cava removed his sweater.

"You wanna walk me home?"

"Yes, I do."

They exited through the backyard, walking around to the side gate and passing some friends and acquaintances of Cava's, all offering a drink or a hit as they passed. He declined, walking ahead and pulling open the side gate, allowing Anjuli to pass first. He looked back and saw a mess of bodies toppling over each other through the living room window. There were bottles, cans, and cigarette butts littering the lawn and police sirens wailing in the distance. A shattering sound kicked the music's roar higher, even outside. He was glad to be out of that mess, but he liked that song.

* * *

The distance that Cava and Anjuli had created from the party smeared the sounds of high-pitched sirens and crunchy bass from the house party to a fading din. He remarked that they were walking through largely unexplored territory, which surprised him, having thought that he knew the city quite thoroughly. He described how much quieter it seemed, without the incessant traffic noise from Eckersley and the homeless rummaging through dumpsters and garbage cans all night long. The tranquility was agreeable, but seemed boring, for lack of a more diplomatic word to associate with the calm placidity.

"Why would you want noise all night? How do you sleep?" Anjuli asked him.

"It's not loud, you know, just a racket. Kind of like little noises that ease you to sleep. Sometimes yelling or sharp noises wake you up. But most times, it's like a lullaby, or ocean sounds."

"Well, I'd like to see that side of Fury. I've been through, but have mostly stayed *here*," she circled her palm. "I've seen some parks and stuff, but you make it sound so different than my uncle. He always talks about Fury, or River City as he calls it, with hope and opportunity."

"Yeah," Quinn said, digesting her words. "I suppose there's some area for development. They say it's only a matter of time before the New Am construction and stuff trickles down. I guess it's good. I haven't really thought about it."

"This is me, here," Anjuli said as they approached a large, beige house with four sedans in the driveway.

"You having a party? Why so many cars?"

Anjuli laughed and tugged him warmly. "You don't know much about brown people, do you?"

Cava felt stymied and ignorant. He glanced around the neighbourhood. All the houses were quite big, similar in shape and makeup, and each with at least four vehicles in the driveway. Almost all of the houses had at least one white van or pick-up truck with a company name emblazoned on the side for some kind of trade: plumbing, siding, foundations, and others. Beyond that, Cava didn't notice anything queer. He'd been told that the smell of curry would be instant as soon as he entered Brown Town, but this was just a typical 'nice' neighbourhood; a panorama of decent-sized houses with well-kept yards.

"I don't," Cava said, honestly. "East Indians, or browns… they keep to themselves. I mean, I know a bunch, but we don't hang out at parties or anything."

"That's fair. Parties are usually a family thing. And to us, family is a bit different than how white people consider it. It's different in Fury, too. Everyone here seems to call someone uncle or cousin. Everyone always knows someone, or knows someone who knows someone. Take my house, for example. My grandparents live there, as well as one of my aunts, my uncle, and their two kids."

"Full house, man."

"Big time. It's kind of annoying... it's too loud when you want to study and you can't throw a bash because someone's always home, and they wouldn't want strangers to come in, with their shoes on, going through the fridge, leaving the seat up... You get it."

"Yeah... Are you guys poor or something?"

Anjuli laughed. "No, we're not poor... but lots of people that moved from India were, so they all split the house costs together. Then, they'd either rent out the house once it was paid off, or give it to a new married couple and start all over again, and again, and again. I dunno if it's a Sikh thing, maybe a Fury-Sikh thing... but we lived in a nice house back home, all by ourselves. Nice and quiet. This is nice, too... It's huge, and I get to play with my little cousins and have chai with my *Nani*. But, I'm still getting used to having so many people to meet, people who already know me and are all of a sudden my family. My uncle and cousin know *everybody*, and it's nice to meet people from school, different people with different... lives."

Cava took the sincerity of Anjuli's last words as an opportunity to pull her in for a kiss. They bumped noses comically, then snorted at the absurd contact. Cava opened his mouth to slide his tongue against Anjuli's. Her tongue moved like a windshield wiper against his teeth and gums, conveying her lack of experience. He pulled away and brought his hands around her, this time with a smaller mouth opening, allowing him to harness the wild thrashing of her tongue.

"Yeah! Get it in, boy!" A car honked as they unyoked reflexively, bashful but smiling.

"I'd better get inside," Anjuli said as she removed Cava's hoodie and handed it to him. "Thank you for getting me home safe."

Cava grabbed Anjuli's wrist and took a Sharpie from his backpack. "That's a 7. My writing is a bit messy."

Anjuli stood ballerina-toed and Cava smacked his lips with hers once more before she scampered towards the front door. Cava waited on the sidewalk, watching her scurry up to her porch, holding her skirt tightly so it wouldn't slide up, and turning back twice before entering through the large wooden and glass door.

Cava felt the warmth of pride and success. For a moment, he was worriless. A hero in his mind. Then, a mental and physical sensation of downiness coated him like a vat of warm molasses.

He sighed and nodded to himself with contained enthusiasm. He looked around the quiet streets, asking himself if the only noise he was hearing was the scraping of cricket legs. He walked to the rounding of the block and looked up at the street signs: Hadden Drive and Amethyst Place.

"What the fuck is Amethyst Place?" he whispered, the cross-street equally alien. He felt a chill and threw his sweater on. It smelled sweet.

KICK

NORMALLY, ON SATURDAYS, Cava would wrench himself from the comforts of his bed and head to the shop with his father to work. He received minimum pay for menial work: sweeping, arranging tools, and providing a second pair of mitts to whatever little restorative operation the boss had been rubbing his chin over all week. Most work could be done with one headphone dripping out of his ear, with the other attentively listening to ways he could sweep more efficiently and arrange more logically.

The already dawn hour at which Cava spilled himself inside his window, the smell of liquor seeping out his pores, and a rare day of fishing for Joe, all combined to allow him to remain in the uterine coziness of his bed until Nora's pacing insisted on his appearance upstairs.

After some coffee, porridge, and downplaying of the previous evening's escapades, Cava returned to his room and flicked on his gaming console. He was into a game that featured an explorer with a fantastically broad sword that sought to save the world from an evil force. A likely premise for a role-playing video game, but one that many of the kids played. He glanced at his book bag. Some minor *devoirs* could have used his attention, but he shrugged off any concerns and opted to put them off until Sunday.

A tap at his window, the piano line from *Shimmy Shimmy Ya*, all followed by the over-powered sliding of the pane presented Luc, his fingers spreading the blinds open with a metallic crinkling sound.

"Shoes off," Cava said, moments before he heard the sound of struggle and the dull thud of shoes landing on the ground behind him. His mother's feet clapped the floorboards above three times. "Easy with the window, unless you want Ma down here."

"My bad, my bad," Luc said, easing his long legs through the opening and landing clumsily on the bed. "You playing this again? Have you even made it any further?"

"It's not all about finishing the game, yo…" Cava responded without looking at his friend. "You have to get your experience leveled up, put your quarters up. Otherwise, you can't beat the bosses. Yeah, you can try, but if you don't have a high enough level, big enough inventory, and weapons and shit, you'll be stuck."

Luc scoffed derisively. "That shit takes so long, just pump in a cheat code and watch the ending. I bet it's pretty dope. It has to be. Why else would they make a three-disc game that makes kid spend like 100 hours on that motherfucker?"

"Because it's a challenge. It's the journey, man…"

Luc rose from the bed and busied himself looking for something. Cava heard him tinker with the books, papers, and pens that he kept in a cup, and his underwear drawer—before slamming it closed. "Snips?" Luc asked.

"Nightstand, top shelf, beside the rollies."

"All I see is a sock and…"

"Top shelf, yo!"

Cava heard the sounds of a Zip-Lock bag unfasten and silver scissors chew through dank, filling the room with its unmistakeably potent smell. Like strongly brewed Cuban espresso beans and freshly hemmed grass.

"You have the vacuum down here? Or… out the window?"

"No, maybe we should bounce... My mom might get choked. She seems like she's looking for a brawl."

Henry, who'd heard the clatter while in the kitchen, headed down after he'd cleaned his plate and washed his hands. "What are you guys doing?" the young brother asked while sitting on the bed beside Luc, keeping his head straight to prevent the youngling from seeing the joint in his right ear.

"Not much, just playing," Cava said. Henry, who enjoyed watching the game, moved up beside his brother on the foot of the bed, leaving Luc against the pillowed end and moving his joint to the inside fold of his baseball cap.

It didn't take long for Luc's legs to itch, watching Henry watch Cava play a video game. He began snapping his fingers, which made him tap his feet, which raised him to a standing position. He started to pace, and eventually found his green and white kickball from beneath a pile of laundry.

"There it is!" he said as he began to juggle the ball—softer tissue and better for inclement weather than a regular soccer ball. "Alright, it's been too long. Let's play some kick. Fresh air, let's go!"

Cava passed the controller to his brother. "Just keep grinding, we need some more EXP." Henry took the joystick and lay himself on his stomach, eyes fixed on the screen.

Luc was already out the window, fighting to squeeze his finger out of his shoe heel. Cava looked at his friend, with the ball under his arm and the joint in his mouth. He was wearing a Hammers cap tilted sideways and a black tracksuit that was painted with tiger-like stripes: white, orange, yellow, and little hints of Alabama red.

"What the fuck are you wearing, Luc?"

"Ha! You're just seeing me now?" Luc spread his arms and modeled the homemade additions to an otherwise fine tracksuit. "I saw an old picture of Randall Cunningham rocking a pair of wild-ass zebra pants. And, Legion of Doom! I thought, I could make them shits, and I did. Pretty fly, if you ask me."

"You look like a damn fool," Cava laughed. "Can you make lids with that style, though?"

* * *

The boys arrived at their school and scaled the fence, then proceeded to the outdoor basketball court. They kicked and juggled the ball for a few minutes to wait and see if Sally, whose window they'd yelled at from below, or Fink, whose window they'd bounced the ball off of, would show up.

Fink arrived with a clanking backpack. Sally followed with an equally full bag that she dumped on the bleachers. They sat in a square on the bleachers, circulating a joint. Moving away from the smoke, Sally mentioned that she had to play volleyball later on, but that it might be the last nice day—a common phrase in her house—so she might as well study outside.

Cava and Luc began their hybrid game of soccer-basketball, which involved trying to shoot hoops with European football-style kicks and headers. The fields always seemed mushy and wet, and neither boy was satisfied with basketball alone. It also allowed them to keep their hands clean for rolling and smoking.

"Why don't you guys just play soccer *or* basketball?" Sally asked in a mocking but sweet way.

"Well, my black side wants to play basket, but my Italian side wants to kick things, so this is what we do," Luc responded as he blasted a right, sending the ball skyward off the backboard, jingling the metal netting.

Fink was still smoking the smallest of nubbins, burning his lips and dropping what was basically resin-covered paper into his tin. "That was fucked about last night," he announced, squinting.

Luc received the ball from Cava, stepped down on it, and turned to Fink. "Word... on your part. Why'd you bring those guys?"

"What happened?" asked Sally.

Luc gave a less-than-quick recount of the details of the party the night before.

"Stabbing?" Sally said with horror.

"Yeah, some cat took a blade in the back and the goons started throwing down... I got my ass out, ain't no time for that. Tried to find the chicks, but I dunno where they went. Tried to find old boy Cavs here, but he was gone with some brown honey," Luc said.

"I saw the storm coming. Tic-Tax wanted to start some shit with me. I didn't want any beef... I'm not trying to get shanked," Cava said.

"Yeah, he don't like you very much," Fink added. "Not sure why. Maybe because you always clown his grill. Maybe some other reason. Sometimes people just don't like you. Sometimes they hate you for no reason. Like me."

"Nah," Luc laughed. "There are plenty of reasons to hate your toy-crossing, beef-starting, fight-running, ass."

"Shut up, Luc," Fink muttered. "Anyways, Ali's meeting me here, so watch your mouths."

Luc made a raspberry as he chipped the ball from the key, hitting the rim.

"What *honey*?" Sally said with her textbook sitting open on her long legs, knees touching.

"Ah yeah," Luc started. "That little Jasmine-from-Aladdin-looking Indian girl. What was her name? Andrea?"

"Anjuli," Cava said, firmly.

"Yeah, cute... not my type. You know: short, long nose, kind of thick... cute. Cava's type. What happened with that?"

"Umm, nothing much. Tic-Tax threw some shade at her, I told him not to, so me and him stared down. When things got heated, I offered to walk her home."

"To Brown Town? How was that? Was it different? Did it smell weird? Did they try to convert you?"

"Normal. It's just some big houses, lots of cars, the same street over and over again... You know, suburbia."

"You fuck her?"

"No," Cava dismissed with a snort.

"You kiss her?" Luc asked, screwing his neck at Cava, who blushed slightly and hesitated to answer. "Oh, shit! Look who's got the moves! Cavs, you got the juice, son!" Luc continued to prod and poke at Cava while moving excitedly. Cava simply asked for the ball, keeping his line of sight far away from that of the lone female of the group. Sally, for her part, felt a tinge of lightning in her abdomen, followed by a small lump in her throat.

"What's up, faggots?!" a nasally voice beckoned from the other end of the court. A childish female laugh followed the off-putting greeting as the boys turned to see Tic-Tax walking up to them with a duffle slung over his shoulder. By his side was Rosee, still wearing her clothes from the previous night. On his other side was a dark, curly-headed fellow. He was darker than Luc, with a wider nose and smaller lips.

"Holy fuck! *Fabienne, comment-ça va, mon frère?*"

The brothers hugged and kissed each other's cheeks. The older brother approved of Luc's custom tracksuit, while Luc asked him if he'd lost weight or seen their mother.

"Nah, little brother. Ali just picked me up from the bus station. I was gonna make some stops, see some cats, and then slide home. You been keeping my room?" Fabi said in his French accented, gravelly voice.

"Yeah," Luc said happily.

"Alright, you back upstairs now. That'll be our office," Fabi said, without smiling.

Tic-Tax was in the corner of the bleachers, shadowed and cooler than the sun-smacked centre of the court that the kids had been occupying. Cava went to sit with Sally before he was summoned as well. He ignored the calls and remained with her for some minutes. He gave her a head shake and a look of concession before eventually heading over, entering mid-conversation.

"Yeah, got this new ride, a Bonneville, guess that makes me Clyde." Tic-Tax laughed. "Cava," he said abruptly. "Beef is bad for business, brother. We cool?"

Cava nodded and agreed as the two bumped fists. Luc handed stacks of fives and twenties to Tic-Tax, who counted them before handing a freezer bag full of weed and some smaller bags with powder and pills over. Tic-Tax then asked for the bag back and handed it to Fink, who put it in his backpack, much to Luc's dismay.

Cava eyed Fabi from the side. He looked emaciated, and his dark skin was ashen. He tried to remember what he'd looked like when he'd left. He'd had short cropped hair and seemed to have a more spirited disposition. His eyes were cloudy and half-open as he swayed, occasionally clapping his hands and moving his arms like an old jitterbug dance move.

Rosee stood behind Tic-Tax, holding his duffle bag and leering at Cava with a look that vacillated between vexation and longing. Cava nodded at her silently, sending her eyes towards the sky.

Luc was having difficulty restraining his giddiness, constantly trying to hug or rub his brother's arm to make sure that he was real. Fabi
switched between reciprocal joviality and circumspect dismissiveness. He
and Fink listened to Tic-Tax's soapbox about how this was some kind of
beginning. Tic-Tax was expertly using his gang connections to get them
access to drugs, and soon, firearms. Soon, they'd be able to supply anyone
with anything, but they needed more people. Good, trustworthy people.

Hearing this, Cava turned back to see that Sally was gone. He looked
up and down the school lot, but didn't catch sight of her. *She must have
made off as soon as he turned.*

"So, that's how it's gonna be. I'll be the *jefe*, and you guys are my soldiers. I'm trying to get some more connects, because I don't know how
long I can work without the Souls finding out too much. I don't want to
deal with the Singhs outright, because they're competitors. For now, Luc
has the Bench and the school. Fink has the walls and wherever he wan-
ders off to. I have Kesq and the brothers doing their thing. Fabi is like
my general. Rosee, she'll sell at the trailers. I can cook at my grandma's
place. The old bitch has no idea what's going on anyways. But, if you
know of a trap house, we could use one to stash all the loot we're gonna
make. We're gonna be huge, guys. The bikers, the Indians, the goddamn
Asians, everybody will be looking up at us."

Cava realised why Tic-Tax had wanted to squash the beef: he was
tight with two of his dealers and would probably try to convince him to
do the same at some point, to be privileged to all his grandiose sermons.

Tic-Tax said it was time to go, and Fabi and Rosee followed him.
Luc asked if he could join, to talk more with his brother and eventually
return to his mother's house with her absent middle son, nearly completing the four chairs at the supper table.

Cava declined a ride home. He wanted to enjoy the sunny day, possibly the last nice day of the year.

* * *

Cava arrived home to find his little brother still killing monsters for experience points. He felt bloated with uncertainty, nervousness, and melancholy.

It was quite the crew. He was now on the outside. Would he want to remain there? Why did Luc care about Fabi so much? Every time he went to juvie, Luc seemed to thrive. He was able to focus on his own interests. The fact that Tic-Tax had said that they were actively pursuing action that was contrary to the Singhs, who Fabi had supposedly been working for, was complicated and nettlesome.

"What you thinking?" Henry asked.

"Uh…" Cava began, but he was interrupted by his mother's heel pummelling the ceiling.

"Quinn Padraig Cavanaugh, come get the phone. Some girl has been trying to call you all day!"

ANJ AND QUINN

CAVA GALLOPED UP the stairs with nervous excitement. He had a good idea of whose voice was awaiting him on the other side of the telephone. He lived within a baseball's throw to his best friends' houses, and they were more likely to tap on his window than call. Nora was beloved by the group, but any chance to bypass a cross-examination from the Cavanaugh matriarch was relished.

The two spoke on the phone for hours, through the sound of the upstairs phone, secured to a cabinet in the kitchen, being lifted and hung up repeatedly by Nora to check and see if the house's only line was free. The conversation continued past the little brother's steadfast gameplay, even as he finally retired for the night. It continued until the battery of the cordless phone beeped, only to signal the fated conclusion of Cava and Anjuli's inaugural chat.

It was the first of what became a nightly ritual. It also quickly became a test of Mrs. Cavanaugh's patience. She had to refrain from gossiping with her sisters back East, prompting her to ask her eldest son if he intended to pay the phone bill in a brusque manner.

At school, the two didn't have any classes together, but they began to see more of each other during lunch break. As Anjuli was a new student—though she seemed to possess a glut of disparate familial relations— and she hung out with her troupe in the cafeteria. Cava, since he'd entered high school, usually stayed outdoors with Luc and the gang in the smoke pit. They all smoked, and Luc always had cigarettes and weed to sell. A small wooded area just outside the school grounds also enabled a better vantage point from which to spot the school's narcs and Furian constables. The group of kids that stood closest to the chain-link throughway would hoot, owl-like, which would be parroted by flocks further down the line, alerting everyone to the buzzards.

Something was changing in the area—*the Trees*, as it was called. Something was changing in Cava's opinion, at any rate.

The Trees had always just been an area where kids smoked and occasionally fought out issues that arose during class or in the hallways; quick, emotionless fights that couldn't wait for the street or an after-school setting.

Still in the nascent stages of the first semester, the Trees became less congenial; traditionally, many kids had provided the service of marijuana or tobacco sales to their fellow students. Whoever had it, sold it. The appearance Tic-Tax, announcing himself as Ali, became a daily routine. He was known and could always have been found behind the school on Fridays, or in the parking lot of a convenience store further detached from the school grounds before weekends, selling party drugs and offering to boot for kids, for a fee. But after his powwow at the courts, he was present every lunch hour, often flanked by Fabi and another crony or two. He was keeping an eye on his 'business,' ordering and taking part in the stompings of anyone who was also selling product in the area. The iron fisted nature of his clamp-down, on top of his salty and unpredictable character, was creating animosity and tension in the once haven-like refuge at school, away from the constraints, self-policed by the unsupervised students.

Cava was becoming less inclined to spend his hard-earned lunch break in such burgeoning hostility with every passing day. He remarked that Fink was presenting a more obnoxious version of his persona, allowing his bravura to replace the insecurity that had always kept him on the quieter side. He'd always had a streak of spitefulness and a conceited sense of pride, which was abrasive, but it had kept itself pinned under the scorn of his group until now.

Luc was also changing. He was showing up to his classes less frequently, both those that he truly enjoyed and the laughably easy courses he simply had to fill a seat in to pass. He still received Cava with a big hug and jaunty, heartfelt greetings, but he seemed like a hollow version of himself. To wit, if he began to reach a level of puppylike excitement, he was given stern looks and censure from Tic-Tax and Fabi—the latter of which, since he'd moved back to his mother's house, shifted between catatonia and intense emotionality. In his deep, croaking voice, Fabi could be heard quietly advising his brother; telling him not to smile so much, to keep his right fist in his left palm, to begin each response by clicking his teeth, and other admonitions against being 'too friendly' with people.

Rosee was always with them, clinging to Tic-Tax the way blood dries to a scab. After not having seen her since the party, Cava noticed that she appeared washed out. Her soft baby fat was depleting and her eyes were somehow more sniping. She fluctuated between coquettish and antisocial. Cava still admired her physical pneumaticity, but found that his concern for her well-being was eroding.

* * *

With quotidian phone-chatting and the change in the dynamics of his long-favoured hangout, Cava made increasingly frequent forays to the cafeteria at lunch. In all his time, he'd never spent more than a tempest or two in the school during his free hours. Sally would join them outside on nice days in the early years, but she increasingly busied herself with practices, tutoring, and extra credit assignments as they got older. When Cava first began spending his lunches inside, many of his acquaintances were surprised to see him mingling with the various tables: nerds, jocks, rockers—basically anyone who didn't smoke or get high at school. When he saw Sally quietly snacking on a sandwich with headphones, buried in a math textbook, she asked him if the four-horsemen had fallen on the Trees, or if an unseasonable blizzard had made him take solace in the clangorous, overly-social lunchroom. He laughed it off, claiming that he wanted a change, watching over her shoulder at one of the brown tables, making distanced, fanciful eye contact with Anjuli.

Cava roamed the tables, choosing a different one daily; some catbird seat from which he could make eyes at Anjuli without getting too close. She was worried about word getting back to her parents that she was interested in someone, a *gora*, as her circle referred to a white boy. Cava feigned understanding. He knew there were complications with people dating outside their ethnic circles and reasoned not to take offense or be insensitive to other cultures, as he was brought up to believe. They'd nod at each other and meet up in less populated hallways to speak briefly, grab one another's hands, and kiss quickly.

Sally, too, began to spend a little more time at the cafeteria, noticing that Cava's appearance wasn't a one-off occurrence. She was lonely and stressed, feeling as though she were the only one going through this process. She also enjoyed venting about whichever teacher or whatever equation seemed to be purposely blocking her progression. She noticed that Cava was preoccupied, staring off into the crowd, and at times grinning with no apparent cause. She figured he'd probably gotten baked before entering the cafeteria. She still sequestered herself to the desk in her bedroom while she was at home, which was only usually after the sun had sunk. During the moments when she drifted away from her calculations and essays, tapping her pencil against her notepad, and staring out the window, she contemplated tickling her nails against Cava's window. She felt out of touch with her friends, but knew that her goals and ambitions were paramount. Her future was being encroached upon by the present.

* * *

Anjuli was able to milk enough of her parents' trust to borrow the family car some nights, with the promise of attending cram sessions, group projects, and other harmless, all-girl outings. An intricate web of yarn had to be woven, with the aid of her cousin Pali, to ensure that the discretion of her whereabouts was secure if she ever returned a minute late.

Anjuli and Cava cultivated their courtship by half-watching second-run movies at the cheap cinema and taking hours to clean out bowls of pho at the Vietnamese noodle house on X. They would also study; Anjuli was intent on graduating with a high enough GPA to choose whichever university she desired, which directly influenced Cava's marks.

On Cava's end, there were no questions about where he was, except from Henry, who continued to toil away at the video game, itching to fight the next boss. On rare occasions, Luc would tap at the window, learn that Cava was absent, and leave, but this now happened much less often. Cava had already established a pattern of either being in his basement room or out with friends, exclusively using the window for access. His parents trusted that he wasn't committing any serious crimes, and they didn't receive the automatically generated phone calls from the school notifying them of his absences. As long as their boy wasn't in a gang or missing classes completely, they thought they were doing the best job they could. He was nearly a man; they had to hope he was smart enough not to be an idiot. For Nora, the phone line was open, and she was free to speak to her sisters about their cousin's son, whom they suspected was joining a cult.

Henry had asked Cava where he'd been spending his time. One night, he was grinding a little later than usual, hoping to progress in the game, but needed his older brother's consent.

"I was out with Luc and Fink."

"Luc came by, maybe… three hours ago. Said you were out. He asked where, but I didn't know."

"What'd you say?"

"I didn't know."

"Good."

"Where were you? Where have you been? Luc said he barely sees you, if at all."

"I been busy."

"With what? I think we have enough points to go to the dungeon and probably…"

"I been seeing a girl."

"Oh, sweet!"

"A brown girl."

"Oh... weird... How's that?"

"It *is* sweet, but she's a little sketchy about being seen with me. Either her parents don't like white people, or they don't want her to date, or something."

"That sucks."

"Yeah... kind of... Anyways, trying to keep it low-pro... So, if you could be a..."

"Yeah, I won't tell Mom and Dad. They'll find out though, you know."

"Til then... Where's this boss?" Cava eased the joystick from his brother's snug mitts.

* * *

"Guess what, Quinn?" Anjuli asked Cava as he sputtered blackstrap-coloured hoisin sauce from a plastic bottle onto his noodles.

"What's that?"

"I told my parents that I might have to start studying later on Friday and Saturday nights. They said that I haven't missed my curfew, that my grades are great, and that they wouldn't mind letting me have the car late on the weekend!"

Cava finally dislodged the treacly sauce, squeezing too hard and over-shooting the hoisin, covering his entire spoon of noodles. He let the spoon sink back into the ceramic bowl of salty broth and looked up: "That's dope... What does that mean?"

"It means," Anjuli said, grinning, "that maybe we could have... I dunno... a sleepover one of these weekends?"

Cava paused. He saw a feisty, playful look in her eyes, like a jungle cat who'd just cut her adult teeth.

"Well... yeah!" Cava said, feeling a warm swirl in his stomach. "I mean, of course. I haven't invited you over because..."

Anjuli suddenly snapped her neck towards the jingling bells on the opening restaurant door. Four men entered the diner: three browns and a black. Cava recognized Fabi, standing behind, looking much smaller than the others. Smaller than the last time he'd seen him. The other three were normal-looking guys; one of them seemed to be the leader, taking the front and approaching the host stand, speaking to the waitress in a low voice. The more Cava looked at him, the more familiar he seemed. He was well dressed in dark-wash jeans, a tucked in, white button-up, and a leather coat. He had a golden cable around his neck, a big gold watch on his right hand, and golden rings on his left. Anjuli's posture instantly shrunk, and she turned her face towards the window. Cava asked her what the matter was, but she responded with a tight-lipped headshake.

The men were shown to their seats. That's when the leader figure noticed Anjuli. He broke from the quartet and came over to the table.

"Anjuli," the man's voice said simply, ignoring Cava. "Cousin, hello."

"Ah, Joti, how are you?" Anjuli responded, pleasantly.

"How are you? What are you doing?"

"I'm good, cousin. I'm just having dinner with a school friend," she replied, in a bubbly tone.

The man, much taller and bigger than he'd looked at the door, eye-balled Cava. He wasn't smiling, but didn't seem angry. He extended his watch hand; it pulled his sleeve back, and a silver bangle and several cloth bracelets appeared. "Hello, young man. My name is Amajot Singh, and you are...?"

"Quinn Cavanaugh," he responded, shaking his hand and realizing who the man was.

"Quinn Cavanaugh. Sounds familiar. Quinn Cavanaugh. Why do I know that name?"

"Beats me... I grew up beside Fabi over there... maybe you've seen me around with his brother or..." Cava trailed off.

"Hmm... perhaps. I'm a close friend of the older Kalou brother, Jan-jak. I know the younger brother has been getting into trouble. I owe it to my friend to try and keep his brothers... safe."

Joti and Anjuli exchanged a few words in Punjabi. Anjuli answered with squinting smiles, albeit affectatious, and noticeably anxious. The older cousin patted her on the shoulder and nodded at Cava. "Nice to make your acquaintance, Quinn."

"Likewise, Amajot."

While they were speaking, Fabi's posture stretched vertically, with his nose in the air like a circus seal balancing a beach ball. As Joti walked back to his table, Fabi lowered his head but kept his dark, sunken eyes fixed on Cava. He nodded towards Fabi, raising two fingers to salute. Fabi swiveled his head around, perhaps not realizing that he was glaring at Cava, sending back a subdued nod, then having his attention arrested by the waitress's order-taking.

"Hey, Quinn?" Anjuli asked.

"Yes, Anj?"

"Do you want to go somewhere else?"

Cava complied. When he went to pay the tab, he found that Joti had added it to his bill. He walked over and thanked Joti for the gift and was told to take care of his cousin. Cava also tried to greet Fabi verbally, whose response was meager, with the same jittery body language.

Cava, while holding the door open for Anjuli, forcing himself not to stare at her backside in front of her cousin, couldn't help but notice the brand new SUV parked in front of the noodle house. *Singh* was embossed on the customized licence plate.

In her car, Cava instructed Anjuli to the Ox's guest parking, lost in his thoughts on the way there. How did Joti Singh know him? What was Fabi's deal? Was he thinking about double-crossing the Indians while working alongside Tic-Tax? What did this mean for Luc? Were they in danger? This was Anj's first visit to the Ox, and his house. Was his room clean? Would Hank be in the room? Did she want sex? Had she had sex? Did she know if he'd had sex before? Would his parents pick this one-in-a-million time to visit his room? Did the lock on the door still work?

* * *

The room appeared empty. When asked why they didn't use the front door, Cava explained that he'd used the window as a gateway ever since he'd taken the room because it avoided his mother's endless questions.

They entered the room and sat on the bed, quiet for a moment, before rolling into each other's arms and pressing their lips together. Tumbling around on the bed, they both exhibited their inexperience. In an attempt to take swashbuckling control, Cava accidentally slammed

Anjuli's head into the nightstand, forcing him to turn on the desk lamp and check for damage. Anjuli tried to play it off casually and accidentally kicked Cava in the nose, still tender from the fireworks night. They gracelessly rolled, kissed, slobbered, and inadvertently tickled each other with moves they'd probably seen in films. They knotted limbs, bumped the walls, rubbed each other, and gyrated in uncomfortable ways, though neither complained.

Suddenly, Cava heard footsteps coming down the stairs. He flung himself off of Anjuli, picked up a comic, and lay on his stomach to conceal himself. Henry entered the room, confused and wide-eyed.

"Hey," the younger brother said, seeing his brother reading with sweat trickling down his temples.

"Henry!" Cava started, "this is Anj. Anj, my little brother, Henry."

They exchanged pleasantries as Henry eyed the console. "You know, your lock *does* work, Quinn." Cava laughed nervously and began to explain that the two brothers enjoyed 'nerding out' with video games. Anjuli admitted that she enjoyed video games as well. She played the same one, in fact. With little other invitation, Henry plunked himself beside Cava, who was feeling the fiery squalls of passion in his body being doused with bucket after bucket of ice water.

Around 10 o'clock, Henry retired upstairs and Anjuli admitted that she had to get home as it was a school night and she didn't want to break curfew. As Cava walked her to the car, they embraced and kissed against the driver's door. She said that she liked Henry and insisted that they chill at his place more often, which was fine by Cava. They had one more perfect lip-lock before she drove off.

* * *

The couple, now feeling like more of a couple, did indeed spend more time in Cava's basement room. They were afforded more secrecy by the younger brother and busied themselves with kissing, reading comic books, watching some television, and doing homework.

At school, they still maintained a clandestine approach to their relationship. Anjuli explained to Cava that his whiteness wasn't a big issue—at least, she didn't think it was. Her parents were over-protective, however, and didn't want her dating anyone, period. She was nervous that Joti might say something, but she hadn't been requisitioned by her parents for 'the talk,' yet. She saw little of her infamous cousin, but still worried that it might leak out somewhere in her extensive family tree.

Little by little, their sexual dexterity and comfort began to align and work in harmony. A staircase creak or heel-stomp still shot them across the room like mice discovered in a pantry, but neither of them felt rushed.

One Friday night, Cava threw a dark t-shirt over the lampshade for mood lighting and climbed beneath the covers. They began to remove each other's clothing, kissing and touching more sensitive areas, admiring the textures and angles. Subtle moans and writhing incubated a heat in Cava, who then started to feel a sudden chill against his bare back. The window crashed open.

"Yo! Cavs! You here?"

"Uh... yeah, man." Cava said, tucking Anjuli's head under the covers.

"Great, I need to talk to you," Luc said as he tumbled in through the window and onto the bed with his feet in the air like an overturned tortoise. "No shoes on the bed, no shoes on the bed!" he repeated as he kicked his runners off and threw the t-shirt off the light. "What you doing? Are you sick? Fabi said he seen you... You jerking off? Whose hair is that?"

"You remember Anjuli, from the party... and your homeroom," Cava groaned.

"Oh shit, girl! Attaboy Cava. Get it in, boy!"

Cava blushed as a brown arm shot out from under the covers. "Hey, Luc." Anjuli's voice was muffled by the blankets. They shook hands and she buried herself back in her cave.

"Anyways," Luc began, then paused. "Aw, man... It's good to see you, where have you been? I heard you been with Sal in the caf during lunch. That's weird. Anyways, I won't take much of your time... I was gonna see if you wanted to have some drink, but you're *busy*. Anyways, I was thinking about you because Fabienne said he saw you... he was with the Singhs, and he said you were with a chick. He's been acting... not his self... Well, I'm guessing you were with *her*. Is she your girlfriend? Anyways, everything is everything on my end... All good, man. But if you have time, I wanna talk with you. Maybe a game of kick tomorrow?

Oh no, you work Saturday. Okay... Well, anyways, I'll leave, but holler at me ASAP, bro. I need to talk to you."

Luc went in for a bear hug and nearly stripped the sheets off his friend. Then, he stumbled back and placed the t-shirt on the lamp once more, gingerly. "*Pardonnez-moi*," he said as he climbed outside. Before closing the window, he whispered, "good job, homie... Remember, get at me." Luc tried to slide the window closed delicately, but it got stuck two inches before it fully closed, so he left it open.

"Does your window lock, too?" Anjuli asked.

"...Yeah. I'll remember that one, too. And some WD-40."

"Am I your girlfriend?"

"Only if you want to be."

* * *

Cava and Anjuli held off seeing each other for the following school week; Anjuli needed legitimate, uninterrupted study time, though they still spoke on the phone nightly. Cava squirmed beneath his skin; her voice sent electric currents through his loins, the tender shanks of lamb boiling in the stew of his underbelly. He had a nerve-zapped way about him for reasons that he couldn't decipher, curling his toes and becoming ultra-aware of his genitals out of the ether. As the weekend approached, a strange blend of anxiety and excitement rollicked him back and forth, like standing in the long queue for the first ride on a roller coaster. He'd begun to sense an air of suspicion in Sally, keenly trying to track what was apprehending his concentration, asking him questions about his hours away from school and whether he'd made any new friends. He didn't know if she knew, but she was too clever and had enough evidence to figure it out.

He deflected most of her questions, answering with hollow, closed responses. He maintained that he was just staying at home, either gaming with Henry or studying. In earnest, though, he did *not* know what he wanted to do post graduation, but it *was* his last year, and if he *was* inclined to pursue the college route, he *should* put more effort into his grades. She seemed eased by such answers, noting that it was *her* influence was finally overtaking that of his other neighbourhood friends.

* * *

On Friday, Cava spotted Cliff's younger siblings milling about the front of the school. He approached them and said: "Lightning, Thunder, long time no see. It's me, Quinn… Cava. How are you? Is your brother picking you up? Do you know if he's meeting Luc?"

The kids shrugged and said that they were fine. The two were closed off to outsiders, to the point of the school board administering tests to see if they qualified as special needs. They never fell within the spectrum, though. When the tests indicated that they were cognitively 'fine' and were left on their own, Cliff put them at the forefront of his priorities. In fairness, they seemed to carry themselves with more confidence as they got older. They still had the dropped-neck, low-hanging gazes of abused children, something that Cliff hated to witness, blaming it on their mother's alcoholism in their early lives.

"We're supposed to walk home today, alone… Cliff said he had a thing to do," Lightning answered. A shoestring with a house key hung around his neck.

"I don't know if he's with Luc. My brother says they don't see each other as much as they used to," Thunder added.

Cava offered to walk them to their apartment, which they neither accepted nor refused. Cava started walking in that direction, and the kids, both holding the straps of their backpacks, shuffled a pace and a half behind him. As they walked, Cava tried to start conversation about school, homework, teachers, sports, and their brother, but he was just given stares and tepid, one-to-two-word answers back. Cava stopped at the corner store near X and O and bought them all popsicles, which the two gladly accepted, mumbling something that sounded like "thank you." As they approached the apartment, the kids were still holding their popsicle sticks in their tacky hands. He gave them little handshakes, feeling the melted sugar momentarily glue his fingers together, and watched them scurry up the stairs.

"Well, aren't you an angel!" a voice yelled to Cava, followed by the unmelodic honk of a horn in a gruesome key of G. Cava's quick spin produced a vision of Cliff behind the wheel of his Fairmont, puttied with fibreglass and chirring like a crow in a cavern. He was smiling behind a pair of Locs tucked under a Hammers caps, reminding Cava of an Eazy-E album cover. "Hop in," Cliff said, shifting the seat back and unveiling Luc riding shotgun. "Had to pick this hooptie up from a muffler-job at the choppers… She's back, baby!"

Cava jumped in the back and smelled fresh herb. Luc, not wearing a seatbelt, spun around and slapped hands with his friend, then bounced back to a forward position. "Yo Cliffy, I seen this motherfucker a week ago *getting it in!*" Luc laughed and flipped the glove compartment down, spilling some green nuggets with wiry red hairs poking out like cowlicks. "How was it, bro? Welcome to the best club in the world… Everything you thought it'd be?"

Cava settled himself into the bench seat and stared out the window. "Actually, I had a friend pop in, and it didn't end up happening."

Cliff laughed and threw a big arm across Luc's chest, who cursed him for spilling some of the bud.

"What?! How long y'all been dating for?"

"I dunno, since the party, or around then. Like a month and change."

"And you ain't fucked her yet?"

"No… I don't even know if I still have rubbers or if you 'borrowed' them all… Actually, I could use some advice," Cava admitted, reluctantly.

Cliff skidded into a shaded parking lot and turned off the engine, leaving the faint hum of snares and kicks playing at low volume from the tape deck. They were in an isolated little lot with a mixture of good and bad graffiti on the brick facades; a fence leading to a plot of tall grass and train tracks was cut and peeled open.

"You know, I can get you a nice face plate and stereo, probably some 10's and an 18, to make this ghetto horse a sleeper sound stallion, son," Luc boasted as he rolled the joint.

"Why would I want to polish shit and get this thing turned out without insurance?" Cliff fired back.

Luc lit the joint and passed it to Cliff, who took a deep inhale and passed it to Cava, asking him to expand on his advice-seeking.

Cava started, "well… I mean a month isn't too long at all, but… we get to a certain point and then we just seem to make out or do other stuff. Which is great, don't get me wrong… but, how do I…"

"Get them panties off?" Luc interrupted. "Get up in them guts?"

"Well, I guess, yeah. How do I go from just kind of playing around to… *getting it in*, as you would say…?"

The two in the front seat laughed, not with pity, but at their friend's refreshing innocence. Cliff deferred to Luc, calling him "the professional," and reminding him that he may have babies, plural, crawling around Fury.

"Shut up, man… I make sure I see it come out when I'm done. On their tummies," Luc refuted. "Well… you're probably dealing with twin virginities, yours and hers. It depends how she feels about her own virgin status. Sometimes they want to give up that V-card like nobody's business; other times, they want to keep that sucker in their purse until they're married." Luc took a big pull, corkscrewing the inhaled smoke in a slow, thick plume from his mouth to his nostril as he passed the blunt to Cliff. "Maybe you guys smoke a little spliff, sip a little drink, and she'll loosen up a bit."

"Nah, that's out," Cava retorted. "I don't want her to… to feel bad about it if she was fucked up."

"Fucking saint this one, huh?" Luc snickered. "A regular knight on the pale horse."

"So, I'm hopeless?" Cava laughed.

"No way, man," Cliff said. "Just tell her that you're ready to take it to *the next level*. A deeper one. Some emo shit, bitches love it when you pull at their heartstrings. Maybe cry a bit."

Cava, feeling the weed both open his imagination and stir his anxiety, began to imagine what he would say and how.

"Cliff's right," Luc said, turning to face Cava. "Be honest, but don't be a pussy. And don't cry, man. That's bitch-made. That's the advice. If she likes you, then she either will or won't. If she does, fucking awesome. You become a man. If she doesn't, she might tell you why and ask you to wait. If she's a trifling-ass bitch, or a coward, she'll bounce, and you'll know that she wasn't real. Either way, you gotta try."

Cava knew he was close, he'd just needed to hear it. Adding peer pressure, something that had always been integral to both good and bad decisions in his life, helped. He stayed quiet for a few moments longer, thinking about how he would bring the subject up. Before they were rolling around? During? Should he just try to be more aggressive? Or let her make the first move?

"Get up out your head, man!" Luc commanded, snapping his fingers.

"So… any moves that I should try?" Cava asked meekly as he put the joint to his lips.

Cliff and Luc howled with laughter. Cliff rested his head on the steering wheel as Luc slapped the dashboard with quick strokes like a drum roll. "*Moves!*" Luc repeated in jest as he wiped tears from his eyes. "Goddamn, I missed you."

Cava sunk low in his seat. He felt immature, but not completely embarrassed.

Cliff finally broke out. "Well, don't do none of that porn shit. You might freak her the fuck out, trying to lick her booty out, or boofing her with a finger. Just take it slow and easy man, that shit hurts the young girls. If you like her, you don't wanna traumatise her, right?"

Luc resumed a normal breathing rate. "I mean, you can stir the pot, flip her on her side, or on her stomach. He's right. Don't daddy-long-dick the shit and tear her ass up… start slow. You nut too fast, and you look like a clown. Make sure she's wet. Probably want a rain coat… probably. Play around with her legs. Lick them. Kiss her in the ears and on the neck. Play with her tits, before and during. Chicks love that nipple work. Don't choke or slap her unless she asks you to, that can get you in some trouble… trust me. Everyone likes different stuff, she probably dunno what she likes, and so, just do you."

Cava thanked his pals, though still felt daunted. Cliff started the car and turned up the music. The tinny speakers crackled as the bass line played and papered over the voice rapping the gritty loop.

"Best album ever. 36 Chambers. If you don't like it, get out."

"Yeah, one of the greatest, but I feel like your weak-ass system is a sin against the Wu," Luc ribbed.

"Want me to swing you back to the Ox, boys?"

"Yeah, I'm gonna nap, shower, and see what Anj is up to," Cava answered.

"I'll get out at the Bench. I got business to take care of," Luc said, without jubilation.

* * *

Driving down Eckersley, the boys passed some cute girls. The warm day had brought summer clothes out: shorts that crept up the bum and low-cut tank tops. Cliff slowed the car and honked the horn. It startled the girls, but they didn't turn around. Luc guffawed.

"Watch this." He rolled the window down, approached even closer, and slammed his hand against the car door with horse-thigh palm slaps. The move waylaid the girls' attention. Luc catcalled them, squeezed a smile out of the cutest one, and they drove on.

"That's the next level shit, Cliff." Luc smiled. "The girls are getting wise, you know, the hot ones know you honking at them. They're used to it, so you gotta be creative. A horn? Ain't nobody got time to turn around for that! But you rail on the side door and they be like 'the fuck is that?' Trust me, this some next level pimp shit... I might have to go holler at them before I head back out, now. Shorty was banging."

"Man, you gonna put a hole in my door slapping on it like that. Then, guess what? You gonna be walking, banging stop signs with your rude ass," Cliff said, trying to conceal his grin.

"Ha! This motherfucker."

Cava and Luc hopped off at the Bench. Cliff gave Luc a pound and pulled Cava close as Luc trod towards the Bench to light a cigarette. "Yo, my brother and sister never walked home before. I was a little nervous. That's some stand-up shit right there. It's good to see you. You even bought them popsicles, man. That's kind, I mean it." He looked to make sure that Luc was out of earshot, pulling Cava's upper body inside the car. "Keep an eye on him. I'm worried. Peace."

The boys sat on the Bench for a cigarette, so close that their legs were touching. There was a silence. Cava looked at Luc, who seemed pensive, despite having spent the last hour smoking and bantering.

"How's things? How's Fabi?" Cava finally nudged, putting a soft elbow into Luc's arm.

"All good, man," Luc said, without making eye contact. "Everything is everything."

"You sure?"

"I guess... I'm confused, man. Fabi ain't his old self. He's dopesick or something, yo... He gets these mood swings and *maman's* getting fed up.

He took the basement and doesn't even let me in there. He's got randoms at the house, and he's fucked up at all hours. You can smell it through the floor."

"He seemed a little blanked out when I seen him at the noodle spot."

"Yeah, man! I been selling shit, and I was thinking we could be hustling, and being, like a team… like two Batmans, cause fuck Robin… But I can't help but feel like I'm just paying some debt for him, or he might be vicking me for my ends."

"How you gonna find out?"

"I don't wanna go looking. He's unstable."

"How's Tic-Tax?"

"T-Squared? I had to start calling him other names… he loses his shit when you call him that. He's getting more rough and sheisty. He just gives me shit to flip, and I do. I dunno how him and Fabi are. I dunno when they get together, maybe at our place, maybe at T's grandma's crib, maybe making runs. They might be going hard cheffing. He keeps talking about getting harder product… I just wanna sell weed and maybe some pills. And it's extra fucked up because Fabi is supposedly with the Singhs, and Ticky hangs around the Souls… But I think that they both stealing from their teams and meeting somewhere in the middle. It's confusing. It's frustrating. It's kind of… freaking me out."

"You need help? You gonna be okay?"

"I'm still on the outside, just a soldier… I wanna keep it that way… but I ain't making no loot," Luc flicked the cigarette and reached into his pocket. "I gotta go, man. Duty calls." He quieted the vibration of his pager.

"What? When did you get a beeper?"

"Eh, a couple weeks ago. It's for business. Here's the number, feel free to holler," Luc said as he wrote it on Cava's wrist in black ink. "Anyways, stay up and I'll try to pop in this weekend, if you're home. Peace."

* * *

Anjuli danced her knuckles against Cava's window at around 8pm. It was later than usual, but she'd mentioned that her curfew had been more generous lately.

Henry had already been exiled to the upstairs, leaving Cava's subterranean quarters vacant with the exception of himself. He'd cleaned his room, neatly folded and put away all of his clothes, slept off the buzz from the weed, and showered, using some of his father's barbershop aftershave. He'd also gone to the store to pick up a bag of chips. Seemed like a good idea.

Cava helped Anjuli in through the window, taking her shoes and gently easing her onto the bed. She was wearing tight black pants and a black shirt with the comic book character *Venom* on it. He tossed her little black and white tie-up sneakers and kissed her.

"Hi," he said.

"Hi." She lifted all of her facial features with a blazing smile, which produced a mirror effect in him.

He began to kiss her, and they rolled, in a controlled manner, proving that their practice no longer resulted in any compromising clunks, injuries, or items on the nightstand being toppled over. Cava proceeded to kiss her on the earlobe, neck, chin, and nose, and moved his hand up her shirt. She giggled. He went to move his hand away, but she ceased the giggling and moved his hand up her ribs. "It tickled," she whispered. "But I liked it."

The two began removing each other's shirts, then pants. Cava paused, waiting to hear footsteps plummeting down the stairs, a rapping at his window, or even a whimsical sorcerer fazing into his room from the astral plain. Nothing. The quiet, the lack of inconveniences, and dearth of disturbance made him feel the eddy of his nerves. He opened his eyes and looked at the close-eyed face that he was kissing, smiling and carefree.

She opened her eyes and laughed, seeing his astonished expression. "I caught you," she said as she ran her hands through his hair and bit his ear. Cava's alarm was becoming panic as he tried to take the next step. His body felt like it was trapped in a sauna, and he could feel himself breathing, trying to remember to breathe, then to breathe with natural cadence. His movements were becoming rigid, and he was clumsily mauling Anjuli with slippery hands instead of fluently caressing her.

She rolled him underneath her, pulled herself up, and looked at him. She rested like the Sphinx, straddling him while kindly looking into his eyes. He could only imagine the sweat that was glistening on his chest and forehead as he looked up and down her smooth, brown body, underneath a modest, black, matching underwear set. His body was soaking the sheets.

"What's wrong?" she asked, looking at him calmly and tenderly.

"Nothing!" he responded. His forceful dismissal proved that even he didn't believe what he was saying, however. "Well... I'm nervous."

"About what? Well... don't pressure yourself. If it happens, it happens... If not, I'll wait however long. I mean, I can feel that you're excited, but, we can take it slow..."

Cava was flustered, realizing that he was leaking in premature increments, but didn't feel the shudder of a climax. She leaned in and kiss him softly on the eyebrow, the ear, and then down his glistening chest. Cava closed his eyes and exhaled. It felt nice. It felt like care. He felt peaceful. He felt his confidence rising.

He swung Anjuli around on her back and took control.

"Do you have condoms?" she whispered. *Oh, fuck. Did he?* He'd meant to buy some, but had felt shy every time he walked down the aisle. Plus, he didn't know what brand was best.

He opened his bedside drawer, and to his amazement, found a fresh box of condoms. There was a post-it note on the box with the overly-embellished curlicues of hedonistic handwriting:

Bon courage, Cava,

Have fun with the rubbers. You'll need them, probably.

Luc, xoxo

Cava smiled so hard that he nearly cried, rattling the box with a shake, then tearing its top flap off. Anjuli reached her hand towards the metal light switch. "Is this ok, Quinn?" she whispered. "I... I just... naked... I'm a little..." Before she could finish, Cava had removed a silver package from the box and opened it with his teeth, releasing the smell of medical gloves and glue sticks.

He placed his hand over hers and clicked the light switch down.

WELCOME HOME

LUC TURNED BACK to catch a quick glimpse of Cava, remaining in the court with the kickball. He walked quickly to catch up with his brother and place his hand on his shoulder. "Have you been talking to JJ much?"

"No," replied Fabi, who continued staring straight ahead.

"Oh. Well, he's getting out soon! Isn't that dope?"

"Yeah, whatever, I guess. I ain't really talked to him since I was in GB. Told him that I was fine, and that's it."

The pair continued walking next to one another, Luc bombarding Fabi with question after question. How was GB? What had he done? Had he informed their mother that he was returning home? Where was he going to stay? Had he heard any new albums? Did he remember the time that they'd wanted to see the inside of a magic eight ball, accidentally broke a window at the school, and stained their hands for a week with mauve liquid? Did he think that the Hammers had a chance? Had he heard that their cousin back East was going to play college ball? Did he know that Luc was saving money to start his own clothing line? Did he remember that Luc was into fashion? Had he found any good plantains or sausages up in GB? Were there many black people up there? Did he remember when they'd listened to nothing but *Hard to Earn* for like two months straight? Did he...

"Luc, shut the fuck up," Fabi said as he gestured Luc into the back seat of the Bonneville, behind the folded front seat. "Stop with all the fucking questions. You're being the annoying, little ass brother."

Luc frowned as he got in. "Okay," he sighed as he ducked in. *It's only excitement*, he thought to himself. It had been forever. He sat nibbling his thumbnail, tasting the filth underneath, and moving it down to his lap. He felt nervous, something he almost never felt around people, let alone his own family.

"And, what the fuck are you wearing?" Fabi groaned, letting Fink into the middle as he took the other back window seat. "You look like a gay cheetah."

The others laughed while Rosee murmured mildly sympathetic sounds. Tic-Tax piled into the driver seat and spun to face Luc: "He might be right, Luc. You might catch heat for being the dealer that looks like some kind of homo in flashy stripes. You need to keep a lower profile, at least for now. No attention or we might all get pinched."

Luc slumped back in his seat, feeling dejected. He began to chew at his thumbnail again. "Cheetahs have spots," he said sullenly. "Fine, whatever, I'll suit up a little more... low key."

* * *

Luc hopped out of the car, fanned the ruffles out of his tracksuit, and waited for his brother.

"Me and Fab have to make a few more stops," Tic-Tax said while opening the middle console. "Here, take this for now."

Tic-Tax gestured for Luc to lean in through the window, and tucked a brown bag into his half-zipped jacket. Fabi instructed him not to mention his return to Fury to their mother. He would be in later to 'deal' with her. In the meantime, he wanted Luc to clear a space in the basement for him to sleep.

Luc walked to the Bench and emptied a few centimetres of tobacco out from a cigarette. He finger-busted a brittle kernel of weed and packed the crumbs in the end of the dart, scraping the sticky crystalline residue off his finger with his teeth. *Just a little something to knock the dust off*, he thought. He contemplated calling on Cava, but decided to return home after the smoke.

He entered the house and greeted his mother, who scolded him for slamming the door. She asked him what was wrong, her forefinger pulling at his cheek-skin as she looked for red in his eyes, remarking his gloomy expression and the smell of grass. He shrugged her questions off, blaming his appearance on being hungry and tired, and said that the weed on his breath was better than the weed on hers.

"I'm making chicken cacciatore, baby. Wash your hands and dinner should be ready in under an hour," his mother said. Her Italian-French accent had a passionate timbre that swung between adoration and cholera like a weathervane.

"Okay, *maman*," Luc responded with a faint smile, making his way downstairs.

He entered the basement and felt uneasy. He couldn't discern the complexity of what he was feeling as he flipped on the droning fluorescent lights.

Broadly speaking, Luc's actions were simple responses to external factors, only delayed by the speed of synapse and neurotransmission. The tissue of his character was easily spotted in his observable demeanour: friendly, loud, excitable, easily engrossed or intrigued, but also easy to succumb to agonizing boredom.

Rarely methodical, Luc existed moment to moment, the way humans envisage rabbits and other uncomplicated biological creatures, grounding their decisions on their desires and the immediate fulfillment of such pulses and drives. Though capable of reflection, Luc would hatch an idea or feel the forked-strikes of inspiration, seeking to capitulate and sate whichever intense feeling he was juddered by at that moment. However, evidence of his ability to carefully essay long-term projects was palpable in the basement, his little atelier: rolls of fabric, cuts of cloth, and textiles that were experimented on with paints and dyes were strewn.

He had shoes, pants, and shirts that had been sliced, patched, sewn back together, and hemmed in non-traditional ways, and material that lay torn apart, like a mad scientist's laboratory full of flamboyant vivisections. There were basic tools, metals, and chemicals that he'd played around with, giving a Doctor Frankenstein quality to the cluttered but tidy room.

Luc was comfortable with this, comforted by his surging impulses and riding the tidal waves of energy that enchanted him with his hobby, usually leaving him puddled with fatigue, prompting him to 'rest his eyes' on the fold-out couch in the corner of the room, whose bedspread always remained in a slattern tangle. To observe Luc as an outsider was akin to watching a half-hungry nighthawk, fiddling at the slightest rustle of leaves in his psyche, the most corporeal fancies and lustful vagaries presenting their bellies as easy prey for his forcible eccentricities.

Within Luc's brain, the nonstop firing was bedlam. He sometimes felt cursed to have so many 'profound' thoughts all trying to pull him in different directions at the same time. He existed as though he was surrounded by the crinkled air of a never-ending mirage; shimmering light waves that distorted and separated him from the outside. On occasion, such as at this moment, he was pulled from *his* bent atmosphere and the world forced *its* reality on *him*. But, to Luc wit da C, this lunacy was normal. He'd developed a mask to hide his inability to focus on the myriad of stimuli that entreated him to follow their beckon; he was at ease within his little world.

What made Luc uncomfortable, where he really lacked preparation, was dealing with the weight of solitary introspection, which tested his shaky emotions like snow on a bough, forcing him to dwell on the abstract nature of his naked heart. He was frustrated, anxious, happy, sad, nostalgic, fearful, and ambivalent when he saw and spoke to his brother. For all his perspicacity regarding his own cerebral kingdom, he was without efficacy when he had strong, singular emotional events to deal with.

Luc sat on the corner of a stool and unfolded a tray table on his lap. He emptied the contents of a brown paper bag onto the table. It contained a few ounces of weed, fluffy and fragrant; the same light green as avocado meat. There were also little baggies of ecstasy pills and white powder. He picked up an orange shoe box, removing a roll of sandwich bags, a packet of zig-zags, a digital scale, and a coffee grinder.

He powered on the stereo and turned up the snapping boom-bap of a mixtape he'd made. Something with horns, he was thinking. The opening to T.R.O.Y. seemed to read his mind and made him smile; he spun the dial further to the right. With the buster plugged in, he began grinding up chunks of herb, the buster wrapped in an afghan to reduce its shrill squeal. He emptied the fine mulch onto a hardcover book, careful not to knock the accumulating kef in the lid. He rolled a scud and lit it, taking a deep pull, then continued to spin perfectly uniform joints; 0.3 grams per. He didn't even have to weigh them out. 1-for-5 or 3-for-10.

As CL Smooth rapped over Pete Rock's classic loop, Luc felt an invisible tug-o-war between his heart and mind, a spiritual conflict with all the belligerents hiding beneath the tallgrass of his soul. He'd listened to the song almost every day since Janjak had been sent away to do his bid, and twice some days, when Fabienne was ghost. He ground more weed and continued to twist the ends his product, not too tight, where it would force cheeks to pucker and yield dizziness, but not too loose, where the small amount of bud would race towards moustaches as the paper burned with hasty wheezes. He prided himself in rolling joints that stretched out the life of the weed and got at least five rotations in a three-man circle.

"When they reminisce over you, my god," played out as Luc put the grinder aside. The lyrics gave him an asphyxiating lump that made swallowing difficult. As he gulped, he felt melted ice crest at the corners of his eyes, stinging his frons.

Wiping his face with his arms, he cursed himself and the effects of the weed. "Damn doja, getting in my feels and shit." The song always resonated with him, but he pretended to have no idea why it was hitting him like this.

He stacked his rolled joints like Lincoln logs to be placed into something else for transport and quick hand-offs. He weighed the rest of the marijuana up and tore baggies from his roll, making little stickers to seal the tops and indicate which ones were a gram, an eighth, or a quarter; red, blue, and yellow.

He could leave the pills in the bag and just stuff them in whichever secret pocket he was wearing on any given day. He'd sliced the tongue of his shoe open, adding a small piece of Velcro to seal the opening. Perfect.

He wasn't familiar with cocaine. It'd never interested him recreationally; he figured that he was already a hyperactive kid. What kind of orbit would such a stimulant throw his mottled, muddled little melon into? He didn't know what units to measure or how to bag them. It seemed like such a small amount of product. He knew that it was usually cut with baking soda; did *he* have to sprinkle the additive in? He could make those little, twisted-end sandwich bag things he'd seen, or he could fold it into a paper flap, or he could buy some multi-vitamins and refill the capsules. He was excited at the prospect of figuring this out, but was completely in the dark about the dosage sizes. He decided to ask Tic-Tax for advice the next time he saw him.

Luc smelled the robust garlic, tomato, and onions sinking down from the kitchen. He wanted to be good and stoned for his plate. He smashed the grinder lid onto the book and scooped the vitreous beige kef into a pipe. He took the entire lot with one giant inhale. A harsh dryness pierced his throat and lungs as though he'd tried to swallow a spiked bat; then, he released a locomotive-sized chimney cloud. He coughed fitfully until his nose ran and his eyes watered. He kept coughing and dropped himself onto the couch-bed, coughing into a pillow and muffling the sounds of snapped kindling bundles.

"Luc, supper's on," his mother shouted down.

Luc raised his head with a stupefied grin and slivered eyes. "Coming, *maman*," he shouted, falling into a fit of fractious hacks once more.

* * *

"Clear," Fink alerted the crew, after having heard a sound like twigs breaking underfoot, keeping six behind a grove at the southern end of the Trees.

"Alright," Tic-Tax said to a 10th grader whose face was mashed against the diamond-cut chain-link fence. "So, you understand, now? This is *my* pussy. If you want to deal, you deal for me. If you make 20, I get 10. What do you have?"

The smaller kid in an oversized Starter coat was shaking like he'd hopped out of a hot shower into a cold concrete room. He reached his hand into his pocket and took out $10 and a yogurt container. Fabi, holding the kid's face firmly against the fence, pocketed the money and passed the container to Tic-Tax. After opening the container and fingering the contents, he put it in front of the kid's nose.

He laughed. "You got this from me, didn't you?" The kid managed a parkinsonian nod. "This must have been in the summer... It's half fucking thyme. My grandma was choked when she went to make red sauce." Tic-Tax tucked the container into his coat pocket, Fabi keeping the ten-note, and they spun the kid around to face them. "Look, now that you know the rules, let's see you follow them. But just to show you that we're serious..."

Tic-Tax steered his fist into the helpless kid's gut, connecting with a liver-shot that dropped him. Fabi moved in to stomp the kid's spine and kidneys, holding the fence to avoid slipping on the wet grass and slimy, muddy terrain.

Luc was standing a few feet clear of the action, watching for anyone approaching from the path to the east. His guard was down as he watched the kid, a random student who he'd seen around and even cyphered a blunt with once, catch a beat-down for dashing a bit of parched green-stuff into another student's removed-cigarette-pack tinfoil. *There's no need for this... I'm not a violent guy*, Luc thought, as he watched his brother foot the kid down into the soft, damp earth. He looked up at Fink. His head was turned towards the direction of the school, not watching the affair.

The echo of female chatter was ebbing from his direction. "Six, six," he called. Fabi concluded his stomping and the four made moves away from the moaning, mired victim.

They broke left and found Rosee gabbing with a couple of girls. "Let's go, Rose," Tic-Tax ordered as the now-quintet slid out of school grounds, settling on a bench near the convenience store.

Luc stood silent, hearing the bell in the distance and turning his body towards the school, feeling the want to attend his sewing class.

"Not today," Tic-Tax said. "Crusher, you can go, run along... Luc, I want you to stay with us."

Luc frowned and buried his hands in his pockets. He shuffled his feet and looked up. "Yo... I get that we need to stick as a crew, but I've been missing some classes. I mean, I always miss class, but I feel like I've been missing more classes than usual. I wanna start going more. I have projects and shit I need to get done."

Tic-Tax and Fabi sat on the table-top and looked at each other. Rosee pulled out a joint, lit it, and passed it Luc's direction. Luc declined and continued standing with an implacable look on his face. The others took the joint and smoked it, continuing to pass it around in compromised silence.

"Well, this is just for now..." Tic-Tax finally said. "Now that I have Crush *in* the school, I have you *outside* the school..."

"That's bullshit," Luc yelled. "He's quiet and weird. No one wants to buy from him. They don't trust him... People like me, I sell all my weed in one day. I *was* supposed to be the school dealer." Luc tossed the brown bag full of cash at Tic-Tax, who dropped the joint to catch the bundle. "I can probably offload the pills by the weekend and... I'm not sure about the coke, though... I don't know what weights you want."

"What coke?" Tic-Tax bemused.

"The little baggie full of white. I thought I could twist some nubs, or whatever, or if you already cut it..."

Tic-Tax and Fabi belly laughed and waved Luc off. "That ain't yae yo, that's meth, stupid," Fabi taunted.

"What?" Luc said with surprise.

"We *could* move into the coke business, but gak is so much easier to make. You don't need to cut it, you can make it with anything, and carry it in whatever, because goddamn base-heads will smoke the pack along with the product, ha-ha. Right, Fabienne?" Tic-Tax said hoarsely, slapping the middle Kalou brother on the shoulder. "I was experimenting with that shit there. Give it away for free, for all I care! Make them beg you for it when I get the lab work perfect."

Luc felt uneasy. Weed? Sure, it was playful and fun. Ecstasy? Why not? A party drug that made people feel great, especially when they fucked. Cocaine? It had allure. It was 80's glam, and all successful people seemed to do it on the weekends. But crystal meth? A dirty, hyper-addictive way to kill yourself and end up like the crag-faced mutants on X.

Luc began to ramble. He was missing time in class. He was forfeiting time he could devote to making clothes. His interest was waning. He wasn't seeing the fruits of his labour in the form of pecuniary gain. He didn't want to deal meth to junkies with switchblades and open AIDS sores. He was having a hard time keeping Fabi's return from his mother. Janjak had even left him a cryptic message where he'd hinted that he knew that the brothers were up to bad deeds.

"Shut the fuck up," Tic-Tax shouted. "You talk too fucking much." He got off the bench and stepped towards Luc. "We've been trying to guide you, here. You're too emotional. You express yourself too damn much. Just keep quiet and slang whatever I tell you to slang, and wherever I point you at." Tic-Tax stood firm, looking at Luc, who returned his gaze with equal firmness. "Alright, give me a couple weeks. As soon as I get more soldiers, you can head back to class and deal from the inside." He looked back at Fabi. "And your brother will be home very soon. He's been helping me figure out cooking. It's a full-time gig, and we're almost there... Need the spices *just right*."

* * *

Lying on his bed, Luc was holding a stack of money, secured at each end with a rubber band, throwing it up and catching it like a baseball. He was tired. His beeper was sitting on the nightstand, dancing in a circle as it vibrated, lighting up the phone number left for him to call, sometimes with another number prompting his journey to a certain location.

He put down the stack of money and wrote another number to call back on a pad of blue line. Eight calls, he thought with despair. Eight deliveries.

He heard jungle beats from the crack in his window and through the carpet, three floors down. A chemical scent wafted up and began to invade his room, making him shut the window tightly. He groaned.

He grabbed his rucksack, opening the flap to check his inventory. He had the weed in his little rolled bags with stickers, he had his multi-colored uppers and downers all marked and categorized, and he had the meth. He took the big plastic bag full of little pouches of meth and put the pouches into his jacket pockets for easier access. 'Probably just more of this shit, again,' he thought bitterly, leaving his bag.

He descended the stairs to see his mother coming up from the basement.

"Can you talk to Fabienne, please?" she implored with tears welling in her eyes. "He won't open the door… He won't stop playing music and making a commotion… He's always with people and they make that awful smell and terrible noises." She looked at Luc, noticed his mastiff-like expression of fatigue, and grabbed his shoulders. "Where are you going?"

"I have to go out for a bit," he responded, not looking at her.

"You're always going out, Luc… Why are you always going out?" his mother cried.

"Just going to have a cigarette and a walk," Luc said faking a smile. "I'll pop downstairs."

Luc made his way down to the basement. The sound of quick, throbbing house music and the smell of ammonia made him wince. He tucked his nose under his shirt and knocked *Shimmy Shimmy Ya* on the door.

The music dropped in volume slightly and he heard fuzzed conversation through the door. The unlocking sound pre-empted the door creaking open. Disorientation from the frantic electronic music and noxious aromas stunned Luc for a moment.

Fabi turned towards his brother, squinting as if he were the sun. "*Frère*, what's up?"

Luc held the shirt tight to his nose and felt his eyes burn. "Can I talk to you outside?" he yelled, making sure that he was heard over the music.

Luc led the way, marching up the stairs, noticing his mother sitting stiffly at the kitchen table on the next floor. Fabi followed him in, shirtless and wearing basketball shorts. They stepped outside into the crisp late-October evening, the temperature long past the clinging few final weeks of a long summer.

"Yo, I'm glad you're home, but you're killing *maman*," Luc said, rubbing his eyes and breathing heavily in the fresh air.

Fabi wavered where he stood with a glassy grin. "What you mean?"

"I mean *maman* doesn't know what you're doing, but she knows you're doing something… Who are those people? What would happen if JJ found out that you turned *maman*'s home into a crack house? I can smell the drugs from *my* room. Why am I making all these deliveries? Where does all my money go?"

Fabi appeared as though he was drowsing off while still on his feet, not feeling the frigid breeze that was chattering Luc's teeth. "I would never thieve your loot, brother."

Luc turned his head in disgust as Fabi smiled; his teeth were terrible. His skin was ashier than a dead moth. Based on the glimpse he'd stolen when the door was open, his sanctified workshop looked destroyed.

"I gotta go move these packs, which should be your job. If you're still cool with Tic… Ali, I suggest that you go back there and take these mutants away from *maman*'s house," Luc said, with despondence that overpowered his anger.

"Or else, what?" Fabi said, too passive to be threatening.

"It doesn't fucking matter, man… Just go."

* * *

Luc made seven deliveries, all along Eckersley Avenue in various parking lots and social housing lobbies. For the eighth beep, he shut the cabin door of a phone booth behind him and rang Tic-Tax's number.

"How's it moving?" Tic-Tax asked.

"It's all copasetic, man… Can I pop by?"

"You out?"

"Nearly, but I need something."

"Five." Tic-Tax hung up.

* * *

Luc went to the rear entrance of Tic-Tax's grandma's house. She was elderly, senile, and virtually immobile. She stayed in her little bedroom upstairs, attenuated and on bed rest almost 24 hours a day. The basement had become a fully-operational meth lab, and the kitchen was used to cook cracks and cut up product. The living room was where Tic-Tax was currently laid-up, on the couch with Rosee under his arm. Fink was occupying a recliner.

Luc handed a stack to Tic-Tax.

"I'll have more tomorrow," Tic-Tax said while watching *Seinfeld*. "You're too quick."

Luc rubbed his face, groaned, and met his hands in a Dürer-like, Apostolic clasp at his chin. "Listen, man… You need to take Fabi back."

Tic-Tax laughed. "Now, why would I do that? It's so quiet here. Peaceful even."

"True, but it's not at my *maman*'s house, and she's passed having it. Which means she'll boot his ass out and you'll have to take him back anyways."

"Will I?" he said, moving his eyes from the screen to Luc. "Will I, now? He's become a useless, jib-head tweaker. He can cook, sure… But he's… on the edge. I don't even know what his deal with the browns is anymore. If he even cares."

"I know, I know… But I'm your best dealer, and if he brings the heat on me, which he is, then I might not be able to do my job."

"I'll think about it," Tic-Tax said, returning his eyes to the TV.

"Tic-Tax, man, I'm serious!" Luc pled forcefully.

"No, I'm serious!" Tic-Tax shot his long body up from his seat and fire-eyed Luc. "You call me that name again, and both of your black asses will be out. Watch your fucking mouth, punk motherfucker. Now, I said I'll think about it. Done. End. Get out."

Luc saw Rosee with a depressed, spaced-out expression, lifting and dropping her head as if it was too heavy for her neck. Fink sat on the chair, smirking under his fist with malignance.

As Luc was leaving, stepping over video game controller wires, Tic-Tax spoke. "I still say you should claim Lamp 7… You wouldn't have to be home, and you could make all the money there is."

"I'll think about it, Ali," Luc said, not turning as he left.

* * *

Luc took a roundabout way back to the Ox. He walked down X towards O, making sales to those that beckoned him along the way.

He was reminded of when he and Cava were young boys and thought all the fiends and mutants were related, like cousins. All those drug-addled men and women whose gray, gaunt faces all seemed to take the same twisted countenance over time. The marionette chins and rice paper lips; the sunken, dead eyes that were proof of inherent or learned schizophrenia; the bulbous foreheads and jagged noses without cartilage; the fault-lines and smoldering lesions, like cigarette embers. The lines of a fiend's face.

Except now, he knew their names. He knew who boosted cars, jewelry, electronics, and meat. He knew who was a new addict, and who'd been turning tricks for years. Who was desperate, and who was diseased. 'Luc with da C,' they called him, as he'd referred to himself when he was more optimistic. He'd already seen pants become looser around shrinking hips, and eye shadow become the smeared, plastered-on battledress of hookers, as opposed to mere social camouflage.

He had around ten packets as he settled up at the glow of Lamp 7, a regular lamppost just off Eckersley with a protruding '7' painted in silver. He didn't know why it had that marking, nor did he care. He had no clue why 7 was 'theirs,' and just stood with a pack in his hand, slapping his closed fist into his open palm, heating his hand with breath, waiting for a fiend.

Five minutes, 11 packs. Luc discovered one in his jacket lining.

The cops rolled by and asked his business. They got out, slammed him on the hood, checked his pockets, coat, shoes, hat, boxers, and under his tongue. He said that he was waiting for a girl. They asked him about his pager, so he explained that his mother used it to keep tabs on him.

"Luc with the C." Officer Collins enunciated each syllable. "Yeah, I know who you are," he said, responding to the feigned look of surprise on Luc's face, clacking his loafers on the pavement. "If I catch your black ass, you're going straight to the clink. They'll check that ass of yours there, and then you'll get that ass checked again," the officer, whose face became ruddier with his temper, wagged his finger an inch from Luc's eye.

The officer pulled Luc by his jacket, slammed his head on the hood of the police car in one motion, held him in an arm bar for an instant, and let him go. Angered by the head-slamming and the racist way in which the cop had referred to his skin colour, Luc sucked his teeth, tasting trace amounts of copper, and made his way towards Oxford.

"That's why I don't motherfucking go to the motherfucking 7-post, motherfucking Tic-Tax bitch-ass motherfucker," he ruminated. "Shit's all out in the open."

* * *

Entering the Ox, Luc passed by Cava's window; it was a school night, but it wasn't too late. The autumn sky only made it feel that way. He saw the dim lamp light leaking out of the blinds and heard a girl's giggle. He stood at the window for some time. He didn't want to disturb Cava and his girl, but he was lonely, tired, depressed, and needed counsel.

He walked towards Sally's; her light was off, and her window was shut.

He sat at the Bench, on the seat, and removed a joint from the secret lining of his jacket hood. Smoking it, he further contemplated hailing Cava. He could wait a bit. He could wait out here all night. He could hear the boom-boom coming from his house. He didn't want to return home to see his perplexed mother succumbing to tears again. Fabienne had only very recently moved back and had already claimed the hill with his flag. He sat, smoking the joint, feeling soreness due to lack of sleep and exercise. It was chilly, but his hood was fur lined. He could wait for Anjuli and Cava to finish their hang. He could wait.

He fell asleep with his head resting down on his arms, on the Bench.

PRODIGY

Reaching for a fresh towel, Sally dried off her slender, serpentine body while still standing behind the shower curtain. She gently padded her face and moved to her underarms, torso, and long legs. She wrapped the towel around her chest and stepped out of the tub, wiped the bathroom mirror with a face cloth, and squinted at her visibly tired face.

Ugh, she thought. *I need more sleep... these crow's feet are appearing way too early.*

She grabbed her little makeup bag and squirted a dollop of lotion onto her palms, gently rubbing the silky ointment into her skin. Sally proceeded to rub another vaguely-feminine scented lotion onto her arm and legs, balancing each leg on the closed lid of the toilet; she then sprayed her still wet hair with Moroccan oil and unconsciously counted her comb strokes.

She was mindful of how much time these new rituals took, sensitive to the increments of time spent moisturizing, oiling, brushing, shaving, blow drying, plucking, tweezing, concealing, shadowing, priming, blending, and all the other beautifying techniques that she'd adopted in Europe. How stupid she'd always thought her sister, spending hours applying makeup and luxuriating herself with expensive compacts of powdered cosmetics and assortments of brushes she used to apply them, probably torn from the lapel of some endangered ibex or chinchilla that lived in a cage like veal.

To be fair, her sister received a lot of compliments for her glamour. Sally did it to look 'normal.'

The little portable clock that she carried with her whenever she left her bedroom read 5:13am. She wasn't behind or ahead of schedule, but the ten-minute shower and additional three minutes of drying and applying gave her a cushion of two extra minutes to groggily contemplate.

Sally was amazed that she'd lived her teenage life, until last year, without attending to a regulated hygiene regimen, until it was forced upon her by her roommates and the overbearing influence of her time abroad. Up until two years ago, she'd only worn makeup a handful of times, when her mother or her sister browbeat her on special occasions and maybe Easter services. She'd never bothered to drag a comb or brush through her hair; the knots were too painful. She showered perhaps once, *maybe* twice a week, only when the smell of dried sweat began to bother her. She hadn't known what depilatory cream was or what its use could portend.

She didn't see herself as vain or self-indulgent. She didn't glaze herself like the other girls, altering their appearances so drastically as to create bases that reflected sunlight like a watch face. She merely adopted a routine that made her feel better, rather than ashamed, of her personal appearance, though she'd never cared about her beauty before this, so perhaps it'd just become another practice to perfect.

The old her would have found the time she was currently spending frivolous. The current version of her looked back on the hairy, smelly creature that she'd previously been with contempt.

While lightly gliding the brush through her hair, the towel dropped. She noticed that her lower section was showing the shadow of growth. As she picked her towel up, she noticed prickly little hairs penetrating from her calves. Trepidation entered her head in the form of imperfection.

She looked at the clock: 5:17am. This meant that there could be time tonight, or tomorrow if she woke up at 4:30am. Why did her hair grow so fast? Why did Rosee call her out on her hair? It'd never bothered her before. It still didn't, kind of.

* * *

She carried her little clock into the kitchen; the smell of coffee and a half-full pot remained from her father's early morning breakfast. She placed the clock on the table and halved a bagel, docking each half in the toaster. She took out the lunch that she'd made the previous evening and cut a banana into medallions. She poured a cup of black coffee and drank two tall glasses of water with a multivitamin. The bagel popped up as she gathered a plate, a knife, and a jar of natural peanut butter. Once breakfast was assembled, she trod back up to her room: 5:33am.

She studied her calculus while breaking her fast, sipping on the strong Serbian-styled black coffee after finishing her plate. Sally never drank while eating, it prohibited optimal digestion. She wondered if she was absorbing the material, re-reading the same equation line several times, feeling that the Greek symbols were changing each time her eyes scrolled over the calculations.

In her room, there was nothing to distract her. Her walls were blank and they'd always been blank. Even when other little girls had tacked pictures of boy bands and pop stars, ponies, collages of pictures, or stuffed animals onto their walls, Sally's walls were devoid of any distinct imagery; symbolic white walls, as the song goes. Her dresser was an old three-drawered wooden fixture, too cheap for its time to be an antique; it was always dusted and held a tape deck, a jewelry box, and a candle. Her table was sturdy enough to support her textbooks and a little framed picture of her, Quinn, and Luc a few years ago at a Hammers game. It'd once held a computer, but her folks wanting to play solitaire became too much of a burden to bear.

The contents of her bookshelf were the items of which she was most proud. The shelf was roughly three feet tall by four feet wide, with three long shelves. Each tier was crammed so tightly that removing one of the horizontally sandwiched books may have caused the entire unit to collapse. To the top, the rows of books were fixed like a screw nailed into hardwood, with smaller vertical stacks wedged into their limits. On top of the shelf were makeshift rows built by pillared textbooks that held in lines of novels and lighter literature, another three rows in height. Beside and in front of the bookshelf were more books, haphazardly stacked waist-high, giving the impression of a second-hand bookstore owned by a compulsive hermit with a hoarding complex.

Sally *needed* to keep all the books she'd read; she used the excuse of research, or that it would be easier to give a novel a second read through with the book still in her possession. Thus far, she'd never read a book twice. The preponderance of mementos that she'd returned from her travels with were books that she'd read; it'd cost her an extra hundred dollars to transport them home, to be placed in new pillared stacks, yet to have their leaves disturbed by her fingers a second time.

* * *

After blow drying and setting her tresses in a smoothed-out, fragrant pony-tail, Sally slid on a pair of sweats over her spandex shorts and a sweatshirt atop her matching sports bra, already covered by a t-shirt. She had two prac-tices, which could save her some valuable time in the afternoon. She also sought to avoid baring any flawed, unshorn pelage in the changing room.

7:00am. She still had ample time to stretch before morning practice, and maybe even study once she'd warmed up. Perfect. She packed her books into her bag and made her way to the kitchen, grabbing her lunch bag and saying goodbye to her mother with a kiss on the cheek. She checked her electronic, shock-resistant wrist watch twice during the procedure, cursing the time for not standing still while she'd had to perform these perfunctory obligations.

Once out the door, she breathed in the cold air and felt her stringy body shake beneath her sweat suit; she was never warm in the chillier months, blaming it on her inability to cultivate or retain body fat. She tucked her hands into her sleeves, then drew her hood over her head and pulled the strings. She giggled to herself that she probably looked like some Fury goon, like her friends.

She passed Quinn's unlit window and wished that he was awake to walk with her, but looked forward to seeing him at lunch. What a nice surprise this year had been; her best friend was spending more time in the communal area, though he always seemed distracted by something. It was a good first step towards him not wasting time in the Trees. Perhaps he would elevate his grades high enough to convince him that college was a viable option. Then, he could leave town. They could leave town.

The bracing autumnal air showed her the little puffs of breath that steamed from her hooded countenance and her eyes watered from the breeze. The fresh leaves on the ground, the browns and yellows, were moist and slick underfoot. Her sneakers pivoted, gnashing the skin from the veins and spines of the dejected leaves, shaken off by the morosely molting trees that separated the Ox from the street.

She glanced at a dumpster that'd been picked through the evening before. Refuse was strewn about the walkway and the street. A cruddy-looking old man carrying two over-stuffed, crinkling garbage bags and a hobgoblin past the acceptable age to ride a BMX stared her down as she walked through the central point of the project.

She shook her head, thinking that it was only a matter of time.

Another grave image: a man, probably a drunk, was passed out on the Bench, head buried under a hood. She scoffed as she walked by, then realized that his jacket seemed familiar.

"Luc!" Sally yelled with surprise.

He didn't stir, but nearing him, Sally identified her friend easily. "Luc," she said in a firm, commanding voice, shaking the trembling boy and feeling the ice-like exterior of his Gore-Tex coat. "Luc, get up... What are you doing out here? It's freezing!"

Luc groggily stirred and raised his head. His teeth immediately bounced against each other as he breathed in. He looked up and faintly smiled. "Hey Sal, I didn't notice I fell asleep."

"What are you doing out here?" Sally inquired, looking at his clasped eyelids.

"Uh, kind of a long story. I was... working, and I didn't wanna go home. I didn't wanna call on Cavs, and I didn't know what to do. I guess I was tired. I fell asleep trying to figure something out."

"Are you okay? Why didn't you want to go home? Is something wrong?" Sally was now deeply concerned.

Luc sat up and tilted his head back to stare up at Sally through crusted sockets. "Like I said, it's a long story. Have you seen Cava?"

"Yeah, I mean, at school… Why? Is he okay?"

"Yeah, yeah… Just haven't seen him much. He's been busy with *her* I guess," Luc said, his eyes slowly closing.

Her? Sally's mind tolled. "You have to get home. You'll get hypothermia or pneumonia, if you haven't already." Sally tried to raise Luc to his feet, the word '*her*' reverberating in her skull.

She walked Luc to his door, the sound of wild techno music, talking, and coughing was leaking out of the window from below. "What's that?" she asked.

"That's the long story," Luc said. He stood outside for a moment and reached into his pocket. He pulled out a cigarette pack and removed one. "I'm gonna… I'm just gonna have a smoke before I go in."

"Are you going to make it to school on time?"

Luc looked, for a split-second, like he was about to cry. He dropped his neck and grabbed a Bic from his inner jacket pocket. Clearing his throat and having his words muffled by the cigarette in his teeth, he responded: "Maybe. Hopefully." He took a puff as Sally began walking away. "Hey Sal, do you need any more?"

Sally stopped and felt her cheeks warm. "Shh," she hissed, pressing her sleeve-covered finger against her lips. "Maybe in a week?"

Luc nodded. "Any time, easy to get."

"Luc!" she shushed him again, with a pleading look in her eyes.

* * *

Sally passed Cava's room again, noticing the faint glow of his bedside lamp. He was still a ways from being ready.

Her.

Sally fought the urge to knock on his window and hurriedly sped away from the Ox, checking her watch dial every thirty seconds. It was now 7:20am. Practice was 7:45am. She was 10 minutes from school. She wasn't going to be late for practice, and they would stretch there. She wouldn't be late for class. She wasn't going to be late for anything. But still, somehow, in the labyrinth of her own mind, she was late.

HELL

THE CIGARETTE SPIRALLED towards the ground; it moved at one-sixteenth speed, as though its revolutions were being slowed by an overly saturated atmosphere, like boxing underwater. The streaking cherry blossom decelerated towards the ground; gradually, dissipating trails of glowing orange swirls that remained long enough to pinch between the fingers and move. Finally, landing on the pavement, he swore that he'd heard the 'boom' of the filtered side, then the smoldered side, as they collided against the freezing pavement. He felt his heart begin to beat quicker and harder, all the way up to the back of his throat and behind his ears and eyes. Taking a deep breath, he hoped that it was just fatigue. He opened the doors to his house. He had no idea what the hour was, but figured that it was early judging by the dim, half-lit horizon.

A step behind the closed door, he felt the dirty, cold deliquesce, a slight throb in his temples, and sounds emanating from the basement. What he didn't receive, which he expected, was the castigating reproof of his mother questioning him on his whereabouts.

Slogging his defrosting, deadwood legs up the stairs, Luc happened upon Fabi in the kitchen with his back turned.

The older brother was holding a spoon and seemed to be putting little scoops of sugar into the coffee pot. *That's not how it works, but the kid might be a genius,* thought Luc.

Various other jars were beside him on the counter, all with the lids screwed off; powdery residue was visible from where Luc was now standing across the kitchen. *Was Fabi baking?* Luc asked himself. *Was Fabi cooking?*

"What are you doing?" Luc asked. A flummoxed look flashed across his tired mug, wrinkling in the middle like a rotting apple.

The spoon flew into the air and powder arced like a rainbow over Fabi's turning head. Disturbed from his concentration, he spun to face Luc. "Hey, you got any stuff?" Fabi disgorged his words with a frenzied, peel-eyed glare. He was grinding his teeth with such ferocity that it sounded like a shovel being dragged over uneven concrete.

Luc grimaced, wincing at the sound of Fabi's teeth, and stared down his cheeks. "Nah, need to get more tomorrow, or today... Sorry, yo."

His brother huffed a frustrated, Neanderthal grunt and began screwing the tops back onto the various jars. He took a dry rag and wiped it wildly on the counter, sending the white powder in all directions. He was wearing bright orange boxers and a tank top with calf-high black socks. Luc recognized each piece of clothing as his own, but couched that concern for the more immediate.

"What the fuck are you doing, Fab?" Luc demanded, more curious than angry.

"Upping the dosage." Fabi mumbled his response without consideration. He continued to wipe, then fastened a lid, put something in the fridge, and flicked the oven dials on and off.

"What dosage?" Luc asked, perplexed, observing his brother's erratic and pointless maneuvering.

"*Maman,*" Fabi answered, absorbed in his addled activity.

Luc took a step forward and noticed a bent spoon and half-mashed pills in an earthenware bowl. He saw that damn near every open jar had some form of undissolved powder sprinkled into it, even the orange juice. Fabi continued to move random kitchen items and sloppily spread the powder out in a thinner layer. He appeared stymied, pressing his hand against the powder and licking his palm, then repeating the cycle.

"What about *maman*? What's all this powder?'" Luc asked in a grislier tone.

"Oxy, mostly…" Fabi said, making more grunts and gurgling noises with increasing exigency.

Luc rubbed his eyes and tried to get a grip on the current situation. His numb face now felt hot, like a sunburn, when he stretched it. He seized his brother's shoulders; Fabi's dark skin was waxy and loose around the bone, as if it'd been deflated. He forced Fabi to meet his gaze; Fabi momentarily rested his glassy, gray-red eyes on Luc's before pulling away. His pupils had fully eclipsed his irises, moving to follow the motions of an imaginary butterfly. An excess of eye water gave them a liquid alloy shimmer and a tremulous, bulging appearance.

He shook Fabi and asked again, rage dethroned by panic, what was going on. Unwilling to ease the grip around his brother, he felt Fabi's muscles and sinew squirm around the rotator cuff and move under his clench.

"*Maman's* been in our business. She's been sniffing around, trying to get in downstairs. She's made it so I can't leave! She threatened to kick me out! I thought I'd given her enough to keep her in bed and too weak to come down, but I guess she got used to the amount I was putting in her coffee. So, I fronted more and now I'm putting it in everything. That ought to keep the bitch down."

Luc's clutch loosened involuntarily and Fabi wriggled out from under his grasp. Fabi moved between messes, creating further disarray, unable to commit to each flit and flutter for more than a few seconds. Luc was struggling to comprehend the situation.

He'd noticed that his mother had seemed like a subdued or restrained version of herself; her emotional hopscotch overtaken by hopelessness. He didn't know the amount of OxyContin that'd been used to sedate her, but wagered that any amount laced into the coffee, spices, and sauces in the house would be catastrophic. Had he not have walked in at this hour, he thought, he would've fallen victim to the gully stratagem as well.

Luc wondered if his brother was even aware of the information he'd just spilled, if he realized that he'd finally crossed the line into insanity.

He reached and grabbed Fabi by the nappy curls on his head, pulling him and feeling the fight of his brother's neck; it felt like a salmon that, though combative for the first few jerks, was soundly outmatched. He dragged Fabi down the stairs to the landing. "You gotta go," he growled through his teeth.

"Where to, brother?" Fabi's face lit up, possibly thinking that he was being sent on a return mission.

"Away," Luc responded without joy. "Away from here. Back to the Indians if you have to."

Fabi broke down. He said that this was supposed to be good for the brothers and the business. He understood that what he was doing was wrong. He was sorry and he wouldn't do it anymore. He would live right and clean up his act. He mentioned that he hadn't been in contact with the Singhs and that he might face fatal consequences, especially if he returned as high as he was.

Luc knew that Fabi was lying. He had no desire to change and couldn't, at least in this scenario, 180 himself out of this hole. Luc wondered if his brother even understood why he was holding him by the cabbage, and if he knew what action he was on trial for. He also didn't know where Fabi *could* go, what he could do, or if he might get even worse. He felt sympathy for his mother, and didn't want his brother to become a body in the river, on top of everything else.

* * *

Three garbage bags were full of condiments, spices, and anything with the manufacturer's seal broken; a cough-inducing bleaching and sanitizing of the kitchen, including the coffee pot; a heavy conscience.

Luc looked at his mother's barren, spotless kitchen and sighed.

He had a list of all the items that he needed to restock, most of which he was sure he could get from the supermarket. His beeper had been going off for the last hour and he questioned himself. "What was all this worth?"

It was 10am and his mother was still asleep. She was a famously early riser, stoking the coals at dawn and ready to pounce on Luc the moment he appeared. He checked on her; she was face down like a rummy at Christmas. He shook her. She stirred, then asked him to get her some coffee and Aspirin. For that, he said, he would have to go to the store. They were all out.

His brother's basement was quieter than usual. Perhaps they'd chosen this moment to have their weekly pass out. Perhaps there was no one there. He tip-toed up to the door and heard faint voices.

"What do you mean? Do you think he'll rat?" an unknown male voice asked.

"Beats me, maybe I'll rat back... Maybe I'll... I'll do something," Fabi's voice returned.

"Should we get up out of here? It's heaty now," a female voice chimed in.

"Nah, not till the cops make us leave... I can't be out there right now," Fabi replied.

Shit.

* * *

Luc rolled over to Tic-Tax's and found him in sweats and a t-shirt sitting on the couch, still with Rosee under his arm, still watching sitcoms. It was that old war show, the one with the guitar, the chopper, and the sad horns in the theme music.

Tic-Tax tossed him a bag. "Everything's already portioned out. You're welcome. There's less weed. Fink has more of it for the school, and since you're in the hole, you need to be moving more money-making product. Volume."

"Why am *I* in the hole?" Luc asked, amazed.

"Your brother keeps fronting so much shit, like a kid in a candy store. Said to put it on your tab. He ain't turned in no loot, so, you guys are a package deal: the Kalou Brothers. Right? Anyways, he's been grabbing pills, shit ain't cheap... He better slow down, or he's gonna end up a useless mutant. Yeah, anyways, you have some work to do. Pitter, patter..."

There was no use arguing. Luc relented before he began. He stated that, from this moment on, Fabi's debts were his own. Tic-Tax laughed snidely. "Trouble in paradise? Thought you wanted big brother back?"

Luc ignored the remark and filled his pockets. He was glancing vacantly at the TV and remembered that he still had to get to the market to replenish the cupboard and fridge, ideally before his mother woke up from her drug-induced coma. He didn't even bother to ask what he owed.

Luc stopped at the door before he left. "Yo, can I also get a bit of Adderall? Add it to what I owe you."

* * *

Luc didn't want to stay at home, but felt his inner voice scream 'coward' every time he thought about going somewhere else. An unthinkable premise had become a waking nightmare. Fabi had, in weeks, gone from being a visible member of the Singh entourage and part-time chemist on the low, to a frail fiend, barricaded in the basement of his drugged-up mother's house. Nevertheless, Luc knew that he couldn't protect everyone.

He'd restocked the pantry and refilled the fridge. Apollonia had only noticed certain things out of order or missing when she finally arose. The missing items weren't coffee and pasta sauce, but random tools, keepsakes, electronics, and appliances. His mother was moody, ill, and didn't know why. She seemed fuzzy and unable to fill in the obvious gaps regarding what had happened. Luc thought about dosing her with smaller amounts to wean her off the opioids, but decided that she should go cold turkey and think symptoms were a run of the mill flu or fever.

Luc played his corners, finding unparalleled success at his lamppost. School seemed like a distant memory to him now. When his *maman* regained her sense of reality, she would receive the mid-term report cards that were always mailed out to the parents. He could only wait for what her reaction to his probable expulsion would entail.

Luc picked up product and sold product. This was now his day-to-day life, paying off the haunting debt that loomed over his head as heavy as the October clouds. He passed by the school occasionally, but it felt like opening a sore.

He longed to go to class, to interact with peers, to flirt with girls, and to listen to a boring math lecture. It pained him to see the soccer or football teams running drills, or the fresh pieces of graffiti artists he knew he could outshine. He groaned at the state of his apparel, which he was cycling through faster and faster, feeling less stylish by the week, missing pieces that he was certain had been lifted by his brother. He mostly conformed to a black-on-black uniform, sometimes sleeping and working in the same clothes for days.

Throughout all this time, he wanted to call Janjak and fill him in; to have him magically perform some voodoo from his cell and have these problems erased. But, as he repeated to himself robotically, he wasn't a rat.

* * *

The day of the week mattered little to Luc, but during one of the sunnier days, while effecting his rounds, a horn honked from behind him. He ignored it, possibly thinking it was the cops, but it honked again. A beat-up car rode up onto the sidewalk, and the thick, sunglasses-clad face of Cliff looked at him. With a cigarette poking out of his mouth, he told Luc to get in.

"Why aren't you at school?" he asked

"Is it a school day?" Luc joked.

"Yeah, it's Friday, man. You look like shit, are you alright?"

Luc avoided answering, asking Cliff about his wheels and whether it was back on the road for good. The two caught up. Cliff apologized for being busy, but said that he was working towards a better life. Luc brushed any questions about himself off; he knew that he was acting guarded, but couldn't help it.

Cliff drilled away, to which Luc shrugged or gave half answers to. Cliff continued to badger; he'd heard rumblings about Fabienne, Rosee, Fink, Tic-Tax, and some kind of gang. Luc maintained his fabricated silence as Cliff carried on, driving towards the school. Luc seemed increasingly distant, ill-at-ease, and nervous the closer they got to Bendis Secondary.

Cliff chirped the tires and swerved across three lanes, taking a sharp right and leading them away from the school. He glided the Ford into a deserted lot and stopped the car.

"What the fuck is going on with you? Who are you? What has happened to Luc with the C?" Cliff barked in a disciplinarian tone, grabbing Luc's door as a safeguard against him trying to escape.

"Fine!" Luc shouted. He reluctantly acknowledged his fears and feelings of the spiked walls and ceiling closing in on him. He hadn't seen Cava in some time. When he briefly saw Sally, to give her study meds, she looked at him with such pity and sadness. His brother was losing his mind, and had even taken to drugging their mother to keep her docile. He busted Fabi as he was arming a dose that could've killed a rhino. Fabi was fugitive to a fire that he'd lit. He had debts he didn't create, or even know the depth of. He didn't know what to do. He was scared.

Cliff listened with staid concern. He said nothing, allowing Luc to pause, contemplate, and then continue to ramble between subjects in his switchback ranting. The silence afforded to him by someone that would and could listen left him venting all his fears. Half an hour passed, and Luc finally sunk into his seat, exhausted, quiet, and motionless.

"Thanks, I needed that... I feel... a bit better." Luc said with his eyes closed. The sun moved into his eyeline, glistening a trail of moisture down each cheek.

"Hey man, don't mention it... but, I think you need to figure some things out," Cliff started. "I can only offer you my help if and when you need it. You always have a couch to crash on or a friend to listen, but I think you need to figure out how you can get out of this. It starts with your brother, but it's not just that... I think you're too deep... I mean, do you even like dealing? It doesn't sound like you do."

"Nah, man... I mean maybe if I made the loot that I thought I would, or if I had time to do other things. But I'm always behind, always in the pocket, and always around mutants and fiends. That's who I see the most. The fucking junkies and base heads. I know, I gotta do something, but I have to figure that out. I just need time."

Cliff cursed. His siblings were done with school and he'd been on his way to pick them up. This was the first time they were to walk home alone, and he wanted to surprise them with a ride. They were good kids, he said, but he was aware that they had a few problems. He was worried that leaving them at the school meant that they might get offered drugs, or worse. What if they were rolled on? What if they were kidnapped?

* * *

Luc rapped on Cava's window. It was about 4:00pm on a Saturday. The window slid open, and Cava's face, in full smile, stuck out.

"Yo, brother! I owe you a million!" Cava beamed, hugging Luc and pulling him cleanly through the window.

"No shoes!" Luc bellowed as he tucked and summersaulted from Cava's mattress onto the floor.

Luc grinned. The grin warmed and tingled his body. The depth of such a grin was like the smallest ring in the mightiest redwood reverberating with joy. His soul grinned. Luc's grin transmogrified into a magnificent, teeth-baring smile, like a Labrador pup owned by rich whites. His smile exercised muscles that had descended in atrophy. His smile was beautiful and genuine; a moment of reverie. He kicked his sneakers off and hugged his friend. "You *finally* did it?"

"Couldn't have done it without you, man… literally. When did you put those raincoats in my nightstand?" Cava said with deference.

"I came by yesterday after we met up. I dunno… wanted to see if you could chill a bit more. You weren't in your room, and I bought those, because as I recall, you had none. Put them in a place you'd see them," Luc said modestly.

The boys cooled in Cava's room and passed the joystick back and forth past dusk. They didn't delve into serious subjects; they joked and ribbed each other, talking about sex, comics, and which Wu solo album hit the hardest. It was the happiest Luc had been in a long time. He changed the conversation whenever Cava mentioned school. He declined his piquing urges to discuss the sequela of his brother's return, his virulent debauchery, or the despair he felt dealing for Tic-Tax. Eventually, joined by Lil Cava, the boys just hung out like kids.

Later in the evening, they gave Henry the boot and smoked a bit of weed, watching the clouds of smoke break apart as they traveled out the window, being untangled by the crisp, still air. They turned the gaming system off and played music at a peaceable level, lying back drowsily on opposite ends of the bed.

"How's school?" Luc finally asked.

"It's good, man. I know I ain't been to the Trees in a minute, as you've probably noticed, but I been hanging with Sal, which is nice. Hanging with Anj, too… well, when we can. She's cutty about being seen by her cousins, all thousand of them. Been studying, actually. It's weird, I feel like I'm learning at school. I mean, more than usual. Sal's been putting thoughts in my head about what to do after grad. She's such a mom.

What a nerd." Cava snickered, staring off for a moment, thinking about something with sentimentality.

A thoughtful look pulled across Cava's face. "Where you been?"

Luc adjusted himself and sat up. "I been busy, I guess you could say."

"How bad is it?" Cava asked in a mellow voice.

Luc gave Cava the same explanation that he'd given Cliff, withholding the more harrowing details. As he spoke, he felt a darkness creep over him and swallow the brief merriment that the visit had yielded.

"It's all a fucking trap, man, that's why they call it that. I have to get my priorities set. Tic-Tax, feels good to use that name for that trout-faced fuck, says that the school is Rat-Fink's spot. I have to hustle on motherfucking X, man. You know what it's like? I'm on a first name basis with fiends *and* pigs. My poor *maman*. I just wanted to slang a bit of herb at school, that's it. Now I can't overstep my set because we have our own territories. Imagine that? Me. W*anting* to go to school, *begging* to get back to a desk and listen to some dude in a tweed jacket say words and numbers. Imagine that shit."

"Do you need any help? You can stay here, yo. We can hang more often, we can-" Cava was interrupted.

"It's not that easy. I don't wanna disturb you and your lady. She seems super nice, by the way. Thicker than I thought too, damn." Luc paused. "Mostly, I worry about what will happen to my *maman*... Even now, I dunno what Fabi's doing, what he up to. And... I love my brother. He's a good kid. I remember my old brother; I love and want that side of him back. It's still in there. But, I see less of that spark every day. He's in such a bad way, man. He's thin as a mop handle and his skin is blue and ashy as all hell. I can't even see any love or respect in his eyes, just the hungry face of a fiend. I want to hate him, I really do. But, I can't. I can't bring myself to mash him out or throw him onto the street. We still have the same blood; we still have the same *maman*." Luc took his hat off, running his hands over his unkempt waves, vigorously rubbing the back of his head and sighing, trying not to tear up.

"I don't even know what happened between him and the Indians, but one day, he just appeared at *maman*'s and barely leaves, if at all. Maybe he stole something? Maybe he just ghosted without saying nothing? He basically said that they'd throw him in the stew if they see him. So, he hides out at his family's place? Putting me and *maman* in danger? He could've killed *maman*. What the fuck! Motherfucker was doping our ma with Oxy, fronting it in *my name*, along with whatever else he's been smoking. I can't make any racks when I'm paying off that skull-faced fiend's debts. I didn't even bother asking how much I owe for his ass. I *can't* just go back to normal, I *can't* just say 'fuck it' and go back to school, act like this shit never happened. I have to keep plugging my corners. I mean, at least I don't use the shit I sell, imagine that, huh? But I'm glad to know that you and Cliff have my back. I don't wanna call on you guys or get you guys involved, but I have no idea how to get out of this."

"Well…" Cava pondered. "You need to clear your debts. You need to get back into school. You need to sever any business with that snake-bitch Tic-Tax. And, I hate to say it, but you either gotta turf Fabi or get him some help."

Luc agreed, but said nothing and pulled his hat over his eyebrows. Luc grabbed Cava's hand for a shake and pulled him into a prolonged hug, burying his chin into his Cava's shoulder, sniffling. Cava mentioned that even though he had a girlfriend, Luc was his best friend, and that he would always have his back. They were brothers, even without sharing blood. Even if Anj was around, even if he was mid-hump, he shouldn't hesitate to ask for help.

Luc exited through the window around 1am. He was emotionally drained and a bit nervous, which was made even worse by hunger. He felt both rejuvenated and relieved, but also anxious and apprehensive. He chuckled to himself and smiled from his heart; Cava had lost his virginity, finally. They could actually talk about sex, for real now. He felt consoled that he still had Cava, and that there were some people outside of his poisonous bubble.

The doubt, the anxiety; it makes you think in crazy ways. Luc was making an effort to grasp a tangible thought that could potentially distract him, or allow him to build a blueprint with which to escape this prison. He was finding no luck, blankly walking a mechanical path without any estimable purpose or feeling.

Looking up, he saw police and fire emergency vehicles parked in front of his house.

* * *

Luc felt a rousing jolt whisk his legs from a drag to a sprint, but he stopped abruptly after the first hard foot slapped the ground in front of him. He paused to take his bag off, tucking it into a shrub at the side of the Cavanaugh house. He peered around to see if anyone was present to clock him, fearing the loss of his product and further bullshit.

Confident that his bag was stashed without witnesses, he booked it towards his house to find his mother with her hands on her chest, disoriented, speaking to a police officer near the car port. "I don't know what he was doing. He was barely looking at me. I smelled something... there's been a smell for a while, but it really got worse. Then, it smelled like burning."

"*Maman*, what's going on?" Luc asked his mother with alarm, putting his arm around her shoulder.

"Back up, back up," an officer said as he moved in, separating the cub from his mother with his cudgel. The red-faced cop and Luc exchanged filthy glances. There was contempt strewn across each of their faces as they drew towards an unblinking stalemate.

"Officer, he's my son!" cried Luc's mother as she pulled him towards her, pressing her head into his chest. "Oh, Luc, your brother's been... infected! He's not acting like the son I raised! He's a... I don't know."

Luc consoled his mother, agreeing with her and stroking her hair. The policeman, one Officer Collins, moved in to pry the mother and son apart again. "Ma'am," Officer Collins began in a drab, emotionless tone. "I understand that this is coming as a great shock to you, but I need to know if you will be pressing charges. Your son is an adult, and he's clearly a junkie. I need to ask you some more questions. You..." he gestured Luc to the left with his nightstick. "Stand over there."

Luc moved away from his mother and the officer. While walking away, he heard the firemen talking about the possibility of an explosion occurring in the basement, saying that they'd arrived on the scene just in time.

There were two ghoulish characters in the back of a cruiser; one's head was slumped forward against the partition, the other's head was tilted back, mouth wide open, with white spit caked at the corners of his mouth. Fabi was cuffed and giving his account to another officer; he looked drowsy and was answering in lethargic mumbles, barely opening his mouth. He was shaken by the officer at intervals, seeming to regain a minimal sense of vigilance before flumping into his own chest again. The officer snapped his notebook closed, shook his head with disgust, and left Fabi leaning his backside against the front end of the police car.

"Brother, what the fuck have you done?" Luc crept over to face the likeness of Fabi. He received no response and slapped him in the face, not a full waist-to-shoulder cuffing, but enough to jerk Fabi's head. Fabi stumbled, forcing Luc to catch him and hold him up against the hood of the cruiser.

"I was… trying to get stuff, but Ali said no," Fabi graveled. "He said I was cut off until I became useful again, but I needed to get a little high. So, I found the hotplate and some chemicals. I thought I knew how to cook with that stuff, but I had to replace some ingredients with others. I guess it didn't work. I went upstairs and left four people downstairs. *Maman* was yelling at me and threatening me, then the house filled with smoke… Can you get me out of this?"

Luc stared at his brother with a feeling dithering between compassion and hatred. He sighed deeply, trying to tie what had happened together in his head. He only saw two people in the cruiser, meaning that another two had probably been taken away by an ambulance or fled. He heard his mother continuing to talk to Officer Collins behind him.

"We'll probably keep you in the hospital overnight, Mrs. Kalou, to make sure that you didn't inhale anything," one of the paramedics intoned.

Another broke away and began speaking to a third. "Run a tox-screen, get her on a drip. Have an officer be back in the morning after this blows over, she might change her tune."

Officer Collins moved in to throw Luc on the grill, asking him where he'd been that evening, demanding a detailed account of the events leading up to the disturbance, and most notably, where *his* drugs were. Collins patted Luc down and ran his pockets with vigor, laying the contents of his person on the trunk of the police car. Collins' meticulous handling of Luc's jacket pockets made his organs plung into a heap in his lower abdomen. Dread accrued with each sound of fissures that split the stitching of his coat's inner lining open. Collins itched and scraped, finding a hole, then opening his fingers to tear a big enough space to probe at the recessive nooks, the spots where Luc had previously found loose cracks and bindles. Collins pinched some grainy specks between his thumb and forefinger, held them to the light, and tasted them. The officer's face contorted odiously: cookie crumbs and pockets lint. He sputtered the flecks at Luc dryly, resuming his interrogation. Luc maintained his innocence, disengaging himself from any culpability with adolescent rhetoric.

Lying in his bed, Cava became aware of the disruption. He was roped in and questioned immediately after he'd jogged over with concern to join the swell. Between Luc, Cava, and Mrs. Kalou, each person gave an account that sought to spare the increasingly lucid and twitching Fabi, who was still leaning against the cruiser, but showing greater disquietude with each passing moment.

Fabi's eyes had gone from being as drooping and cloudy as an old dog with cataracts, to a tumescence that seemed to be plotting an escape from his own head. He gestured Luc over. Despite his intent to ignore his brother, Luc nonchalantly moved backwards towards Fabi, coming within earshot.

"Yo, brother. Keep six. I gotta break out," Fabi hissed.

"Fuck that! You need help, son. Maybe this is what should've happened a long time ago." Luc whispered, his consonants manifesting his rage. He scoffed and walked towards Cava and his mother. He was stopped by Collins again, who repeated the same round of questions.

"Yo, why you giving me the third degree? I wasn't here! I was playing video games and talking about pussy, like a normal kid!" Luc said, succumbing to agitation.

"Because, I've seen you on the street corner. I've seen your fist balled up, shaking hands with druggies. I know who and what you and your brothers are. I know patterns, and I know that you're headed down the same road that got your oldest brother put away, that will get your middle brother put away, and will eventually see you dead or behind bars, too," Collins fumed. "Your poor mother." A puddle of venom pooled beneath him. He breathed heavy, and the red blotches on his face turned ruby with anger.

Luc wanted to punch the cop. He wanted to slam his fist into his jaw and watch his front row of teeth float beneath the streetlight, like a swarm of flies disrupted from a carcass.

"Luc, can you stay with Quinn tonight? Quinny, is that okay?" Apollonia patted him on the shoulder. He felt her little hand through the protracted tension in his body, emanating from his wound fist.

Cava nodded, preoccupied, patting Luc's other shoulder and rotating him away from the action.

"What the fuck do you mean he's gone?! Wasn't Scarpelli watching him? Scarpelli! Where the fuck is he?" Collins began to scream fervently; his face resembled a raspberry as the blotches met like drifting islands. Tactical flashlights illuminated and most officers dispersed hurriedly. "Get the fuck out of here, Luc with the C," Collins' purple lips shimmered.

As Luc and Cava walked away, two officers in a car, detached from the scene, conversed while blowing on coffee. They were evident latecomers to the fiesta.

"Well, if she's not pressing charges and they don't know what the hell that donkey was trying to mix on that portable stove, I don't know what to tell ya," said the cop in the driver's seat.

"Goddamn projects. No one says shit, not a single person talks. Not even the mom. She's probably in on it, too," said the other.

"Let him run... try to light a crack-pipe with his hands in cuffs. Ha-ha!" said the first.

"Yeah, one less criminal with hands is a win for us. Let him starve. This city is just one junky fuck after another. Terrible parents."

"What can you do? I mean, we keep doing the same thing over and over again. Fucking immigrants."

"Send 'em all back on the boat; Africa, Asia, India, Mexico, wherever. Make my life easier- fuck that's hot! Do they have to make the coffee so hot? And they forgot my Danish. This night is ruined."

Luc dead-eyed the seated cops, unaware of his passing, as Cava directed him towards his house. They crept back in through the window and didn't say a word as they settled in, back-to-back on Cava's futon.

* * *

Luc was restless. He tossed and turned, occasionally waking Cava up, apologizing, and listening to his friend's breathing slow and settle into a hollow rhythm. As the room began to fill with lines of light, sliced by the blinds like a delicatessen, Luc collected his bag and shoes and walked over to his house.

He unlocked the front door of the house and went straight to the kitchen. Everything seemed as it had always been upon a cursory glance. The cabinet beneath the sink was left ajar, and Luc opened it to notice that all the cleaning supplies had been removed; a half-package of sponges, a coarse bristled floor scrubber, and a mop bucket were the only items that remained. He was disgusted by the mephitic odor, which had elements of cat urine and rotten eggs. It was faint but omnipresent, as though it was soaked into the wallpaper.

As he made his way down to the basement, the effluvium gained potency. He covered his nose with his shirt and continued. The door was axed into smithereens and pieces of cheap wood laid on the floor in fragments.

His eyes and septum began to sting; the sulfurous, ammoniac pungency was overwhelming, but the state of his one-time workshop was even more ruinous.

His sewing machine, basic tools, electronics, weed paraphernalia, and clothing were missing or difficult to recognize amidst the spectrum of smashed and defiled conditions. His posters were torn from the walls, and mangled canvases bestrew the floor. Cigarette burns pockmarked the couch and floor like rocks picked out of a man's face after a motorcycle accident. A sooty plume streaked up the rear wall, appearing to start at the element of the scorched hot plate. Closer inspections revealed a blackened saucepan with solid, carbonized residue rutted at the bottom. The smell was heinous. Luc nearly wretched into his own shirt. He discerned an organic component within the miasma of noxious charred chemicals.

There was a metal bucket filled with human excrement to the left of the hot plate. His fabric rolls were torn and had been used as toilet paper, laying in the bucket and scattered around the room. More feces were pearled at random, trodden over and mushed into the short-haired carpet. *His fabrics would carry the smell of death forever,* he thought. All of it was useless now.

Some of his needles and thread were punched into the wall to create an eerie scene, like a macabre detective's pinboard. Parts of the walls were spray-painted with grimy, gangland-styled graffiti that was void of any aesthetics: thin, jagged lines that were just words like "help," "fuck," or "salvation."

The windows were covered up with cardboard. Luc tore the duct tape squares off and exposed the finer details of the warzone. Heroin needles and crack pipes. Soda cans with their centres thumbed down and perforated. Singed pieces of tinfoil and pen tubes, emptied of their ink cartridges, like dead fruit after the harvest. More of his clothes and fabrics were hacked up into sinister figurine cut-outs, or callously torn into ribbons.

Luc began to wonder if inanimate objects could feel pain, or whether the pain he was feeling was anything like how Jesus likely felt when he looked down on all the sinners, his bastard children, who didn't care what evils they did.

In the last corner, he found even more of his fabric wadded into dense cylinders. They were imbued with a brown-red colour, something like rust.

He noticed drips of what he calculated to be blood, based on the colour and metallic scent, which somehow cut through the chemical odor leading from the crumpled, napkin-sized pieces of fabric. His socks had been turned into tampons.

He drew closer and thought that he saw something. He prayed that his imagination was exaggerating. His eyes spun away as soon as he peered into the bin.

The inside of his closed eyes continued to flash the half-image of a twisted, petite, crimson deformity. Something incomplete.

Luc wobbled halfway up the staircase before his legs could no longer bare the weight of his heavy head and heart. The smell had made him ill, and his tears burst without control. His body quivered, and streams continued to pour out of his overtired eyes, now tucked inside his sweater. Luc fought the stench and the visuals until he fell asleep on the stairs, holding himself within his sweater like a turtle shell, still shedding tears in his sleep.

NEW LEAF

"I REALLY WISH you weren't involved with all that hood-rat shit," Anj said. Her lower half was half-draped off the bed, one leg touching the ground, her arms and chin resting on Cava's stomach. "I mean, I like Luc, and I get that he's going through some serious things right now, with his family, with his gang, or whatever... But, I don't want my cousin to have even the slightest idea that me, or you, are involved with any of that stuff."

Cava had been brushing his hands through his girlfriend's long, black hair, half-listening and half-daydreaming. What she said didn't surprise him, but the manner in which she said it did.

"He's my best friend," Cava began, staring at the ceiling. "He doesn't have many places to go, with his house being condemned and all. His brother is on the lam and his momma's heading to Montreal until the place is fit for living in again."

Cava adjusted himself and sat upright so that he could face Anjuli, pulling her onto the bed. "He can stay here sometimes, at Cliff's sometimes. Put yourself in his position. Can you imagine the shit he's gone through? He shouldn't be alone."

Anjuli grabbed Cava's hand and kissed it. "Look, Quinn… I'm not saying it's him or me. I know that you love him and would do anything for him, I get that, I do… It's just that I don't want you to get dragged down with him. I want…"

A rap at the window made the young couple jump.

"Hey buddy—oh, buddies. How's it going?" Luc asked through a crack in the window.

Anjuli and Cava welcomed Luc inside. Cava took Luc's shoes and tossed them to the side as he sat cross-legged on the bed.

"I should probably go, it's getting late," Anjuli said with a strained smile, the wrinkles on her forehead divulging her feelings. Cava walked Anjuli to her car and promised that he would get everything settled in the next little bit. He would figure out a plan that would make everybody happy, and that if she was still interested in meeting his folks…

"Oh babe, of course, but you know that mine are…"

"I know, I know… but I'm sure that mine are more than curious about the beautiful, smart, and funny girl that I've been stealing away with whenever I'm not at school." Cava kissed Anjuli and shut the door. When he walked outside, he saw Sally's silhouette at her desk.

A pang of worry washed over him, as if he'd been caught for doing something wrong; it made him feel nauseated. His eyes widened and vibrated for a moment as he stared at her, staring back at him. Her light shut off as soon as he'd raised his hand to wave.

Cava walked back to his room with a lowered head, feeling the heat racing towards him as he entered his open window.

"It didn't smell like sex in here. Did I come too early?" Luc asked while pulling a sandwich out of his pocket and taking a bite.

Cava shook his head and closed the window. Luc noticed his heavy expression and drew a look of concern. "Yo," he asked with a strand of iceberg lettuce hanging from his mouth. "What happened? Did she just end it?"

Cava shook his head again, leaning with one arm against the wall. "Nah."

Luc pressed him.

"Well, it's my own fault… I didn't really want Sal to know about Anj. I don't know why; I didn't know how to break it to her. She probably knew, but only in her mind. But, I think she just saw us making out at the car, and shit."

"Oh. That's it? She's a big girl, and whatever, it's not like she wasn't going to find out."

Cava agreed, but felt a knot in the pit of his stomach.

"So, how *are* things with Anj? Gonna walk her out in front of Nora and Joe? You know, if you guys need some nights, I can ghost, easy. Cliff's couch ain't so bad."

"Yeah, I want to invite her over for a dinner. Don't worry, I'll tie a sock around the window if we're busy getting it on."

The boys chuckled. Cava grabbed the lettuce still hanging from Luc's mouth and tossed it in the trash. They were silent for a moment.

"Fabi turned up," Luc said, aloof.

"What? Where? What the fuck? How?"

"Well, I guess he'd been bouncing from crack house to crack house, from gutter to gutter, and ended up in jail. Not prison, mind you. Just a normal cell. Long enough for him to get the dope out of his system, more or less. He's back at Tic-Tax's, cheffing."

"Is that a good idea?"

"Fuck nah, it ain't a good idea. When's a meth head cooking crystal ever a good idea?" Luc said with incredulity. "Even stickier, the Singh's caught up with him when he was locked up. Had a beating put on him, to wisen him up, maybe…? Maybe JJ ordered it, I dunno. Either way, he said he's got it under control. Yeah, right."

"Jesus H. What next?"

Luc contemplated for a moment, scratching his chin. "Well, Imma call this semester a total write-off. Go into the school and see if I can get back on board next semester. What's one more semester, right? Find out what the deal between me and my 'debt' is, see how long it'll take me to pay that son of a bitch off. Get some wood and paint and try to fix up *maman*'s house during the days, save her some money, un-condemn that thing. Try and get my life right before my oldest bro gets released. Beyond that, scale back my own operations and just chill, man."

Cava gave dap to his friend, pounding their fists together.

"Got papers?" Luc asked.

* * *

It'd been weeks since the fire and its fallout. Luc had been staying at Cava's regularly, though not as often as Nora and Joe were aware. He was making efforts to have a place to crash every night, treating his dealing as one would a regular job, punch-in and punch-out. He tried to eat and sleep routinely. He made efforts to be diligent and detached with Tic-Tax, grind away at his debt, and focus on taking care of himself. He still played the post all night at times, on weekends or when his hand was feeling hot. Cava was thankful to have some alone time to be intimate with his lady, whose tone always defied her words, seeming to be less accepting than Cava had hoped. Luc could climb the fire escape to Cliff's house if he was stuck on X, or scale the lattice to Salomea's room and catch a few winks on her floor. In dire circumstances or times when he felt sentimental, he moved the loose two-by-fours of his own bombed-out abode and slept in his mother's bed.

Even though Luc had grown up close with the Cavanaughs and was far closer than any of their detached extended family that resided in the East Coast, Nora and Joe expressed their suspicions and apprehensions about Luc staying at their house to Cava. This troubled Cava, but he understood. The fire, Fabi, and the general air of Luc's character had undergone a metamorphosis of sorts; the harmless antics of a once hyperactive, prone to mischief—though harmless—kid, were now tainted, from their perspective. They were being swayed by the gossip more than anything else. Cava argued the fables and backbiting, at home and at school. He said little else than what needed to be said; Luc's story was his own, and Cava felt that it wasn't his place to relay the misfortunes and adversities that had befallen his friend.

When talking to his parents, Cava put Luc on his back and took all responsibility, saying that he'd never bring drugs or any negative elements into their home. He suggested that if they wanted the raw facts, they should ask Luc himself. Until then, they should reserve judgement.

To Joe and Nora's knowledge, Luc spent a night or two a week at the house. On those nights, he appeared at the dinner table, lauding the overcooked, Irish meals and thanking his hosts for being so hospitable. Cava was also able to use Luc as a means of deflecting questions about Anjuli, whom the parents wanted to meet in the flesh. Cava wasn't worried about anything other than being embarrassed by his mom showing baby photos of his bare ass on a bearskin rug, or his dad getting wobbly from booze and insisting that they have a sing and strum. He'd never brought a girl home.

The clandestine nature of Anjuli and Cava's relationship had begun to grate his nerves as of late. They'd only been seeing each other for a couple of months, but it increasingly felt like he was a dirty secret. There were only certain, select places that they could go and only certain friends that they could see. Anjuli insisted that it wasn't the difference in skin colour, but a complex ethno-cultural restraint that kept them separated at school and some public spaces. Cava sensed that people knew, but the code kept them quiet. Anjuli was adamant that another code governed 'her people,' and that if her parents found out she was dating, it would be difficult—nearly impossible—for them to see each other. Cava wondered if her parents could really be that naïve or stupid, or perhaps it was just her.

Anjuli and Cava discussed post-secondary scenarios. She thought it made sense to look for schools in another city, far away. Anjuli had much better grades than Cava, but he was proving that he was no slouch in his senior year. Her parents had a distaste for their new city and wanted her to travel to Rockford for school; Cava had never seen anything outside the Four Fingers. Willful ignorance annexed a more mature, medium-term thinking, which kept them boxed in the present.

The only veritable contentiousness that the two otherwise experienced was Cava's attachment to his street friends—specifically, his best friend. Anjuli maintained that she thought the world of Luc, that she thought he was charming, funny, and a true friend. She was worried about Cava getting caught up in gang or drug-related violence, getting sucked into the trap himself, or sacrificing himself for the sake of his friend. Cava would counter that his influence and steadying presence had already helped Luc start to dig his way out. Anjuli maintained that it wasn't just Luc, that he was surrounded by unsavoury characters, greedy and shifty people. Now that she'd frequented the area more often and seen more of his side of town, Anjuli was amazed that Cava hadn't become an addict or a thug. Cava could do little but agree and make his usual promise that he would, if not only for Anjuli, stay the course.

* * *

Cava groggily mounted the steps, smelling coffee and recognizing that his family was making little effort to mute their heels against the linoleum that shingled his ceiling. He looked over to see Luc still sleeping, his mouth agape.

He exchanged good mornings with his little brother and sat at the table, forking over a broiled tomato and toast, waiting for the rashers.

"Not saving some for Luc?" Nora chirped as Cava put two pieces of toast on his plate. "I assume that was *him*, the window, last night: open, close; open, close..."

Cava paused and tossed a piece of toast back onto the little circle plate in the middle of the table. "Hank, wanna wake Luc up? I wanna ask Mom and Dad something," Cava said as he poured coffee into his mug.

"If it's about Luc, we know that he stays here more nights than not, Quinn," Joe said, sternly. "The four horsemen have yet to bring plague upon the house, so maybe we'll bring a chair up from the garage... Though it is funny watching you two lads split a chair like you were five again." Joe's face softened as he chuckled.

"Aye, we kind of thought about what you said, and, if he's not going to do the smart thing and head back to Quebec for a spell, he might as well have some place safe. Plus, I can start nattering at him to do some chores."

"Well, the window wasn't just Luc..."

"You're not to smoke darts in the room, boy," Joe shot.

"No, no... I mean, I had my *girlfriend* over. We were all just hanging out."

"Ahh, he finally admits that he has a girlfriend. So, it's official that you're seeing the phone girl," Nora teased. "Does your little tart have a name?"

"Of course she has a name. She doesn't not have a name—that'd be weird. What kind of person doesn't have a name?"

"Well?"

"Oh, right... Anj. Her name is Anj."

Joe and Nora repeated the name back and forth.

"What?" Cava bemoaned.

"No, nothing. Well that's nice that you have yourself a little squeeze," Nora hummed.

"I said it because we've been dating for a couple months." His parents' faces looked a bit stunned. "And... maybe you guys want to meet her. I dunno, have her over for a plate or something."

"How very mature of you, Quinn. You aren't afraid that we'll embarrass you in front of your little chippy?"

"Well, don't call her a chippy, for starters... That might help."

"When do you see her next?"

"I dunno, maybe tonight?"

"Then tell her to use the front door and come for dinner. I can make something special. How about Shepherd's pie?"

Cava despised his mother's Shepherd's pie. He felt that its textures fought against each other. Luc and Henry came up the stairs, and Joe began to flip rashers onto everyone's plates.

"Um, no... How about just something simple? Fried chicken, or stew and soda bread, or sandwiches..."

"Nonsense. Your ma's Shepherd's pie is why I married the dingbat."

"Shepherd's pie? What's the occasion?" Luc asked, bumping Cava over on the chair and grabbing a piece of toast and a tomato.

"Quinn here is going to invite his little sweetheart for Sunday night dinner. Oh my, I have some frozen meatloaf in the ice box I can use for the base."

"Anj's coming for dinner? *Here?*" Henry asked.

"Aye, Luc, you gonna be here for dinner?" Joe asked.

"Hell yeah, I'll pick up the dessert."

"I can grab the chairs from the garage," Joe said, extending his fingers as he began to list off names. "Me, your mother, Quinn, Henry, Luc, Chippy, Salom..."

"No!" Cava grunted. The room fell silent. Those around the table paused their chewing to stare. "No. Sally's studying for midterms. She has enough on her plate, I mean."

"Joe, get the extra leaf for the table, too," Nora said with glee, shaking Cava's comment off. "Make sure you dust it off, we haven't used it for two Christmases."

Cava sat back, listening to Luc breathe through his nose loudly, smacking his mouth while eating his breakfast. All his items were loaded onto one piece of toast. Luc smiled at him and went to rub his shoulder.

The situation had slipped out of Cava's hand like a tadpole. He was daunted, but decided that baptism by fire would be the only way that such an introduction could be done.

"Quinn, take your brother to the store and get a sack of potatoes, some butter, a few sprigs of... I'll just write you a list. Luc, you dust and sweep. I don't want her thinking that we live in a pigsty. Lord only knows what she thinks after seeing that hovel." Nora was buzzing. Joe had already gone to find the table leaf and wrangle some chairs. "Oh! Has anyone seen the photo album?"

* * *

Nora paced around the cramped kitchen, shifting the mismatched silverware on the table and lifting the tinfoil from the glass baking dish full of Shepherd's pie to fluff the creamy mashed potato top layer. With each swish of the spatula, she sprinkled her secret ingredient: a few pinches of paprika, just for colour.

Cava wasn't the skein of nerves that he'd been on the telephone earlier in the afternoon. Anjuli was more than familiar with over half the attendees: Henry, who was cursing the Band-Aid he'd placed over his knuckle after peeling potatoes, and Luc, who'd come home from hustling with a banana cream pie, currently busying himself in conversation with Joe about carpentry. Luc was as high as gas prices, whereas Cava had declined the opportunity to get 'nice and baked' for dinner, feeling that he needed to be on his toes.

The table was set atop the nylon, flower-print tablecloth. There were six plates, cutlery, five glasses, and one mug, Joe would be damned to drink his coffee from an Englishman's cup. A pitcher of water and a two-litre jug of orange juice sat alongside a big wooden salad bowl containing tongs, thickly cut red peppers, celery, cucumbers, and red onions. Plastic bottles of ranch and French dressing were beside the salt and pepper. There was a stack of rolls and butter on the counter, placed in the inherited crystal butter dish. Cava always wondered why the butter was left in the cupboard, but the margarine was kept in the fridge, and why they only served butter when company was over.

Three meek, almost pusillanimous knocks at the door meant that it was time to meet the *bourreau* and the basket.

Cava answered the door and felt the frost. Anjuli was wearing a parka, smiling nervously, and standing still. Her parka was too thick for the weather, like using a missile to destroy an anthill, but she was still shivering. Cava hugged her and kissed her cheek quietly, smelling her sweet, freshly showered hair.

"Come in, come in. You look freezing," Cava said, trying to smile through his revamped nervousness. "Leave your shoes on. This is a white house." He laughed.

"I brought *gulub jamun*," she said with a timid smile, holding up a clear plastic bag. The bag was steamy, and the bottom contained a greasy, orange syrup.

"Is that this Anj I've heard about?" Nora yelled from the kitchen, quickly dousing her cigarette under the faucet and throwing it in the garbage. She grabbed an aerosol can of air freshener and shot a few blasts of fragrant mist into the air.

"Mom, Dad, this in Anj."

She was conservatively dressed in tight black slacks and a collared shirt beneath a maroon sweater. She'd hounded him on the phone about what to wear, what to bring, and whether his parents liked flowers. Understandably lacking experience, Cava provided little by way of answers.

"You already know my brothers."

"Hey, Anjuli," Henry waved over his head without turning to face her.

"What up, Anj?" Luc smiled dumbly, peering over the couch through eyes like paper cuts.

"Hey, guys." Anjuli's ultra-stiff posture was noticeable to Cava, who was glad that she was as nervous as he was.

"This is for you, Mrs. Cavanaugh," Anj said as she passed the plastic bag over to Cava's mother. Noticing her confused expression, she continued. "It's a Punjabi dessert, *gulub jamun*, like… little donut holes in maple syrup."

"Sounds lovely, dear. Thank you very much," Nora said, removing the container and placing it on a plate beside the pie.

Cava noticed that his parents seemed tentative, which took him by surprise. They had home field advantage and were welcoming a lamb into their lion's den. They exchanged rigid pleasantries.

"Are you hungry, Anj?" Nora asked. "Am I saying that right? Anj?"

"I am!" she replied, smiling. "Quinn said that you make the best Shepherd's pie on the West Coast! And, Anj is perfect. My full name is Anjuli."

Nora affected a bashful guffaw. "Well… I mean, *I* think so. How sweet of you. Please take a seat. Anj, honey, thank the Lord you call him *Quinn*. I named him that because I love the name, and all these little hoodlums and urchins don't even use it."

"I love his name. You were the one that picked it out?" Anj replied with sincere eye contact and an exuberant smile. "It's funny, it just suits him so well. Did you have it picked out before or after he was born?"

"Aye! Before, well… I had a couple choices. Quinn or Colm for a boy," Nora placed her hand on Anjuli's. "Kathleen for a girl. To be honest, I really wanted a girl. I still would if I could."

"I don't have any siblings. I always wanted a sister, too."

"An only child? Oh, you poor thing. You never got to fight over the last piece of chicken with any siblings?"

"No," she replied, laughing. "But, I have lots of cousins. There's always some kind of fight for something going on."

"I have six sisters—let me tell you. Maybe your parents figured it out."

"Oh wow, so does my mother!" Anj responded with a glowing smile. "I have so many aunties!"

"Well, maybe we have a lot in common. I love your sweater; it goes so well with your skin tone. Quinn, you didn't tell me that your little belle was such a fetching young woman. Look at your figure, you're very pretty. You look so exotic."

Anjuli blushed. "Thank you, Mrs. Cavanaugh."

"Please, sweetie, call me Nora," she responded. "Would you like to see pictures of Quinny when he was just a babe?"

"Mom!"

"Right, right… After dinner."

* * *

The plates were scraped and piled beside the sink. Desserts were enjoyed with coffee and Earl Grey tea, with cream and sugar cubes in crystal caddies that matched the butter dish. The family was surprised at the sweetness and texture of the innocuous looking dessert that Anj had brought. She joked that when she'd asked Quinn which flowers were his mother's favourites, he'd responded with "carnations?" His mother and girlfriend concluded that no one really liked that detestable filler flower, and that Anjuli had made the right call in just bringing sweets.

The entire feast took on a more formal tone than the rustic food would normally elicit. Nora and Joe bombarded Anjuli with questions about her culture, much to the chagrin of Cava, who apologized for his parents' impertinence. Anjuli answered gracefully, with courteous, open-ended answers, usually followed by a question of her own about his family's own heritage.

After the mugs held nothing but grounds and slumped teabags and the boys had excused themselves to play video games, the Cavanaugh family bid farewell to their guest.

"Anj, it was so nice to meet you," Nora said with sincerity. "I'm so glad that our Quinny is able to make some right decisions." Joe, nodding off slightly, agreed and shook her small hand.

"Mrs. Cavanaugh," Anj started, before noticing the raised eyebrow. "Sorry, Nora—thank you so much for the dinner. Everything was so delicious."

"Now, you can use the front door when you visit," Nora said, squeezing the young woman in her breast. "And please, visit any time. You're such a positive influence on my son. And, I'm very interested in this eyebrow threading! I love how yours are done."

"It does hurt quite a bit, but you need to tweeze far less often. Maybe I can make dinner sometime. We can have the korma or vindaloo that I was talking about."

"Sounds lovely, dear."

Cava walked Anjuli out to her car. She began to gush about how nice his family was, how little he had to worry about, how Luc seemed 'normal,' and how funny and charming his mother was. They embraced at the car, feeling the heat from each other as they pulled closely, tightly. Cava's attraction to his lady had been magnified by her appreciation of his family. He wished that they could have a few moments alone, in his room, but she giggled that it would be too obvious, and she didn't want to kick any dirt on the reputation she'd just built at supper. Smitten, they kissed again. Cava closed the car door behind her. She smiled and kissed the window before starting the engine and driving off. Everyone was on their best behaviour, and he felt closer to them as a result.

Entering the house, Cava heard the rattle of his mother putting away the dishes and his father still sitting at the table. It was past his usual bed time.

"So?" Cava asked, trying to repress a smile. "What did you guys think of Anj?" Cava quickly told his mother that she didn't need to put away the dishes—she cooked—he was more than happy to clean up.

Nora turned around with a nervous expression and put another plate away.

"Mom, stop. Are you alright? You seem weird."

Cava removed a saucer from his mother's hand as she stiffly walked to the table, grabbed an ashtray, and lit a cigarette.

"Seriously," Cava said, now with alarm. "What gives? Did something happen in the five minutes I was saying goodbye?"

Nora let a big cloud of smoke out and darted her eyes at her husband once more, sighing. "Quinn, let me say that I loved Anj. She's smart. She's beautiful. She's respectful. She seems very kind and very fond of you. There's almost nothing bad that I could say about her."

"But...?"

"Quinny," Joe said, dryly. "We assumed you were bringing home an Andrea. Maybe an Angela."

"So?"

"Honey, it might be difficult for you to date, short- or long-term, a girl like *that*," Nora spoke with regret on her face.

"I don't get it," Cava returned, as though he'd been trapped in ice and the world had changed while he'd been dreaming.

"What your mother means is that… Now, we thought she was a great young lass. She really has her head screwed on, and probably has a bright future. But, we're older than you. We see things in a different light. You being white, and her being, well, Indian, might be a little difficult."

Cava took a step back with alarm. "That doesn't make any sense. It's the nineties for God's sake! It's not like they're the only brown family in the city—they're *half* the city! I'm sure this isn't the first time the two races have dated."

"Of course not, baby," Nora replied, dolefully. "But, do you know anybody else that has? Do you know how much more difficult it might be to get on? Their community is very different, a little more… closed off… Quinny, do her parents know that you two are dating?"

Cava was now leaning against the counter with his arms positioned like a swimmer about to push off in a race. His triceps were taut, and his facial features were pulled up with shock. He thought for a moment before responding. *No, he didn't know any other mixed couples in school. Yes, the community was quite different, but he didn't know to what extent. No, her parents were under no circumstances to learn of their relationship.*

"Well… I don't know every single kid, and their entire backstory, at school. There's like a thousand students," Cava said firmly, selecting the easiest point to refute.

"Will she tell her parents that she was at her boyfriend's house tonight? Eating supper and meeting his folks?" Nora asked innocently.

"No," Cava responded dourly. "She said that they weren't allowed to know. But… she said it's not because I'm white. It's because she's not supposed to date anyone. She's not really to see anybody while she's in school, or something."

The parents looked at each other again, dismayed. Cava slumped with dwindling resolution and plummeting confidence.

"Look, we think that she's great—"

"But you wish that she was white?" Cava shot back.

"Heavens, no!" Nora cried. "This is a world of colour, and if someone makes my boy happy, I don't care if she's white, black, brown, red, yellow, blue, or even a *he*." Joe gave Nora a funny look. "We just want you to be careful. We have more experience than you. There are things you can't hope to control. White people aren't the only racists, you know. There are deeper things than your feelings about her, and hers for you, Quinn. If your father was an Orangeman, we would have been shunned back home. Just for having a near same religion. People aren't as open-minded as you want them to be. There are a lot of old believers, and people who put culture or appearances above their own family. I don't know her parents. I don't know much beyond what the people and papers say about the barbaric things like honour killings and…"

"Enough!" Cava yelled, stamping foot.

"Quinn Padraig," Joe leaned forward. "You will watch your tone and respect your mother. We're looking out for you. You don't need to get emotional. Do not—I repeat—*do not* try to intimidate the woman who carried you."

Cava breathed out sharply. "I wasn't."

"It's okay, Joe. Look, son… we're not saying that you can't see Anj, but we're saying that maybe you shouldn't get too invested in this."

Cava stared at the ground angrily. He fought the snarls and curling of his lips. He could feel his eyes trying to smuggle tears out of their ducts. He cracked his knuckles and rubbed the sweat from his palms.

"Why don't you get ready for bed, maybe go downstairs and hang out with the lads for a moment," Joe said, allowing his sternness to leave and sympathy to enter his words. "We'll put the dishes away."

Cava continued to look at the ground and made his way to the landing. He went out the front door to get some air.

He sat on the Bench, noticing the cold but not feeling the brusque wind against his bare arms. He took out a cigarette and lit it. Clearing his throat, he noticed his hands shaking—not from the stinging cold, but from the surge of anger and hurt that comes from the sting of words.

He didn't hear the footsteps approaching him.

"Quinn, are you okay? Aren't you cold? I saw you from my window and brought you a quilt. Are you crying? What's wrong?"

"I'm not," Cava stuttered. "It's just the cold on my sinuses."

"Oh," Sally responded. "Then, why are you sitting out here in a t-shirt? You'll pick up the devil in a cold, you know." She draped the quilt over his shoulders and rubbed him as a parent would do with a child fresh out of a lake.

"I just needed some air," Cava mumbled. "A little space, I guess... The house is pretty full these days. Luc's basically moved into my room, which is great. He seems to be doing a lot better. Not perfect, but he's eating and has a place to rest. But, I don't exactly have a lot of time alone to just sit and think."

Sally nodded. "That's true, you do like your solitude... You always have."

"You know me so well, Sal."

"Do I, though?" she said frankly. "You seem a little... I don't know what the right word is... distracted, I guess, as of late. Maybe it's just me. I haven't been totally present either. Not the best friend. I've just been so drained from school, and tutoring, and sports, and..."

"No, no. You're right. Safe to say I've been a little distant, too." Cava heaved a sigh and decided to apprise Sally in a stream of consciousness. Like tearing a strip of duct tape off a bearded muzzle, he winced as he spoke about his relationship with Anjuli. He felt the bite of cowardice, perhaps because he'd waited for so long. He was finally able to breathe when he reached the conclusion of his rambling.

"Well," Sally said, not sitting on the Bench, but standing, with her hands folded and looking away. "I did *kind of* know."

"I know I can't keep anything from you for too long."

"Please, don't give me too much credit. I had my suspicions about something going on. I didn't really know what it was. At first, I thought you were always distracted in the cafeteria, the same way a child who was raised by wolves might have a difficult time acclimating to the civilized world. Like I said, I've been so busy on my own little planet, I never

really gave much thought... It was just really nice having you around."
Sally cleared her throat.

"I enjoy being around you—"

"*But*," Sally spoke over her friend's attempt to wrestle the conch away.
"I went to call on you one night, and I kind of heard, you know... noises."

Cava's eyebrows jumped towards his hairline with haste. He felt his
jaw drop. "Yo... I, uh..."

"I didn't know who it was, to be honest, because I never saw you
with anyone, not that I ever went looking. But, later, I saw you with a
girl from some of my classes." Sally cleared her throat again, sniffing.
"Anjuli, I believe. She's really nice. She's also very beautiful... It *is* cold
out here," she concluded, using her sleeve to wipe under her eye.

Neither of them spoke for a moment. Sally had one hand retracted
in her sleeve, blowing hot breaths onto her fingertips, while Cava lightly
scratched the Bench with his forefinger.

"She is nice," Cava finally acceded. He told Sally about how they'd
met at the party. How they'd seen each other secretly in school and clan-
destinely in public. Who her older cousin was. He spoke without glam-
ourizing, but as if he was reasoning why she was an adequate selection of
partner. "And, I'm really sorry that you had to find out *that* way. I didn't
tell you because..."

"You don't need to say anything," she said as she grabbed his hand,
stopping his scratching, which had become more conspicuous. "I'm glad
you told me, Quinn. And, you can talk to me about it. You sound a
little on the fence about it, if I'm being honest. If you need any advice or
anything, I promise I'll be a better friend."

Luc, who'd been standing just to the side of Sally and Cava, finally
wanted to be noticed. "Hey, guys," he began. "I didn't want to interrupt,
but Cava never came downstairs. I heard a loud thud. What happened?"

"Pull up a stump, bud," Cava said, sliding down the Bench towards Sally.

* * *

"Well, they're not wrong to be a little cautious," Sally said stoically. "The
papers do sensationalize things, and you know how the older ones take the
news like the gospel. But, you're also right. You guys are a newer generation."

"She's a dope chick, Cavs. Truthful." Luc hopped in. "But, it's fucked up how she ain't about to tell her mom and pops, and how you guys have to be all covert-ops and shit."

"Does it bother you?" Sally asked.

"Course it does," Luc chimed in. "My man invited her over for dinner already… Cava's gotta roam free."

"Quinn?" Sally leaned forward to look at Cava.

"Yeah, I mean, maybe? It was on my mind, but the fact that my folks picked that up, after one evening, dropping the gavel and kind of going off the way they did, it got me all hot." He paused and scratched his chin. "It pisses me off because… maybe they're right? Not about all that overblown media type bullshit, but maybe there is no future. But, why would I care about the future when I enjoy the present? Why would I start doing dumb shit now, fucking up what's still been pretty sweet, for what might or might not happen a year or two from now? I know that I have the tendency to get in my own head and overthink things to death. They know that, too, and they couldn't keep it to themselves."

"Well, they love and care about you," Sally added.

"I know. But just let me enjoy this small thing that I have, so far. I don't need them coming down on me while her seat was still warm. I just… I just know that they probably had some good points. She's been telling me that the brown-white thing isn't a big deal, but what if it is? I seem to be the only one who thinks it's stupid and old school, but the proof is kind of starting to pile up. What if they're right about that? What if it's destined to fail at some point because we have *differences*?"

"They seem stupid, but they *are* real," Sally said. "Maybe her parents finding out gets her in a lot of trouble. Maybe it's something that you can only ignore for so long. Short-term versus long-term…"

Luc scoffed. "Long term…? Man! He's 17 years old, man! What's the worry? What's the hurry? The only long-term thing you should be thinking about is what you're having for breakfast tomorrow; maybe what we're doing next weekend. You plan too far ahead, you're gonna trip on your laces, walk into a lamppost, know what I mean? I've had mad dads get salty that their white daughter is with a black dude. I don't give a fuck. I'm like those dinosaurs that eat plants *and* animals, an *omnisaur*... I don't care what colour you are, everyone's pinkish or purplish on the inside!"

"Perhaps," Sally drawled. "But, there's nothing wrong with a little planning. Maybe she's already made up her mind about some things. She could have decided on a university and her future before you'd even met. Have you?"

"I have no idea," Cava acquiesced. "I don't know about school, about Anj, or about anything for that matter. I know what makes me happy, in small doses. I like hanging with you guys, all of us, together; Cliff and even Fink, sometimes. Am I not allowed to fuck up? Am I not allowed to be a goddamn kid and enjoy goddamn kid shit? Why do I gotta either have my life planned out until I retire or fly by the seat of my pants until I die all of a sudden? Can't I just be me? Am I fucking crazy or something?"

Cava looked at the blank expressions on his friends' faces.

"No, man, you can do you. It ain't a biggie," Luc said.

"Of course, you can just wait and see how it goes," Sally added. "That's no crime."

"In time, sure this might not work, and I might have a nice little bender to cap off what was a good first experience. Luc, I'll holler at you for that one," Cava said as Luc grinned. "So far, I went from thinking that college was stupid and unnecessary to giving it a real look; Sal, you can take credit for that change in my thinking. I started off the year the only virgin left in my crew, and now have an actual girlfriend, albeit one that's kind of a secret and might prove to have some difficulties down the road, with the differences in our skin colours, which I still think is fucking dumb as a motherfucker... At least I don't give two shits about Rosee anymore. That's gotta be a win, right?"

Luc and Sally nodded. "Well," Cava started, returning the quilt to Sally and bracing himself to rise to his feet. "I'm now starting to feel frost building on my arms. I'm gonna go see if Mom and Dad are still up. No sense going to bed angry. That's what Mom always says, anyways. Luc, I guess I'll see you in bed. Sally, I'll see you at school tomorrow." He walked a few paces and turned back, "Guys," Sally and Luc turned around. "Thanks," Cava waved as he slid his feet across the glassy pavement like ice skates.

With Cava firmly out of sight, Luc placed his hand into his pocket and removed a translucent orange prescription bottle.

"Here ya go," he said, passing the pills to Sally, rattling the contents within. She snatched and palmed the bottle, grasping it tightly to kill the noise. "I don't know why you like those things. I took some to see if I could use them when I get back to designing again... I felt zeroed in, but so... uncreative. I was going to bleach stain an old black shirt, but just zoned out on a loose thread and couldn't activate my third eye."

"Well," she said, coiling her hand into her parka sleeve, "I don't *like* them, they just help me focus. They're supposed to be for people like you who can't sit still in class."

"Oh." Luc stretched out his vowel-rich utterance. "I guess that makes sense, kind of felt my soul die, you know, the parts that make you *human*."

"Yea, Ritalin, Dexedrine, all those things are basically given to kids now, to clamp down on the shenanigans in class. Like a class full of zombies."

"Like a class full of mutants after they get stoned, more like it."

The two were silent for a moment before speaking at the same time. "You alright?"

"You first," Sally said.

"Yeah. It's been nice staying with Cavs. His family seems to feel like I'm trying, and isn't all weird or bugged out, for now. I plan on going back to school in the New Year. Mom is still back East, I dunno til when, maybe until the city fixes the house up? I'll have to tell her about this semester, sooner or later. I really want to start sewing and stitching again. I've had some crazy visions about some gear that'd rock cats this summer. What else..."

"Are you still dealing drugs?"

"Well, yeah... I mean, I gotta. I have a debt, it's a big number, thanks to my fuck-up brother, but nothing I can't crush. I decided that this probably isn't the life for me. Maybe it could've been, but it's gone so bad, maybe it's a sign." Luc lit a cigarette and took a big pull, breathing the air through closed teeth. "I gotta take care of me. Look what happened, look at my momma's house. You probably heard about Fabi.

Shit, look at JJ even, who's the best of all of us. This trap shit, man, it just takes and takes and takes. I told Tic, when I'm caught up, I'm done... I'm out, I'm ghost."

Sally pondered for a moment. "Is it that easy to leave?"

"He's got his own problems, dug his own grave with the Souls... last thing he needs is a soldier who isn't buying into his plan, falling in line. I've mentioned it. He's actually been really cool with me since I said that. I can still sell a lot, but I just don't put sales above my own mental anymore."

"That's good."

"So, how you?"

"Busy, stressed, tired, feeling like every day is the same."

"Well, maybe it's those pills? Every day might be the same if you always have tunnel vision."

Sally laughed bitterly. "I have tunnel vision without those things. I was born in a mineshaft. I only hope that the light at the end doesn't keep running away, making the tunnel longer."

"Course not. You're the best one out of *all* of us. For sure the Ox. Maybe even Fury! You're so smart and dedicated. That's probably why Cava was always in love with you."

"Pardon?"

"Don't act like you didn't know. You can fool him and maybe yourself, but I know you're smarter than that. You probably knew about him and Anj before he did. That's probably why you stay in your room and look out the window like an owl."

Sally began to protest but, noticing her own voice getting louder and shriller, she resigned from her objection. "Yeah, I mean, sure, but..." confounded with her own inability to string together a sentence and having been made aware of her blushing by Luc, she sighed. "Of course I knew, or rather, I had an idea. Then, I found out the hard way, like *we* always do. I'm happy for Quinn, of course. But, I was so happy thinking that he was sitting with me to be *with me*."

"I've had so many conversations with both of you about the same things... both of you, saying the same things about the other. To me, it's kind of funny."

"Ha... ha, Luc."

"Don't worry, it'll all work out." Luc smirked and rubbed Sally's arm. "Remember, I come from a line of Haitian voodoo priests. I can see your future," he concluded in a dressed-up Carib accent.

"Thanks, man. Maybe I will make the effort to try and hang out more often."

"I talked Cava into the drags on Friday. You want to cut in?"

"The drag races? Fuck that!"

"Salomea Doktor... you cussed." Luc laughed in awe.

SIMPLE FAVOUR

LUC WOKE UP feeling good. He'd had to go pee around six in the morning, and had decided to stay awake to cook the family that'd been boarding him, rent free, some of his favourite breakfast foods. He wanted to chef the Cavanaugh family some banana pancakes, salsiccia, and spicy eggs.

"Damn Irish," he muttered to himself. "Ain't got no spices, no flavour, no nothing up in this pantry. What do we got: onions, baking stuff..."

He always purchased bananas and plantains for the Cavanaugh home, which only he seemed to eat. Since it was too early to bop to the grocery store, he remembered that his ice box probably had frozen Sicilian sausage; there would also be a shaker of Maggi and hopefully some dried peppers that might still be edible. He slipped out the door as quietly as he could, removing a joint from his ear, lighting it, and taking a couple puffs, remembering to check if there were any cans of coconut milk—or at least condensed milk.

"Fuck is going on," Luc said aloud, pinching out the cherry and sliding the extinguished joint into his pocket. Approaching his house, he chafed at the soot on his fingers and wiped them on his pants, then picked up his pace towards the door. He clocked three white vans and a pick-up truck parked outside of his house. All the boards were torn from the front door, and men in coveralls appeared to be moving in and out of the premises. The nascent flush of dawn exposed the singularity of the figures. Luc continued to approach, surging with adrenaline.

"Hey!" he hollered. "What are y'all doing in my house?"

The characters largely ignored his appeal, some of them conversing in a language that he didn't register.

"I said, what the fuck you doing?" He placed a hand on the collar of a man wearing a surgeon's mask and carrying an abused wooden chair.

"It's okay, it's okay." A man's voice came from behind Luc. He said something to the man in the mask that Luc didn't understand. "You must be the son. The younger brother, Luc, yes?"

Luc turned to face the man. He was brown with curly hair and a full-bodied mustache, wearing a plaid shirt tucked into jeans with a giant, brick cellphone at his waist. He was carrying a clipboard, and he extended his hand.

"My name is Sunny." The man gave Luc's semi-raised hand three prompt shakes. "These are my men, and we're restoring the house."

Luc looked at the vans closer: Dhaliwal Restoration Services; Gupta Finishing; Singh Wood and Concrete.

"We were hired to come in and finish everything as soon as possible. Remove all the garbage and debris, replace what needs to be replaced. It shouldn't take us long, it's mostly the basement, though it's quite bad. It's a horror show, but, I'm sure you've seen it. We have the contract and can submit it to the city. It should be fit to return to very shortly."

Luc's exasperation was evident.

"Who hired you? Who's paying you?"

"We're privately contracted. The bill has been settled. All that remains is to complete the work and get a locksmith here." Sunny noticed the pager on Luc's own waist and pointed to it. "I can page you when the keys are ready, after the locks are changed. When you'd like to move back in, you may do so at your own leisure."

"Wow, yeah… That sounds incredible," Luc said, stunned. "Can I grab something from inside?"

"Of course, my friend." Sunny smiled and bowed his head slightly.

Luc squeezed by the workers, trying not to get in their way. He heard all kinds of activity from the basement—power tools and jawing from the workers. The carpeting on the stairs was being removed, torn up along with the thin layer of foam underneath. The living room and kitchen looked the same, untouched by Fabi's malefaction.

Luc removed the frozen sausages from the freezer, finding the spices and some scotch bonnet peppers that appeared serviceable. He felt a cloudy, surreal, almost hallucinatory sensation; he wasn't entirely sure if the morning tokes had hit him like a blunderbuss, or if he was still dreaming, possibly urinating in the bed next to his friend.

"Luc?" Sunny tapped his shoulder. "I have a phone call for you."

"This is Luc wit da C," he said hesitantly.

"*Fre.*"

"Janjak! *Kouman ou ye?*"

"I'm good, bebe. Are you?"

"I'm doing a lot better. I've been staying with Cava. Things are on the up and up."

"That's good. *Maman's* back home?"

"Yeah."

"Good. I heard that Fabi did a little bid. That he's awaiting trial. He may run. Either way, he's not to step foot in the house. You need to be strong, especially with *maman*. She loves him, as I would imagine you do, but he's brought nothing but harm."

"Will… will he be okay?"

"He's a black cat; he's bad luck and must have had nine lives. I don't know how many he has left, so I can't answer that. I no longer wish to protect him. I also don't know if he has a life worth protecting, or even living, for that matter. He may just twist the blade by himself."

"Should I fear the Singhs?" Luc whispered.

"Who do you think is fixing *maman's* rest?" Janjak said. "No, you must fear the low-level crimeys and snakes that you've jumped in the stew with."

"I'm dealing with that now, don't worry."

"I have to. Too much time to think. *Mwen renmen ou, fre.*"

"Love you too, brother."

* * *

"Luc, this breakfast is delicious. A little spicy, but absolutely wonderful," Nora chirped, picking her and Joe's dishes up.

"Yeah," Henry added, his mouth full of eggs. "It's real good."

"You all ruin it with syrup and ketchup. Now I know how all the Italian *mammas* feel when whites come over for dinner," Luc said in a contrived tone, to the enjoyment of the family—particularly Nora.

"Oh, I'm already late. You boys want a ride to school?" Joe asked as he poured the remainder of the coffee pot into his slate-coloured thermos.

"Hank's riding bitch," Cava said, blowing out of his pursed lips due to a pepper seed he'd bit squarely.

"Mouth!" Nora chided.

The boys assembled their bags as Luc and Nora began to clean the kitchen. Luc reminded Cava of his English paper and Henry of his science test, still wearing Nora's apron, which he'd used to cook the plates. "You know, I bet I could design a practical, but still ill, set of aprons for men and ladies. There's some real money in that."

"Ha! There he is," Cava said, sliding his shoes on. "Thanks *Moms!*" he said sarcastically.

"Cava, still down for tonight?" Luc said softly, so as to not be heard by the parents. "It's Friday, so I got, uh, work to do, but it's the first one of the year, should be a fucking rager."

"Should be good. Anj didn't seem too jazzed up on the idea..." Cava trailed off.

"Probably not her vibe, to be honest. Bunch of booze, bunch of broads, and some roadsters just getting whipped? Yeah, I can see how your lady wouldn't be too into that. The nice girls aren't into that for some reason."

"Well, I told her that I might be able to hang after, which would mean that she'd be crashing here, which would mean—"

"Yeah, yeah, yeah. This guy's got the couch, I get it. Joke's on you: I like the couch."

"Okay, man, well, you can sleep there every night, then."

"No. There are phantoms."

Cava scoffed. "Nah... Anyways, I'll beep you or whatever later on."

"Have a nice day, honey," Luc said, waving a dishrag like a handkerchief.

"Thanks, darling," Cava blew a kiss to his friend as Joe blasted the horn.

Luc caught the kiss. Nora shook her head before laughing up the stairs.

* * *

Luc received a page and met Fink just outside the school grounds to head over to Tic-Tax's house for pick up. Luc noticed that Fink was wearing a new Northface jacket with a fur collar. *Real fur.* He had a chain over the coat, a long Cuban link cable that would probably hang to his navel without the topmost layer, and a pair of brand new Jordans. *Flu Game Jordans.*

"Yo man, you popping fresh, dough-boy," Luc said, petting the soft fur around the collar of Fink's bubble-goose parka. "You got the rope, out the box J's, shit's looking crispy. You must be making all kinds of sells."

Fink scoffed. "You just ain't doing it right."

Luc waited for him to continue, but he just looked straight ahead and kept walking in silence.

"I got some Pippens and Air-Maxes, too," Fink finally said as they neared the sliding door of Tic-Tax's house.

"Shit, those are my favourites," Luc said, envious.

"Yeah," Fink responded as he wiped his shoes on the mat outside. "I know."

Luc, about to remove his sneakers, noticed that Fink remained in his shoes. He decided to give his a second, vigorous wipe on the mat and followed his cohort inside. He hadn't visited the house as regularly as before, since his brother's exodus, which coincided with his living at the Cavanaugh residence. The house had the dichotomous arrangement of nice, leather couches, an ostentatious, massive glass coffee table, and a big screen television. All of it was housed in a place that looked and felt mysteriously damp and smelled unpleasant—in some areas, straight foul. The laminated floors were sticky and stained, the carpets were visibly grimy, and the walls had a greasiness about them, like a teenager's fore-head. From the living room, Luc could see that the kitchen was noth-ing but dirty pots and Pyrex. Pizza boxes and Chinese food containers foamed from the garbage can, nearly licking the ceiling from the stacks on the dinner table.

Fink walked in through the living room, peered down the hallway, and walked into the kitchen. He raised his foot and stomped three big boots to the floor, raising his knee as high as his chest and slamming his foot down on the vinyl tiles. The tiles were not-quite-brown, not-quite-grey; they weren't any discernable colour, like gruel, and were omnipres-ent among the Oxford houses.

Luc cringed. Footsteps ate the staircase steps with what he perceived as anger; an apparent misstep and curse halfway up, aggravated the furi-ous ascension. *Great*, Luc thought. The only thing he liked less than a drug lord was an incensed and vengeful drug lord.

"I told you not to do that, Marek," Tic-Tax cried, wearing goggles and the same mask as the men in Sunny's crew.

"I need to get back to class," Fink responded, pompously. "It's my final year, you know."

Luc choked on his own breath, coughed, and shook his head. He wondered what tree Fink had torn the nuts from to speak to Tax like that.

"Ah, Luc, my man," Tic Tax said, removing his plastic glasses and lifting the filter onto his head. Luc noticed that his head was shaved to the roots. It kind of looked like an alien head, oblong and misshapen, with some random bumps that emphasized its unevenness. "What are you looking at?" Tic-Tax barked.

"N-nothing, man. Just ain't seen you without any lettuce before, is all." Luc scanned his boss and noticed that he seemed skinnier. Maybe it was the razor-job, but he looked gaunt and his complexion was greyish-yellow.

"You wanna see your big brother?" Tic-Tax asked, jovially. "He's doing great, I been keeping him under my thumb. Just cheffing, nothing else. I give him a little sniff of the good stuff, here and there. It's good for everyone to put a little in their nose from time to time. But no meth, no crystal at all… That's the brain-melter."

"Nah, I'm cool," Luc said, coldly. "Do you guys all have shaved heads?" he asked, having noticed that Fink's chestnut locks had been stripped to the scalp when he'd removed his hood.

"Yeah, it was Fink's idea. Like actual soldiers... Besides, the chemicals soak into your hair and it's hard to wash out... It really reeks."

Luc noticed that Tic-Tax seemed scrambled. His usual hostile temperament seemed to have given way to a state of easy confusion. Maybe the cooking chemicals had poisoned his brain. Luc had worked hard to keep his interactions very simple: pick up, drop off, wait until the money was counted, and leave.

Luc and Fink zipped their packages into their respective backpacks and set to the exit, when Tic-Tax motioned them over to the couch. "I just got this new system, you sure you guys don't wanna stay?"

"Nah. Class, remember?" Fink said as he slid the glass door open. "I'll holler at you later, Ali."

"Sit a moment, Luc," Tax said as Fink left. "I need to ask you a favour."

Luc was startled. Not by the possibility of a favour, which could be, optimistically, parlayed, but by Rosee's head, which he nearly squashed when he went to sit on the smaller loveseat.

"Jesus, Rosee. Have you been there the whole time?"

She didn't respond and simply looked at the television's screensaver, an insignia bouncing from side to side. Her thin eyebrows and little fox mouth were slightly illuminated when the logo threatened to hit the corner of the screen.

"Beside me is fine," Tax said. "I don't bite."

Luc fought back the urge to make a comment about his teeth.

"Business is going well... Well enough, I suppose. Perhaps too well. I don't really have a way to figure out how well things are going. To me, it's a success. Look at this room, look at these toys. It's nearly perfect. Except for the mess, fucking lazy-ass Rosee. I haven't left my humble abode very much. I'm tired, I feel like I'm almost a prisoner here. It's good for your brother, who as I mentioned, seems to be much better. He's getting his colour back." Tic-Tax chuckled. "But, I suspect that the Souls have an idea that I'm selling behind their backs, if they care. I haven't been at the chop shop or the tattoo spot for a minute, and though they probably don't give a shit, they tend to eliminate people like me, rather than, you know, talk it out."

Luc raised an eyebrow and rubbed his hands against his knees. He had no idea where this was going.

"I need a bigger crew. I don't want to take them on, that's fucking retarded. And your bro's scared shitless after getting dummied in the cell by some brown dudes."

"What are you driving at...? Ali?"

"It's where *you're* driving, and that's to the docks, tonight... I have a plan and I need all my boys in on it." Tic-Tax leaned forward. "I'm getting us some good fucking stuff, and I need you to drive my car and help me pick it up. It's a two-man operation, and you're the other man I trust the most. Crusher has become disrespectful, and I'll deal with him. I have some crackheads pumping dope and shoving ice picks, but they're far from trustworthy. I'll have Fabi with me; I need his skills. But, I need you most of all."

"What kind of good stuff?"

"Don't worry about it," Tax smiled, sharpening his devil's chin. "We'll all be good to do whatever once we get it."

Luc sat back and scratched the back of his head. "Look, yo, I already told you... If I'm going in any direction, it's out. I wanna go back to school, I wanna live a normal life again. Look what's already happened. I want out, man... I told you this."

"Do you even know what you owe me?"

"No, I mean, I have an idea, but..."

"$10,000."

"Fuck off."

"Watch your fucking mouth," Tic-Tax blustered, hunching his shoulders like a vulture.

"That's impossible. I been selling and selling and selling and not spending barely any of my ends."

"Brother," Fabi's voice rang. "Long time no see. How is ma..."

Luc leapt from the couch and speared his brother against the stairs. Luc easily overpowered his brother and began choking him. The poorly lit hallways showed nothing but the whites of Fabi's rolled back eyes.

Tic-Tax placed Luc in a sleeper hold but was lifted from his feet as Luc turned and flipped the lanky attacker onto his back. Luc was breathing heavily, thinking that he could very easily eradicate all of his problems, right here and right now.

"Okay, okay, hold on!" Tic-Tax screamed, having narrowly missed his head on the sharp-cornered coffee table. "I get it. You're fed up." Luc noticed a legitimate fear in Tic-Tax's eyes. He glanced and saw his brother trying to recover his breath. Rosee was still catatonic on the couch.

"Do this for me, and you can be done," Tic-Tax said, rising to a seated position.

Luc stood silently. Was this a trick? Would there be recrimination? Would a favour turn into a set up?

"Alright. I'll do it."

"1 am, the docks. The keys will be in the transmission out front. We can talk about what comes next, after. Meet me at the races beforehand so I know you're good."

Luc made his way to the front door, fighting the magnificent urge to burst into smiling tears. He heard Rosee mumbled something, probably about the rebounding emblem. She was promptly slapped. Luc heard a second, and then a third clap. After the third collision came a piercing scream, then a series of whimpers. He stopped as his fingers closed around the doorknob.

"Be easy, man," Luc lifted his palms. "She ain't do nothing."

"Fucking bitch! She *don't* do nothing!" Tic-tax turned to Rosee. "You never cook, you never clean, you just lie there like a fucking toadstool. What fucking good are you?" Tic-Tax screamed and snarled. Displacement, as Freud would have it. "Ain't your business, Kalou. Turn your head, or the deal is off."

Rosee remained vacant, as if nothing had happened. Luc chose to exit, glancing to see his brother recovering from his near-suffocation. As he left, he heard some muffled yelling, mostly male, with a few feminine objections.

Though ethically torn, Luc was cautiously optimistic about the evening. He had a hard time believing that Tic-Tax would let his cash cow walk, just like that, for a simple driving favour.

The reality of Luc being an unlicensed driver hadn't even entered his mind. All of the Kalou brothers had driven their mother's car to the store with a note to buy smokes since they were knee-high. He was as comfortable driving a car illegally as he was walking.

He took a left, not wanting to even pass by Mama Cavs house with a backpack full of dope. His head was in a complete fantasy. He thought about staying on, selling drugs, and actually pocketing profit. He thought about giving it up, rebuilding his atelier, and weaving the dreams that he'd been so miserable without. He thought about doing both, how drug money could buy all kinds of new tools and cloths. Briefly, he thought about JJ's impending release, and how he would handle finding out that his baby brother was still moving units.

He suddenly remembered that he'd had sex with Rosee in the back of her dad's truck only months prior.

* * *

Anjuli and Cava had decided to meet after classes were dismissed for the week, two blocks from the school grounds. Due to the distance from her house to the school, Anjuli, like many other older teenagers in her area, elected to park off school grounds to avoid paying for the school lot's parking pass.

Cava gave Anjuli a head start, extinguishing the minutes by conversing with Sally and Cliff, the latter of whom was rolling through to pick his siblings up.

"The drags?" Cliff repeated after being asked about his weekend plans. "Yeah, I might be able to swing that. I've been stacking up some chips, laying low, and working. It might be time to upgrade this slab." He threw his palm against the side of his car door.

"You know," Cava started, "you'll actually have to insure the next one."

"Of course I will." Cliff chuckled. "That'll be phase two."

"Phase two?" Sally inquired.

"Yeah. On getting me and these little squirts the hell out of Fury, once and for all." He spun in his bucket and looked at Thunder and Lightning. "You guys wanna go live in nature?"

"Yeah," the two responded in unison, mildly enthused, which was a level of animation uncommon in the children.

"Moving?" Cava blurted. "But, why?" Even as he asked it, he felt that the question was redundant.

"Cause this ain't no place to raise young ones. How can everyone be so broke, but the cost of everything keep going up? It don't make a lick of sense. Soon as I get my Grade 12, I don't want to leave these two to fend for themselves while I work half the day to scrape by. Lots of jobs up North. Trade schools, work and learns… I can get a ticket and have an actual house, all while doing my years. Maybe the fresh air, the trees, the animals… maybe all that will have an effect on the kids. Lots of work there: the dams, the plants, the oil… everything."

"Well, I mean, it's rough to lose you, big guy," Sally responded. "But, your mind seems made up, and you seem excited. Besides, with any luck, we'll all be going our separate ways after this year."

Cava looked at Sally puzzlingly, who, after giving him a dispirited smile, continued. "The sooner the better, in my opinion."

"See?" Cliff said, leaning his head towards Cava. "That's why she's always been the smartest. Gonna miss this bag of bolts… You wanna come for its little send-off, Sal?"

"The races?" she sneered. "Ew. God, no. It's so dirty and illegal."

Cliff pulled a pack of darts from the visor and lit one. "Yup, smartest person I ever met. Later, guys. See you in a few, Cavs."

Cliff drove off, while Cava and Sally remained. Cava felt a prickling sensation in his lower stomach. Sally had been so indifferent moments earlier, about everyone 'going their separate ways.' She watched Cliff's car maneuver out of the parking lot and looked back at Cava, smiling with more muscle.

"I only made it sound like we were all going to be travelling different paths next year, you know, so he wouldn't feel as though he was missing out." She turned her head and grabbed both her backpack straps. "For him, getting out of town is really the only option. What does he have here? Nothing really. An alcoholic mother who he doesn't even let near her abandoned children. No, he needs our support, and the best support is to solidify his resolve."

Cava looked dreamily at Sally. "You really are the smartest. So, the band isn't breaking up?"

Sally laughed. "Well, we can always do solo projects, like that rap band you and Luc love so much." She twisted her sneaker into the ground. "I'll be your Method Man."

Cava laughed. He wanted to wrap his arms around her and lift her up, or tackle her into the nearby patch of grass. Instead, he bumped his knuckles together before stuffing his hands into his pocket. "You don't even smoke weed."

"Oh, is that what he does? Is there one that likes books?"

"Probably all of them?" Cava chuckled. "They're quite smart, in spite of what you think about rap."

They stood in silence for a moment, looking at each other.

"So," Cava said as he scuffed the sole of his sneaker against the concrete. "Drags?"

"Ugh," she exaggerated the sound. "What are you doing now?"

"I'm supposed to meet Anj at her car. I spoke to her in passing today, and she didn't seem too amped about the drags. I don't know why you people hate it."

"Because we're classy ladies. But really, those things are kind of gross… It's just skids and gambling. I went once, remember? We—I included—almost got jumped because Fink slashed someone's tire for no reason."

"Oh yeah. He keyed like seven cars."

"Anyways, she probably had them where she used to live, and it probably invited the same trashy elements as this one." She thought for a moment. "I just don't get it. You barely see the races. It's just a bunch of fights, drinking, drugs, and illegal stuff. Why do you like it?"

"Cause all my idiot friends like to jump off bridges, and it's lonely on the guard rail."

"Do what I do: bring a book, the sunsets are rather nice… probably a lot nicer if you watch them with someone."

They both reddened.

"I have to walk a couple streets this way to meet Anj. Want to come?"

Sally corked her features and hummed a thoughtful melody. "Okay, I guess I could say hi. I also want to grab some nibs before I tutor."

Cava laughed. "You tutor on Friday night? What a network of nerds." He chuckled again, repeating her word. "Nibs… cute."

* * *

Sally and Cava approached Anjuli's stationary car in a cul-de-sac, a neighbourhood beyond a catwalk. As they approached, their conversation echoed down the graffiti-covered corridor of wooden-fenced yards that sat snugly against the waist high chain link fence. They weren't talking about anything important, but both noticed the peeking head of Cava's girlfriend emerging from her car window.

"Hey Anj," Cava said, chummily.

"Hi! Anjuli!" Sally waved enthusiastically.

"Oh! Salomea, hi," Anjuli responded with equal verve.

"Call me Sally," she said with a kind smile. "People only call me Salomea when I do something wrong."

"Absolutely… I can't believe Mr. Miller's assignment this weekend. I feel like he actually wants us to fail."

The girls continued talking as Cava drifted away into his own mind. He could make out their chirpily, good-humoured banter, but retained little regarding the subject matter.

"Quinn!" the girls bellowed in concert.

"Hello…" he answered with the affable candor of one who was too simple to be evil.

"I don't think he was listening."

"Yeah." Sally smiled. "He does that sometimes."

* * *

Cava hopped in the passenger seat and gave his lover a peck on the lips, ensuring that Sally had begun walking up the street and had her head turned the opposite direction in the rear-view mirror.

"How was your…"

"She is *very nice*," Anjuli intruded. "So *nice* and so *beautiful*. Also, very *intelligent*. Does she have a *boyfriend*?"

"Sally? I'm pretty sure no. She fills her time with school, and sports, and all kinds of extracurricular activities. Like, all the time. I never really see her much these days. Kind of a shame. She leaves when it's dark and comes home after the sun sets. Hard worker."

Anjuli sighed.

"What?" Cava asked with a knitted brow.

"Oh, nothing. She just seems to really like you."

"Of course she does! We've been homies since we were babies. Me, her, and Luc. We all grew up yelling distance from each other's stoops. They're my day-ones."

"Has she always been so..."

"Smart? Nice? Pretty?"

"Yeah..."

"Smart and nice, yes; she's been a total geek since day one. Saved me from getting into a lot more trouble than I would've otherwise."

"*Beautiful?*"

"No! She was always the hot older sister's not-so-hot younger sister. She kind of... changed over the last year when she was abroad. Came back looking like a totally different person."

"Do you think she's hot?"

"What? Me? No... I mean, I can see that she's attractive, sure... But, she's been my closest friend, other than Luc, since we were both in diapers. I don't really see her that way, you know? If anything, I'm worried that guys will only see her for her looks now, and not the cute, bookworm, straight-edged weirdo that I know. You know?"

Anjuli checked the rear-view mirror and fired the engine. Cava eye-balled her and asked her why she seemed angry.

"I'm not, I'm not... I just didn't know that you guys were so close. She's been talking to me more lately, about you, about us, and I just didn't know why."

"Well..." Cava studied his lady. "She just found out about us being together on Sunday. Maybe she's looking out for me? Maybe she's just curious about who her friend is dating? I don't know, but you don't have anything to be—"

"I'm not worried."

Cava worked to reinstate his good favour with Anjuli, which had seemed to take a hit from something beyond his control. He'd often dealt with feelings of jealousy, suppressing them into the acid bath in the pit of his stomach. He'd figured that if he'd attracted a jealousy-prone mate, that it was something desirable as it clearly demonstrated that he was cared for. However, he wasn't titillated by her anxiety; he was annoyed by its preposterousness.

He joked, tickled, sponged her with compliments, and broke the knob while turning up his charm.

She eventually succumbed to his wiles, which ranged from maudlin to self-sacrificingly cloying. When he finally exhumed her smile from the depths of her doubts, he felt that he needed a dart.

"So... what are you thinking for tonight?"

"Well," Cava began, prepared to batten the hatches again. "I mentioned earlier in the week, and today, that I was going to go to the drags with Luc, that is... drag races. You're welcome to come..."

Without looking to his left, he felt the rise of quills once again.

"I promised Luc I'd go, it's the first one of the year."

After a pause, Anjuli broke her silence. "No. We had something like that back home, and they were just full of older guys that never graduated, who only worked on cars. It was always a big drunk. Kind of stupid, if you ask me. A total waste of time. The only people that would go were like, hood-rats and skids." Her tone was firm and emotionless.

"Maybe I'm a hood-rat and a skid then."

"No, babe, you're not," she responded with conviction. "But some of your friends are. I don't want to assume anything, and I know you've grown up here and it's all you know, but you're better than all that pseudo-criminality that your friends are into. You're smarter than that. You're just going to wind up in trouble, in prison, or even dead."

"I haven't yet."

"No, because you're smarter than them. Or lucky. But, look at what's happened to your friends this year. I like Luc. He's better than this life, too. But, he doesn't know any better. You do."

"But, he's my best friend. I'm not just gonna let him waste away."

"I know that, Quinn. I respect your loyalty. Now that I've met your parents, I see where you get it from. I love your mother. I respect her for raising you well, in spite of all the temptations for you to be a bad guy. But, having met them, and knowing them, liking them, feeling as though they liked me, I have a harder time now... watching you put yourself in situations, or surrounding yourself with tough people who like to do immature, illegal bullshit."

"But, if I am better than all that, why do I enjoy it? Why don't you enjoy it with me?"

"Do you enjoy it? You might have been nervous, but being with your family, and Luc, in your house, safe and surrounded by people that love you, you seemed so happy. It was such a nice side of you. You're not a thug, babe... I think you've learned how to act tough in order to fit in with all the delinquents that you've been stuck around all your life. I think you want people like me—Sally as well—in your life."

Anjuli continued. "And, I wouldn't enjoy that stuff... I don't like being around people I don't trust, people that only want to take advantage of you or hurt you. It's not fun, and it's not safe. I don't know why you like it. Maybe you're lying to yourself. You have all these different interests—reading, writing, sports—and I bet you even like studying."

"If I would have spent my life doing only those things, I would have grown up alone. I would have grown up alone and without anyone to watch my back. You didn't grow up here. You grew up in a nice, big house with your family in Rockford. You live here, sort of, but you still live in a nice big house with your family, have multiple cars, and your dad has a business that he doesn't need to work at 70 hours a week to put food on the table for his wife and kids."

"My parents work damn hard. They came to this country without a dime in their pockets. They were highly educated back home, from respected families. You know what that gets you here? A job driving cabs or making sandwiches. They clawed and studied and pursued their dreams here. I'm indebted to them, and fortunate to have parents that built something from absolutely nothing."

"I didn't say they don't! Maybe if I met them, I'd have a better understanding. They worked harder than I can imagine, built a good life, and raised a great daughter. Who, you, will in turn have a great life, guaranteed! You will get in to any school you want. You can have any guy that you want. In a few short years, you can have any job that you want. If

I'm such a street urchin, such a low-level, two-bit piece of shit, then why me? You can do a lot better than some *Fury*."

She paused and looked as though she wanted to cry. "Because I *want* to love you, and there are parts of you that I do love. There are parts of you that I'm fucking obsessed with. I'm attracted to you more than you could ever know. You get me. You're the only person I've ever felt comfortable to be myself around. You usually make me feel like I don't even deserve *you*, because you're so nice and kind to me. But, you don't love yourself. You think that you're sentenced to a life of mediocrity because of where you were born, so you just go with the flow and let yourself think that you're a victim and a product of your environment. You're not! You're so much better than that! I want you to be the man I know you can be."

Cava listened blankly. He felt a reservoir of indignation find a crack in the wall. "The man you *want* me to be? I'm only 17, man. It takes time. I need to figure some things out... I can't rush headlong into life without a plan or with the mediocrity I've settled for thus far. I've wasted a lot of time, and a couple of months isn't going to build a bridge that leads me anywhere meaningful."

"You're almost done with school. *So close.* And, you're getting great grades in all your classes. You're not a kid, or a boy, or anything but a man who's afraid to knot his shoes and be a man. Don't make excuses, you always do."

"Why are you saying all this to me now? How long have you been bottling this up for?" Cava snapped.

"It's not that I've been bottling this up, it's just that I care about you and I want to be with you. Some of the stories you tell me, about growing up, about what kinds of things you and your friends did and do for 'fun...' they scare me. I want to think about us in the future, but I don't want..."

"Me to hold you back. Is that it?"

"No. I have to look out for my future first. I owe that to my family. And, I don't want to feel like I'm dragging you by the arm, like I'm taking you somewhere that you don't really want to go."

"I'm not dead weight. I make my own choices."

"I want to believe you, I really do… But what do you do as soon as I leave? Smoke marijuana and cigarettes with Luc?"

"I don't need weed when I'm with you."

"You don't need it at all. It's not you that I don't trust, it's the influences that are all around you. The influences and your inability to control yourself when I'm not around. The decisions that you make when you're left on your own… I can't babysit you. I want to, but I can't. It's not fair to either of us."

"What are you saying…? You don't trust me?"

"I do! I trust you, babe… What I don't trust is how you deal with peer pressure. How often do you lie to me?"

Cava felt a petulant heat douse and dour his being. He searched for a counter-argument but found none. He wasn't willing to admit that the precise logic dealt upon him had been drawn with careful forethought and plucked with the expertise of Oliver Queen. The velocity of each release left Cava unobservant of the arrow; he only felt each Bodkin point hit the bullseye.

"Quinn? Is there anything you want to say?"

Cava responded with a shrug. He knew from experiences with his mother that he needed time to dwell on her bombarding rebukes and barrages of disapproval; anything he might say would be an emotional disaster or easily picked apart. He stayed silent, battling within his own mind, thinking about how to prove her wrong, but finding little internal reinforcement that could assist him in such a fruitless endeavour.

"No. You're right. At least at this point."

"It's not about being right. It's about being honest and open. Do you have anything that you want to say to me?"

"No. You're perfect."

"Quinn… that's sweet, but I'm not…"

"Fuck sakes! Can't I still hold onto one belief about me or us today? Damn."

Anjuli was stunned.

"Sorry for cussing, but I wasn't prepared for any of this. I care about you, too. I care about us. I hate to admit when I'm wrong, and I hate to admit when other people are right even more. I have to, kind of, sleep on this, but I don't think that anything you said was wrong. That's frustrating to me, you know? I just found out that I'm a shitty dude."

"You're not…"

"But I feel like one, which is about the same." Cava pondered for a moment, realizing that he was in the visitor's parking at the Ox. "Look, it's a work in progress. I want to change for you, but you can't destroy who you've been for your whole life and change instantly. I don't even totally understand how I'm supposed to change. I don't have a red cape and a telephone booth. I can only promise that I'll work on it."

"Are you still going to the drag races tonight?"

"I am, because I said that I would. A Cavanaugh don't break their promise. But I'll keep it low-key, play the wall… No hood shit."

"You swear?"

"Of course," Cava said. *I'll do my best,* he thought.

The two teens exchanged a tense-lipped, bird-beak kiss. Cava went to exit the car, but turned and pulled Anjuli into a longer, more passionate embrace. He didn't feel that it was warranted, but felt a great swell of lust and affection for her. He *was* cared about by someone else.

"Be careful," Anjuli said with a sympathetic smile and feeble wave.

She just jinxed me, Cava thought as he made his way home to soap and sup.

STAY HOOD

THEY WERE OFF to an industrial park down by the river, where the temperature was colder and windier than in the centre of the city. The boys usually hitched, took a bus, or rode bikes. When they caught a ride, there was always a 50/50 chance that the car might get impounded, that the driver might become too impaired to ferry them back, or that a post-drag party might lead them somewhere else, so the following morning would be the time to salvage a way home.

Luc rattled on the window as Cava slid on a workman's insulated flannel over a long-sleeved shirt. He popped the blinds open to see Luc dangling a set of car keys with a big smile on his face. Disengaging the window, Luc asked if he was ready and whether he had any food.

"I forgot to get much groceries, so I used the water-in-the-shampoo bottle technique on the milk… I don't think the milk was good and the cereal tasted like ass," Luc said.

"You're allowed to use the front door like a normal human, you know."

"Yeah, but, your mom's going to ask me what we're gonna do, I don't wanna have to lie to Mama Cavs."

"Fine. I'll come through the front door. I'll get you a banana and some bread or something."

No one was upstairs to sniff around and ask him questions. He grabbed his bigger Starter coat with the giant Lakers logo on the back: all-black except for some purple and gold piping around the sleeves and trim at the bottom, which hung below his waist. His father's scarf was draped over a kitchen chair. Cava eyed the scarf, a useful and warm invention, but was unfortunately 'gay' according to Fury's code of masculine ethics.

Cava grabbed a banana and a granola bar. He inspected the pantry for anything else that was easy to carry and quick to consume. He grabbed a half-full pack of saltine crackers and closed the cupboard door quietly.

Luc was standing outside the front door with a lit joint. "You take forever, bro. I lit this when you said you'd be right out." He passed the bone to Cava, who took it and handed Luc the various snacks that he'd amassed from inside his pockets.

"You wanted snacks from an Irish house, you fool," Cava snickered. "We don't keep fun food in the walls… Why are you blazing? Don't you have to drive?" Cava's tone changed from mockery to concern as Luc peeled the banana from the bottom end instead of the stem.

"Take the edge off."

They made their way toward Tic-Tax's grandmother's house.

"Don't worry. I can't remember the last time I whipped a chariot not high, in fact. That time we took Rosee's dad's pickup to get hash? High. That time that girl was too fucked up to drive her mom's MPV home from Fig Beach? High… and kind of bent." He swallowed the rest of the banana and wiped his lips with a scarf-tail buried in his jacket, leaving the frilly black and purple ends exposed. "I'd be more worried if I had to drive sober."

Cava took a few more pulls of the joint before passing it back, allowing himself to be persuaded by Luc, and they hopped in the car.

"You'd make a fine girl, Cavs," Luc said as he noisily munched a saltine. "You passed the door test."

"This ain't Bronx Tale, Sonny. And I don't think I'm your type."

"We get caught by the pigs, you might just have to do, babe."

* * *

The plan was straightforward: maintain a low profile while driving to the drags. Get off of any main boulevard as expediently as possible, and cruise the backroads and alleys until they could drive under the sparsely lit, rarely patrolled flats. From there, it was a quick boot to the industrial arcade where the drags were to take place that week.

Much of the industrial park was owned and operated by gangsters, mainly the Souls. One would assume that the opportunity for the police to bust an illegal drag race in their sphere would be too hot, but the cops generally left the area alone as long as no one got hurt. The added gravity of racing on biker land meant that the racers and spectators kept their disputes and vandalism to a minimum. With the attention on the street, it also meant less scrutiny for the buildings that appeared closed, prompting a superior opportunity for the real greasy shit.

The Souls profited from the races by having their foot soldiers play the corners and put a premium on their product. They bought and sold stolen cars, with at least one notorious chop shop being located in the area beside a tattoo parlour. They also played bookies, taking bets and giving odds for races; all activities that core and even peripheral members could earn a little coin off of.

Luc wisely parked outside the industrial area. It was much cooler, and the air was thin and ghastly. Luc brought his scarf around his head like a Tuareg, and Cava pulled up his hood.

"Why are you wearing a scarf? Aren't you afraid to be called gay, or something? This is a pretty tough crowd."

"Who gives a fuck?" Luc responded, his words slightly muffled by the scarf wrapped around his head. "In MTL, no one gives a shit if something is ugly or gay in the winter... When it's cold, you bundle the fuck up! People out here have never been cold, or they'd know that these things save lives, man." He tightened the scarf. "Besides, this one even matches the stitching on your jacket. Speaking of which…"

"Fuck you."

Cava picked up his pace.

* * *

The sound of engines revving and people yelling superseded the visuals of the drags. The next sense to be activated was the temperature change, enabled by the building blocking the slicing winds and trapping the body heat of the crowds and warmth from the continuous churn of car engines.

The smell of gasoline, weed, and liquor breath was palpable as Luc and Cava shouldered their way through smoking circles and people crowded around various boomboxes. The cacophony was undesirable without alcohol; tinny speakers rattled out either punk guitar on the whiniest of trebles, or rap songs on blown speakers that made kicks sound like static and the bassline humid and hollow. This outer ring catered to the casual crowd, there more for the party atmosphere than anything else. The boys slapped hands and sipped bottles with a few acquaintances, asking if anybody had laid eyes on Fink. Cava was keeping an eye on Luc's bottle-tips, making sure that he refrained from jeopardizing their trip home.

Continuing through the throngs, the two shoved their way to an area where people opted to pop trunks and open doors to show off their rides. More of a show and shine, these cars rattled with abyss-deep bass, leaving the track undiscernible to the average ear. Airbrushed paint jobs of everything from Sailor Jerry-styled tigers and dragons, all the way to lifelike portraits of the Virgin Mary, adorned the lowriders. There were whitewalls, chromed-out grills, and piping that were turtle-waxed to a gleam, and spotless plush or leather interiors. The owners leaned on their cars and nodded as people stopped to show their respect. Some conversed about the Pioneer or Rockford Fosgate amps, the velour interior, or the wood grain grips. Many of the slabs had a shivering girlfriend inside, her arms tucked into herself, waiting for the egocentric fiesta to end.

Luc's attention was always kidnapped by the studded-out, customized cars; anything with care, craftsmanship, and style. In the distance, the high-pitched squeals of cars leaving from their mark, stuttering as they shifted and shrieked out of sight, caused heads to turn uniformly.

The boys continued wading amongst the people, acknowledging the turnout, which was even more impressive given the weather. They stepped over a passed out youngin' lying atop three BMXs. A questionable guard dog if the friends had ventured off to explore.

"Cavs! Luc wit da C! What up homies!"

"Yo! Bertie, man you everywhere! What's good?" Luc said enthusiastically as he brought Bertie in for a hug. Cava followed suit and locked his right hand while throwing his left around the tall, Swedish-looking teen, his hair now longer.

"Not much, not much... Dad's old shop is right there and the boys are all losing their minds... They can't be bothered and are in a seriously bad mood, so me and the lady decided to check on some metal ponies. You guys remember Claire? I met her at that messed up party. I think that was the last time I seen you guys."

The boys introduced themselves to Bertie's girl, a tallish blond with ocean blue eyes. They hadn't remembered her, but agreed that it'd been too long and that the last time they'd seen each other it'd been under some unfortunate circumstances.

"Luc," Bertie said, throwing a big arm over his shoulder. "Now, I've heard some pretty wild things coming out of your guys' area. Are you okay? Are you straight? I tried to reach out, but no answer at your house. Cavanaugh, sorry, I lost your number. I've heard some pretty scary things involving you. Are you okay?"

Luc patted Bertie's hand. "I wasn't, nah, I was far from okay... Lots of shit went down... Got myself in some pretty fucked up situations. It's getting better. Not *all* good, you know? But, I'm pulling myself out. Had to leave school, but I'm going back and was living with Cavs and his fam-a-lam. But! You know me, man. I ain't going down without a fight, and I'm finnin' to punch my way out."

"Cava, I heard you got yourself a lady. Congratulations, my friend."

"Jesus, Bertie, how do you know all this stuff?"

He laughed and slid his hand around Claire's waist and then into her jean pocket. "I hear a lot. I guess I maybe just listen a lot. Dope scarf, Luc! Me and you, we're the only ones that understand this winter business. What's wrong, Cava? Think scarves are gay?"

They all laughed and caught up, asked Claire some questions, and craned their necks whenever two racers lined up and skidded from the start position as some brave soul dropped his hands to signal 'go.'

"Yeah, we both live in Vincennes. Different schools, but she was out with her ex that night, a Fury boy. He was acting a fool, needed a talking to, and here we are."

"Aw man, good old Bertie. You a solid dude, man." Luc beamed at his friend. "Say, have you seen Rat-Fink anywhere? He was supposed to meet us, but he didn't tell me where?"

"You mean Guppy's peg-boy?" Bertie laughed. "Nah, he probably can't leave his master for too long. Which reminds me… Luc, can I talk to you for a moment?"

Bertie and Luc walked a few paces away to leave Cava and Claire to exchange token smiles. Cava assumed that he was safeguarding his lady from hearing whatever he had to tell Luc.

"Know anyone that needs a car disappeared? You need a ride? Tires? Stereo? Speakers? Summas? Anything, baby, anything?" A guy in a long coat and black Hammer hat came up to Cava.

"Uh, no man, need a better job first," Cava replied, surprised.

"Payment plan? I got you. Price to fit your budget? I got you. Whatever you need, you see me first. Take my card." The guy thrust a business card into Cava's hand before disappearing.

Jux Whips: Whatever you need, I got you. Cava showed the card to Claire, who seemed just as surprised, before popping it into his inner pocket.

Bertie and Luc returned. They looked serious, but without anger; resilient, but without cheer.

"Good looking out, homie. I'll take it and see what I can do."

"Not saying you have to do anything, but just watch your back. Protect your neck and all that stuff," Bertie responded with an equally thoughtful look.

They dapped Bertie goodbye and made their way deeper into the action. Cava stared at Luc, who looked ahead, pinching his eyes as he glanced around for Fink.

"So…" Cava started, "what did you guys talk about?"

"Not here. I'll tell you after."

* * *

The boys passed by the grimiest area of the drags. Here was the line of stolen cars, boosted items from trucks and backseats, and odds-makers that set up bets for the race. The off-the-books nature of all this activity was what usually led to brawls, broken limbs, and long car rides to bank machines in town.

Some of the cars were brought to be written off or stripped for metal. These people had to be sure that their cars were either completely destroyed or assured to be taken somewhere to be fleeced entirely. An insurance scam couldn't work if any foul play was suspected, or if the vehicle was still able to be salvaged.

Many people came to peruse the flea market of anything stolen or salvaged from the cars. Almost every time, there were dust-ups over articles that went missing from someone's car or truck, only to be found here.

Many of the vendors were crack and base heads. You could pay a mutant to shank a cop, after all. Some of the vehicles, parts and accessories arrived as run-off from the gangs themselves, who'd set up either an addict or entry-level member to sell off the merchandise.

"Boys! Come and say goodbye to the stallion!"

Luc and Cava turned and saw Cliff, wearing his Eazy-E shades and a flannel with just the top button attached, waving them over.

"What are you doing here?" Cava asked.

"Well, I doubt this piece of shit could make the drive up North, and I have enough money saved to buy a truck," Cliff said merrily. "Off the lot, you snakes… Jesus, I ain't taking a hot car anywhere. But, this is just about it for your boy!" Cliff waved off some encroaching salesmen.

"You be careful, man" Luc warned. "What are you doing? Writing her off? You don't want this shit to come back to you."

"If I insure it, for what, the weekend? It goes missing, ends up in flames in the marsh? They're gonna think I did it. Nah, I'll flip it to some crackhead, probably to do some dirt, pocket the money, and give my ass an alibi."

Cliff had the slight twinkle of liquid courage in his eye, which made him absolutely sure of his plan. Luc and Cava expressed their lack of faith, but to no avail. Cliff's car had already rolled out of the area and he had a sweet stack of 20s in his pocket. "Five hundy for that bondo boat! What a steal."

"What are you doing now?" Cava asked.

"I put a bill on the little Civic to take the RX. Something tells me she's a sleeper… Got 2-1 odds on the bitch. I'm heading to catch the last bus from this dump after that. Working tomorrow. You boys?"

"Not much," Luc stepped in front of Cava. "Supposed to meet Rat-Fink and smoke a bit of Buddha."

"Cool, well, fuck that herb, but cool," Cliff said as he watched the cars idle up to the line. "Goddamn rotary engine, blow out now, you little fucker… You know you wanna…"

Cava spotted Fink leaning on some crates out of the way of any action. They bid their friend adieu, who waved them off, yelling at the cars as if they were humans. They all promised to meet up before Cliff's departure and wished him luck.

"Yo, what's goodie?" Luc approached Fink, who was putting out a joint as they approached. "Percy, huh?"

Fink shrugged indifferently. "Alright, where'd you guys park?"

"Two blocks from the front, you guys?"

"I got my mom's car. Ali got a fiend to cop a burner… I came with him to make sure he didn't fuck us over. Rode to meet Ali, then bombed the way back. You guys are late.

"Man, fuck you, man… What's the fucking plan you rat-snake -fuck-shit-punk?"

Cava, startled, laughed without restraint. Fink breathed out sharply through his nose.

"Plans changed a bit… It's too hot here. We're all gonna meet at the docks. You know where the Dutch containers are? We painted them… maybe a year back? The orange ones? Up from the bus yards?"

"Yeah, of course… Just say the Nike boxes," Luc answered.

"Oh, right. Anyways, we're all meeting there."

"Hey, boys… Luc, right? Quinn? Umm, I can't remember, but you're the Russian kid." A middle-aged man approached the crew. "Have you seen a '74 Ford F-100? It went missing from my driveway…"

Fink decked the man as he was hurriedly, though warmly, asking them about the truck. Five random fiends came from the car accessory area and began to swarm on the man.

"Yo, Fink, you fucking psycho, that's Sluggo's dad… chill, man, chill!" Cava cried. He and Luc began tearing the fiends off, some of whom Cava recognized from the party, and pushed Fink backwards into the crates, toppling them, and him, over. The two boys defending their schoolmate's father, standing over him protectively, told the attackers to calm down, and tried to explain that this wasn't a big deal.

Two of the random assailants helped Fink to his feet. "Motherfucker called me Russian. I'm Ukrainian, you worthless piece of shit. Fuck you. Fuck your poor, white trash family, and fuck your ugly, hairy, retarded daughter. Cunt." Fink said as he rallied the men and made his way towards the back of the last building.

"Thanks, boys," Slug's father said. "I was just hoping to find my truck, I even have my last monies to try and find it, or another one."

"You don't want one here, Mr. Suggs," Cava replied as they struggled to help his giant frame onto its wobbly stilts. "You'll get pulled over and that's that."

"Maybe you're right. Fuck sakes, boys… Things ever go right in this goddamned city?"

The boys shrugged. "Not really, sir. You just have less worse days."

"Jesus H." The man pulled his frayed flannel sleeve above his broken-faced wristwatch. "I'm gonna miss the last bus. You boys don't happen to have a dart for an old-timer? I ain't boughten any and the old lady tooken mine after supper."

* * *

It took no more than 15 minutes of twists and turns to reach the docks. Luc knew the area well from painting with Fink. It was an amusement park for graffiti artists: a stock yard with trains that traveled cross-country, storage containers to get their ups in Europe, or wherever, and the bus depot, which would allow their tags to be seen for up to a week by all the

Fingers if the authorities weren't quick to repaint the buses. Security was heavy in all the areas; specialized enforcement units patrolled each part with hostility. One bomber had been beaten by the bulls, the rail cops, and left on the tracks instead of taken into custody; he was struck by a train like a damsel in distress and remained paralyzed from the waist down.

Luc knew that Fink had been referring to the open lot near the Protestant-orange cargo containers owned by some Dutch holding's corporations; it was dark, far from any sensitive property, and unsupervised in their previous visits.

"Weird," Luc said, holding the wheel closely, turning the music down, and peering over the dash. "Ain't no pick ups, and I don't see Fink's momma's hatchback."

"How does Rat-motherfucking-Fink have his license?" Cava asked.

"His folks paid for it," Luc answered. "Cat drives like a maniac... Like he's being followed by an axe murderer... The question is, how that dude *still* has a license."

They pulled into a spot facing a forest. The view of the marina and dock activity was a football field away.

Luc lit a scud and rolled the windows up, leaving the console light on and playing one of Tic-Tax's g-funk tapes at a low volume.

"See..." Luc said, holding a big toke in, "we used to sneak in there and walk over to the south gate. We'd hop it, usually having to lay a blanket over the barbed wire, or sneaking through if someone cut the fence. The security was bad... You could hear everything, so you kept six while one guy dropped a throwie, and then taking turns. Me and Fink, we would paint all night, passing bones, not talking for eight hours."

"That's the best way to hang out with him," Cava laughed, smoking a joint that was testing the extremes of the zig-zag. He coughed and passed it back to Luc.

Luc was scribbling his tag on the window, fogged from the humidity in the car. His finger squeaked against the glass as Cava watched through the thick, smoky cab. Cava turned to his mirror and placed the knuckle of his index against the window. Cava had tried to paint with his friends, but had very little artistic ability or creativity. He enjoyed the art; the walls were the canvasses of the pauper-Rembrandts and gutter-bred

Monets of his city. Having tried many times, he understood the difficulty of the craft; to be clean and fluid with the imperative of celerity, and the overlying threat of being pinched.

Cava's knuckle had already warmed a little circle around its resting place, as he thought of what to write. *What's the first word that pops in to your head?* he asked himself. *Sal...*

"Who's that?" Cava said as his attention shifted to a moving figure in the side mirror.

"Oh fuck!" Luc leapt to his senses, turning the inside lights off and putting out the smoldering blunt. "The bulls!"

The boys scrambled in their seats and saw the man illuminate a flashlight aimed at the car. They saw the spotlight invade the inside of the car as the beam moved jerkily. They cursed aloud and to themselves. The car was fumigated with weed smoke, and it wasn't theirs. Neither Luc nor Cava had a license.

"Fuck, fuck, okay... Fuck," Luc said. "I got an idea."

"What?!" Cava whispered with the full force of his diaphragm.

"You not gonna like it."

"Well, fuck man..." Cava began to plead but saw Luc's hand come around the back of his neck and thrust his head into Luc's lap. He fought to remove his face from Luc's crotch, but his strength was astonishing.

"Dude! Be easy. I got a plan..."

The figure approached the window and seemed stunned as he leaned in to tap the pane with his flashlight. Luc matched the man's amazement and finally allowed Cava to release himself. Cava flew upright and lunged for breaths. His eyes were wide and full of rage, but he shrunk into his seat.

The man began to say something imperceptible to the boys, pacing around before leaning in. "What doing?" The man was now firmly visible. He wore a burgundy turban and had a full grey beard with strands of black. He appeared elderly. His bony wrist had a metal bangle and held a small, department store flashlight, not the long, metallic police-issue lantern.

Luc whispered the words "rent-a-cop" to Cava and leaned towards the security guard. "Sorry, sir," he began with a nasally, lisp-voiced whimper. "My boyfriend and I, we just wanted some privacy. Our parents don't know! Please don't tell them."

The security guard stood up. He appeared to scratch the back of his neck with the flashlight handle and reached for his walkie-talkie. He then moved his hand towards his face to scratch his beard.

"Oh my… I don't know… You shouldn't be here… It's private property," the security guard said with acute exasperation and a thick accent.

"Listen," Luc continued the charade, "we'll leave… I promise. We just need a couple minutes so the battery recharges."

The guard mumbled and muttered. The only word the boys could make out was "gay," but eventually the confused old man came back to reality. "You leave, 10 minutes. No police-cops," he appealed, flustered.

Luc watched the aged guard trot with the fleetest foot that his limp would allow. He saw the beam from the flashlight dance nervously on the ground two paces ahead.

"Wow, he was rattled… Good thing it was only a rent-a…"

Cava punched him in the shoulder.

"Homophobe!" Luc joked, unfazed by the duke thanks to the layers underneath and the padding of his coat.

"Fuck was that?" Cava demanded.

"A good fucking plan!" Luc retaliated, as he picked up the joint and held it against the flame in front of him. "Sad, man… He gotta be 60 or 70, and working in the middle of a freezing ass night." He put the joint to his lips and took a puff, wincing at the cherry hitting his bottom lip.

Cava wrinkled his eyebrows and crossed his arms.

The sound of incoming vehicles, four altogether, led by a Nissan hatchback, entered the lot. The boys turned their heads to make sure that this was the convoy they were waiting for.

"Yo," Luc tapped Cava's leg, who was staring out the window, "maybe next time you let me unlock my own door, ha. Calogero."

* * *

The cars were all parked in a disorganized, broken manner. Tic-Tax leapt out of the cab of a gray truck, beat up and rusted around the wheels. Rosee was visible for a moment as the interior light went on when he opened the door. She appeared lifeless with her head pressed against the window. A half-dozen guys lifted their heads, rose from a lying position, and hopped out of the tailgate. Fink emerged from his mother's car followed by the five people who'd jumped in when he'd popped Mr. Suggs, they tripped out of the tiny 4-seater like it was a clown car. The other two vehicles, one old, two-tone brown van and an unidentifiable American car, liberated eight and six men apiece.

Cava looked nervously at Luc, whose demeanour was calm, studying the cars and cats.

Tic-Tax stretched his long legs and walked around the group, nodding and greeting the various men. Cava only faintly recognized some: they all seemed gawky, hawkish, and pale. *Fiends,* he thought, *and a pretty sizeable collection at that.* He recognized the thugs from the party, but as for the rest, he couldn't place any identities. They appeared older, but also appeared to either be mutants or in the process of mutating. Aspiring X-men.

"Now everybody shut your gobs," Tic-Tax began with his hands raised. "Yes, I have what you came for, and yes, as long as we're all in agreement, you may all have one."

Cava looked at Luc again, who maintained an unblinking, iced-forward look at Tic-Tax.

"Now, this more than officially cuts my ties with the Dead Souls. Piece of shit motherfuckers. They'll get theirs. But, for now, we get ours. Luc, my keys." Tic Tax walked over to Luc who flipped Tic Tax the keys. Tic-Tax thanked him, grinning an awful Green Goblin grin that, under the reticulated running lights, made his pointed features appear even longer and sharper.

Luc now appeared slightly confused as Tic-Tax walked past him to the back fender. He popped the trunk with a click of the keys and the boys saw the pith of Tic-Tax's upbeat, unflappable composition.

"I know you probably shouldn't... But hell, Cava, you can tell all your little friends at school... Luc, isn't this beautiful?" Tic-tax said with his arm rested on the open lid.

Cava saw his friend's features in the soft glow of the trunk light, his stone-faced countenance was melting away with a face of fear, appal, confusion, regret, shame, sorrow, and maybe a little excitement. His lips remained stiff, but his eyes were vibrating with the tumult of dynamic emotion.

With his mouth agape, Cava turned and looked at Tic-Tax. His Germanic jaw bone was outlined aggressively by its proximity to the lightbulb. His irises were near spirals as they danced around, looking at the contents of the trunk. His teeth were now, more than ever, like a thousand tiny needles that overlapped as they latched tightly to form an incubus' smile.

"Baby," he shouted, "baby, look what hard work does!" Tic-Tax said as he stomped over and opened the door. Rosee spilt out of the truck and landed hard on the pavement. He gave her a stiff toe in the ribs. With the help of a nearby crony, he rose her to her feet and brought her over.

"Hi Cava," she said with a yawn.

"Dumb little bitch," Tic-Tax jeered. "Look at all these!"

Cava felt Luc's hand press against his abdomen at the opening of his jacket; it was unbeknownst to Cava that he'd advanced forward.

"So, I been driving around with *these* in the trunk all night?" Luc asked.

"Ha-ha, no," Tic-Tax gave him a pat on the shoulder. "Well, yeah, I guess." He drummed the trunk lid with his fingers and stared at Luc. "Stand-up move, Luc. Tell you what… you can pick first."

Luc looked at him, then looked in the trunk. He looked back at Tic-Tax, and then looked back in the trunk.

Finally, Luc let out a long breath. "Ali, man… I dunno… If you have it, it means you have to use it."

"No it doesn't. It means that people know you have it, and will think twice before fucking with the crew."

Tic-Tax reached in and pulled out a nickel-plated gun with a black handle. "Here. Take it. See how it feels in your hands." Luc accepted the gun. "Banging. Looks like you were born with it."

Luc palmed the gun, looking at it. "I don't even know how to look at the bullets."

Tic-Tax seemingly ignored the comment and stared at Cava. "You like?" He snuck his hand in and pulled out an all-black piece with a hockey-taped handle. "Try it on… I bet it fits."

He proceeded to pass out handguns and rifles to his crew. They appeared equally as inexperienced as Luc had announced himself to be, but replaced their words with actions. They fumbled with the weaponry, seemed confused about the safety, and pointed them at each other. Not every cat had received a gun. They squabbled and protested, but Tic-Tax was ready to address any concerns.

Tic-Tax kept a shotgun for himself. With the barrel over his shoulder like a town sheriff, he walked in front of the group, telling them to shut their mouths. "Now, you have the guns… you have to *earn* the ammo. Having a heater will make you seem legit, trust me. Ain't no one but the big boys rocking this kind of heat in the city. I need to know you're loyal, I need to know you're down for the cause. The people I trust, well, they can have bullets. Everyone else, work for it. Everyone that doesn't have a gat, earn it. We can get more."

Tic-tax then strode slowly over to Cava, still holding his gun in his two palms, like a guinea pig. "So," Tic-Tax leaned in. "You want in?"

Rosee, who was warily on her feet, decided to speak up. "No, leave him out of this. He's a good one, a good boy. He doesn't need this bull-shit. He doesn't need you."

"Shut up, you fucking fiend," Tic-Tax said.

"I'm a fiend, because you made me a fiend, pussy!" Rosee screamed at Tic-Tax.

He swung the barrel and gun-but her in the shoulder, spinning her to the ground. "Put that mouthy slut in the truck. We're almost done here."

Cava felt Luc's hand hold his down. He didn't notice, but he'd squared his grip into a shooting position.

Tic-Tax caught sight and pointed the shotgun at Cava's head. "Mine's loaded, boy."

Cava stared over the barrel into Tic-Tax eyes. He wasn't scared. He didn't have time to be. His look was stale and unamused; as an instinc-tual reaction, he didn't think that Tic-Tax would pull the trigger.

"Nah," Cava shrugged. "You don't need to point that thing at me, Ali. You can give this pistol to one of your goons. I don't want one. I don't need one."

"Big man," Tic-Tax said without sarcasm, nodding and appearing impressed. "You surprise me. You ever want a job, I got you."

Cava bowed his head slowly, now feeling the hyperactive engagement of his valves create a pulse that felt like a drumroll behind his ears. His chest was palpitating so hard and rapidly that he was sure his voice would tremolo if he spoke.

He eyed Fink, staring back at him and Luc, scratching his temple with the nozzle of his pistol.

Luc stepped to Tic-Tax. "Ali, I don't think I should have one, either... I'm trying to pull out, you know? This is some real crimey shit... I was always happy just being a normal hoodlum and vandal."

"Sleep on it, sleep with it," Tic-Tax said. "Maybe you were always on some goon shit, and now you just need some time to tuck it and see how it feels."

Luc rotated his hand, holding the gun, looking at it from various angles.

"Nah," Luc said, holding it by the muzzle. "I'm good, homie."

Tic-Tax took it and spun around, throwing it to sullen-looking man without a firearm. "More guns for the goons!" The man caught it; a wide, chipped, and missing-toothed smile enlarged on his weathered mug.

"Hey, what doing?" The old security guard slowly limped up, flashing his light at the group.

"Keep walking, you old Hindu," Tic-Tax said with his shotgun aimed at the guard's chest. "You turn your head, or end up dead." The crew flashed their various guns at the man behind their leader.

Behind them, Cava looked at Luc again. His face had aged twenty years and had the angular severity of a Spartan's helmet. Cava still felt his heart bumping against his other lungs, oscillating his breathing. For once, he couldn't read his best friend's mind. He couldn't tell if Luc was feeling resignation, wrath, or just trying to repress any feeling of any kind.

"Damn, man..." Luc finally spoke. "That old dude should be at home with his grandkids."

UNCOMFORTABLE

SATURDAY'S DAWN CAME far too soon for Cava. He got a lift
back to the Ox from Fink—a tense and wordless journey of 20 minutes
between the two in the front and Luc in the backseat. From the rear-view
mirror, Cava clocked Luc sitting, slumped against the side panel with his
hood up and head tilted back. He normally occupied the middle of the
bench with his head precariously forward, able to see and converse with
the driver and front passenger. Now, he looked like a crumpled heap of
failed introductory paragraphs. Cava also discerned Fink's idiosyncratic
petting of his pistol grip, the handle poking slightly out of his waistline
at each red light. Fink also wore a narrow-eyed malevolence the entire
ride, accompanied with an eldritch snigger every time he stroked the
half-sunken firearm.

"You guys should've kept the guns," Fink said when they arrived.
"Even just to have. Kind of stupid, if you ask me."

Cava stared blankly at Fink.

"Nah, man…" Luc shook his head. "That's bad news, man… That's out."

"No… it's bad news if everyone has a heater, except for you," Fink maintained. "It's worse news if people who you got beef with have them, and you don't."

Luc smacked his teeth. "I ain't scared man… My brother always said that guns were for scared people, people who can't handle their B.I. Why would I have something if I wasn't never gonna use it?"

Fink scoffed and pulled up his sagging pants, ejecting the handgun on the ground in front of him. "You ain't gotta use it, just kind of have it… and I ain't scared of nothing." Fink picked the gun up and shoved it back in his waist. "You saw the type of people who you *now know* are packing heat. Ali changed the rules of the game. You picked a side. I'm just saying, be a little careful."

Luc nodded. "Maybe you're right. Maybe I could've kept it in my sock drawer or taped under a table. You know, just in case. Maybe, one day, I'll actually need it. But, maybe not."

"Yeah. Maybe, maybe not."

Fink nodded to Cava again, who reciprocated with a two-finger, army-style salute. Fink appeared to have trouble as he tried to walk towards his stoop. Fink wore exceedingly baggy attire: XXL on his lankily medium-sized build. Ill-fitting pants and oversized shirts were ubiquitous in Fury; usually hand-me-downs and five-dollar 'fill 'em' bags at the Salvation Army or the Catholic Church clothing line. Fink wore new clothes, purchased three sizes too large. Because of this proclivity for cartoonishly drooping garb, his customary stride was comparable to a bow-legged hobble; he limped as though one leg had been injured in a car accident and metallic rods were riveted to his hip to allow him to perambulate. With a gun tucked in his waist, he struggled to keep the piece and his pants from falling. The gawkily clownish lurching he carefully manufactured made Cava think that he looked like a duck who had to take a shit.

Luc and Cava walked away when Fink's hand made contact with the handle of his screen door. Cava desperately wanted to comb through the night's events, the glut of activity that was crammed into several hours,

like a White Owl blunt. He noticed the rippled forehead of Luc's thinking face.

"So…" Cava began, carefully. "Quite a night, huh?"

Luc affirmed the comment with an autonomic, closed-lip murmur.

"Cliff's really leaving, I guess," Cava tried, with a more upbeat tone.
"That's good… And, Lil Bertie has himself a fine lady, good for him…"

As they reached the split, Cava grabbed Luc's shoulder to prevent his
robotic canter from completing its course. "Hey man, I know this was all
fucked up. It'll be good to sleep on it… but, what did Bertie say to you?"

Luc's eyes awoke, even though they hadn't been closed. "Oh," Luc
began, "it was just something about Tic-Tax."

"Well? What about?"

"Well, it wouldn't have influenced my decision either way. I wouldn't
have took a bammer… Like I said, if I have something, I'll make a reason
to use it, even if it doesn't call for it."

"And?" Cava said, with less patience.

"Well…" Luc blowing heated breath onto his hands. "He said that
the Souls are aware they're missing some weapons. They also know that
Tic-Tax has gone AWOL after being a dick-sucker and bitch for however
long. All I can say is… he's lucky that he stayed away from the drags…
Obviously, it was on purpose." Luc smirked ever-so-slightly. "I wouldn't
wanna be the guy that vicked guns, bullets, and whatever else from the
motherfucking Dead Souls… and I wouldn't wanna be caught with any
of their toys."

Cava looked back at Luc with uncertainty. "So, you didn't take any
of that whole gun talk and showing off as a threat?"

Luc considered this. "Nah… I mean, I know what the point was…
I ain't no slouch, I ain't no dummy. If Tic-Tax wanna act like a real big
boy, that's fine. I'm gonna stay out of his way, front like he's the man
for a minute. Maybe make some loot off him. Before the real HNIC, or
whoever, steps up and paints the wall with his sheisty ass."

Cava shot Luc a look that said he was begging to be convinced. Luc
stared back boldly, though without arrogance, as if he knew the outcome
of the fight before the bell.

* * *

"Why? What's wrong?" Cava repeated into the mouthpiece of the home phone after hearing no response.

"I have… family issues." There was another silence on the other end. Cava heard Anjuli breathing; the exhalations of repressed dialogue.

"Is everything okay? Are you okay?" Cava asked with genuine concern. Whether the concern was for her or himself, he was unsure.

"Yeah, I'm fine. It's just that one of my family members was attacked last night, and the whole house is pretty shook up about it."

Cava was still in the process of removing his steel-toed boots at the kitchen table with a half-full, half-cold cup of coffee he'd poured as soon as he'd walked in the door. He mashed his palm against his tired face, feeling the three hours of sleep from the previous night drain instantly. "Attacked? Is he, she, okay?"

"Yeah, it was my uncle… He wasn't hurt, but he was really scared." Cava heard the voices in the background dissipate. "I want to see you tonight. Maybe I can grab the car and come over later. They're still talking about it all, and I'm getting in shit for being on the phone."

"Yeah, I want to see you, too."

"Okay, well, I'll call you back in a bit. If you aren't home, I'll try to come out to your place for 9pm. Is that cool?"

"Of course. I'm just going to nap. I had a mega late night and I'm fucking slapped."

"Okay, baby… I'll see you soon."

"See you soon, Anj."

* * *

"Hey, you awake?" Henry asked as he stood over Cava's dozing, fully clothed body. "Hey! Hey, are you up? Hey!"

Cava stirred. He dazedly pruned some incomplete words from his mouth before wiping the sleep and drool from his mug.

"I was outside, and Luc came running over. He told me to tell you to get over to his place, quick fast."

Cava groaned. "Is it dark out?"

"Almost," Henry replied impatiently.

"Ugh, I couldn't even get three hours, goddammit… Thanks."

He balled his feet like fists, a trick he'd seen in a movie, and stretched his arms towards the kitchen. Cava trucked himself towards his bulky workman boots and yawned as he pulled the door open. He was instantly greeted by Luc, standing on the stoop with a valiant smile.

"Good, Lil Cava woke you up," he said, making very little effort to contain his excitement. "I didn't wanna wake you. You're like a hibernating bear when you nap."

Luc began to ramble about nothing that could be easily interpreted by an untrained ear as they made their way to his house. He gave Cava a cigarette and lit it, speaking so quickly that his words seemed to hang in the air, even when his mouth was closed.

"What the fuck are you talking about?"

"Well, *maman* gets home this week, which is cool, because I miss her, and I'm excited for her to see the house." He grabbed the cigarette, taking a couple quick blasts and handing it back to Cava, half-eaten due to his voracious pulls. The cherry was abnormally long and pointed, like a spearhead. "And then I received something this morning, on a Saturday! I dunno where it came from, or who from, but... You'll see."

"Fuck sakes, you soaked the filter," Cava said, pinching the brown tip and rubbing the moisture from Luc's saliva in between his fingers.

"Shoes off," Luc half-joked. "This ain't no white house."

Cava peeled his boots off by the heel and gave Luc and unimpressed glare. "This better be good, you punk bastard. I was having the weirdest dreams."

The boys made their way down the stairs. Cava acknowledged that Luc, since returning home, had kept the house pristine. He spotted the vacuum plugged in at the top of the landing, and there were no dishes on the counter or in the sink. The place even had a pleasant scent—not overpoweringly sweet, but something like lavender incense.

"My mom had incense," Luc said, noticing Cava's nose poking upwards with a few disharmonious sniffs.

They made their way to the basement. Luc paused for a moment, took a breath, and opened the door. "Look at it! Isn't she beautiful? I think I'll call her Jean... You know like Jean Gray, like the Phoenix. Because she raised from the dead, or something."

"Ashes," Cava said. "And when Jean Gray was the Phoenix, she tried to kill the universe."

"Okay, the name isn't important. But look at her!"

"Well, I know what it is. I don't know what's special about it. Other than you didn't have one before."

"Well!" Luc began with one sharp clap. "The ones at school are busted and old, like a trick, man... Everybody's used them there. This came in a box. It has a warranty on a piece of paper and an instruction manual." He held the plastic wrapped booklets up, still unopened. "It looks pretty new. It says that you can do all kinds of crazy things, like program certain shapes, switch the thickness and textures, and a whole bunch of shit I don't even know! And, the best part is, it's mine... I can stay in here, listen to music, get high as the Eiffel Tower, and make stuff until I can't make no more."

Cava smiled. "That's dope man, ultra-dope! Who's it from?"

"Maybe *maman*? Maybe it was supposed to be a Christmas present, and I fucked that up. It's December in a couple days, so it's only barely early. And I don't care if I never get another pack of socks or deodorant again if I get this bad girl."

"Yeah, but this seems pretty expensive."

"Think so?"

"Everything new is."

"Maybe it's not new, but it's new to me," Luc countered. "Maybe JJ? He does send me things, or get them sent to me... Who cares?"

Luc tore the instruction manual open and sat on a chair he'd imported from the kitchen. The basement was still barren. Cava stood over his friend's shoulder, watching him flip between the French and English pages, nodding to himself when he was able to figure out the instruction, and lightly smoothing over the buttons with a delicate touch.

"Well, I'm gonna leave you with Jean," Cava said as he patted Luc's shoulder. "I gotta meet up with Anj and I wanna rest and shower a bit. Sounds like she was having a tough day."

"Yeah, they'll do that," Luc said, too absorbed in the manual to give a thoughtful response.

"Alright, brother. I'll holler at you tomorrow."

Luc waggled his fingers without turning.

"Sicker than your average..." he began to sing to himself.

* * *

"No, Quinn. I'm not really in the mood right now. Can we maybe just read or watch TV or something? You can turn up the music and we can just... I dunno." Anjuli slid her body out from under Cava and squirmed into a seated position against the wall.

"Sure, anything you want... Do you want to talk? Do you want to tell me what happened to your... uncle, right?"

"Yeah, it's kind of bothering me... It's pretty scary. I guess it's true that either you or someone you know has been attacked in Fury." Anjuli grimaced.

"Well, I mean... these things happen in every city."

"Perhaps." Anjuli's lips tightened. "But, my uncle never had a gun, let alone 10 or so guns, pulled on him back home, or even back in India."

"T-ten guns, you say?"

"Yeah, he was doing his rounds at the docks, and he said that he stumbled upon a gang or something, and they all had guns, and had them all pointed right at him... My uncle's old. He was a veterinarian back in Chandigarh and had to take a ridiculous security job here. Why? I don't know. I guess he wants to contribute or not be bored. But... I don't think that he'll be going back now."

"Jesus..." Cava said, unblinkingly. "Is he okay? I mean, did he get away? What did he say? What did he do?"

"They didn't lay a finger on him. He was patrolling and found two, well, men, having sex in a car. He told them that it was private property and that they should leave, or else he would call the cops. He probably just wanted to give them the impression he would. Then, when he came back, there were a whole bunch of vehicles at the same spot. He got closer to see what was going on, and they all drew their weapons at his head! He turned around and walked away. He said he didn't even know if he called the cops. He just left, and to his recollection, ended up at the house."

"That's crazy. Did he get a good look at anyone? Any license plates?"

"No, he's almost deaf and blind as it is. He can't even get a license with a bribe to an Indian DMV worker. That's how bad his vision is. He was still in shock when I was talking to you on the phone today. He was asleep when I left. My auntie is terrified. My mother was running around the house waving her hands around, and my father was saying that all the money in the world isn't worth putting his family at risk. After we hung up, another uncle had to talk him down. Just crazy!"

Cava rubbed Anjuli's knee and tried to hijack her gaze as she peered over his shoulder. "Are you okay? Are you scared as well? How do you feel?"

'I'm… okay, I guess," she said as she put her hand on his. "I mean, muggings and thefts happen all the time around here… But, when it happens to someone you know and care about, it's really kind of traumatic. It's this kind of thing that makes me want to find a university far away enough from all the dangers here."

Cava frowned. "I mean, it's not all bad. Even in this area, there are good people. Hardworking people who own their own businesses and want to do good by others. Not everyone is a shark or a snake, you know."

"No, I know… I didn't mean to offend you. I just feel that even the normal people here have seen some pretty graphic things or had some unnecessary encounters that they wouldn't have if…"

"If what? They didn't live here? They had more money to live behind a gate in a nice neighbourhood?"

"Think of how much further along you could be if you'd never had these influences around you, Quinn. You're finishing up your first semester of your senior year and are only now realizing that you have a brain that works well."

"I begeth thy pardon, my lady?" He sat up rigidly. "You know, I know you're a little freaked out, but stuff like that always happens. I been jacked before, lost a sick Hammers lid, and Fink got his Saint Christopher tooken last summer behind the Trees. This isn't just a bubble of badness. Bad things happen everywhere. You can't hide from bad luck."

Anjuli sighed. "*Tooken* isn't a word."

"If you're that scared, I can protect you. You can even buy a razor. Most girls carry some kind of blade in their purses. I think even Sal has a boxcutter that she keeps stashed in her backpack."

"I don't need or *want* protection. I shouldn't even have to think about it. Can't you see? That's not normal. People shouldn't have to be scared to walk around."

"It's not fear… It's being prepared, maybe. I don't carry anything sharp, or blunt, or whatever. But those that do, maybe they have a reason. Or maybe they know that everything is random. That's why they're called *random attacks.*"

"*Here* they are. Not everywhere else." Anjuli moved herself further from Cava. "I don't want to talk about this. It won't go anywhere. Thank you for offering to protect me, but I'd rather be somewhere where… it just wasn't an issue."

Cava tried to grab at meaningful thoughts, like catching tears in the rain.

"I care about you, a lot… like, a lot, a lot," Anjuli said, putting her hand on the back of his shoulder, sidling over and wrapping her arms and legs around him from the back. "I just think to myself, what if you'd ended up like one of the people who was there? What if you had all those guns pointed at you? Or if you were one of the people who was holding one? I don't even know what's worse."

Cava's face twisted dolefully away from Anjuli. "Thanks, baby… I know you care about me. And I care about you, too."

"My god. I honestly don't know which side of the gun is worse."

Cava nodded, unaware of how his face was currently arranged, but relieved that Anjuli couldn't read his expression.

"How were the drags, babe?" she asked, kissing him on the back of his ear.

"Good."

ASSEMBLY FOR THE DEAD

"I DON'T KNOW, man… I apologize and shit, but she still seems distant. I feel like we're drifting apart. I mean, I know we have finals, and she needs to concentrate on them, but I can't really focus on much when I'm thinking that she's mad at me. Does that make sense?" Cava was lying on Sally's bed, tossing a volleyball and pondering his own question.

Sally, with her highlighter streaking across a textbook, squeaking as the neon yellow passed over the glossy pages, contrived a few audible mumbles whenever he paused.

"Hey! Are you listening? Is the perfect student really defacing a school textbook?" he teased.

"I bought this one from the school," she said indignantly. "Sorry, I missed most of that."

Cava repeated himself.

"What does Luc say?"

"He's too busy with his new toy. He got mad when he sewed his sleeve to a tablecloth and started tripping. Besides, with his mom home and him trying to make all the money he can before he ducks out of the trap, he's not fit to give any advice. He just said that she should respect where I come from, kind of called her down for coming from a family with money, and said that I should be happy with who I am." Cava held the ball at his chest, then rolled onto his side to face Sally.

Sally paused thoughtfully. "Well, he's not totally offside. You are who you are. But I can see where Anj's coming from. She cares about you and doesn't want to see you embroiled in any kind of seedy or danger-ous activity."

"Sal, you know I'm not the type to go looking for trouble. If I'm in some kind of hot water, I didn't set out to drop myself in the pot."

"I know that, but you have a tendency to associate with people that seem to… habitually create high-risk situations. She obviously sees that and doesn't want someone she feels so much affection for to be caught in the crossfire. I know the feeling. I've worried about you for my whole life."

"Why did you never say nothing then?"

"Because. Lots of reasons, I guess," she rotated her chair and slid closer to Cava. "You guys always called me a stiff, or a nerd, or a square…"

"We never called you a square. That's from the 60s or some shit."

"Whatever! Anyways, I was still happy to be part of the crew. To feel like I belonged. Later, when you started following Luc around like a shadow, I always wanted to tell you that some of the hijinks you guys were up to would lead to trouble, but I didn't want to be 'that guy.' Do you know why I went to Europe?"

"Cause it's dope, and you were smart enough to get a scholarship?"

"Well, thanks, but, right before I applied, I was hanging out with you and the rest of the guys at that weird little park by Cliff's old place, you know? The one with the little path and the barrel you guys always used to start fires in?"

"Of course. Owens Park."

"Sure. Well, there were a bunch of people there, and a fight broke out between those two girls. Remember? They were fighting over a guy, or something?"

"Uh, kind of… there were so many…"

"One girl took a cheese grater to the other girl's forearm and tried rubbing out the tattoo she'd gotten of the guy's name?"

"I think so. I don't think she *totally* got it."

"She got some. She got a good bit of flesh before they were separated."

"Jesus H."

"Yeah, Jesus H. What's crazier, Quinn, is that a moment like that, where two girls are fighting, clawing, ripping each other's hair out at the roots, and trying to slice each other's arms off, is something you have to strain to think about."

Sally wasn't entirely worked up, at least not to her melting point. She was clinical and decisive in her delivery.

"I like you guys. I really care about you guys. I love you guys. I just didn't want to be one of you guys."

"That makes sense. But we all knew you weren't. You were different... better and smarter."

"Your friends are your friends. If you hang around with a certain kind of people... you can hide yourself away, you can ignore the warning signs, heck, you can even pretend like you're outside of the culture... But eventually, it will catch up with you and drag you in. Law of association."

Sally paused to collect her thoughts.

"Quinn, I always respected you and thought of you differently. Everyone has their charm, but you were different. I never wanted to intrude and risk losing you as a friend... as anything. So, I never expressed my worries or fears to you. But, I can tell you, I know exactly how Anjuli feels."

Sally continued before Cava could interrupt.

"*You* are also *better* and *smarter*. She hasn't known you since you were a little hellion... She probably knows you as a quiet, sweet, intelligent, and handsome guy. She comes from a different place, where this hood stuff you guys do for fun isn't normal; there, only the criminals and delinquents act that way. Luc will always be Luc; he needs to keep his hands busy. But you, you need to be... you need to keep your brain busy. Look at you, this year. You're getting awesome grades and seem to be enjoying school. I haven't worried about you much this year, for the first time in ages. Why do you think I always used to write to you, and call?

To make sure that you hadn't been led down a road that got you killed or thrown in juvie... If we never saw each other again, and you left with her, and started a nice and boring life somewhere else, it would make me so sad, but so happy."

Sally began to tear up. Cava twirled the ball nervously.

"I had no idea, Sal. I appreciate it, and I'm sorry for ever making you worry about me, worry about whether something bad would happen or not." He looked at her and noticed her sleeve lightly pressing at the folds under her eyes. "I'm sorry for... well, everything. I'm sorry for distracting you from your cramming session."

Cava placed the ball on the ground. He wiped her eye with his calloused thumb and wrapped his arm around her.

Sniffing back the sounds of her sobs, Sally closed her long arms around Cava's head. "Please, no... Don't ever be sorry to come to me about anything, at any time. I, too, like distraction... that's what studying has always been. Guess we're not all so different."

Cava looked at the wet spot on his shirt. "No mucus, don't worry," Sally laughed.

Sally and Cava maneuvered onto the bed, his arms firmly wrapped around her as she held his hands tightly.

"Quinn," Sally sniffed. "You'll always be the most important thing to me. Don't forget that. More important than studying. More important than tests and term papers."

* * *

A general assembly was gathered on the following Wednesday to mourn the loss of a student. The entire student body and faculty was summoned to the bleachers and folding chairs in the gymnasium to announce that Amanda Crystal Suggs had passed away.

As was usually the case with events such as this, the cafeteria and school yard had already determined the causes of her death, even without being able to put a face to the name.

The principal spoke in brief, unequivocal statements at the podium, flanked by grief counsellors and the parents, Gary and Cindi. The parents declined to speak. A projector displayed the girl's most recent yearbook picture—ugly beyond repair—which no doubt caused a jolt of remorse within the more empathetic students who'd, in one of many ways, transgressed against her.

The father was staring at the top row of bleachers angrily. The mother had dressed in something other than a housecoat for the first time in recent memory. She appeared to be in a daze, with her eyes widening and narrowing and her head whirling around like an animal that'd been torn from the wild and placed in a zoo.

"Amanda was a lovely young girl," one female teacher said.

"Miss Suggs was always full of questions and answers," another male teacher said.

Cava was seated beside Sally. He saw that she was on the verge of tears, so he grabbed her hand.

"I could have done something," she whispered. "I could have… I have no idea… Been there, talked to her. Just been a friend."

Cava shook his head. "No, stuff like this just happens. You, her parents, teachers… no one can really predict this kind of stuff."

Fink was seated in the top row, casually exchanging a quarter ounce of marijuana for $60 with another student. He looked down to count it, pocketed the loot, and returned his gaze to the illuminated portrait. He visibly and audibly shuddered.

Half of the school band played a small rendition of Pachelbel's Canon as the picture on the drop-down projection screen faded into the year of her birth and death. The mother, still stupefied, suddenly began to weep without restraint. "My baby, my baby." She repeated those words until the song was over. The father, whose ruddy face had become a Malbec red, squeezed his eyes and lips together to fight the tears. It emphasized his Yeltsin-esque, varicose-webbed nose, giving it an elephant seal-like prominence.

The students guessed that she'd taken her own life, which was correct. There would be no reports, no attempts to make such information public, but given the melancholic and surly habitude of the girl, it was nowhere near a stretch of the imagination.

Why Amanda Suggs—Slug—would commit suicide opened the door for conjecture. She'd been a loner, though not by choice; an unpopular and disenfranchised teenager. She'd been unattractive in appearance and in temperament. She'd been poor, and her parents were alcoholics and pill poppers.

The verdict had arrived before the evidence had been thoroughly combed and tested. Once the initial disbelief and shock of her suicide subsided, the black humorists emerged. Already, Fink and the lad to whom he'd sold the bag begun to converse about her unibrow, hairy arms, gunt, and greasy mane. Some students looked at them with caustic, chiding expressions, though others had their feelings of remorse replaced with reluctant snickering by the pinpoint strikes of ruthless adolescence.

Gary couldn't hear the vitriol. At that moment, he could hear neither the music, the caterwauling of his wife, nor the blend of weeping and flu-born sniffles that the crowd and staff were snorting back. Gary wore a fixed look that blazed from his seething, little black eyes.

The assembly concluded with the principal making an open plea for donations to the Suggs family. "This is a tragedy, for the school and, of course, the Suggs family. Being that it's this time of year, the approaching of Christmas..." the principal coughed and corrected himself, "holiday season, we can all give a little something back to try and help Amanda's parents cope with the sadness of losing their only child."

* * *

After the assembly concluded, Sally approached the parents and the principal as they exchanged gratitude and condolences.

"What'd you tell them?" Cava asked when she returned.

"Oh, just that I was sorry and that Amanda was a sweet, nice girl. And, that I'd be able to collect donations of any kind: money, food, blessings."

"Isn't that a little... patronizing?" Cava asked with sincerity, unhappy with his word choice though unable to find a better phrasing.

"Well... in some cases, maybe... But, they're really down on their luck. I'm sure anything would help."

"You figure they'd piss the money? That why?"

Sally didn't answer, but her lips creased a slight frown that projected a subtle endorsement. As the two were exiting the gymnasium, Sally complained that she'd heard some laughter during the assembly.

"It's just kind of incredible, you know... that people would speak, even crack jokes, during something so serious. Like... what's funny about suicide?"

"I dunno, man. Maybe some of the kids need to have some kind of way to make themselves laugh so they don't get sad and cry in front of their peers. Like, how you laugh when you catch a dead arm."

"Maybe... Perhaps it's because they don't have the maturity to deal with something so serious and close to home. Maybe some people are just jerks."

The secretary's voice croaked through the speaker abruptly. "Students will report to their homerooms for schedule changes, please. Good day."

"I guess it must have to do with finals," Sally said, narrowing her eyes. "Hey! Luc?"

He slapped Cava.

"Guys! I was hoping I'd bump into you," Luc said, hugging Sally and dapping Cava. "That was really emotional... Really sad, man. I mean, I didn't know her all that good, but I always felt this weird feeling in the lower part of my stomach when I saw her. It was like... I dunno, like diarrhea, but made me sad."

"That's pity, Luc," Sally said with a soft smirk.

"Yeah, I pitied her," Luc repeated, pronouncing the word as though it was a new addition to his lexicon.

"What are you doing up in here?" Cava asked.

"Making sure that I'm registered for classes. Step one, right? I also heard about Slug, er, Amanda, and I wanted to, you know, pay my respects. Teared up a little. That was nice. Except for Rat Fink whispering through the whole damn thing. He'd probably do that through his own momma's funeral."

"Kalou, Luc?" The same bullfrog intonation that had blasted out of the speakers earlier summoned Luc. "Please step in. The vice principal will see you now."

"Psh, been gone a minute and they forgot who I am... Don't even get to see the top dog," Luc scoffed. "I'll meet you guys out front after your little class thing. We'll chill. Wish me luck!"

They wished him the best. Sally refrained from saying that she had to study, and Cava assented.

"I'll be one minute," Luc said to the impatient secretary. "Sally, I wanted to give you this—you know, for that dead girl's parents…. Okay! I'm coming, one minute!" He handed Sally a little envelope and entered the office.

As Cava and Sally walked towards their homeroom, she opened the envelope. "Holy moly! There's like a thousand dollars in here!" Her face was momentarily radiant. The radiance faded as she and Cava looked at each other. "Quinn…"

"Yeah, more than likely… But you can say that it was from a bunch of people. It definitely was. Still nice of him."

* * *

Just outside the teacher's lounge, two greenhorn teachers, new to the school and still without the tenure required to secure a homeroom, conversed near a potted fern.

"You know what I heard?" the teacher with a coffee cup in hand whispered to the other with a plastic water bottle. "I heard that she took her own life on the weekend."

The other teacher responded in less-than-a-whisper. "Oh my god, I heard that, too! The parents hadn't checked on her for a couple days. Didn't even notice that she wasn't at school. It's the school's policy to call students who miss two or more days of full classes without a note."

"Can you imagine?"

"No, I really can't. How can you be so, so… so…? I don't even know? Careless? Unconcerned with your own child's welfare?"

"Makes me sick to even think about. My own little Gregory has a cough, I have the thermometer in his mouth, lickity split."

"Well, they do live *there*, and you know the stories about what happens in that trailer park."

"You need a license to operate a vehicle, but not to have kids."

"Unbelieva…" The principal abruptly exited her office with the parents of the deceased.

"Mr. and Mrs. Suggs, we're so sorry for your loss. Amanda was a gentle and friendly girl."

"I…we… everybody at the school wants to give our condolences. This must be tough."

Gary walked away silently, dragging Cindi away from the two teachers.

"Think he heard us?"

* * *

"Yo, that shit smelled like the bomb, Marek," the student beside Fink in homeroom told him.

"Yeah, my hook up's pretty tight with whatever you need," Fink said smugly. "We got weed, pills, powder… Whatever you need… we got it. I mean, *anything*. Not just drugs. Feel free to call me Crusher."

"Okay…" the student replied warily.

"See how I'm fly? New jacket, new lid, new rope, new kicks… Everything brand new. Business is good."

"Seems risky. I mean, I'd do it, but my mom would kill me, or I'd be afraid to get jumped and lose my stash."

"That's why you need to pack, son." Fink pulled up his jacket to reveal the handle of his pistol, still without a bullet in the chamber.

"Jesus Christ! Are you nuts? You know what happens if you get caught? Why do you even have that?"

"Those are the new rules of the game. You rule or get ruled. Me and my crew, we're the kings. Just last weekend, we stomped Slug's dad down at the drags because he owed my connect some money. Then, we pulled up on some old Hindu security guard at the docks. Fifty guns pointed at him like 'better move old man, or *blaow*.'"

"No way. That didn't happen."

"Did so," Fink said bitterly. "You can ask Cava or Luc or anybody that was there… Those guys were shitting their pants. Pussies."

* * *

After the cursory homeroom class, not even half an hour of seated attention, school was dismissed again.

"So, finals are staying the same. I was kind of hoping to space mine out, but whatever, just more studying in the next bit," Sally said to Cava and Luc, hoping to impress her need to shut herself away for the day upon them. "I have five in three days, so… I'll probably be lying very low."

"There's a shocker," Luc said.

"Five?!" Cava blurted. "But, we only have four classes!"

"One is an advanced course done in partnership with an open learning policy for the universities. It means I can fast track some of the 100 classes in my first year."

"My god, woman," Luc laughed. "You're at super-nerd status!"

"Ha, shut up! Luc, thank you so much for the… donation. You shouldn't have."

Luc looked at Cava with a side glance. "Ah, well… Maybe I could've done more… Not just stood by, you know?"

"You donated?" Fink approached the crew. "Waste of fucking money, man. However much you gave, the girl still ain't having a casket. It's turning into pills and booze faster than you can say—"

POW!

Just like the visual-sound effects in Batman, the slapstick *crack* of a hard, wide fist connecting with Fink's dome filled the area. Fink was lifted out of his shoes, a size and a half too big, and dropped like a shuttlecock a foot from his unlaced sneakers.

Nobody jumped in to restrain the stout, barrel-chested father. Cava and Luc stood for a moment, admiring the anger puffing out of the snot-rimmed nostrils of red-faced Gary, before bending over to inspect their friend.

"Well, he's breathing," Cava said. "So, it's only assault."

"You got knocked the fuck out, man!" Luc added. "Get it? Friday! The Ice Cube movie."

Cava shook Fink's shoulder. He stirred and reached for his eyes; his tears were beginning to accumulate as he shook himself from the daze.

A chorus of students began to whoop and applaud the attack. Other students stood on their toes to see what they'd missed. The school's security guards meandered over without great concern once they saw who was laid out, eventually securing Gary, still vibrating with rage, and escorting him back into the school.

"Look at his feet," Luc began, grabbing one of Fink's toes. "They're so small… it's like the Wizard of Oz."

A few minutes later, Cava and Luc helped Fink to his feet. Fink shook his head and used his sleeves to mop the water under his eyes. "Must've hit me square in the nose, probably broken." He shuffled his heater beneath his shirt.

"Nah, man," Cava retorted. "Right here, side of the head. It's already swelling."

"He's gonna pay for this."

"I think he already did," Cava remarked. "Pretty sure that was an I.O.U."

Fink groused as he tried to gain his equilibrium. He grumbled about heading home, getting some ammo, and several unattractive things about the father and his departed daughter. "Fucking stupid. Everybody hates me. Good… Now, everybody loves the dead girl. Brilliant."

ANJ AND QUINN II

CAVA WAS EXPECTING Anjuli at his place that evening to study. He knew she would be extremely keen on the idea of only studying, with the first semester finals looming very near, and took care of his own needs before she arrived to make sure he'd be able to concentrate, if only for a bit.

He knew that things had been a little bit rocky over the last couple weeks. He knew that it was due to the fact that he was with the crew of thugs that had endangered the life of one of her uncles. He'd wanted to tell her something about it. But what?

He couldn't bring himself to face the fact that he'd lied. He felt like a coward twice over. He thought about telling her just enough to make himself look brave, as though he'd tried to be the voice of reason.

He didn't want to lie. He didn't know if he could. Anything beyond his rapidly beating heart, or sense of trepidation and impotence, would certainly be a vainglorious building up of the character that he lacked. It was too late to play the lion, the lemming, or the chicken.

He didn't hate himself, but the happiness that he felt when he was with her was beginning to unravel. As his guilt grew, his ability to take the most out of each moment that they spent together dwindled. His affection felt tarnished and insecure.

He was angry that he'd allowed his fear to dominate him. He questioned his intelligence and his worth. He carried a completely selfish anxiety, one that would cause him such emotional pain should he tell the truth. This self-centered care, void of altruism and respect for his lady, made him all the more sour.

"You selfish asshole," he said to himself. "You aren't telling her anything because you don't want her to leave you. You're a fucking coward! You're afraid that she'll end things with you, and you'll be alone. You won't have her. And so, what? Do you deserve her? Do your lies deserve her? You fake!"

It hadn't even been a week, but Cava was already being digested by the acids of his conscience.

A soft tapping at the window shook him from the delirium of his own self-reprimanding. He pulled the blinds up and saw Anjuli. *Strange*, he thought, figuring that she would at least say hello to his mother, which she'd accustomed herself to doing since their meeting.

He pulled the window open and offered his hand. She seemed apprehensive, but accepted, and sat on the window sill as he slid her shoes off.

He carried her tiny runners and placed them gently on the floor. "Hey, Anj, I know you probably want to get cracking on the studying, so I wanted to tell you that I'm going to be perfectly professional tonight. Has to be what's best for me, too, am I right?"

He turned and saw that she had streaks of mascara racing each other down her cheeks. She was staring away from him with her hands folded. She was clutching her upper arm, as if she were cold.

"What's wrong? Do you want me to turn the heat up?"

Anjuli sniffled, bit her lip, and shook her head.

Cava dropped to his knee and took her hand. "Babe, what's wrong? Are you okay?"

"No."

He felt a knife twist in his heart as he saw her eyes glisten. Cava stood up and crossed his arms.

"What's it about?"

"You know exactly what it's about, Quinn," Anjuli pushed out, almost hyperventilating when she said his name. A split second of wrath shot across her brow like cannon fire. "Your rat friend was bragging about it in homeroom!"

"Look, sure. I mean... yeah, I was there. But I didn't know any of that would happen. I didn't have any control over anyone. Luc and I were out of our element."

"Luc and I," Anjuli said spitefully. "Luc and I..."

"What? I just went with him to see some..."

"I don't give a fuck! You promised me that you would cut all that hood-rat, stupid shit out. You swore. You lied to me, Quinn. You *lied* to me. The more I know you, the less I feel like I actually *know* you."

Cava felt as though he was hovering in dead space, his head unable to determine what any of the right words would be.

"I wanted to tell you, honestly."

"*Honestly,*" she said in a sardonic tone. "Do you *Furies* even know what honesty is?"

Cava dropped his neck with resignation. She could verbally or physically harm him; curse his friends, his family, anything at this point. He wouldn't try to defend himself or block her blows.

"I do," he whispered. "But, if you know any way that I could have told you about that, any way at all, I'm open."

"A better idea is not to put yourself in situations where you're pointing guns at elderly men. *A better idea* is to remove the phrase 'Luc and I' from your vocabulary."

"He's actually on the up and up."

"I don't give a fucking shit! If that, and I don't know what else happened, but if that's the 'up and up,' then... I don't even know, Quinn."

Cava moved to sit beside Anjuli. He placed an arm around her and felt a shudder.

"Your touch is grossing me out. Get off me."

"I'm sorry. I'm sorry for lying, or for withholding the truth. I'm sorry that I did what I said I wouldn't. I'm sorry that I hurt you and that I hurt you so bad, without even knowing it. I'm sorry because... I love you."

His head lowered as her sobs evolved into wails. He turned and saw that her hands were covering her face, and black tears were leaking through her fingers.

"Here," he said, passing her a white t-shirt.

She took the shirt and buried her face in it, crying the way that infants do until their throats go hoarse and their heads ache.

"It's okay," Cava said.

"No. No, it's not."

"I'm sorry," he said, increasingly desperate.

"I am, too. I'm sorry that I never even got the chance to love you back. I almost did. I really thought I might. I was so into you. I've never felt this way about another person in my life. It felt like we were put here to find each other. Now, I feel stupid. Now, I feel like any other high school kid that has these fairy tale feelings, too quickly, for the wrong person. I don't think I ever want to feel that way again."

Her voice steadied.

"No, Quinn, *I'm* sorry. I'm sorry that you never let me love you. That you care about your friends and your city, or whatever, more than you care about me. You're selfish, Quinn Cavanaugh, and I'm sorry that I can't see your parents, who are excellent people. I'm sorry, Quinn. I'm sorry for you."

Cava was gutted. She hadn't even looked at him as she spoke.

"My parents were trying to get me to move back. They kept asking me if I had a boyfriend, and if I was in a relationship. I lied to them, said that I wasn't and that I didn't want to go home for the last semester. Now, I don't have to lie, to them or myself. I'm leaving Fury, Quinn. I'm leaving and I don't want to come back. You were the one good thing that I had here, and now I can't even look at you."

She got up and slid her shoes back on. "Please, don't try and contact me. I have the luxury of putting this whole experience behind me, and that's exactly what I plan to do."

She walked across the blanket, shoes on, and cranked the window open, shaking all the panes of glass.

"Quinn," she said as she pushed herself out of the window. "I don't want to regret us, and I will always have a spot in my heart for you. But I can't forgive you."

She cried a little longer at the window ledge. After a few deep breaths, she spoke again without wavering. "You need to put your priorities in order if you ever want to be happy and get out of here."

* * *

Cava had no concept of the time that had passed as he sat there, emptied from the stomach to the soul. He repeated the words that he'd heard clearly back to himself, cycling them over in his head. He wanted to feel like the victim, a hero that'd had his love snatched away, like Spider-Man. He tried to rally all of his defense mechanisms to stop the bleeding from the words that had ripped his spirit apart.

He couldn't.

He wasn't able to feel like some kind of valiant hero. Even now, he was nowhere near certain of how his priorities had made enemies of each other.

He put his head in his hands and felt a lump in his throat swell. His cheeks tightened and felt hot. His sinuses stung. His mouth was dry. He sobbed. He tried to fight the sobbing, but felt his whole upper body tense. He grabbed the t-shirt, trying to contain the wellspring of emotion, and smelled her.

Superheroes didn't cry. Neither did supervillains. Cava realized that he was neither super, nor a hero, nor a villain. He was weak, and now, he was alone.

* * *

The students' exam period had started, and lacking any classes with his former love, he was able to pass through the periods without seeing her. He knew that she would've already taken precautions to not be where she knew he would be. She was smart like that. Damn, he already missed her.

On Monday, Cava did have an exam, not first thing, but around the time that second period normally started. He was prepared enough, without really having studied, and he needed a good breakfast to make up for the calories burnt quivering in self-loathing the night before.

"Quinn," Nora said. "Are you ready for exam number 1?"

"Sure."

He responded to her other, related questions with one-word answers. He barely touched his food and felt his organs clench, trying to purge the tears. He was hungry, but couldn't so much as look at his breakfast.

"Quinn," Nora said with a raised eyebrow that Cava didn't see. "What's wrong with you?"

"Nothing."

Nora stopped, about to become angry, but then asked another question. "How's Anj?"

Cava stammered and then went silent.

"When did it happen?"

"Last night."

"I thought I saw her car. Thought it was strange that she didn't say hi, or nothing. Why?"

Cava grumbled and made little attempt to answer. He felt the clouds roll in on his eyes and cleared his throat.

"It's okay, son. You don't have to answer if you're not ready."

He didn't. He didn't respond to her, or to anybody else, for the following week. He tried to study when he wasn't taking exams, but found it impossible to concentrate. He was upset and angered by his own sadness. He wanted a second chance. He wanted to call her, or climb her window and give her one last kiss. He couldn't just be thankful that he'd finally experienced the joy of love. He'd tried.

He fought to be positive. To not lash out at his mother, who was busily trying to cheer him up. He pretended that he was absent when Luc came calling. He didn't try to reach out to Sally. He simply holed himself up in his room. He cracked a book and ignored it, pulling the sheets over his shrimp-curled body, both sobbing to himself and resenting his own sobbing.

He completed his exams on Friday morning. Nothing spectacular. His diligence throughout the semester had given him better footing than he'd ever had before. He cared, but his results were overshadowed by his sorrowful character. He saw daylight and living as a chore, only wanting to crawl back into his bed and hibernate until his winter was complete.

* * *

"Get up, boy. We got work to do," Joe's voice came from the doorway. It was Saturday.

"Can't," he groaned. "I'm sick."

"What? Were you out partying? End of the semester is no reason to miss work," Joe growled. "Come on, up, up… We'll get coffee on the way. Come on!"

Cava dragged himself out of bed. He threw on a padded flannel and a cap and marched out to the idling truck. The air was stiff, frigid, and the truck was defrosting the windows noisily as it spat out exhaust.

The father and son said nothing as they drove to the shop. Joe stopped for bagels and coffee. Cava left his bagel untouched and lightly sipped the burning, sour mash from the store.

"Swear to Christ, they just use the same coffee and change the water," Joe said, gruffly. "You good?"

Cava nodded, not saying anything.

The rest of the drive was silent, except for talk radio. Joe had an affinity for talk radio that explained how cold the temperature was every seven minutes. It gave sports scores every ten, and news whenever those two were in intermission. Every time the Hammers' season was lamented and the negative weather was addressed, Joe took advantage of the moment to harangue the team and cavil at the weather. Normally, Cava would roll his eyes and tell his dad that he was a sucker for punishment, but today, he remained as silent as a morgue.

Several wordless hours passed as the Cavanaugh men retreaded tires, changed rims, polished tools, and swept. Lunch came, and Cava passed up his father's offer of half a sandwich. He also declined the bagel from earlier, and kept sweeping. He sniffed away in silence until his father could no longer stand it.

"You're moping, huh?"

Cava said nothing.

"So, you and your little girlie broke it off, huh?"

Cava kept sniffling and sweeping.

"Damn it, boy, talk to me! What'd you do? You kiss another girl? You mess around on that little angel?"

Cava replied with silence.

"Hmm, so I raised a cheater? Famine to feast, eh, Quinny? The girls love a man that's spoken for, you gotta learn…"

"I didn't fool around, Dad."

"Oh, he speaks!" Joe said mockingly. "I'll have to tell your mother."

Cava turned away.

"Hey, boy-o, I'm just giving you a hard time," Joe said sincerely. "You wanna tell me what happened?"

Cava explained, carefully, that Anjuli was unhappy with his choice of friends, activities, and environment.

"She go making a mountain out of a molehill, it sounds like. Maybe she was just in a bad way, you know, exams and whatnot, and—"

"No. There's more." He proceeded to recount the night of the drag races with as much face-saving as he could. As he relayed the tale, he felt like crying. Not the same sorry-for-himself tears that'd been wetting his lashes for the past week; he was finally realizing that his actions, the events, everything, were his own doing.

"Well…" Joe said, startled, pulling a cigarette of his own and sporting a face of restrained anger. "That's quite the story. So, I didn't raise a cheater… I raised a goddamn criminal."

Cava contested, meagrely.

"Look, boy. You played with fire. It didn't just burn you, but burned the girl you cared about. That kind of fire, you know, burned up your friend's basement and got his mother sick. I know you're sad, but you aren't the victim. She is. You got what you deserved. You're lucky it was just that."

"But I didn't set out for that… I didn't want to be there, I didn't—"

"You gotta stop making excuses, son. I was a man by your age. You're acting like a spoiled little bastard. Your mother and I didn't bring up a sad sack who blames everyone else for his problems. You make your own decisions, and until you make the right ones, you'll always end up like this. You think it's easy for us? Knowing that when you leave the house, you get into nonsense like this? With these idiots? These people who are going to end up in prison, or dead?"

"I just—"

"Cut the bullshit, Quinn Padraig!" Joe thundered as he grabbed his son's hand, nearly crushing it like a vice. "Smarten the fuck up. Lord forgive me, but you're better than this. You know that. You think this is real pain? Huh? This isn't real pain; this is one girl, when you're 17 years old. A 17-year-old who thinks that he knows everything, and the world owes him something. Real pain is when *we* die. Family death. You remember… Real pain is when you have to leave your family, your country, and everything you've ever known. Real pain is people banging on your door and taking away the people you love because they think that they might be hiding information. Don't insult me, my family, and the rest of the people who feel real pain, every day, because you were a stupid moron and your little tart knew better than you did."

Cava was silent. He knew his father well, to the point that no matter what he said, he would be blasted, rightfully, for immaturity.

"You're right," Cava finally said during a long breath out. "I'm just an idiot, and—"

"Look, you're not an idiot, Quinn. That's your biggest problem. That you're not stupid. You do some really dumb things, really dumb, but you aren't an imbecile. Prove her wrong. Grab your broom."

Joe slapped his son's knee and pulled himself up. "You can ruin a lot of relationships that way."

For the rest of the day, Cava tricked himself into being angry about his father's stern words. He was relieved to feel something else. Deep down, he knew that he wasn't angry with Joe. Why would he be? He enjoyed the thrashing. It was almost like penance.

As they left, Cava felt a burning hole in his gut. It was different from the intestinal surges that had hampered his appetite. He was hungry; this was his stomach dissolving itself and his ribs crossing their phalanges.

He picked up the old, rock-hard bagel and shook his head like a dog to eat it. He took giant chomps and mashed his teeth against the dried, starchy dough. He ate the bagel like it was the cause of all his problems.

Joe smiled. "You know, before I left the old country, I had a woman. I loved her. Before your mother. I really did. She had fire red hair, sky blue eyes, and looked like a mermaid. I cared for her and she cared for me. I've never told anyone here, that."

"So, what's your point?" Cava asked between two enormous mouthfuls.

"I guess that… at the time, I had to leave. I had to leave her. I was down. Very down. I didn't think that I would feel that way about anyone ever again. Then, I met your mother."

"Okay…"

"Well, the point is, until you'd mentioned this thing with Anj, I hadn't thought about her since I started dating Nora, some twenty-odd years ago. I guess what I'm trying to say is… you're young. You have a whole life of ladies ahead of you. Don't hang your hat on the first hook you see, and don't worry if you never put it on again, son."

PUPS

"AWW MAN, REALLY?" Luc asked with excited disbelief. "Just like that? Like, poof? *She gone*?" He shook his head and took the joint back. "Man, that's trifling. Like, no more one-more-chances with these bitches anymore?"

Cava puffed the smoke out and snorted. "I was kind of already on the last chance, man. Don't call her a bitch."

"My bad, my bad... Man, is there anything I can do?"

"Nah." Cava shrugged. "I can only help myself."

"You don't want me to get one of these mutants to suck your dick? They owe me favours."

"Ew, nah!" Cava laughed. "I don't wanna catch AIDS or nothing."

"You can't get sick from oral, yo."

"Uh, yeah you can, dude."

"Okay. Maybe, just maybe, if the chick has, like, a cold sore, but I dunno... We can always ask Sal. She'd probably be interested to hear that you're single." Luc punched Cava stiffly and winked at him.

Cava laughed nervously. "You know, Anj probably wasn't wrong... I gotta get myself straight and be better for the next broad. I wouldn't want to bring Sally down... I just want to do me, try not to be so..."

"Bah. You're fine, man. And, you couldn't bring Sal down with torpedo; that girl is on her *game*. But in all seriousness, I hollered at Lil Bertie and he said we should come watch the fights on the weekend."

"The fights?"

"Yeah man, near the drags. Well, right down the street and a bit. They have dog fights, man. I always thought that was a myth, but he says the shit's mad fucked up. I gotta check it out."

"Dog fights? What the hell is that about?"

"You ain't heard of them?" Luc sprang up to his feet, excitedly. "Yo, they have like, dogs, in a ring. They train them, and they fight like boxers do. People put bets on the motherfuckers, and it's like when Mike fights in Vegas, but probably Fury celebrities and shit. Aww man, it'll be hella-fied dope. Come on, man. Come with me. I don't wanna go alone."

Cava scratched his chin. "I dunno, man, it sounds like a hassle. Do the dogs get hurt?"

"Nah man, I'll scoop us a ride!" Luc beamed. "Hurt? I dunno... boxers get hurt. Except in the Olympics. Maybe they have head gear, and fight for points. Either way, when you go off to university and start wearing tight khakis and hollering at all them nerd bitches, you don't wanna be all like 'Damn, I wish I'd watched dogs fight with my boy Luc.' Instead, you can be all cultured and be like 'Damn, I watched dogs fight with my boy Luc, the illest homie in Fury!'"

Cava laughed. Maybe there *would* be a girl there that was even better than his ex. Maybe he *did* need to let off some steam. Maybe he *shouldn't* be such a pussy and have some fun while he was off school. At any rate, the peer pressure was working. He needed to open the valves, and what's the worst that could happen?

Fink strode up to the Bench. "What're you guys laughing about?"

"Oh, what up, champ! The Knocked-Out King! The Crush-ed One!" Luc rang shots off at Rat-Fink, still sporting a swollen jaw.

"Shut up, man. I'm lucky I didn't have to get my jaw wired because of that poor ass psycho. My mom said that we're gonna sue the shit outta that bitch and take him for everything he's got."

"Which is what?" Cava asked. "He ain't even got a truck to his name anymore. You'll be trying to squeeze blood from a stone."

"Either way, he can rot in a cell. Fuck him. So, what were you guys talking about?"

"The dog fights this weekend, you want in?" Luc said, rubbing Fink's shoulder. As he raised his hand, Fink trembled, then raised his own in defense. The boys laughed and whooped at the shook Fink.

"Yeah, I'm down. Probably a good place to unload some product. It's been slow for me. You?"

"Nah, I ain't been on my game. *Maman*'s home, and I'm gonna be a student again soon. I always have a bit, probably need a bit more, but I'm phasing out like Kitty Pryde, son. And, it's pretty fucking sweet."

"I'm headed to Tic-Tax's right now if you wanna boot along."

"Yeah, why not? I'll check on the boy, see how all that arsenal is treating the crazy... you just call him Tic-Tax?"

"Yeah, Imma call him that until he gives me some fucking bullets. I been walking around with an empty gun for a minute now. Not to his face, though. And don't tell him I said that."

Cava shook their hands and watched them go, smoking a post-joint cigarette and feeling the vapour lift him a little higher. Combined with the cool air, he felt refreshed. The cigarette flavour had a rejuvenated taste that marijuana tended to endow them with. He was fighting his negative thoughts and had a plan traced out for the weekend, sure to further distract him.

Cava collected himself and started towards his house. He had nothing planned for the evening and figured that he'd see if Henry was up for putting some time in on the console. Henry had been essentially banished from the basement while Cava stewed in self-loathing, but he was feeling like company now.

"Hey! Quinn! Hey!" Sally shouted from her window, waving her hand like she was setting sail for Normandy. "What are you up to?"

"Not much, was gonna see if Hank wanted to play some vids, but pretty quiet otherwise. You?"

"Nothing. I'm actually kind of bored... I can only study so much, and now that finals are done, I'm *actually* bored," she sounded enthralled with the idea of boredom, as an activity and state of mind.

"Okay, weird... Well, you're more than welcome to come down in a bit. I'm gonna sup, but come knock on my window."

"Okay!"

* * *

Luc and Fink walked the short path to Tic-Tax's grandmother's place. Cava had always wondered what those two did when he wasn't around. One seemed to get along with everyone, while the other couldn't seem to stand—or be stood by—most human beings.

When they were left without other friends, they refrained from speaking for as long as Luc could stand the silence, before the needling in his nerves propelled him to break it.

"You know when you wear sweatpants? Or like, track pants?" Luc started.

"I guess, yeah," Fink responded mechanically.

"When you take a piss, do you pull your balls out along with your dick? Or just your dick?"

"What?" Fink asked, annoyed.

"Like, for me, it depends on the string. How tight it is. Because, if it's tied loose, then I'll just take my pesh out, but if the waist is tighter, I find I always have to throw a thumb down and squeeze my nuts out, too."

"What the fuck? Is this the kind of shit you and Cava talk about?"

"I dunno, I guess... It just popped into my head," Luc said innocently.

"That's stupid. You're stupid... Can't you just be quiet?"

"How long you known me for?" Luc smiled.

"Jesus Christ," Fink scoffed. "I ain't Cava."

* * *

It wasn't long after Cava had recruited his brother to play a few rounds of video games that Sally knocked on the winow with the quick energy of a woodpecker.

"Do I gotta go?" Henry asked, disappointed.

"We'll see," Cava replied as he opened the window.

Sally knew the drill: she tossed her shoes and slunk onto the bed, ending up cross-legged at the back near the pillow. "Hi, Henry, long time no see! How was your first semester?"

"Good, thanks. Yours?" he asked while absorbed in a dialogue box on the screen.

"He gets pretty into the game, sorry... Runs in the family, I guess."

The two friends bantered for a bit about finals and what'd been happening with their friends. Henry eventually seemed to become annoyed and excused himself. "Sally, it was nice to see you... Quinn, I'm going upstairs. Let me know if you wanna play tomorrow."

Cava and Sally said goodnight to Henry, and Sally apologized. "I'm sorry, I didn't mean to come in between your guys' game. Is he mad?"

"Nah, he's used to getting tossed. Trust me. We'll play another time. I have lots of it now."

Sally frowned and pulled her hands into her sleeves. "I heard about that... Are you holding up okay? Do you want to talk about it?"

Cava gave Sally a play-by-play of their discussion, including Anj's chief reasons for ending the relationship. He explained how he knew she'd been right and that he'd fucked up, bad. He began to run down a list of his own deficiencies, trying to lay the blame on himself, not focusing on the outside influences.

Sally looked at him with measured empathy. She knew the problems; she saw them herself. It hadn't been long since they'd discussed them. She knew that he'd indeed fucked up, and that he was wearing a badge of guilt he'd sewn himself. However, she didn't want to see him so sorrowed.

"I kind of know what you're going through," she said, after allowing Cava to verbally wear himself threadbare. "When I was away, I was seeing a guy. I thought, 'Yeah, this is it. I could be happy like this. This is great.'"

"It wasn't?"

"No, it was fine. But, obviously, I'm here. At first, I... it's hard to say. I was happy to have someone that I felt cared about me, put me above anything else. It makes you feel special. When it ends, you never want to put yourself in a position to be hurt like that again. But, after a while, you start to miss that feeling. You start to miss caring and having someone care about you."

"I care about you."

"And I care about you. You can distract yourself, tuck yourself away. You can do anything to try and forget something or someone. You can read. You can study. You can run. You can't hide from your own mind, though."

"What'd you do?"

"Well, you just go on living, and you have to be patient. It hurts, but you have to accept the hurt. Almost cherish it, cherish the time you had with someone, the experiences, no matter how it ended. Learn from it, and eventually, you'll feel normal again."

"Why would I want to open myself up to that kind of... I don't know what to call it... pain, again?"

"Because, Quinn, pleasure can't exist without pain, just as good needs evil."

"What happened between you and your guy? You've never talked about it."

"Well... I was cheated on. And that takes a while to get over."

"Jesus, I bet... Who the hell would cheat on you?"

"Well, someone who I thought was trustworthy and caring, who ended up being a slick talker, shady, and very selfish."

"Man, I don't think I could ever do that to someone."

"I didn't think it would happen between us, but sometimes you think you know someone, and you don't. He was sweet, endearing, a good listener, handsome... so many great qualities. I actually thought that I was in love. Looking back, no... I was happy that someone was paying attention to me. I know that I look different than I used to... Maybe I'm a little put off by any attention I get now. I still don't trust men in general, their intentions, but they're not all snakes and sharks, as you would say... liars and pervs... They can't be."

"And Anj thought she knew me, I guess. I wish I could tell her how sorry I was, I am... I feel like a villain."

"You're not! Don't ever say that! You're my favourite person in the world."

"Hero to some, villains to others, just like Victor Von... I just feel like I wanna close myself up. Just curl up and stay there."

"But you can learn to trust again, to open yourself up to love."

"I don't think Anj even loved me."

"Trust me, she did. You're an easy person to love. Give yourself some credit. You have flaws, you're not perfect, but that's what makes you who you are. I mean, Quinn, you're only 17..."

"So are you."

"Sometimes I actually wish I went out with you guys more, so I could feel 17, not 70."

"Most beautiful 70-year-old I know."

"Shut up."

"So... should I try and get her back?"

No, she thought. *He shouldn't.* She saw Anjuli's perspective, but would never forgive her for making her friend hurt. *No, he shouldn't.* Sally said nothing, choosing wisdom as the wise word not spoken.

"No... I need to go forward," Cava said, with resolution. "Yeah, this sucks... but so do a lot of things that I've lived to see the ass of."

"That's my boy," Sally said as she, as if by reflex, hugged Cava and pecked him on the cheek.

She withdrew before Cava could squeeze her back. They were both red in the cheeks. They exchanged curious smiles.

* * *

Luc and Fink arrived at Tic-Tax's and entered through the sliding door in the back, noticing Rosee lying on the couch beneath a quilt, watching cartoons. Fink kept on while Luc stopped and sat beside her.

"Hey Rosee, how ya doing?"

She stirred and rolled onto her back to look up at her old friend. "Are you here to take me away? Am I going home?"

"What?" Luc said, puzzled.

Rosee flitted her eyelids, then seemed to blink a second, almost imperceptible set; the secondary blinking didn't require the use of her yellow-brown eyelids. A serene flicker transfigured her azure eyes, appearing to be caught in between waking dreams, wandering in some invisible wonder, before they returned back to a strained, pained reality.

"Luc, hi. How are you?"

"I'm good Rosee. Are you doing okay?"

"I'm tired. I just want to sleep. I think I'm sick," she whispered as she fell asleep, her miniscule ribs rising and falling like a ladybug's.

Luc left her and went into the kitchen, where Fink and Tic-Tax were talking.

"Well, I feel as though I've been patient enough. I feel like a phoney, like a mark," Fink said. "You said you'd have something for me to put in my heater... It's been weeks, and it still only makes clicking noises when I pull the trigger."

"Well, clearly you're not ready, if you're pulling the trigger. Look, I need more time, I need more everything... Luc, haven't seen much of you, kid. How have you been? Got anything for me?"

"I'm paid up, Ali," Luc answered indifferently. "Just coming in to say what up."

"Your brother is downstairs, if you guys wanna have a little family chat. Heard through the grapevine that Mrs. Kalou is back in town."

"Nah, I'm straight. Besides, if I see him, I might snap on him. He knows to stay away from the crib."

"So, what's the play?" Tic-Tax asked as Fink, arms crossed, turned his attention to Luc.

"What play? What game are we playing?" Luc ask, confused.

"Fink tells me that you're going to watch the pups this weekend. What's your angle?"

"To watch motherfucking dogs fight motherfucking dogs. Or robots, or crocodiles, I dunno... Whatever them shits are. A buddy invited me. Lil Bert... I think you've met him."

Tic-Tax picked the crud out from a fingernail and sucked his teeth. "Can I come?"

Luc blew a loud raspberry. "You? Did I not just say who invited me? Considering recent *you know what's*, I don't think I'd want to be seen with you there. I don't know why you'd want to be seen either, unless you want to start trouble. And even then, you'd probably find more than you bargained for. You'd be fucking insane, bro."

* * *

"How the hell do you want to get there? It's even *further* than the drags. It's down by the badlands and all those creepy-ass, old warehouses. Transit doesn't go there… Shit, man, I don't think the police even go there." Cava took a little puff of the joint and handed it back.

"Oh ye of little faith," Luc took the joint and smiled with his head tilted towards the heavens. "I told you, baby Cavs. I'll take care of it."

Cava stood up and sat down a few times. He felt a strange, pulsating sweat in his perineum, as if the butterflies in his stomach were falling like buzz-bombs onto the floor of his gut.

"Why the hell you so nervous, brother? This'll be dope! You said it yourself. You need a night of fun and excitement."

"I didn't say that. You said that," Cava fired back.

"And, you should always listen to me. I'm a doctor… like Ivan." Luc removed a plastic bottle and unscrewed the lid, taking a sip and making a pained face. "Want some? The ride should be here soon."

Cava took a swig and cringed. It didn't have the warming sensation of brown, but the emetic sting in his sinuses from dirty clear booze. "How much loot you bringing?"

"I got $50, but I'll make more there. I have some shit. Something tells me dogfighting fans like their meds. Plus, I'm Lucky Luc. I'll make dough off the fights."

Two narrow lights approached them slowly; they were jerking, like in a claw crane arcade game. The headlights were little and beady—ugly, in fact. Cava imagined the car as a peevish Englishman with a comb-over and malnourished mustache, complaining about the dryness of his crumpets.

"You got yourselves a ride," Fink said from the driver's seat. "Hey, don't even think about smoking in my ma's car. Leave the tissue box alone. Don't tag on the windows. Don't move the floor mats."

Fink navigated the car with convulsions. Though he was the only one of the boys who had his license, his ability to negotiate brakes and gas needed practice. He raced red lights and hammered on the brakes. He tapped the stopper around corners and chirped the tires at every takeoff. The filthy hooch and weed were churning in Cava's head, making him choke back his tuna casserole dinner.

Luc sat in the middle, tugging on the head rests. He proposed numerous scenarios about St. Bernard's fighting Dobermans, German Shepherds squaring off with Great Danes, maybe even a Chihuahua having a cute little dust-up with a Springer Spaniel or Jack Russell. Maybe they had costumes. Maybe they had weapons. Did dog fights have ring girls? Were they canine ring she-dogs? Did they use mutants from the X to clean the shit up and hold score cards?

"You sure it's this far?" Fink asked, halting the vehicle on a barren road with tall brown shoots on either side. "We passed the drags spot like, 20 minutes ago, Luc."

"Word. Bertie said that you follow Mercer Road until you can't follow Mercer Road no more, then you hook a Rudolph and follow that motherfucker 'til you see the floodlights."

The boys continued down the lightless road. It was dark, but the nocturnal influence only accounted for part of it. Cava felt chills as they moved over the bumpy, pot-holed road; little shacks with barely any light emanating from within appeared sporadically. There were virtually no powerlines, and driveways were scarce.

"How do people drive up to their houses?" Cava asked. No one answered.

They passed a bigger lot. There was a tin-roofed shack that was stitched together like a doll made out of spare parts. An oil drum burned as several men turned and watched the car move along the road.

"Man, this area is creepy," Luc murmured. "Oh, the end of Mercer! Go right, Finkie!"

They continued down another vacant road with what seemed to be abandoned houses. Luc had to pee, but he'd be damned to pull his pesh out in this area—or so he said.

A light in the distance began to unveil itself, like an infant moon ringed by mist. They continued down the road they couldn't discern the name of; the poles with the street names had been fleeced.

"This has got to be it," Luc said, bouncing up and down.

* * *

The boys pulled into the lot, Fink trying to ride the brakes as the ground beneath them became more unstable. The lot contained a number of structures. To call them buildings seemed a stretch; they were wood and tin squares of various heights. The rust and rot were visible in the pitch black. Among the dilapidated erections were busted, broken down cars, farming equipment, cranes, backhoes, cages, and other broken pieces of hardware for all varieties of work. Timber and foundation forms were piled up, and the loose fencing was standing merely for show: it seemed as though a strong enough push could topple the entire area like dominos.

Fink found a clearing near other cars. Among the heaps of scrapyard vehicles were dozens of Harley Davidsons, some luxury sedans, SUVs, and trucks. Just as common were rust-buckets and hoopties. All in all, a quick count showed somewhere between 20 and 30 vehicles.

"I guess this is a pretty big deal," Luc said, barely feeling the teeming liquids in his bladder that'd been threatening release mere moments prior.

Cava took a deep breath. "Smells like… sawdust. Like the docks, that freshly cut wood smell… Where the fuck are we, exactly?" Cava liked the smell, but remembered Ivan always saying that if you can smell the docks at night, you might want to turn around.

"We must have taken a big loop or something," Fink said, admiring the open walls on the some of the larger buildings. "Gimme a smoke."

Pissing into some bushes two feet away, Luc replied, "You don't smoke." This was punctuated by the sound of torrential urine and a satisfied gasp.

"Yeah, I know, but I need something to do with my hands."

Cava, having just lit a dart, pulled out another and held it to the cherry of his lit cigarette, then passed it to Fink. He snickered as Fink took it between two willowy fingers and held it to his overly pursed lips, taking a small, quick drag and ejecting the vapour with the same breath.

"You might want to work on that. They'll call you a homo."

Luc finished and wandered back, smacking his hands against his denim. "Fuck me, I needed that."

The boys looked around the area. One warehouse had a number of floodlights lighting up the entire parking area. Other structures seemed inactive; some lights leaked out of crooked panels, and the faint sounds of saws or other tools could be heard.

Luc let out a gush of air and smiled. "You guys ready?"

The closer they got, the more audible the jagged symphony of masculine yelling became. They heard yelps and gnarls from dogs.

A giant blocked their entry.

It was colder than in the city centre, but the giant was only wearing a leather vest over a t-shirt. His arms and neck, up to his chin, were covered in tattoos. He wore leather padded gloves and held a can of beer in one hand, a Rambo blade in the other. The knife looked small in his hand, but easily measured any of the boys' forearms in length and width.

"Fuck you want?"

Fink shot his head down the moment he felt the radius of the giant's glare graze his face. Cava got one syllable out, which dragged on for far too long. Only Luc was able to form full words. "Here for the, uh, fights."

"Best be fucking off," the giant barked. "Don't think you guys get it."

"A friend invited us. Lil… Bertie Lévesque."

The man eyed Luc up.

"Alright," the giant stepped aside. "Don't fuck around."

* * *

The first thing that struck the boys was the smell; more than the heat, which gave the venue a sticky, sweat-lodge-greenhouse effect. The odour, however, was hard to pinpoint.

"Iron," Cava said, licking his teeth, "like a cold spoon."

It was fresh and organic; the smell of fresh blood and poor ventilation. And shit. The sour and earthy smell of mounds of dog shit.

The activity had seemingly subsided from 'the ring' for the moment, so the boys peered around the environment. Knee-high planks of two-by-fours were nailed to pikes that were driven into the hard-packed soil terrain underfoot. The currently empty ring contained smatters of blood and chunks of fleshy fur.

Around the area, which was much larger than it appeared from the outside, were workbenches and random car parts that were pushed against the walls and covered with sheets. The sheets, Cava thought, were strangely cute, with blue flowers and harmless canary colours adorning them.

"I may..." Luc started, aghast, "...have pictured something completely different."

"Yo, all I smell is dog shit," Fink said, scrunching his face.

Cava spotted Lil Bertie near a workbench, speaking with a man in a vest. The boys approached and saluted their comrade.

"Yo, boys, glad you could make it. You see that last fight? Friggin' brutal. Glad I don't have to brain these poor things."

Beside Bertie, the man was feeding a raw steak to a tawny Pitbull that was too large for its cage. Across the room, two Filipino men were carrying the limp body of a gargantuan Pitbull out the back door. Another two men followed with shovels and a shotgun.

"So... all the dogs... are Pits?" Cava asked, trying to make polite conversation.

"Well, why do you think they call them 'Pit' 'bulls'?" Bertie threw a friendly slug at Cava's shoulder.

Luc rubbed his arm, almost as though he had a sympathy pang. "This is different than I was thinking, Bert."

"Yeah, I won't lie... not exactly *legal*, but uncle Dino, here, has been taking me my whole life," Bertie said as his uncle continued to force the steak into the dog's mouth, like a slack rope through a hole.

Uncle Dino raised himself and stood as tall as the giant. "Friends?" he asked in a thick French accent.

"Yeah, from school," Bertie replied. "Luc wit da C here is from Quebec, too."

Dino and Luc exchanged greetings in French while the other two looked around. Lots of patches. Lots of degenerate gamblers. Lots of drug dealers and gangsters.

"You guys wanna drink?" Bertie grabbed a bottle of whiskey from a nearby desk. He threw the cap away. "Gotta finish it, now."

The boys fought their booze-cringing faces, not wanting to look weak, and posed some light questions to their friend.

"Who's all here?" Cava asked.

"Well, think of it like this. Some of the bikers. Some of the browns. The Flips. The Nammers. Some Triad-looking Chinese dudes. And then, the rest. Lots of shit goes down here because everyone is kind of kept honest. It's like… anyone here could kill you, and everyone is in some way affiliated or tied in with everybody else. Sure, there are gangs and drug lords and all that crazy stuff. But, in here, there's kind of a gentlemen's agreement. People make trades, sales, et cetera, and the cops wouldn't dare intervene. Kind of cool, you know?"

"Do the dogs dress up? Are there judges? Are there ring girls?" Luc asked, shakily.

"Nope," Bertie responded with a laugh. "Just two Pits trying to murk each other. The secret is… the winner doesn't die."

"Die?" Luc asked in horror.

"Well, yeah, die… Did you think this was like professional wrestling or something, Luc?"

"Hmm… Maybe a bit. This seems kind of sad now."

"Reserve judgement until after you throw some loot down and watch the craziest thing you've ever seen. Oh, wait, only… no selling drugs and no welching on a bet. Two rules. Aside from don't start a fight and general etiquette. We aren't savages, you know."

The boys agreed.

* * *

Bertie introduced the boys to all his family in attendance: Uncle Dino, Uncle Henri, Uncle Claude, even Uncle Damian was there, giving Fink the evil eye. Cava spotted the Browns but didn't see Anjuli's cousin. A small win.

"You seem a little shook, Finkie. You okay?" Bertie asked.

"Yeah, I'm fine. Tired is all. Big family. Who's that?" Fink asked, pointing at a stout, Arabic-looking man with a neck full of fat twist-chains and fingers full of stones.

"I dunno," Bertie scratched his head. "Looks like a pretty fancy fella to me." Bertie left to ask one of his uncles and returned with the answer: "Name is Omar. Apparently, an enforcer from Fig. Look at him, his hands are like textbooks… Probably don't smudge his sneakers."

People began to huddle towards one of the blood-stained boxes, and Bertie asked them if they wanted to throw any loot on the fight. Luc gave him $20 and the others shook their heads.

There was little fanfare; no entrance music, no big-haired manager, no robes or belts, no Bruce Buffer.

A Vietnamese man and a fat, white biker walked two Pits to the edge of the ring, unbuckled the leash, horse-collared them in, and that was it. The dogs fought as dogs do, but without the owners eventually pulling them apart. The gray dog clipped and erased the ear from the brindle-coloured dog's head. They snarled and gnashed at each other's snouts; the teeth on teeth sound made Luc's urethra recoil into his gut. The dogs tore at each other's craniums, throats, and legs. Pieces of dog cleaved from both them like shredded beef under the strength of their jaws. Worst of all, it continued. It just kept going. The front row had a combination of avidly engrossed men with pundit expressions that were smoking darts in European and Asian styles and scratching their chins, alongside emotionally invested spectators, either owners or people with serious loot riding on the outcome. Both jostled for a view and couldn't forge a blink.

The boys didn't try to pry and jump as others near them in the back row charged forward. Bertie had positioned himself on the shoulders of two of his uncles and was turning red from cheering.

"Which one you got?" Cava asked, twisting his brow.

"Dude," Luc said, shielding his eyes. "I don't even care."

The match concluded with the brindle-coloured Pit incapacitating the gray one. It'd drawn enough blood to the point that the gray Pit was lying on its side and leaking its insides in a steady stream. The same Filipinos that'd escorted the previous dog outside picked the gray dog up and carried it out the same way. Luc saw the dog's miserable and violated expression glare at him with the pain of death. Its eyes then rolled into its massive cranium, and its tongue bounced with the gait of the men. Luc sniffed and quickly spun, swigging at his fire water.

"That was..." Cava started.

"Bloody rad!" Bertie finished his sentence. "I mean, they're probably going to have to cap the winner, too. He took a ripper and might not be of any use... Man, he took a beating. That was like Rumble in the Jungle, yo!"

Luc held his stomach. "Dude, I don't think this is my scene," he said to Cava softly.

Cava nodded. "I know, homie. It's all good. We came, right?" he looked around. "You notice there ain't any chicks here? Not a one?"

"No shocker, homes. Why would they want to see doggies get deaded?"

"Where's Rat-Fink? Must be pissing. Oh, hey, that's Mr. Suggs, right there. Hate to say it, but I guess we know what he did with the money."

A loud buckshot was heard from outside the building. Cava cringed as Luc jumped.

"Man, that guy shows up at the greasiest goddamn places. Help yourself, first, man."

Gary Suggs walked towards the boys, counting some cash. "Hey boys, how are ya?"

"Good," they said in stunned unison.

"We're sorry about Amanda," Cava offered.

"Yeah, it must be tough," Luc followed.

"It's been... It hasn't been easy on my wife or myself," he said with his head down. "But, the Lord and our community has seen it fit to give us a donation, for us to use to improve our lives. That's what that gypsy girl told me. Anyways, I bet $500 on the brownish thing and it was an... underdog!" Gary laughed, to the chagrin of the boys. "I just won $1,500! Now, I can get a truck and get back on my feet," he noticed the boys giving him a strange look. "Boys, nothing will bring my daughter back. She was... special. But, this is step one to a new life for old Gar."

The boys hesitantly congratulated the man.

"Listen, I want to use some of the money to do something nice for the memory of my daughter, like a bench or a plaque or something. If you have any ideas, let me know. And thank that gypsy girl for me. Her father is a madman, but I think she lives near you."

"Will do."

"One more thing. Have you guys seen that Russian friend of yours, Mark?"

"Marek?"

"Rat-Fink?"

"Yeah… that's the one," Gary narrowed his gaze. "Tell him I better not see him, ever. Got it?"

The boys agreed. "Hell did Finkie do to old man Suggs?" Luc asked. "*That* dude can't take an L? Where that fire been at?"

"No clue. Where is that pinko-commie fuck-rat? He's our ride."

* * *

About an hour had passed, including more fights, resulting in more dead dogs, and still no sign of Rat-Fink. The boys could only plug their mouths with so much whiskey and feign watching so many fights.

"Seriously, dog. I mean, man, where is that little bitch?" Luc asked. "It's like 1 am, and getting home is only gonna get harder."

Like at a house party, the movements and actions of the attendees were becoming sloppier and surlier. Loud hacking laughs and fat fingers pressed into strapping chests were beginning to mushroom.

"Until there are no more pups to put out," Bertie slurred in response to Cava's question about how long these events usually last. Bertie threw his arm around the boys and tilted a generous gulp of brown back. The bottle now rattled with only a light auburn splash at the base.

Cava felt his vision start to double and his legs become weightless. His four sneakers were criss-crossing as he looked down to watch his steps.

"Luc," he said. "I'm wasted."

Luc was licking the yellow adhesive strip on a joint backwards. "Me too, brother. We're fucked for the night." The weed spilled on to the floor.

They agreed that walking home would take them past daylight and tried to plot alternative measures.

Cava shook his head, hoping to destroy the blurred scenery and set his spaceship back to a more tranquil ebb. He leaned against a work bench and lit a cigarette backwards. The bitter, vinegar taste of the filter made him spit the dart onto the ground in front of him. He squashed it under his sole and retrieved another, pirate-eyeing the tube to make sure he had the right side.

"Maybe we can score a lift with Suggs?" Cava suggested, looking up and noticing that no one was around to absorb his parole.

A large circle of men had formed in the distance. Not near any of the stinking, red-painted rings, but closer to the front door.

"We caught them snooping around out back, and they got heat... Think it's our heat!" Uncle Claude said, holding a kid by the hoodie, wearing a ski mask.

Uncle Henri pulled the gun out and opened the chamber. "Fucking idiot's running around with an unloaded gun. Who the fuck are you?" He tore the ski mask off one of their faces.

Cava squinted and recognized the face as being one of Tic-Tax's crew. He looked frightened, like he might piss himself. The other fella had his ski mask ripped off, too. He was another one of the cats who'd been at both Drew's party and the dockyards the night Tic-Tax had handed out weapons.

"What do we do with them?" Uncle Dino asked, cracking his knuckles.

Where's Luc? Cava thought, his anxiety outweighing his intoxication.

A shower of bullets tore through the brittle wooden planks, and everyone hit the dirt.

Cava didn't duck, but was tackled down by Luc, who'd been standing within shouting distance the whole time. All colours of criminals dug their heads under their hands and threw themselves onto the soil. The noise from the gun blasts didn't last long, but there were enough perforations in the siding to feel the frigid air seep into the musty structure.

Once it stopped, the two masked characters had vanished; their masks and guns gone. Men began raising themselves and checking their organs for holes. No one had seemed to catch a stray. Luc and Cava remained on the ground for another moment, their eyes firmly sealed, before getting up and brushing themselves off.

"What the fuck happened?" Cava asked.

"Well, somebody clearly fired some rounds into the building," Luc replied calmly, patting himself down.

The men began to exchange heated words. The heated words bubbled over into screaming matches. Everyone blamed everyone for the attack.

"You've had beef with us for years, you do this?"

"I just got here, it didn't happen until I walked in! It's a set up."

"It's y'all bringing that big city shit to the flats. Pathetic, you fucking bitch-made cocksucker."

"Everyone calm down, we can figure this out."

"Who the fuck are you? You probably set this whole thing up!"

"You're accusing me? I'll kill you."

"Kill me? I'll kill you!"

"Who brought the strap? We all agreed, no guns!"

"My glock's in the whip, but I'll..."

What the boys saw was the yearly fireworks brawl, if it were played out on Monster Island. The bikers, the Browns, and every other organization were throwing uppercuts and mega jabs. There was double and triple-teaming, knives and bats; every dirty trick was being pulled out. Dogs were barking from their cages. Foam could be heard flying from their mouths.

Luc and Cava were left without dance partners. They stood back-to-back. Even Luc, who momentarily wished he had his *snukts*, was scared shitless. They locked fingers and kept themselves tight. They watched grown men swing and connect with powerful shots that would tear their heads clean off. They heard the sounds of feet moving on loose dirt, the gurgling of chokeholds that were meant to kill instead of subdue, and the whistle of swinging blades and chains.

One or two of the lights had been knocked out, either by the gunfire or by titans bumping into them. The boys were frozen. The circle of mayhem was tightening around them. They looked for any spaces to use to free themselves, but each one opened and then disappeared, imprisoning them on their shrinking peninsula.

Suddenly, Cava felt Luc fly out of his hand, and didn't have any ability to pull him back.

Cava spun around and tried to remain on guard. He felt dizzy and sick; whether the booze or the threat had made him light-headed, he didn't know. He heard footsteps approaching him from the rear, looking in time to see someone tackle him like a strong safety. He skidded and bounced several feet. He glanced to his right for something to hammer his attacker with. Nothing. He glanced to the other side.

To his left he saw Fink, curled up under a work table with his pistol white-knuckled in his slim hand.

"Fink…" he gasped.

Fink didn't move. He merely backed up closer to the wall and held the gun near his face.

Cava looked up and saw the face of the attacker: a big, round, Moroccan-type head with a gold tooth and summas, his Rakim-rope dangling in his face. Omar.

But I didn't even step on his kicks, thought Cava.

He felt the man's big, meaty paws land on him. It hurt. The rings felt like they were denting his forearms with every bash. He felt the fingers of Omar's watch hand loop around his neck and start to squeeze.

Cava felt his eyes bulging out, ready to burst. He couldn't make out colours or shapes. He managed a tiny breath in, but felt his pipes begin to buckle.

He was going to die. It felt like an hour since he'd last taken a full breath. It was getting dark, and his turbulent thoughts were slowing. He might already be dead. His hands floated above him like sentient vine from a plant; like Doctor Octopus' tentacle.

He wrenched his head back and took in a bit more air; he was seeing stars with his eyes closed, like travelling at light speed through deep space. The body on him weighed more than a truck. He couldn't twist himself an inch.

He'd been holding the wrist of the hand that was slowly working to join its brother. It was thick, with a Cuban link bracelet. That was the strong hand. If it connected, he really was dead.

He inched his way to the palm and the fingers. The hand still descended. It felt just as hard as the ground beneath him, with thick fingers, each like a sausage casing packed with concrete.

He managed to get his hands around two fingers apiece. Time was running out. Cava had his ring and pinkie in his left hand, his middle and index finger in his right. He felt the weight of the rings and the stiffness of the fingers driving closer.

Cava pulled and snapped the fingers apart. He felt them tear like a wishbone. He heard a gruesome tearing and ripping as the man flew off him. That must be what ripping apart an alligator's jaw feels like for Colossus.

He could breathe. He looked up to see Fink, but couldn't make anything out besides swirls of dark, wispy shadows. He pulled himself by the table leg and under the table, blindly. He felt around for a sign of Fink. There was none.

A large hand secured itself around his ankle and pulled him out. "Please, god, fuck, no, no, not again." He looked up and saw the stern and wrathful face of Joti Singh. He grabbed Cava by the collar and lifted him to his feet. He dragged him around the still-active fighting and threw him out the side door.

Cava landed surrounded by dog carcasses and freshly-dug, half-covered holes. A few shovels were speared into the dirt and Luc was lying on a soil mound of a freshly sealed dog grave.

"Homie, you okay?"

Luc raised his head and blindly placed his palm on his friend's head. "I'm straight."

Cava sunk his head into the cold, turned earth and thought about the mineral odour once again before closing his eyes.

* * *

"Guys, guys! Get the fuck up! We gotta get the fuck out of here before they see us."

Cava dragged his right hand from his forehead to his chin; he felt the morsels of dirt crumble and break apart under his palm. His hands were freezing, but his face had a recently whistled kettle heat to it. He groaned, and heard Luc release a similar grunt simultaneously, feeling the cold, loose soil shift and kick up just above him.

"Seriously, you motherfuckers," the voice was now Fink's. "We gotta get the fuck up out of this fucking place."

Luc shot up, his face filled with confusion and pain, then panic. Cava's vision and senses returned to him as he felt his body lifted by the preternatural, wiry strength of his comrade. He spied Fink marching around the side of the building towards the car, holding his jeans up at each hip, high enough to show the stripes of his socks.

Luc and Cava were still dazed, one from head shots and the other from asphyxiation, but sped their canter up to a gallop as they saw Fink hop into the driver's seat of his mother's idling car.

The inside lights brightened for a second, and the boys saw the silhouettes of two more figures in the car, one in the front and one in the back.

The door flew open, nearly striking Luc as he approached, and the guy in the front pulled the seat forward. Luc shot in. Cava looked back. A quick appraisal only showed him cold dust swirling at the floodlights like a sandstorm. The sound of angry shouting, Pits barking, and two shots in the air accompanied the sight of small-statured Asian men fleeing the structure and fanning out in multiple directions.

"Get the fuck in!" the passenger screamed, hoarsely.

Cava hopped in and landed partially on Luc's lap. Fink peeled away with the passenger door flapping wildly. The rear axle warped and pivoted violently, sending the three in the back to the left, then crushing Cava to the right. The car made a petulant, nasally wheeze while trying to catch up with the pedal already mashed against the floor.

"That was fucking stupid," the guy in the front seat said, his ski mask pulled up to his nose, exposing a bloody nose and chipped teeth.

"I dunno," the man in the back said, his ski mask still fully around his mug. "I think it probably got our point across."

Cava felt his face. His right orbital bone was tender, but it'd been worse in previous fights. His arms and paws were tight, tighter than after a day spent with a ratchet and rig wheels. He was still trying to catch his breath; his oesophagus felt like the crushed soda cans they used as makeshift pipes when they were younger. The skin around his Adam's apple was raw.

Luc was rotating his jaw, testing its flexibility and biting power. Cava figured that he must have taken one hell of a slug. Luc was also blinking and routinely shaking his melon, as if trying to knock some dust loose.

"Did you do your part? Crush?" the guy in the passenger seat rolled his head towards Fink. Not a scratch on him.

"Uh…" Fink started. "I couldn't see shit. I couldn't, uh, see any targets…"

"I don't think we hit any-fucking-body," the backseat guy said, lifting his mask over his head after checking the empty road behind him. "Lucky we didn't get hit. We weren't supposed to be in there, even."

With two fingers pressed against his jawbone, an audible click sounded as Luc lifted and descended his chin. Finally, he asked, "Wait… that was a fucking plan? Were you guys trying to hit someone? Some cats? Who? What the fuck were y'all thinking?"

Only silence followed his question. The only sound that was heard was the strained whistling of an over-burdened exhaust and the bumpiness of the road beneath the blading tires.

"No one in particular," said the guy in the front seat, continuing to stare straight ahead. "We were finally given some clips and told to get inside and start firing at important looking guys when the outside shots started coming in."

"I think I hit a dog," chuckled the guy in the back seat. "You lost your clip, idiot. The fuck were you gonna do with an empty gat? They clowned you good!"

"Fuck you," he shot back. "It fell out of my pocket. All you did was shoot in the air and hit a dog like a bitch, bitch."

Cava now fully recognized him as one of the guys from the party: Sketch, a fairly well-known crackhead and blade-sticker-for-cheap. He observed the guy in the front seat from his position. He wore a paint-crusted hoodie and had a pistol on his lap, finger still looped around the trigger.

Luc appeared as though he was about to say something. The car skidded to an eventual, semi-abrupt stop, reversing about 10 feet.

Headlights flared on a car pulled off the road in a clearing, and two doors swung open. Fink kept the engine running as the passenger hopped out, gesturing Cava and Luc to follow suit.

"Well, you guys managed to get out in one piece." Tic-Tax's voice could be heard before he appeared. "Boys, you're always in the wrong place at the wrong time, huh?"

Cava and Luc leered at Tic-Tax, but exhaustion and disbelief punctured anything threatening in their countenance.

Tic-Tax came into view and put a hand on Luc's shoulder. "Thanks for the idea, bro. This masterpiece is owed to you. How else could I have guessed that anyone who hates me or I hate back would be in one spot?" He shifted his attention to the crackhead and the other guy. "You guys hit anyone of note?"

The two men looked at one another, then back at Tic-Tax. "Guaranteed," the one swith his mask still on suggested, "at least, someone caught a stray. Not just dogs," he said as Sketch snorted a laugh.

Cava was stilled with garbled notions and sentiments. He looked at Luc, fist balled and shuffling his way towards Tic-Tax.

The cat in Tic-Tax's passenger seat intercepted his march and pulled his shirt up to his chest, revealing a sawed-off shotgun. "Don't be a stooge," he whispered. "We all got one."

"I'm driving, Crusher. You drive like a crazy old woman," Tic-Tax said to Fink as he stepped out, his gun falling to the ground.

"I got shotgun, then," Fink replied.

"No, I got shot gun," laughed the man who'd warned Luc just moments ago.

Cava stared at Fink venomously, who was walking over to him and Luc.

"Dude, I… I couldn't help you… I'm sorry," Fink said quietly.

Cava couldn't even make a fist. He swung his sore right hand from his left shoulder and spun Fink's head 180 degrees, putting him on his knees. His hand throbbed.

"Whoa there, whoa," Tic-Tax laughed. "Though, that was one hell of a pimp slap, Cavanaugh."

The shot gun concealing guy lifted his ski mask to his forehead and picked Fink up. Another memorable face, but Cava couldn't put his finger on it.

"Okay," Tic-Tax said assertively. "We all pile in with you, Fink. Luc, you and him can drive my car back to Ox. We'll ride with Crusher, and you guys can get yourselves back in my whip. I'd hurry, too. Never know who's gonna come looking for answers. Gangsters… cops…"

"Fuck that," Luc said. "We'd rather walk all the way back."

"Show him," Tic-Tax said to the previous front seat passenger, still masked.

He went to the backseat and pulled Fabienne out. The middle Kalou brother wore an expression of dishonour and guilt.

"What are you doing here?" Luc demanded.

"He helped us light the place up." Tic-Tax belly laughed. "Not a bad shot, either."

Luc was soul-slugged.

"I thought you might want to drive your brother home, but if you faggots are going to be difficult, he can ride with us. And if you don't bring my car back to the Ox, I'll either kill him or turn him into the cops or the Browns. Choice is yours." He got in the front seat and rolled down the window. "See you soon, boys."

* * *

The two friends watched as the car's rear lights faded into the thick darkness of the misty night.

"What," Cava began, slowly pronouncing each word, "the fuck, just happened? Luc?! What the fuck happened? Were you in on this?"

"Fuck no, man! This is my nightmare. This is the absolute worst case scenario. Brother, this is bad, real fucking bad. Like… I don't even have anything to compare it to!"

"Thanos?"

"What?"

The distant sound of police sirens could be heard mulching through the humid air. How distant or going in which direction, no one could tell.

"You gotta sober up, fast," Cava implored.

"I can't drive, yo." Luc put his hands to his temples. "I can't see straight. I hear this weird beeping… I think I have a concussion. It's gotta be you. My head is bumping."

The whirling ebb of sirens edged closer; like a tide at night, they didn't know how long they had, but were feeling the ocean lick their heels.

"Fine!" Cava crowed. They boys hopped into the car and immediately rolled down the windows.

"Ugh." Luc grimaced. "I've heard of liquid courage, but motherfuckers on meth? That smell is nasty. Buckle up."

"Which way?" Cava asked.

"Click your belt in, man."

"Fine. Which way?"

"Uh, left. No, right out of this spot, then left, then another left."

"Holy fuck, man. It's crazy with all this black ice. Feels like I'm driving in a hockey rink."

"Racist." Luc smiled.

"I don't know why you're smiling, bum bastard."

"Well, what else can I do? What else do you want me to do? Say I'm sorry? I'm a lot more than sorry. I know this is my fault. I know this may go down as one of the worst nights we've ever had. I know that we got tooken for a motherfucking ride and that we're nowhere near out the woods yet. So, what do you want me to do? Cry? Like a little bitch? That's out, man. I'm trying to keep it light."

Cava stayed silent, wiping the window in front of him to clear the condensation.

"You're mad, ain't you?"

"Man… it's been a shitty couple of weeks."

"You telling me, man… Been a shitty couple of months."

"You ever wonder if you're cursed?"

"Me? Nah, just a stroke of bad luck, is all. Maybe some bad decisions."

"Maybe it *is* Fury," Cava pondered. "Or, maybe it's just *you*."

"Me? Well, I did promise you a night you'd remember."

"Yeah, not a night I want to forget."

"What are you trying to say, Cavs?"

"I dunno man… Anj thought you were a bad influence. I get the feeling my folks get all worried whenever I'm with you. Maybe you've changed. Maybe we *are* just getting older, and our little misbehaviours are getting more and more serious. I dunno, man."

"I'm not the bad guy! I sampled it, wasn't for me! I'm trying to get myself out of the game. The trap. This was fucked up, and no one can take any blame except that Rat-Fink fuckboy and that shark-toothed, punk-ass bitch. I didn't want this. You think I wanted this? Nah, man. We're brothers, we're family, and we stick together. All we've ever had is us and our own."

"I had someone else. Very recently. Now, she's gone."

"You gonna blame me for your break up? You had months. We've had a lifetime."

Cava stopped talking. He needed to concentrate to straighten out the thousand, slick tire-shifts that were creeping up from the ground through the wheel. He placed his hands at 11 and 1, as Fink did. He remembered that he was drunk. Not like he could forget, but the reality of driving, underage, without a license, inebriated, was sneaking up on him like a fiend.

"You know those goons with Tax?" Cava asked.

"Yeah, some of them. Sketch was there... some booster and a stick-up kid. Guess he graduated. The kid with the shotty was one of the Delaneys, so my guess is the guy in the front was another Delaney. There was Fabi... I can't believe Fabi would do that."

"You can't believe?" Cava asked cynically.

"He's still my brother. He's still my *maman*'s son."

They continued to play over what'd happened, preserving the memories that they still had. The chill made them roll up the windows.

"I dunno who snuffed me. I took a stiff shot and then a couple kicks. I think one of Lil Bertie's uncles threw me to the side. I was in the dog ring, probably covered in blood. Then, I crawled my way out the door. Goddamn Flips just stared at me. I was laid up on a dog carcass." Luc shuddered.

"I had some ham-fisted 'roid monkey choking my lights out. Thought I was gonna die. Was ready for it. It would've been peaceful if it didn't hurt so fucking much."

"Then what?"

"I dunno... I grabbed his cheque hand, it was *only* the watch hand that was strangling me, and I pulled his fingers apart."

"How?"

"Like this," Cava told Luc to grab the wheel and showed him what he'd done.

"Ugh! Jesus fucking Christ! That's grisly! How'd you think to do that? How'd you have that in you?"

"Sink or swim, I guess." Cava shrugged. "Oh, fuck."

"What?"

"Then, Anjuli's cousin, Amajot, came through and saved me. Threw me outside."

"Anj's cousin is motherfucking Joti Singh."

"…yeah."

"Well, ain't that a kick in the head?"

Luc delicately massaged the soft spot where his pulsating headache seemed to be coming from.

* * *

The Bonneville chugged through the hazy backroads. Cava occasionally flicked on the high beams, but they only made the fog more oppressive.

"Thick as porridge," Cava said as he wiped the sweat trickling down his forehead. "Can't even turn down the de-frost, or it'll cloud back up again."

"Ugh," Luc groaned. "The heat and the road are making me dizzy… I could puke."

Luc rolled down his window; the air circulated and smacked the boys like a whip, waking them up from the dreariness.

"Better?"

"Kinda," Luc mumbled. "Can you go faster?"

"I don't think so. No. The street lines and shoulders seem to get narrow, then wider. Plus, it's slippery as hell."

"Mind if I spark a J? My head is swimming, and it might help."

"Nah, man. I need to concentrate. I catch a little contact and this bitch goes in a ditch."

"What about a dart?" Luc asked, removing his head from the freezing wind.

"Yeah… Can I have one? Might calm my nerves."

"Yeah, of course," Luc responded, removing a couple of cigarettes from his pocket. "Oh, shit…"

"What?!"

"Ah, nothing… Just dropped my fire. Maybe it fell under the seat. These old cars, the seats are starving for lighters and pocket change."

Luc dangled himself over the hump and started feeling around for his lighter. He became mildly concerned about pricking his hands on stray needles, or whatever foreign matter might be living under the seat, and he voiced his concern.

"Man," Cava said. "I kind of get why Fink was driving like a grandma. Cliff always told me, if you drive drunk, connect your thumbs at the top of the wheel and make sure they stay straight. The shit is really working, but I want to make 'pew-pew' noises, like I'm shooting aliens."

The tires buckled, and the car shifted diagonally. Luc was thrown onto his head, his legs squirming in the air like tendrils. Cava steered with his whole body to try and correct the car, going from one harsh drift to another.

"You okay?"

"Ow. That'd a been dope if I wasn't already close to puking." Luc burped and choked back vomit. "Got the... what the fuck?"

"What? What is it?"

Luc climbed back into his seat and fastened his belt. He was holding a pistol in his hands.

"Woah," Cava exclaimed. "Careful, brother. Do you know how to check if it's on? Like if there are bullets? If the safety is on?"

"Not really," Luc said while rotating the gun, handling it like an unknown artefact. "There's a button on the side. I would've thought they'd a emptied all their..."

Bang.

The sound of the gun blast in the car couldn't be done justice by any onomatopoeia. It was a full body sensation that started in the ears, quickly incapacitating them. A seismic shock carved through the entire vehicle, deadening each sense in a series of corporal paralyses. A bullet tore through the roof as Luc and Cava were blanked out.

Cava struggled to breath. He rubbed his eyes. He gasped upon opening them and saw perfect white. He blinked, saw absolute gray and snatched the wheel, pulling himself abreast to the column. He inadvertently chirped the brakes and the car began to fishtail. He let off. The soft shoulder rumbled beneath the tires on his left side. He squinted, trundling his jaw and purposefully hyperventilating. He then pulled the car back onto the road.

After blasting the orphan round left in the pistol, the gun had fallen from Luc's lap. He quickly ducked his head in between his knees and pressed his palms against his ears, screaming. He couldn't even hear the abdomen-tensing shriek that was erupting from his diaphragm. A searing pain, an equator-long line cut with a scalpel, forced a deformed expression on to his face. He couldn't feel the side-to-side swishing of the car.

Cava still couldn't hear his gulps of air, but felt incrementally refreshed. His jaw hinged up and down, and his chest heaved as his lungs swelled greedily. The pain in his hands wasn't recognizable.

The road and its conditions were still no friendlier. Every time Cava seemed to even think of feathering the brakes, the Bonneville's shaky axles buckled, and the bald tires caught edges like a speedboat.

Cava tried to say something to Luc, but not a word could be heard. A continuous *beep*, not just a ringing in the ears, but a fire-alarm from the jaw to the sinuses, obfuscated any sound. Luc tried to say "what?" but only heard a dull phonetic sound somewhere near his head.

Luc noticed Cava clutching the wheel; his knuckles looked inhumanly knobby and violet. He seemed to be yelling, but the *beeping* was aggressive. Luc felt that the traction was becoming fully liberated. He gripped his lighter and the handle above the door. His breath was staccato.

The beeping subsided slightly, the clouds around his eyes dissipated. He saw the dread-scored expression cleaved into Cava's moist eyes.

"…hold on…" Luc was able to make clear.

He saw Cava fighting the wheel like a whaling captain. Momentary flashes of determination deliquesced into something beyond panic: the red seal of one of a million unresolvable, injurious destinies.

The car hit something. It may have been a tree stump, a pot-hole, or debris from one of the Fury residents dumping their discarded junk in the flats. They began to spin.

Cava's auditory buzzing quieted. "Fuck! Sorry, that was loud."

The Bonneville tweaked at something—ice or a bump in the road. It leapt from flat land and began to fly.

Weightlessness. The boys felt as though their belts kept them from outpacing the arc of the car towards the sky. It felt like a divine hand had snubbed physical laws, deciding that the two friends should be whisked away from the carnage.

The car began to spin upside down. Cava felt his hands become one entity with the steering wheel. He looked at Luc. His Jesus-piece had slipped out of his shirt and was dangling towards the roof; the crucifix hanging magically in mid-air. "Are we dead?" he asked.

"I think…"

The swallowing calm had regurgitated them. A constellation of choppy images flooded in, overloading their senses. The kaleidoscopic visuals were a blender of tenebrous ambiguity; only different shades of gray and black. The sounds of crinkling, crunching, and various scraping textures were devolving towards chaos. Dirt, grass, tree, metal, body, bone; the ears could only feel movement at this point. Then, the movement stopped.

* * *

Cava opened his eyes, blurry and disconnected with the darkness around him. The sound of the blinker clicked his mind into action; its metronomic pace guiding him back to the world. He glanced dazedly at Luc, his cross hanging between his lips and nose. Each hinge of his branches was slack, his lifeless wrists were curled in against the roof, the lighter in between them.

Cava tried to rouse Luc, saying his name and shaking him. Anxiety, the kind that feels like an elevator free-falling down a shaft, set in. He wagged Luc's flimsy arm, lifting it and watching it fall flaccidly against the roof.

"Fuck."

Cava unbuckled himself and fell onto his head and arms, crawling to unlatch Luc. *Careful*, he thought, not wanting to deal more damage to Luc's battered dome.

The driver's side window had been blown out during the impact. The frame was dented and warped, but enough room remained for Cava to worm his way out. He stood up quickly, nearly falling backwards, securing the fender and allowing himself some big breaths to conquer the stars in his eyes.

Scurrying around the other side, he made physical contact with Luc's neck, checking his pulse. It was beating, whether too fast or too slow, Cava had no idea, but the diminutive bulging of the vein gave Cava hope. He submersed himself in the car and clicked the belt button, dropping the full weight of Luc onto his back. He released himself, making sure that he did as little injury as possible to his friend's neck and head, before carefully freeing Luc, inch by inch.

The black mists above and damp, frigid soil below weren't even picked up by his sensors. Cava was semi-familiar with CPR—something about pumping the chest, pinching the nose, and breathing into the mouth. Beyond such basic knowledge, he knew little of the steps. He wanted to cry for help, but who would hear him?

Luc grunted and wiggled his fingers.

"Hey, whoa. Are you okay? No. Wait. Don't move. Can you move your toes? Your hands? Feet? Legs? How many fingers am I holding up?"

Lying on the cold-pressed soil, Luc groaned and slowly heeded Cava's instructions, taking a valuation of his limbs.

"Yes, yes, yes, yes, uh three?" Luc whispered with half-closed eyes.

Luc reached for Cava's shoulders and pulled himself up. Cava braced his hand against the ground, now feeling the topmost layer of frost, and steadied Luc to a seated position.

"How you feel?" Cava asked.

"Well…" Luc began. "My head ain't doing any better. I feel… okay, actually. Maybe not in the morning, but… okay."

Cava stood up. "Yeah," he said with surprise. "Me too. Legs are a little stiff, kind of dizzy, but I don't seem to have anything poking out of me."

He offered Luc a hand. "Careful. Take it slowly."

"Argh, my mitts," Cava yelped as Luc pulled himself up.

Luc stood up and immediately vomited.

"Fuck me," he said. "I been holding that back for a minute, now." He vomited another little splash, steam rising from the pile.

The friends slowly followed the path of destruction back to the lightless road. They both sighed with defeat.

"Now what?" Cava disdained.

"I guess… we're hoofing it."

They lifted and dropped their feet twice. Cava stopped.

"Why the fuck did you let off that gun?"

"Yo!" Luc used a sizeable amount of energy to respond. "I didn't mean to... You hit a pothole and the trigger must've been sensitive." He winced and put his hand to his forehead.

Cava scoffed. "This is what I was talking about. You know what I could be doing right now? I could be cuddling up, having an after-sex mint in my window, watching Anj's fine ass walk to her car, about to lay my head on my nice warm pillow. Nah... I'm in the motherfucking flats, beat the fuck up, probably have some very dangerous people at least somewhat interested in my whereabouts, walking however many miles down this freezing, haunted-ass road full of fucking inbreds."

Luc struggled to follow Cava's words. "Look, my head is bumping... like, worse than before. Are you still blaming me? Like, you can't get over yourself for a split second, and admit that you made the choice to come, too?"

"Okay, sure... I chose to come. I chose to follow you, again, to try something that I knew was a bad idea, again, to almost be sure to end up in some kind of trouble, or injury. Again."

"Don't be a pussy. Can't you just be happy that we made it out in one piece? That we get to live another day?"

"That ain't doing it for me this time, man... I think I'm done."

"Done, huh? Like, that's it?"

"Me and you? Yeah, I'd say this fuckery about does it."

"Well, once we get back then, that's it then."

"Good."

Cava began to walk two paces ahead of Luc, flipping his hood up and rolling his hands into his sleeves. He felt the cold, now. He blew hot breaths into his sleeves and buried them in his jacket. His hands and arms were already stiffening, worse than before.

"Wait. You hear that?"

Cava shook his head. They stopped for a second. A slight rumbling could be heard with fair effort.

"Oh shit," Cava said meekly.

Luc turned and saw the circular glow of red strobe lights in the distance.

"In here," Cava said, grabbing the slow-witted Luc and hiding in the bushes, just off the road.

* * *

"Yup, right here. You can see the skid marks where they lost control, the dirt off the shoulder where they spun out, the punched-down grass…" a young cop said, on one knee, his flashlight tracing his observations.

"I fucking hate this area," an older cop said. "Goddamn lawless wild west. Poorer than Africa, these people."

The cops disappeared from the boys' view for a moment. They looked at each other, shushing back and forth spitefully.

The young cop tapped his nametag with the flashlight. "Either they evaporated at the time of impact… or they made away on foot. Everything still feels warm; the lights were still on. Found a Magnum in there. One bullet in the chamber."

"Thieves pulling a heist?" the older cop asked. "Or, maybe some dumb fucking kids tobogganing… and lost control."

"Well, they couldn't have gotten…"

Beep Beep.

Luc's face flexed with intense fear. The pager in his breast pocket was rumbling and tweeting. He and Cava froze.

The officers pulled their guns and pointed their flashlights at either side of the crouching boys. Drawing the lights towards the poorly hidden duo, Luc pushed Cava backwards. Cava tumbled over a lowly felled log, and Luc sprang up, hands in the air, to walk towards the expectant officers squinting at their spotlights.

"Keep 'em there. Turn around, and get on your knees." The young cop quickly cuffed Luc and dragged him to his feet. "You have ID, son?"

"No, no need." The older cop approached with his gun aimed at Luc's head. "I know this piece of shit."

"Fuck." Luc saw the older cop take shape as he entered visible light. Collins. *Fuck.*

"Luc wit da C," Collins smiled. "What a lovely surprise. And me, off my regular beat. Would you look at that? All the way out here."

Cava lifted himself to see the action. The younger cop lowered his pistol. Collins marched towards Luc with his gun still pointed between the eyes.

"Officer," Luc said, as Collins snapped the cuffs onto his wrists.

"You been joyriding, you black son of a bitch?"

"No, sir. Got stranded at a house party and was walking home."

"By yourself? Awful long way back to the dregs, you monkey."

"Collins," the younger cop said with some force. "We should take him in for questioning."

"Look here, rookie. This is what we call a gift from God. A lone, miserable piece of shit, out in the middle of the flatlands, with no one around, late at night, clearly in violation of several laws, with a gun."

"We don't know if the gun is his," the young cop said. "Actually, we don't even know if he was driving, if it's just him…"

"Rookie. Listen. You wanna save the world, it don't start with taking every two-bit fuck into custody. Sometimes, to make Fury a better city for the mothers and the kiddies, you have to… I used to be like you. I had a veteran show me the way."

"Collins! This isn't how it should work."

"But it does." Collins clicked the gun, looked Luc in the eyes, and shook his head. "Take his cuffs off, so it looks like he tried to shoot at us. We can plant the Mag."

The rookie cop withdrew the handcuff keys, reflexively. He stopped as they jangled at his side.

"What are you waiting for? Whatever, I'll just radio Mitchell and Barnes for shovels and lime."

"No!" Cava ran out, tripping over the log, but pulling his body towards the fray with his fingers. He stepped in front of Luc and looked at the cops, heart racing. "I'm a witness," Cava said meekly.

"You're just another body," Collins hissed.

"This is Officer Murdoch. We have a black male suspect in custody for drunkenness, possible reckless driving and weapon possession." The rookie cop, Murdoch, was speaking into his walkie-talkie and receiving confirmation from the female voice on the other end. "Officer Collins and I have the suspect in handcuffs and will bring him back to the station. Requesting holding cell upon arrival. Out."

"Fucking asshole." Collins pointed his gun at Murdoch, then suddenly turned and lashed Cava across the face. Cava fell to the ground.

Collins kicked him in the ribs before the still-cuffed Luc threw his body onto his friend's.

"Well, isn't that cute?" Collins picked Luc up by the collar and moved him to the cruiser, slamming his unprotected head onto the windshield. "You lucky little monkey."

"What are you doing here?" Murdoch asked Cava.

"My boyfriend and I... We were heading home from a party. The people there found out about us, and they started to hit us. It was awful. We were walking, and they chased us. Tried to hit us with their car. We dove out of the way, and they crashed. They... they ran through the forest, and we kept going. We heard another car, so we hid for a second. Please don't tell my dad. He's Irish and told me he'd disown me if he found out."

"Hmm. Well, we have to take your... boyfriend... into custody."

"You little fucking liar." Collins gripped Cava by his throat. "You tell him the truth!"

"Not... the... neck..." Cava gasped.

"Hey!" Luc cried, pulling himself from the hood. "Watch his..."

Collins' fist cut across Luc's face. Cava knelt down, gasping, and picked his head up. "What have you done?"

"Collins! What are you thinking? You've tainted the investigation! Now, this is a hate crime on you!"

"Fuck you, rook... They begged me to get you right. You're weak. Load the unconscious queer into the car."

"And the boyfriend?"

"This one can walk back to the city. You told them we had one black male in custody, not two queers."

* * *

Cava watched the cruiser instantly outrun his wobbly legs. He rubbed his throat and coughed a dry, splintered hack. "They just left the car?"

He got several paces before turning around and returning to the overturned vehicle. He collected the gun, the lighter, and the pack of cigarettes. *I'll dump this someplace where no one can get it.*

As he walked, painfully smoking a cigarette, he sighed. And sighed.

He passed dark, shuttered houses, and he sighed. He felt the soreness in his limbs and a line of bruise where the seatbelt had saved his life.

He couldn't decide if he was angry with Luc, or disappointed, or neutral. He'd used the fumes of liquor in his gut to mount a fit, denouncing his lifelong friend, dismissing him as a piece of shit and a bad influence. Did he deserve a lesson? Was it even a lesson that he should have to learn, again?

With little else than the rustling sounds of nature at night, Cava heard his footsteps go from an ungainly clop to a slow, rasping drag. He heard each laboured breath and felt his intoxication continue to leave him. Crossing a bridge that lifted his path over the river, Cava thought it a fitting place to drop the gun. The infinite murk wasted no time in gobbling the heavy pistol up; only a subtle splashing noise sounded before it was gulped up by the waters.

Cava made out sirens ripping through the tranquility of the night ahead of him. Cava stepped onto the shoulder, separating himself and the street with a thin blanket of vegetation. Two cruisers whizzed by, their wails peaking deafeningly, before fading behind him.

Glad I dumped that piece, Cava thought. It was the first stable thought he could remember having since trying to pry Luc from the wreck. He had no idea what the time was. It felt late, or early. The desolate atmosphere told him that the sun was still fast asleep. He remembered bending this corner on the way in. At least he was going the right direction.

Everything was pewter. Something between a liquid and a dust. The grass, the trees, the shanties, everything was die cast. As he approached the sparsely planted streetlights, their glow was anemic, a pale silver hue instead of the orange tinge that gave you four shadows. The entire perspective that Cava beheld was akin to a film, silent era. A 35 millimeter, where the slides scroll slowly, making the actors' movements seem jittery and spastic. An ashen quality, like the vista that seemed covered in dried, crumbled dragonfly wings.

Cava buried his head and kept walking. The mist and fog began to break as he felt the road steepen to a slight, perpetual grade. It wasn't warm, but he felt sweat release itself from every pore beneath his layers. The pewter ambience and ancient cinematography defrosted beneath the radiance of tangerine lighting. He saw two crackheads sleeping and one rocking back and forth in a cross-legged position, beneath a rickety garbage-bag shelter, supported atop a thicket. He saw the pervading light of the Fury middle finger welcoming his return.

SUPPER

"QUINN, I'VE BEEN stomping on your head for over an hour. Get up! You have to help clean," Nora's shrill voice made Cava's eyes close harder. "And close the damned window. We're not trying to heat the whole block!"

Cava turned with painstaking effort to position himself in view of his alarm clock. It wasn't late, though by no means early, and he wondered why he could never secure himself a good sleep in after such implausibly rough nights. How would he grow?

His mother's heel shook the lightbulbs on his ceiling. It was freezing. Why on earth was his window open? He moved to close it, feeling his whole body ache. He saw one shoe still outside, cold, atop the barren soil in front of his window. The other was on his bed. Sitting in his boxers, he looked at the brown strip of bruising that streaked down his torso. His hands were stiff, and he was barely able to rotate his wrists. His forearms were like battered plantains. His legs looked fine, but felt like he'd just finished the first practice of the season after a long layoff. He fingered his neck like he'd escaped the gallows just in time—the noose had left its lipstick stain.

Luc. What happened to him? Was he okay?

His mother shook the floorboards above him, once again. First things first.

Carefully hiding his war wounds, he was reminded of the annual dinner with the Doktors on Christmas Eve. The families had had a little dinner and drink with each other for as long as Cava could remember. The time had flown. Cava had done his Christmas shopping with Anj leading up to the time of their break up. He had something for every member of his family, and he and his friends rarely exchanged gifts of monetary value. He also had a few things for Anj: a necklace, a pair of high socks, a comic book, a hoodie. Just thinking about them made him remorseful.

Another bang.

With his wounds covered, Cava emerged to the playfully derisive taunts of his parents. He had a coffee and smoke and was given a list of chores. He chose to go to the store first, giving him the chance to sneak out and check on Luc. He pocketed the shopping list and bee-lined for Luc's house.

He knocked: nothing. He rang the doorbell: also, nothing.

He was concerned. He could try his pager when he returned home, but it offered no certain update on his status. This also meant that his mother was away. Collecting him from the station? The hospital? The meat locker?

* * *

Returning with a trunk's worth of brown paper bags, an obscene amount to hand-bomb the couple blocks, Cava returned to Luc's stoop again. He banged on the door and hammered on the bell: still, nothing.

He saw Sally in her window. They exchanged greetings and were both happy to be seeing each other later. She wore a big smile and a towel wrapped around her head; her big eyes beamed like searchlights.

Cava returned and set to doing the minor chores that remained:

sweeping, dusting, and giving an extra polish to the guest china. He was in a daze, reliving the night before in his head.

"Quinn!" his mother shouted. "What's wrong with you? Are you on something? Clean yourself up! Company will be here soon!"

Cava nodded, apologized, and assured his mother that he was straight, just tired. He explained that he'd been held up the night before and had had to walk home from Vincennes.

"You know you can call us for a ride if you're ever in trouble," both parents chimed in.

"I'll remember that."

He got a good look at himself in the mirror. His face was near pristine: he had a bump on his head, but nothing major, and covered by his moss. His body was another story. He was various hues of black, brown, blue, purple, and red from his neck to his hips. The strangling, the belt marks, the punching, the accident, all had given his shell an abundance of welts and dents. "Like Tony Stark's armour," he mused to himself. He tested some movement: achy, but still pliable. If the bruising stuck around for awhile, he'd get checked, but for now, he considered himself fortunate. What of Luc? How many lives did he and his other cat have remaining? If this were a video game, how many men did he have left?

* * *

The Doktor family arrived as Cava finished trying on his Easter gear, pulling up the lapels on his shirt to mask the discolouration on his neck. He hoped that he could get through the meal without anyone noticing.

They entered and Cava took view of Sally; her long, straight, dark hair with highlights was fastened with a cute bow and she wore an equally charming dress. Removing her jacket, Cava fixated on her long, smooth legs and arms.

The families greeted each other and the fathers set to drinking beers. The beers would be followed by wine, and then, "Whatever you have in the pantry, Joe." The mothers set to the kitchen, and Henry, with his confirmation suit and hair gelled like a young Brando, asked if the older Doktor sister would be coming.

"No, Henry," Sally replied. "She has plans with her fiancé."

"Drats," Henry said, running his hand through his slick part.

"Quinny!" Ivan shouted. "You been with a lady? Look at all those hickeys!"

Both families began to ridicule Cava, who deflected the insults and questions.

"You're back with Anj! I knew it. Who could stay mad at that face?" Nora said.

"Nah, just... you know, some girl at a party," Cava laughed nervously, scratching the back of his head.

Sally was looking at Cava with a wretched stare, almost vengeful. He looked back at her with alarm.

"Well, gotta get back on the horse somehow," Joe remarked.

Ivan laughed. Nora scoffed and commented that she didn't want to hear it. Danuta simply whisked a bowl containing the ingredients of what would later be gravy.

"Sally, no..." Cava touched her arm, confused as to why he was about to explain himself with such anxiety. "It was *not* a random girl."

"So you *did* get back together with Anj," she said, forlorn.

"No." Cava looked around and suggested that they move to his room. The story was a doozy.

* * *

"Are you serious? So much of that is wrong... Did you two really think that dog fights were something different than what it was?"

"I had no idea. Luc was pretty convinced that it was a... lighter-hearted affair."

"Oh my god, Luc!" Sally put her hand to her mouth. "So you haven't seen him since—"

"Since he was decked by that racist-ass cop and poured into the back of the wagon, no... I called on him twice, but no one was home. Not even his mom."

Sally took her time to process the information.

"I don't know if I can even be friends with him. It just keeps getting worse. It just keeps getting more serious. I know it wasn't on purpose, but... come on."

Sally pulled Cava's collar down and saw the bruising. She noticed more and opened his shirt. "Oh my god. You should go to the clinic."

"It only seems skin deep, and the muscles and joints are just sore. No breaks. No deep wounds. I'll wait it out."

"Well, I know you're probably mad, but give it a bit of time. Maybe you shouldn't throw away a lifetime of friendship. Maybe just refrain from following him on his journeys."

"It could've been far worse if I hadn't been there. I need to watch out for him."

"You say that, but you always seem to get the worst of it. What happens when you're not there once, or twice? He's a big boy. He can take care of himself. You need to do the same. Just, do me a favour. Don't throw the baby out with the pram. You love him, and he loves you."

Cava remembered telling the officers that him and Luc were lovers. "What's a pram?"

Sally was feeling Cava's tender skin. She laughed at the question. He added the part of the story about their 'relationship.' She laughed again.

"Well...uh... what's your assessment, Doctor Doktor?"

The door opened, and Henry entered. He let out a noise and tilted his head down. "Damn, brother... Dinner time, guys."

* * *

After a dinner of lamb and potatoes and a dessert of apple strudel, the young ones always cleaned the dishes as the parents savored shortbread and hot black coffee. The mothers waited for their husbands to retreat to the garage and start playing their twangy, howling folk music.

Sally and Cava returned to his room and relaxed on the bed while Henry got his video game fix. They spoke lightly about nothing in particular.

A familiar rhythm tapped against the window.

"You guys done dinner? Any left?" Luc asked.

"You can help yourself. It's all packed in the fridge."

Luc tossed his shoes into the room, exposing a plastic hospital bracelet.

"Lil Cava, my boy, you near a save spot?" Luc patted the immersed younger brother on the shoulder. "Got some big boy stuff I gotta ask your brother."

Henry cussed and saved his game. "Never get more than a damned area before you guys kick me out."

"Listen, Cava. I'm really, really, *really* sorry about dragging you into that fucked up situation last night. Like, that was fucked up, even for me. Mad fucked. I know we left things a little heated, at least that's most of what I remember before that bitch-ass cop snuffed me. Man, I was out. But, I'm genuinely angry at myself for putting my main man, my truest brother, in that fucked up situation. I dunno if you told Sal yet, but it was a motherfucking episode, man. I didn't think any of it would go down like that, like anywhere near that type of way. I'm sorry, brother."

Cava felt his anger dissolve and a stupid smirk grow at the sides of his mouth. "You fucking loveable little mutt."

"So, you told her?" Luc asked, surprised.

"Most of what I could remember. I'm tired as fuck. That was a long walk back. What happened to you?"

"Well, it's pretty hazy, man. I remember leaving, after all the gunfire…"

"Gunfire?!" Sally shrieked quietly.

"Ah, I left anything to do with guns out. Salomea, when I said fight, I meant gun fight."

Sally's big eyes grew even larger, and she listened intently to Luc's retelling of the story.

"Then, it was black for a while. I remember waking up for a split and hearing *maman* just giving it to some pigs. I dunno where I was, but I remember her just cursing the pants off all that bacon. That was like, gray; then black again. It was black until I woke up in a hospital bed with an IV and this cool bracelet. You like? I was thinking about making them for sale. Remember how dog tags were cool?"

"I called on you a couple times today," Cava said, concerned.

"Oh yeah," Luc said airily. "I woke up some time in the after-noon. *Maman* was still there. They had to get some fresh oinks to get my statement."

"What'd you say?" Cava leaned in.

"I said fucking nothing." Luc smiled. "I said that I remembered getting a fist to the head from a cop, must be where this—he pointed to a big bubble on his head— came from." But, the rest, I said I had no idea. Just that I came from a house party, a fight happened, and I walked home. They didn't even mention you. Or us, being dick jockeys."

Luc laughed. Sally smiled nervously and looked at both friends. Cava nodded with an expression that contained both relief and gravity.

"I gave them my statement. When they mentioned a gun, I just said 'what gun?' It actually took me a while to remember that we found one in the whip. I'm sorry about bucking that thing. I totally have no clue how it went off. What *did* you do with it?"

"I sleeved it, then tossed it over a bridge. The water seemed deep and dark, so I hucked it in and kept walking."

"My man." Luc smirked.

Sally sat with her hands on her little knees. It was hard to tell whether she was repulsed or merely stunned. Her face went blank. She squinted, and her eyes went up into her forehead. Thinking, seemingly.

"You're quiet." Cava finally patted her hand.

"Yeah," she said, slowly. "You know... they, the police, I mean, are probably going to watch you, Luc, and by association, you, Quinn, like hawks. If you know the cop, Luc, then I'm sure he has a vendetta, or at least a bone to pick, with you. You may want to... turn a... go legit. I think... I think that maybe this is the sign that you should play it extra safe. So, you, or anyone you care about, doesn't get implicated and picked up for anything, and put through the system with prejudice."

"My girl," Luc smiled. "Way ahead of you, Sal." Luc took a bag of weed out of his pocket. "It's just this stuff now, and not even selling it. I'm done. I'm retiring my beeper and focusing on getting out of school. *Maman* said that JJ's coming home on the third, and I couldn't be more pumped. He'll be *pissed*. No doubt he's heard of all this shit that's happened to me, and that base-head brother of ours. I could actually use a good, old-fashioned beat-down from Janjak, just to put me back in line, like the old days. But, mark my words, I'm done with that gangster, hustling shit. I'm too pretty. Starting in '98, me done."

Sally smiled. "Our little man is growing up." She tickled at Cava's arm lightly. "We're such good parents."

Cava was lost in his own mind. It was 1998, nearly the year 2000. Crazy. Flying cars and shit should be unveiled by the Japanese and German companies soon, with the Yanks sure to release their lesser-quality, more affordable model after.

"What you guys doing for New Year's Eve?" Luc asked, looking for snips and papers in Cava's nightstand. He shuffled a box of rubbers and smiled at Cava.

"I hate New Year's Eve," Cava said, snapping himself from his thoughts, shaking his head at Luc's unspoken, suggestive rattle of the box.

"No plans," Sally said.

"Well... Uncle Cliff's gonna have a baby rager. Nothing too crazy, just the people he likes, but it's doubling as a going away party. He told me that he leaves on the second, right before big brother comes home. Kind of... what's that word, ironic?"

"I don't think—" Sally started.

"What about Tic-Tax's car?" Cava asked. "Won't he be pissed that we mangled his ride? Left it to be found by the pigs?"

"Well, it was him that paged me when we were hiding, asking me where the fuck I was... When I got out, I met up with him before coming here."

"What'd he have to say?"

"He was okay. I tried to spin the situation in my favour, said that the Bonnie was getting too many looks. Since it was insured under his grandma's name, he had Rosee fake her voice and report it stolen."

"So..."

"So, I didn't mention that he left a bammer in the back seat, and it's whatever. I told him that I didn't rat him out, even after such a cocksucker's move... blasting up a goddamn den of goons."

"So, he's chill?"

"Cats like that..." Luc sucked his teeth, "...they never chill. But, I got a pretty strong feeling that he's gonna have way bigger problems, and probably pretty quick."

Everyone in the room nodded.

"Luc," Sally said with a mild strain of confusion visible on her forehead, "how do you know what's been going on when you've been in the hospital?"

"What can I say? I'm Luc wit da C. Things just have a way of finding me."

"For real, though," Cava added. "In another world, you'd make a dope-ass Batman."

GOODBYE, '97

IT WAS ALWAYS difficult to read Marek Kosh's mind. Unlike the fraternal bond that'd made Luc and Cava brethren with pseudo-telepathic interconnectedness, Marek, who'd known them just as long, was always something of an outsider. They knew his baseline interests of graffiti and rap, but little else that spoke to any goals or passions.

He always played the wall and made himself an afterthought.

The boys were rarely privy to his home life. They knew he was the only sapling of two Ukrainian immigrants, who even in spite of their poor English, seemed like a shady pair of parsimonious and dour people to everyone else. The scarce instances when he'd invited his friends into his house—always tidy and ensconced with crocheted doilies and framed cross-stitched banality—were always met with his mother trying to offer the kids *khrustyky* or the father staring at them contemptuously. Marek always answered his parents with brief Balto-Slavic phrases before cursing at them in English. Whether this was meant to impress his buddies or to genuinely demean his progenitors was a valid subject for debate.

After a few years of inviting the family to Ox-based gatherings and open houses, the other parents lost any shred of desire to include the Kosh clan. As the kids got older, the parents of the local kids looked at Marek with derision and mistrust. He rarely smiled, almost never said "please" or "thank you," and had a haughty disposition. Ivan called him 'Devil's Hoof,' Apollonia was certain that he was a sociopath, and Joe and Nora simply ignored him, as if he would likely just disappear one day.

Marek wasn't a dolt. He was spoiled and not to be trusted, but not an idiot by any means. Marek marked well with little effort and flew so far beneath the radar that teachers left him alone, thinking that this was the kid that might set their car on fire in the back of their minds. He grew up with both parents telling him stories of how they were able to immigrate; how many necks they stepped on, how few people one could trust, and that once one compromised their soul, there was no point trying to retrieve it. His father spoke of his successful arrival with the pomp and grandiosity of one who'd fallen asleep to the reading of their own legend, an attribute that the son and his proclivity for imperious-ness drank like amrita.

Unlike Luc or Cava, Marek reveled in solitude. He rarely felt the need to chill with 'associates'—the word he often used in place of friends. He held himself with the same air of outward contempt as his father: *These* people were beneath him and should rightly owe him for the luxury of his association. His spare time was mainly spent crafting stickers, working on ideas in his sketchbook, and bathing in a skull full of antipathy that he never questioned.

After the shootout, at which he'd felt greatly duped as *underboss* by his only superordinate, he felt that he should try, though minimally, to make amends with his old associates; to bury the hatchet, sensing that Luc and Cava were probably a little angry about what'd taken place.

"You goddamn right I'm mad, motherfucker. I'm mad as hell. You set us up!" Luc was trying to hold back from screaming at Fink, seeing a young mother pushing a baby and tugging another by the hand on the path near the Bench. Dart in her mouth.

"Look," Fink said with his hands out. "That bitch *still* didn't give me any ammo, man… You think that I would've gone into a battle *and* stayed inside, for a barrage of bullets?"

Luc scoffed. He looked at Cava, who wore a glower supported by crossed arms. "Then, why would you feel the need to bring 'em out? You think he was just gonna walk in with a nice Sunday shirt and sell Bibles?"

"Yeah," Cava broke his silence. "None of it makes sense."

"What he told me was that he just wanted to know where that place was, to see if it was a stronghold, if they had anything he could vick— you know, just recon." He shuffled his feet. "If I would've known that he was planning an assault, honestly, do you think I would've been there? Without a single fucking shell?"

Luc and Cava maintained eye contact for an extended period of time, silently working out his level of honesty. Fink watched them. He knew this game.

"You're a pussy," Cava finally pointed at Fink. "You were gonna let me get the ghost choked out of me, and you just stayed there."

"No bullets! Remember?"

"Still, you were nowhere to be seen when the ski mask dudes were caught, and then you disappeared when the shooting started."

"Well," Fink crossed his arms, "I'm not gonna apologize that you guys got so starched that your common sense was thrown out the window. A blind mouse could see that shit was about to go down."

"I'll give him that," Luc said.

"Besides, I woke you guys up and got you out of there."

"Barely," Cava added.

"What happened to you guys anyways?" Fink sought to change the subject.

"Ah man, I'm tired of telling it," Cava groaned.

"Yeah, it's sorted," Luc piped in.

Fink nodded and pushed his hands into his hoodie pocket.

"So, what's with you and Tax now?" Luc asked.

"Ain't no real *us*, to be honest. At least, not anymore." Fink scratched his chin. "I make money, I get dipped, but if he's gonna be going all cowboy on everyone's ass, I'm not about that. I been avoiding him… He's coming unglued a little. Too much sniffing, maybe. Like, everybody

is out to get him, now. Maybe that's true, and if it is, I ain't hanging around."

"Rats flee the sinking ship first," Cava said, bitterly.

"Actually, Luc bounced first. Anyways, I apologize for the night. I'll
take half the blame."

Luc gave Cava a puppylike look that wordlessly suggested that half
was more than nothing, and that he normally imparted zero blame
on himself.

Cava sighed, frustrated. "Man… just don't fuck us."

"Affirmative. Well, it's been a slice, boys, but I gotta mosey."

"You coming to Cliff's party?" Luc asked.

"What party?"

Luc filled Fink in on the plan for the year's end. It would be a farewell to their friend, a tight-knit social event.

"Maybe I'll make an appearance," Fink said coolly. "Catch y'all later."

Once he left their sight, Cava turned to Luc. "Why you always go
easy on him? I thought you hated that fucking rat."

Nah, Luc thought. "Well, sometimes… I kind of *pity* him. He's just
so… angry. So alone. Don't you ever sit back and think that we're all
he's got?"

"Nope. I usually think 'Fuck that guy, why do we give him chances?'
Dog, we nicknamed him Rat-Fink for a reason, and it ain't because he's
a stand-up guy. It's because time and time again he acts like a coward, a
pussy, a liar, or just an overall piece of shit. I bet he waited for us to get
nice and baked before coming out to test the water."

"Well it worked, didn't it?"

"You just have so much mercy, Luc wit da C. A regular Saint
Jane Francis."

"Who?"

"From Catechism? Saint of Forgiveness?"

"Nope, nothing."

"No matter. Better off keeping an eye on him. He's gotta earn any
trust from this point on. Friends close, type thing."

"You're worrying about nothing, Cavs. *He ain't a crook, son, just a shook one.* What you should be worrying about is who you gonna kiss at midnight."

Cava shook his head while fighting a smirk.

* * *

Dresses piled up on Sally's bed the same way that Danuta was carefully laying latke after latke on a serving dish a floor beneath her in the kitchen. Given the gift of an entire day, without studying or sports pressing her with a sharpened spade, the teenage girl had time to guise herself in a variety of costumes, makeup, and jewelry. She clothed herself, deciding on a colour palette and assortment of trinkets, only to strip down to her undergarments and take a warm, wet towel soaking in a metal bowl to gently remove the cosmetics.

With each revitalization, she found a different hair follicle or dry spot on her long arms and legs to remedy. The entire process was causing trembles of anxiety that were spreading from a pit in her stomach.

"This is so stupid," she said out loud, blowing a ribbon of hair that'd spilt from her bun from her face. "I'm just going to an apartment in the centre. It's not a *formal* affair."

She turned her lips and bent her head, making a self-mocking kissy-face, then scoffed. She grabbed her right buttock and maneuvered her body inward around the saucy, heroine fulcrum pose in which she'd been inspecting herself. She was wearing a matching white bra and high-waisted panty set. She pulled the waistband forward, took a quick look and let it snap against her hips.

Sally groaned.

* * *

After scraping the bones from stewed chicken thighs into the garbage, Luc excused himself from the kitchen, pecking his mother on the cheek and thanking her for another delicious meal. Food tasted better since his *maman* had returned, and Luc knew that it'd taste even better with the complementing conversation that Janjak would soon provide at the supper table.

The mother and son spoke eagerly of the return of the oldest Kalou brother, each relinquishing the opportunity to discuss the other missing seat at the round table. Luc thought, during the wordless moments of chewing, that it'd *still* be nice to have all three of them around the little table. The brother that eventually rose first for another spoonful of peas or lentils would become the errand-runner for whosever empty cup or plate had the patience for the other to stand up. Same with taking the garbage out or leaving to buy a pack of darts.

He knew that his mother thought so, too, no matter what hellish tortures Fabienne had put his family through: the lying, the stealing, the drugging, and the condemnation of their residence. Luc was his mother's son; they were merciful beyond rationality. For how many times Luc had fucked up, which by his count was in the millions, his mother had always loved him, forgiven him, and held no grievance. He viewed himself as no more special than his siblings in any way. While they were certain of JJ's innocence, even if he were verily culpable, even if it'd been a worse crime, they were family. Family didn't turn their backs on each other. Fabi had always been a little *different*, as middle children tend to be, but he'd always received the same love and indulgent clemency from their *maman*.

Luc stepped onto the stoop for an after-dinner mint. He was excited, and a little sad. Cliff would be gone, maybe forever, and this might be the last chance to have the whole crew together, ever again. He supposed that he could visit Cliff, maybe bringing Sal and Cava along, and make a nice little road trip up North. Maybe they could even see bears, foxes, or snow leopards. Were they extinct? Did they even live there? Maybe an owl, then. The North *had* to have owls.

The plan was to shower, vest, and drop by Cava's house. His mother would be with Sally and Cava's parents. Luc was making her go. She was always invited to events, but usually declined. Apollonia, such a shy little woman. Luc wondered why she never dated anybody, though to be fair, no one would be good enough, and such a man would be entering the gladiators' arena, if he ever showed his face. They reflected the love that their *maman* gave them with protectiveness, perhaps an excessive amount. As the water splashed his face, his thoughts drifted. *How could he have put her through so much grim this year? How had he put her through so much trouble throughout his whole life?* He felt his eyes sting. Tears were lapped up and confiscated by the pouring showerhead. He sniffed and smiled.

Dried, dressed, and ready to step, Luc made his way to the kitchen.

"You're going to the Doktor's, *maman*?"

"Of course. I said that I would, so I will."

"I'll tell them that you're coming. That means you have to."

"Yes, Luc. Yes, I know."

"It'll be fun."

"You know, I'll be home right after the ball drops. I'm usually in bed by that time… I'm no partier anymore, my love."

"I know, but it's good to have a social life. I can't keep partying for you and JJ!"

"Yes, yes. You party just for us two? You have the social life of an army."

"Not my fault people like me."

"Well, I love you, baby."

"I love you too, *maman*."

"Be safe, and take care of your little friends."

"You be careful, too. Ivan's moonshine is something crazy."

Luc gave his mother a smack on the lips and a big hug. *When a mother is all you've ever had*, Luc thought, *you love them more than most kids love both parents.*

* * *

Humming the little tune along with the knock that he usually applied against Cava's window, Luc elected to enter the house through the front door to wish the Cavanaugh family a happy New Year, and to further solidify the expectation that his mother would get out of the house for the night.

"Oh, that's wonderful Luc, hun," Nora said in a robe with her hair in a towel. "She knows that we're going to Danuta and Ivan's, yes?"

"Yeah, I told her. I said you were all expecting her."

Luc descended the stairs to Cava's room, who, upon seeing his friend, smiled.

"Look at this guy. Coming through the house for the first time in years."

"You wearing that?" Luc referred to Cava's blue jeans and white t-shirt.

"It's a classic," Cava replied. "And... we're just going to a third-floor walk up on X."

"Check this fly little ensemble." Luc separated the teeth of his coat to reveal a tucked in dress shirt, a matching set of burgundy suspenders, and a bowtie.

"Where the hell did you get that stuff? You look so..."

"Fly? Ill? Dope? Chocolate boy wonderful?"

"Nerdy is the word that you're searching for. You're one pair of black-framed cheaters with white tape around the bridge away from looking like the real thing, Urkel."

"Hater," Luc said, in good humour. Cava laughed.

"Yeah. If anyone can pull something like that off, it's you, Luc wit da C."

"We grabbing Sal?"

"Yeah, we'll head over to hers in like half an hour. She said she needed more time."

"She needs hours, and you're rocking a motherfucking d-boy, fla-vourless, white crew neck and denim? Step it up."

"What? Why?"

"'Because she needs all that time to get dipped and dolled for you, you dummy."

"Nah..."

"Word."

Luc went into Cava's closet and shuffled his garments from side to side. "You ain't got much besides hoodies and... well, that. What about this?" Luc pulled out a baby blue dress shirt.

"Easter clothes," Cava replied. "I hate that shirt. My mom always makes me wear it with khakis. I hate khakis."

"I give up. At least you smell alright. Joe's aftershave?"

"Yeah, stole a few squirts. Are we meeting Fink at any point?"

"I called him. Said he would come down after dinner with his folks.

They went to some Ukrainian thing to have cabbage rolls or pierogies or whatever."

The boys looked at each other with visible reticence.

"I'm sure he's coming alone," Luc affirmed.

"Yeah… What are you looking at?"

"Those new kicks?"

"Yeah, why?"

"That burgundy swoosh would look great with these suspenders and bow tie."

* * *

Luc and Cava hailed Sally a little later than 8:30pm, giving her an extra handful of minutes to put herself together.

"Boys, boys, come in," Ivan waved his hand at the friends jolilly. "You two look like you're going to different places. Quinny, you're going to watch a Hammers game, and Luc's going to a spelling bee or a science fair." He chuckled.

Sally yelled something from her room, admonishing her father for taking the piss of her two cohorts.

"Salomea," Ivan began, the way a Greek restaurant owner welcomes an old patron back through the door, "I'm pulling the legs. Don't worry about it."

Ivan offered the boys a glass of homemade clear liquor, which each of them begrudgingly accepted. It was free, but the cost would be immediate gut rot.

"Better than usual," Cava said.

"Yes, yes," Ivan cooed pleasantly. "I added sugars and fruits, give it a better taste, still working on it, but much better."

"You wanna grab Sal, Cavs?" Luc asked. "Or get an idea of how long she gonna be?"

Cava trudged his socked feet up the stairs and gently rapped on Sally's door. It opened slightly, and he caught glimpse of her putting on a pair of earrings.

She turned around and smiled at Cava effervescently. The back lighting from her lamp lengthened her svelte silhouette and gave additional sparkle to her eyes. Cava could only muster an audible open-vowel syllable.

"Looks okay?" she asked, pivoting her toe into the carpet and rotating her slender leg inward. "Sorry about the mess."

Cava gawked at her tidy elegance: a simple black skirt and matching top. Unassuming, but perfectly complementing the stunning specimen's physical frame. She stepped towards Cava in modest heels with a strap over the top of the foot that she'd bought in Amalfi. The gold buckle on the heels matched her golden baby-rope and thin hooped earrings, more restrained than the flagrant circlets donned by her contemporaries. Her hair was flattened and combed straight down with a braided portion that looped from the centre of her head to the back. Cava looked at her light mahogany waves, rebounding the light and shimmering like the ocean at sunset. He hadn't realized, as her hair was almost always coiled in a bun or pulled up in a taut ponytail, that it reached down to the small of her gracile back.

"Man…" Cava uttered, smelling the sweet, though not sugary perfume scent wafting about the room. "I feel underdressed."

"Too much?" she asked with concern.

"Not at all, you look… you look… gorgeous."

She walked across the room and he felt the heat radiating from her face. Flattered and bashful, she took his hand and put it around her. With the pumps, she stood a few inches taller than him.

"Should I lose the shoes? Put on some flats? I feel like a beanstalk," Sally said, putting her head on Cava's shoulder.

"No. They add to your outfit, and you look amazing."

"Shall we?"

* * *

Fink was already posted up on a couch with a big bottle of vodka and a carton of orange juice balanced on each knee. Cliff and his siblings were present, alongside a few other acquaintances.

"Thanks for coming, guys!" Cliff welcomed them with a big, spine-cracking hug. "Sally! Luc! You guys look amazing. Cava—well, you smell nice."

They stashed their booze and admired the barrenness of the apartment.

"Yup," Cliff said. "Got the moving van parked a few blocks down, full of our shit and locked down. Everything here, you guys can help me dispose of, Fury style, sometime early in the morning." He was referring to the practice of leaving couches, mattresses, and anything that couldn't fit in a dumpster in an alleyway. Luc and Cava happily agreed.

"Don't worry about breaking anything," Cliff said. "I mean, don't go putting holes in the walls or ripping the pipes out, but don't stress it. No, Sally, leave your shoes on. What'd I just say?"

"So, are you excited about leaving?" Sally asked Cliff, gently pressing her lips against a glass, leaving a slight imprint of her lips in red.

"Yeah, well… it's salty and sweet, you know? Lots of friends, lots of memories in this place. Not the apartment, this place fucking licks, but Fury, in general. You know, if you asked me two years, maybe a year ago, what I'd be doing, I wouldn't know what to tell you, or how to say it. I guess you have to find something you care about, something that means something to you, and work towards taking care of it."

"You talk to your mom?" Luc asked.

"Why bother? I took the kids to see her on Christmas. She can barely hold it together for a few hours. I told her the plan, and she just acted like it was a weekend trip, or something." He rubbed the heads of the quiet children. They seemed so much younger than first-year highschoolers. "They have some different schools with programs in the North. I already got them in this developmental learning thingy… I dunno, but it seems like a fit for these two. Beyond that, I get to use my hands, work and learn, you know. Make a career out of something."

"We're proud of you, man," Cava started. "You've come a long way, and you're the living proof that people can turn their lives around."

"Any of you guys been in touch with Rosee for the past little bit?" Cliff asked the three closest to him.

"Haven't seen her for a long little while," Cava answered.

"Not since the beach for me," Sally added.

"Yeah," Luc reluctantly declared. "She ain't… she ain't look so great."

"I asked Fink to let her know, if he'd seen her, to come down for a drink or just to say hi," Cliff explained. He nodded at Fink, who returned a thumbs-up and acknowledged that he'd let her know.

"I dunno if she'll make it, man," Luc began. "She's kind of... well, prisoner isn't the actual word, but she's always doped up and loopy, on a couch. Pretty sad. Wish I could do something... we could do something, but you know how it is. She made her choice."

Cliff sighed. "She always had this spark, you know? I always tried to take care of her. Her shit-ass parents, her brother, fuck... I just... I wish that I could've done more, you know? Whenever I tried to explain something to her or teach her something, simple as right from wrong, she'd just rebel. She was always so attracted to bad influences and bad people. If I could mash that drug dealer boyfriend of hers, I would. I really would. But, what happens then? You know? It's fucked up."

The crew nodded and took a sip.

* * *

A few more people had begun to hand-slap and bear-hug their way inside. Perhaps it was the sight of Cliff's little dachshunds pawing at his knees, the sublime nature of a farewell party, or the complexity of the *Reasonable Doubt* record playing in the background, that were simply too cerebral for the more primal areas of the brain. In other words, it wasn't a rager; but it was still early.

Cava and Sally seemed content to stay within an arm's pull of each other, allowing the usually awkward bouts of silence to feel natural, weightless, and warm. As they piled cups, their physical communication became more playful and overt.

Luc was enjoying playing spectator. He bounced around the room, receiving critiques and compliments on his plumage. Watching Sally and Cava, though, brought him a contentment that penetrated his selfdom.

Cliff was emotional, drunk, and with each lap of his apartment, his lumbering gait slowed. He raised the music's volume with every pass and checked the television to see what time it was.

Fink stayed on the couch. He spoke when spoken to, but seemed apprehensive; something Luc was able to pick up on early in the night.

"What's up, man? What's with you? You like a black cloud, or something."

"Chilling, man. This is how I chill."

"You sure, homie? You seem quiet."

"I am quiet. You should know this by now."

"I meant quiet, even for you. You all good? Pierogies got your tummy in knots?"

"I'm chilling."

An hour or so passed, and Luc returned to see that Fink's litre of vodka was draining steadily. He was taking mouthfuls of vodka, then pressing the carton of OJ against his lips, swishing the mixture in his mouth, then swallowing.

"The old mouth-mix, huh?" Luc asked.

"Don't need a cup this way, plus, no one will vick my drink when it's in my hand."

"You ain't even got up to piss, man… How's that?"

"Got a bladder the size of a football. You been watching me?"

"You acting weird."

"Maybe."

"Why?"

"I *did* invite Rosee when I popped by Ali's place. She *did* want to come and say goodbye to Cliff." Fink's face seemed to carry a shred of regret. "She *can't* really come alone. And, he *never* steps solo… So…"

"Aw, shit."

* * *

Around 11pm, Rosee made an appearance, trailed by Tic-Tax and two grubby-looking cats behind him. Gasps dotted the room. She was rakish, dappled with sores, and ashen. She floated in under a stupor; squinting and sniffling, rubbing her red, crusted nose with a coarse denim jacket sleeve that hung past her fingers. The skin on her face was rubbery and hung in loose orbit under her eyes, as if one could manipulate her jowl like clay.

An anxious hush crept in. Some people did not even have to know Tic-Tax or his grimy companions; their appearance was threatening in a room replete with the nonbelligerent.

The quartet made their way to the kitchen, where Luc and Cliff were jawing with some cats.

"You putting booze in there?" Cliff asked one of the black-hoodie wearing brothers who was diving straight for the fridge door.

"Nah, I, uh… looking for chase."

"Got a sixer of Sprite you can have, but if you don't have nothing in there, stay out," Cliff said, sternly.

Rosee stumbled up to Cliff timidly and grabbed his heavy mitt with her little paws. "I can't believe that you're leaving. That's so sad."

"Yeah," Cliff said, his lip quivering as he looked at his young friend. "It's just time. How have you been? You been holding up okay? How's school?"

Rosee blinked lazily and smiled. "Everything's great. Me and my boyfriend are planning a road trip. Right, Alistair?"

Tic-Tax nodded. Luc looked on, seeing the Tic-Tax's other friend hold himself steady against the wall. *Fuck*, he thought. *These guys are already blowed. Suckers need bodyguards.*

Cliff was speaking with Rosee slowly, trying to catch up as best as he could, to pry information out of the little girl, with her handler bearing on her like a shadow. Cliff eventually excused himself, finding Luc and asking him how it got so bad.

"I dunno… It happened fast. One day, she was normal, and the next, like… fucked up."

"It makes me want to cry. Looking at her, seeing the pain and sad and drugs and shit. I want… I want to kill that guy she's with."

"Listen, man. People make their own decisions. They choose their own paths. Look at you. You're leaving in two days, man. You're drunk, and this will all be like a bad dream, I promise. You probably ain't the only cat that wants him minused."

The Delaneys found Fink and sat beside him. They asked for sips, which he declined, not wanting to receive whatever viruses they might've been carrying. Frustrated and disinclined to obey the rules of a regular party, they stepped outside to smoke.

Rosee made her way to Cava and Sally, standing in a corner, happy to be left by themselves.

"Hey guys," Rosee said, appearing a bit more lucid than when she'd arrived.

"Hi, Rose. Long time, no see," Sally said with all the forced jubilation that she could muster.

"Hey, girl," Cava said. "How goes it?"

"Cavanaugh," Tic-Tax nodded morosely.

"Sup, man?"

Seemingly unaware of the reaction that she was drawing, Rosee began to speak, defiantly upbeat. "Not too much. Might go for a road trip, not sure where, but to get away, you know, from the city. Where would we go, Ali?"

Tic-Tax shook his head and shushed her.

"That sounds really neat," Sally said nervously.

"Sally…" Rosee caressed her arm. "You look so beautiful. I'm glad this is finally happening, between you two."

Cava and Sally blushed and looked at each other.

"We're just friends," Sally said.

"Well, Cava is a dope dude. I had my chance and blew it. Don't do the same."

As she uttered those words, Tic-Tax's shoulders hunched.

"What?" Cava asked.

"Don't get any ideas, bud," Tic-Tax said, putting his long, crooked fingers over Rosee's shoulder. Cava raised one eyebrow and shrugged.

A silence followed. Rosee and Tic-Tax sauntered off, leaving Cava and Sally to themselves.

"That guy is so creepy, Quinn," Sally said, grabbing Cava's arm. "Like, creepier than last time, even."

"Yeah, he's a real piece of shit."

* * *

Closer to midnight, the brothers returned from their smoke, showing the effects of what they were inhaling, either stumbling or crashing into people and things.

The entire party was drunk, but not raucous. It was energetic in a way that wasn't destructive. Cava felt his palms moisten as he glanced at the TV, showing the time remaining until midnight.

Luc was performing his duty as unofficial life of the party, hitting on girls and trying to find the right candidate for his midnight kiss.

Rosee was visibly shaking her head and raising her voice, showing a more animated side than what she'd come in with. Cava and Sally watched, but they couldn't make out what she was saying.

Cliff was within earshot. He wrangled Luc and they approached the pair. "What's the matter, lovers?" Luc asked, jokingly.

"Stay out of this, man." Tic-Tax shot Luc a virulent stare.

"He's trying to make me drink the drugs, but I'm tired of drugs. I want to have a good time and not be a sleepy starfish." She turned back to Tic-Tax. "I'm sick of it, Alistair."

"It's medicine," he said, patronizingly, trying to press a cup to her lips. "You'll feel sick if you don't."

"No!" Rosee stomped her foot.

Cava left Sally, who'd finally won the right to use the washroom, to join Cliff and Luc around the argument.

"What, you guys gonna jump me?" Tic-Tax said crabbily.

"No, no, not at all," Luc said with his hands up. "Just… maybe the girl doesn't need her mind melted, tonight, or you know…"

"Yeah, I mean, look at her," Cliff boomed.

Meanwhile, the brothers had stepped in from behind. A standoff.

"Look," Luc said, calmly. "We're all here trying to have a good time, so let's do that. To a good time?" Luc grabbed his cup and held it above his shoulder. Sally made her way over and did the same, as did the rest.

"To a good time," Tic-Tax took a sip and then tried to place it to Rosee's lips, who again, turned her head away. A vein protruded from his reddening forehead.

The crowd dissolved and returned to their separate areas again.

"Shh," Cliff hushed loudly as he turned off the music. "TV's going on. It's about 5 minutes to midnight."

In spite of the tension that was still looming in the stuffy apartment, many people were unaware of any potential fracas. The crowd huddled close to the television; some expensive spectacle was in full motion as the announcers in thick, down jackets and heavy headsets began to recite antiquated poems and read from their bromide script to ingratiate the viewers at home to the magic on stage.

The countdown began. The entire room bellowed along with the slowly descending disco ball on the TV. Luc had his arm around the waist of a sandy-haired girl. Cliff had his little siblings under each arm. Rosee and Tic-Tax were sitting on the couch next to Fink. Rosee was lip synching the count.

At five, Cava stiffly grabbed an equally rigid Sally by her hand, feeling her damp perspiration complement his own. Their fingers slowly interlaced. Standing side-by-side, he pulled her in to face him.

Happy New Years!

He pulled her down for a kiss. At that point, he realized that that was what she'd meant by putting on flatter-soled shoes. Sally bowed her head to meet his lips. She moved her hand from his shoulder to the back of his head.

Cava released her wet hand and put his fingers around her hips. *Incredible*, he thought, both at the present action and the tensile muscularity of her waist. As their lips parted, their foreheads touched, and their eyes met.

"You two need a room?" Luc whooped.

Sally and Cava blushed. She ducked her head onto his.

"Quinn," she said. "I feel weird."

* * *

"Sal...?" Cava asked, concerned. "I'm sorry, I shouldn't have kissed you... I didn't mean to make it weird, I..."

"No," she pressed her index against his mouth boorishly. "The kiss was perfect. I just feel... swimmy."

It was visible to Cava that the booze had seemed to hit Sally like bumpy knuckles wrapped around a roll of quarters. The way she gracefully held equilibrium was suddenly compromised and she began to slur her speech. He looked into her eyes; they looked more stoned than drunk. *Guess this is what happens when you don't get out the house much,* Cava thought.

Luc could be heard wishing everybody in the room luck and happiness, dragging a blond girl by the hand and planting pecks onto everyone's cheeks. He arrived at the corner where Cava was supporting Sally and wrapped his arms around each of them. He hugged Sally and was then forced to act quickly, catching her as her knees began to wobble and her legs gave out.

"Woah, girl," Luc rattled. "You okay?" He turned to Cava. "She okay?"

"I dunno. She was fine just before midnight, and I guess the booze hit her pretty hard."

"*Yeah, the booze hit her pretty hard,*" Sally repeated Cava's statement with sopping sarcasm. "Aww Quinn, so cute!"

She stumbled from Luc's arms to Cava's, rubbing his chest and smacking a little kiss on his chin. "What a slice of cutie pie. And me, without a scoop of vanilla."

"You gonna go?" Luc asked.

"Yeah, I probably should. Pretty quick, I guess."

He left Sally with Luc and went to bid farewell to his friends.

"Cliff," he said with compunction, placing a hand on the thick, sloped shoulder of his comrade. "I think I gotta get Sal outta here. She's fucking gooned."

Cliff began to protest, glancing over to Luc, who was struggling to keep the bleary-eyed girl from toppling over. "Oh, yikes. She went from 0 to 100, quick fast. Well, you gotta do what you gotta do, friends and family."

"Holler at me if you need help moving shit, or whatever," Cava said as Cliff wrapped him in his big, sweaty arms.

"I'll check you out before I leave," Cliff sniffled. "You're a good man, Quinn Cavanaugh. Watch the kids for me."

Cava made his way to the couch where Fink, Rosee, and Tic-Tax were sitting. "I'm out."

"Already?" Fink asked. "Going soft, homie?"

Cava made a nod in Sally's direction.

"Oh shit, the nerd can't handle her liquor, huh?"

"Guess not. I'll catch you soon," Cava said, slapping hands with Fink.

"Word."

Cava shifted his attention to the other two, uneasily. Tic-Tax was sitting with a sulking, sour face. Rosee was seated on the end and seemed spritelier than before. Almost present.

Cava held his hand out towards Tic-Tax, cleared his throat, and said "Ali." Tic-Tax scorned the attempt and shot a quick burst of air out of his nostrils. Rosee looked up at Cava.

"Cava, you're leaving? Already? Why so soon?"

"Uh, Sally is a bit too bent. I gotta get her to her bed," Cava replied.

"Not your bed?" she winked.

"Ha... Nah."

"Cava," Rosee grabbed his hand. Visible sores and scratch-lines were apparent. "I miss the crew... I miss you. Please make the next year... one like how we used to be."

Cava looked in her eyes nervously. He felt a tweaking pain, like a liver shot. Sympathy surged like an exposed nerve ending; it coursed from his toes to his ears. Hot sadness. Amidst his hope was a realization, whether or not she was cognizant of it, that there was no hope. Had she ever known happiness? Love? Actual friendship?

"Of course," he finally nodded. "Of course, I still have the same, well, everything. I'm always around, you got it!" He forced a smile that creaked like old turbines to falsify a satisfactory lip-turn.

Tic-Tax seethed next to her, shooting the two friends loathsome scowls. He looked at the physical connection of their hands and sneered. As Cava turned to collect Sally, he heard Tic-Tax begin to castigate Rosee in a low hiss.

I wish someone would just murk that pebble-toothed cocksucker, Cava thought.

* * *

Cava led Sally down the three-floor staircase, passing puddles of piss and broken bottles. "Someone must have had themselves a go," he said.

She looked at him with a glazed smile. "You're cute."

They didn't have far to go, but at the pace that Sally was clumsily pushing herself forward with, the journey would extend by reams.

Mutants, X-men, and women approached the swaying couple,

offering backpacks, stereos, and whatever else they'd managed to swipe from residents who'd made their way downtown, whether leaving their homes or cars unattended. Sally was in another world. She had the airy, careless demeanour of a happy drunkard who was interested by anything put in front of her. She tried to peruse the stolen items held in front of her, begin conversation with the fiends, and request to stop for greasy food as they passed pizza joints and kebab shops. She repeated how cute Cava looked. He steadied her as she squatted in an alley to relieve herself, giving a crisp $20 to a lady crackhead to use a few sheets of her toilet paper roll.

He raised Sally to her feet. She teetered and covered her face with sudden embarrassment. As he consoled her, she moved her attention to a Chinese restaurant, stating that she hadn't had chow mien in forever. As they continued, she became groggier.

"Here." Cava slid off his shoes. "Put these on."

"What? Quinn! We just walked over a haystack of heroin needles! I'm fine..."

Cava grabbed her hand and hip as she nearly tumbled over, kicking one leg out and snapping her planted heel.

"See, I can just crack the other one off and..."

"Salomea, put my sneakers on," Cava said in a serious tone.

She caved, sliding the right shoe on. "Ha-ha, so loose!" Cava was forced to laugh, charmed by her adorable innocence. She put the other sneaker on, and they continued. "It's so cold, Quinn. Are your feet okay?"

"I'm alright, Sal."

"Quinn?"

"Yes, Sal?"

"Nothing."

* * *

Sally walked more comfortably as Cava watched the ground meticulously to avoid hypodermics and piles of shit. The thunderous sound of shopping carts prompted Sally to ask Cava if they could buy one so he could push her home. He responded by bending down and offering his back.

"Like a camel?" she asked, with delight.

"Like a camel, Sal."

Reaching the intersection of Eckersley and O'Connor, Sally's head was planted onto Cava's back. The little food stands near the train exits bubbled with fiends, kids, teens, young adults, and everything in between. A few fights were already in progress—some fair, some leaning towards random assaults. Cava watched, holding Sally's skirt tightly over her bum as she rotated her head, still laying against Cava's back, to see the disturbance.

"People are dumb," she hiccupped.

"Yes, they are," he said stoically.

"Hey, Quinn?"

"Yes, Sal?"

"Nothing."

* * *

Cava listed towards the Doktor house. The lights were still on, and the sound of metal strings and handclaps were apparent.

"Quinn, no!" she bulleted.

"What? What's wrong?" he responded, concerned.

"You can't take me in there! My parents can't see me like this! Even if you walked me up to my room... I can't."

"Then, what?" he posed.

"Can I... sleep with you?" she asked coyly.

The two had shared a bed all their life, even after puberty. Cava had never felt strange about allowing her to partake in his sheets and pillows. Tonight, he felt more than a sliver of apprehension.

"I mean..." he mumbled.

"Please!"

Cava opened his window and eased her in the best he could. She fell onto her back, her long legs pointed in the air.

"No shoes on the bed, Dad," she flailed with laughter. Cava removed his socks, charred with street, and threw them towards the deepest chasm that he could see.

"I'm gonna run my feet under some hot water," he said as he removed his kicks from her feet easily.

She'd already begun to drift off.

The black and blue colouring of his feet slowly gave way to a ghastly white, then red. He dried them and shot himself a sincere look in the mirror as he brushed his teeth. "You're a good man, Quinn Cavanaugh."

The room was dark as he entered, with only a few slashes of street light leaking in from the blinds. The room smelt of Sally's sweet aroma. He could hear her stir and gently moan as she rustled under the covers. He felt her clothes at his feet. He debated what to wear to bed; normally, it was boxers and, at most, an undershirt. He thought, perhaps, that this time he should don a few extra layers, however. He saw Sally's side profile, lying with her back towards him—her limber, oblique body resting motionless.

He crawled into bed carefully, trying not to disturb her. He noticed his breath entering and leaving his lungs at a quicker pace than normal. Before he could continue that line of induction, he felt Sally turn towards him slowly. She grabbed his left hand, moving him onto his side, and placed it on her breast. She was naked. He could see that her eyes were open, looking into his, as she moved his hand down. She kissed him and put her leg over him. Cava felt a rush of guilt. His heart began racing and, though his mouth was penetrated by Sally's tongue, the breath from his nose was sharp and panicked.

"Sally," he said, pushing himself away. "I don't think I can do this."

"Why?" she responded with annoyance.

"Because, you're not in your right mind. You're not sober... Way past the test."

"What? Foolish. You're being mean."

"How?"

"Listen. I want this. I want this when I'm sober, and I definitely want it now. Please, can we just... please?"

Cava shifted. He moved his hand back up to her hip, then to her hair.

"Sally, I really care about you. Of course, I want this. I have for... maybe forever. I just don't want you to regret anything. I don't want you to not remember. I don't want you to be embarrassed or hurt or anything."

"Then... —she pulled him on top of her and cinched her legs— ... do me."

"Do you?" he flustered.

He saw her face in the little light that was fissuring from the outside. She was nodding and biting her lip with her eyes closed.

"I can't." As he said it, he tried wriggling out of her leglock. She was strong. She was beautiful. He had no issue in motivating himself. But, he couldn't. Not like this.

"Quinn Cavanaugh, you're an asshole," Sally said bitterly, releasing him and turning away.

Cava was nonplussed. *How am I the asshole for being the good guy?*

She rolled back over and straddled him. Lightly tracing her finger over his forehead, she kissed him.

"Quinn?"

"Yes, Sal."

"I..."

"Sal?"

Sally crooked her torso and vomited. She just missed Cava's head and the bed. It wasn't a deluge, but enough that Cava felt her athletic body tense at once and heard a light drizzle hit the floor.

She rolled back and began to weep drunkenly. "I'm sorry, I'm such a goofball. Sorry, Quinn... I feel so loopy."

Cava used a towel to clean up what he could in the darkness. He threw the towel and the bits into the hamper. He was tired and not too concerned about the smell.

"It's okay, Sally. You don't have to cry. It was just like baby spittle. Just a few wee drops. Really! More cute than anything."

Sally sniffed. "Please don't hate me."

"Never," Cava wrapped his arm around Sally. He wiped the water under her eyes and held her naked body close to his. She tugged at his forearm, making him squeeze tighter, and moved her head to kiss his chin.

Before he fell asleep, he remarked to himself how difficult that was, how strange this has all been, how beautiful she was, and how bad her breath smelled.

* * *

It was late. The noise at the neighbour's house had been muffled by exhaustion. The streets, though never desolate, were left to their crepuscular kings and queens, rambling about at an unusually late hour.

Cava and Sally hadn't budged an inch, still conforming snuggly into each other like mess hall trays.

Out of nowhere, a weak tap struck Cava's window. An attempt to peel back the stubborn pane was abandoned for another series of feeble taps. Cava was roused, but Sally was immobile. Cava declined the visit he knew would be a late night or early morning cannon-sized joint with his friend. He wanted the feeling of Sally, squeezed into his chest, to last as long as it could.

Another languid tap, as if by the fingers, followed by a streaking sound, finally made Cava rise. Like a cobra slowly waxing its vertebral column from a wicker basket, Cava moved onto his knees to check the window and to wave his friend off until the morning.

He detected a strange blemish on the window. A smear of something, but no Luc. He clicked his light on and fell, dumbfounded.

Daubs of red, like a child's finger painting, were streaked viscously on the glass.

"Sally!" Cava repeatedly shook the sleeping girl. "Sally, get up. Sally!" His voice grew frantic as she stirred.

"What?" she asked, weakly.

"Call an ambulance, please!"

"Wha…"

"It's Luc," he said, throwing his clothes from the previous night back on.

* * *

Cava flew from his window as if he'd been discharged from a catapult. It had begun to snow since he'd fallen asleep; the light powder barely frosted the projects, but he saw Luc's footsteps and a trail of blood.

He ordered Sally to go upstairs and use the kitchen phone. She fought her delirium and made her way upstairs, unclothed. Cava set to a sprint, seeing a hunched over figure in a parka sitting on the table of the Bench.

"Luc!" Cava cried as he found his friend trying to light a joint. Luc was holding a lighter, trying to get a flame, shaking, clutching his side.

"Why are you here? What... what the fuck's going on?"

"Hey, brother."

"What happened? Sally's calling the paramedics."

"You and her? Nice." Luc coughed.

"Luc, what happened?"

"Well... can you light me a cigarette?" Cava took the pack from Luc's jacket and lit one, made sure it was going, then placed it in his lips.

"Can you hold me?" Luc's voice cracked. Cava hopped on the Bench and wrapped his arm around his injured friend.

A moment of silence took over. The hiss from the cigarette and the stillness of light snow were the only sounds. Even such brevity bore the weight of a life sentence.

"You're going to be okay," Cava said, rubbing Luc's head.

"Yeah..." Luc sighed. He showed Cava his blood-drenched hand before putting it back on his side.

"Who..."

"Tax..." Luc began, with effort. "He was pissed that Rosee looked at you some way... He got in the cups. And the powder. And the pipe. Wanted to have a chat with you."

"What?"

"Told him not to. Shark-teeth pulled his gat. Fink said he had no bullets left. Said that the brothers were dropping pills in girls' drinks... probably Sal's... Cliff lost it... kicked them out. They started getting wild in there... Those cats almost got snuffed out. Tax left Rosee behind. Me and Fink left soon after. Didn't want... didn't want anything to happen to you. Found them. Said I'd... said I'd burn one, you know. Bygones and shit. Fink went home. Stuck up for you. Those guys were mad fucked-up. One of the brothers pulled a blade and twisted it. I dropped... they ran..."

It was quiet again. Cava felt Luc's breathing begin to slow and falter. There was a blustering, wheezing sound as he tried to inhale and a splintering, coarse noise at the exhales.

"It's okay... you're gonna be okay!" Cava tried to sound positive. "A wagon should be here soon, they'll fix you up, good as new!"

Luc sniffed sharply, almost laughing. He coughed. Little spatters of blood landed on the white ground beneath them.

"You spent your time... trying to keep me from getting hurt. I owed you at least one," Luc said as he put more body weight into Cava.

"No... we look out for each other... Hey. What's that GZA lyric? I got ya back..."

"So you best to watch your front. That's my favourite album."

"Remember, we stole that album and the purple tape from JJ with a few weed crumbs and played it in the Trees, before we were allowed to hang out on the Bench? We smoked the bud out of the pipe you stole? We weren't even going to Bendis yet..."

"More," Luc groaned.

"He beat our asses bad. You worse. But then he gave us the tapes after all that... and the pipe."

Luc groaned.

"When we were like, 10 or 11, and our moms got wise to us vicking their cigarettes, so we stole bags of cans from crackheads, took them to the bottle depot, and bought cartons from the Asians. Then you would sell loosies to mutants, and we'd buy more smokes. And cassettes from the pawn shop. And we did that for a whole summer. Then, got our asses beaten by our folks?"

"Course," Luc smiled weakly.

"Remember when we were real young, you'd just moved here from Montreal, and we collected all those dope needles. We didn't even know what they were. We tore the lid off a pizza box and drew a dart board on it, and tried to hit the bullseye? Both our parents beat our little asses bad that day, too."

Luc let a little burst of air out of his nostril and coughed. Blood wetted his lips.

"Remember how, before she went to the smart classes, Sally let us cheat off her? How she'd tap her foot in multiple choice questions and write mega large so I could copy her and you could copy me? Because she wanted to hang with us over the break instead of us having to go to summer school?"

"Your writing was... is... terrible..."

"Remember when I finally got a girlfriend and, even though your life was a living hell, the worst shit that I've ever heard anyone go through, ever, you still snuck into my room and put a box of rubbers in my night-stand with a note wishing me good luck, because I was too much of a pussy?"

Luc made a wistful, approving sound without opening his mouth.

"Remember when my papa died, and I just wanted to be alone. I used to take my Mongoose out, ride to the docks, and just sit there. Remember, you kept following me? I didn't want you to, but you did. I wanted to be alone, but it wasn't safe, and you just kept following me and sitting like 20 feet away from me for, like, eight hours at a time. You didn't tell anyone because I used to go cry there. So no one would see me, because I was ashamed."

Cava's eyes began to water, blurring his vision.

"And then... every couple of days... you moved like a foot closer, thinking that I wouldn't notice... I did, because we were the only two there. I was lonely. I was sad. I was angry and I'd never lost anyone so close to me. And, finally, you just sat right next to me, put your arm around me, and said, 'Next time you see him, you'll have so much cool shit to explain?'"

Cava felt tears steal down his cheeks. Luc's breath was slowing even more.

"And..." Cava was now gasping breaths to try and stop his voice from breaking, "after this year, we'll have way more stories to tell. We can tell some to JJ. He gets home in two days, right?"

Cava couldn't discern if Luc had affirmed him faintly, or if he was just hanging on.

The sound of sirens began to ring in the distance, a timorous echo that neared with each swirl of sound.

"Hear that, brother?" Cava squeezed and lightly shook Luc. "That's coming for you."

Cava held hope that the incoming siren was indeed theirs, but it seemed to fade away as soon as it became more distinct.

"It's okay," Luc whispered. "It's okay..."

"No," Cava grunted. "It's not okay, it's not. I love you. I love you so much."

"I know," Luc said. "I love you, too. I don't feel like I need to prove it anymore."

"You never did, you never had to…. Not even once."

Luc slumped deeper into Cava—this time, with more slack. His hand began to drop from his side.

"Don't!" Cava said, repeating himself in a courageous tone. "Please, don't."

Cava squeezed his friend and placed his hand where Luc's had been. "No, I'm not letting you. Don't go."

"Don't go… please… don't…" Cava sobbed repeatedly.

* * *

Sally was standing two meters behind, wearing a pair of sweats, Joe's work boots, and a flannel that she'd grabbed after calling the ambulance. Her face was buried in the sleeves, pulled over her hands. She was crying, without any ability to control herself. She watched the backs of her friends; one increased the intensity and strength of his grasp while the other's life was draining from his physical body and slumping away.

She wanted to go up and wrap her arms around the two, but she couldn't. They were best friends, and she'd never seen someone die. She couldn't move. If she did, she would fall.

The ambulance arrived. A paramedic pried Luc from Cava's arms, and another joined to load him onto a gurney. Cava's face was deep in his palms. Sally noticed a look of desperation and resignation on the medics' faces, shaking their heads with austere eye contact as they peered at Luc.

Officer Murdoch was the policeman on the scene, arriving as the ambulance was preparing to speed towards the hospital.

Sally had moved in to console Cava, who was beyond crestfallen and absent to the newest addition.

"Your friend was stabbed?" the officer asked Cava.

"I have to tell his mom," Cava looked up with tears in his eyes, his face red.

"No, son… You'd better let me. That's her door?" he pointed.

Sally confirmed.

The officer wore a pitiable expression. He was glum, but seemed to have a degree of empathy that most police leave on the hooks at the station. He asked some questions, received some answers, but didn't press. He seemed to know that this would work itself out on the street, and that nothing he could do would stem that reality.

"Look," he turned his attention to Sally. "I'm going to grab Mrs. Kalou. If either of you know anything, call me, or find me at the station. My name is Shawn Murdoch. Please. You two seem like good kids, and we can handle this in a way that sees that justice is dealt. *Safely.*"

"Can I come to the hospital?"

"No. I'll take the mother, but I don't think that you should. I don't think…" Murdoch bowed his head and sighed for a dreadfully long time.

Things went dark for Cava after that. He didn't faint or pass out, but the night was a blur. Sally said that she'd taken him to his room. He'd still been damp with sweat and blood. She'd told him to shower; he didn't recall any of this when it was told to him later.

Waking the following day, he and Sally emerged from the basement to see his mother in tears. His father was biting down on his jaw stiffly, and Henry was weeping with his head on the table.

"I know," Cava said, feeling his face contort.

Nora hugged them both. Joe cleared his throat repeatedly. Henry went to his room.

Luc's mother had called and told Nora that her baby had died before she and the cop had arrived at the hospital. There was nothing they could have done. Blood loss. Stabbing. Tic-Tax. Brothers. Cava was only able to maintain one syllable thoughts at a time.

He returned to his room and laid in the fetal position. He shut the lamp off and marinated in the darkness. His eyes were busted faucets, dripping no matter how hard he turned them to the right.

"Do you want me to leave?" Sally squeaked, mouse-like, through her sobbing, sitting on the side of the bed.

Cava pulled her down and wrapped his arms around her as she began to convulse. The sight of his bloody shirt on the floor forced him to shut his eyes.

BLACK FLOWER DAY

SALLY AND CAVA laid without as much as a sound for the day, and most of the next.

"I have to see my parents," she sniffled.

"Okay."

"Can I sleep here tonight?"

"Please."

She kissed him softly and left.

Left alone, Cava was drowning in thought. His anger boiled the waters that his sorrow would chill, freezing the squalls and caps in rigid, mountainous pinnacles. He felt lost. He felt an instinct of revenge, but anything done would be sloppy. He knew it was out of character to think about such things, but he also knew the identities of the attackers. Prison would be too nice.

* * *

Sally returned that night, and every night thereafter. The two became nearly inseparable, usually succumbing to laying on their sides and holding each other tightly. The parents seemed to understand their despondency, rarely issuing a word, allowing them to work things out.

On the fourth, with school looming under a week away, Cava's mother entered the room and told them that the funeral would be held on the sixth, two days before classes began. Cava was asked to give the eulogy, and Sally a reading from the Bible.

Cava needed to get up, write, and clear his head. He had to immortalize his friend in front of the most important people in his life. He declined Sally's assistance; it was his duty to Luc, his best friend.

Sally and Cava finally parted ways the next afternoon. She went home, organizing herself to the point of distraction with school and scripture. It was what she knew. It was her meditation.

Cava decided to go for a walk. He hadn't seen the outdoors since *that* night and needed to stretch his legs and mind. He spotted Fink sitting at the Bench, by himself.

"Jesus, been waiting here for you for days, man. You been holed up, or what?" Fink asked.

Cava nodded morosely.

"I'm sorry… I mean, he was my friend, too. But, I'm sorry."

"Yeah."

"Well… that sent those three into hiding."

"What do you mean?"

"I mean, murder. All three. They knew they would all turn on each other, quick fast, so they all ran off."

"Where?"

"Dunno. The cops came looking for Tic-Tax at his grandma's, and it was a huge scene. You didn't see it?"

"Nah."

"Oh man, guns out and everything."

"The Delaney two?"

"Bolted. Probably hiding in some crack house."

"Word. You still got your piece?"

"At home, yeah. Why?"

"Can I have it?"

"Why?"

Cava stared at Fink as if he should know.

"No. Hells no."

"Why not?"

"Because. I took one because I hate getting my ass kicked. Makes you feel powerful, like everyone's your bitch. There's a fat line between a whooping and a murder. Now, I wanna get rid of it. Seeing Tax pull a gun with no bullets on… It looked stupid and weak as fuck."

"Tell me what happened that night."

Fink explained the story in greater detail. After he and Sally had left, the trio began getting amped on whatever drugs they had. The Delaneys were seemingly trying to shake gold in their pans from their drink-lacing escapade, and Tic-Tax was becoming increasingly vicious with Rosee. Almost all the girls at the party were beyond a normal level of alcohol intoxication, and one girl caught a brother dropping something into her cup, red-handed in the act. Meanwhile, Cliff was confronting Tic-Tax about the way he was treating Rosee. The brothers and Tax eventually found themselves in a corner, and Luc stepped in the middle. Tax pulled his pistol out waved it around, saying that anyone that got near him was getting plugged. He tried to pull Rosee from the couch, but she fought back, wanting to stay at Cliff's house. Tic-Tax then commented that he was gonna have Cava's head to teach him a lesson for hitting on his girl. Luc stepped up, and the gun was pressed to his dome. Fink calmly stated: "It ain't loaded." He was more than aware that they'd been ruing themselves for using all their ammunition when they'd lit up the dog fights, failing to secure more. Also, they'd been unable to equip Fink after he'd waited so patiently and obediently. Surprisingly, they made it out in one piece—Luc brokered their exit. Everyone who'd stayed was working on coming down, trying to continue the party and decompress from the episode. Rosee was emotional, crying and breaking apart as drug addicts do when they feel reality creep upon them. Luc said that he had to leave, stating that he had to stop Tic-Tax and that he could cool him down. Fink joined him, just wanting to go to sleep. They caught up with the trio, and Luc began to talk them off the ledge. It seemed fine, and Fink went inside as they were sparking a peacemaking joint.

"Honestly, man," Fink said, after a pause. "I'd just call the pigs. You know who did it. *They* probably know by this point. Just do it."

Cava nodded and thanked Fink for telling him the story. Fink asked Cava if he knew how to throw a gun away, and Cava told him to find a deep enough hole, like a well, and let it go.

Cava left the Ox. He walked down to X and O, not even taking notice of the mutants scabbing their way up and down the street. He looped the area and returned. He felt no more inspired or better than he did before he'd left. He just wanted to go back to bed.

"Quinn Cavanaugh," a deep voice spoke. "You've gotten big."

Cava turned. "Janjak?"

* * *

Cava followed Janjak Kalou into his mother's house. He battled tears as he accepted a big hug from little Apollonia, who thanked him for eulogizing. The eldest brother asked for a moment alone with Cava, which she granted after leaving them a plate of biscotti. Baking helped her.

"She's a wreck… What a year. I'll move her home after this is all said and done. It's not healthy for her to stay here. With all the ugliness, with all the terrible memories. She needs a fresh start, and a man."

Cava nodded.

"Quinn," Janjak said, staring through Cava's soul. "I've been gone a while. I know my brother was getting into trouble, and though I doubt you were part of all of it, I need you to promise me something."

"What's that?"

"Please, don't try and seek retribution on behalf of my brother. Those who had anything to do with his death will be swiftly and right-fully punished."

"But—"

"No buts, young man."

Cava took this seriously. *How did Janjak know?*

"I've seen this too many times. Something happens to someone and someone without a record, without priors or a violent bone in their body, does something foolish and ignorant. Clumsy and emotional. I don't want that for you."

"But, won't you go back to prison?"

"No. So, trust me when I say that everything is taken care of. Names. Who was it? I know my brother worked and rowed with a small-timer named Guppy? Alistair or something."

"Yeah. Tic-Tax. We called him that because of his fucked up little teeth."

"Who else?"

"These two brothers. The Delaneys."

"Already done. Anyone else?"

"No one else I heard of that night."

"Okay, then. How are you parents?"

"Good."

"Salomea? You two married yet?"

"No." Cava blushed.

"Liar. Are you getting good marks?"

"Better than usual."

"Good. Got a job?"

"With the old man.

"Business booming?"

"So-so."

"Nervous?"

"Yeah."

"Don't be. I have to make the flower arrangements and speak to the priest. I don't mean to be rude."

Cava was startled by Janjak's directness. He hadn't cracked a smile, and spoke with such flow and tact. His accent had seemingly changed. He was massive, weightlifter big, but his words fell softly, like water drops from one leaf to another.

"We'll be in touch, young Cavanaugh. You were like a brother to my brother, so you will remain as such to me, brother. I know this is hard. Be strong. He will always be with you."

"What about—" Cava was about to inquire about another brother.

"Don't ask, please."

* * *

"I'm nervous, Sal," Cava whispered to her while they lay together in bed, her head on his chest.

"You shouldn't be. Is it the people? Having to speak in front of a whole mass?"

"Kind of… I still don't fully know what I want to say. How do you start? How do you finish? I hate class presentations, but I've never had to give one about my best friend. Usually it's something like Tibet or Animal Farm."

"Well, sure… This is different, obviously… And, I wouldn't want to take you back, but, I heard what you said to Luc, about the memories you guys had shared, you know, when you were holding him on the Bench."

"Do I talk about that moment?"

"It might be too grim, but it depends if you're trying to be, well, grim."

"I don't think I want that."

"Well, you can still share your moments, your favourite times, the memories that you two built together, why he was your best friend, why you loved him, why we all did…"

Sally was drifting off as Cava ran his fingers down her hair and back. He could hear the rhythm of her breath slow, the cadence normalize, and then a little snort that preluded her adorable little snore. *Like a kitten*, he thought.

Cava's brain couldn't rest, and his eyes couldn't close. He fought the urge to try and sleep, realizing that it would be an unproductive scrimmage of stirring that would wake Sally in the process.

Cava grabbed a pen and a pad and went to the kitchen. The oven clock mocked him. He put the writing material on the kitchen table and flicked the light on.

Staring at the naked blue lines, he wondered if this was even productive. He was tired, but at the same time, it felt as if he'd taken a spike of adrenaline to the neck. He was nervous—unnaturally so. He was scared to begin, and worried about what he might leave out.

He picked up the pen and held it. He wrote an introductory statement. Scribbled it out. Another, which was met with the same fate. Cava lit a cigarette and allowed himself to zone out momentarily.

He began to write.

* * *

Sally and Cava were seated in the front row along with the Kalou family members. Cava held Sally's hand, while JJ wrapped his bison-sized shoulder around his little mother. Fabi sat silently, his hands folded on his lap, drifting in and out of consciousness.

Saint Antoine, the Roman Catholic Church, was packed with friends, teachers, and the congregation members who'd known Luc and were showing support for Apollonia. The overwhelming number of teenagers there was a testament to Luc's charm and popularity—so said the Monseigneur, who delivered the opening address as a family friend.

Sally and Janjak read scriptures. JJ did a reading from Psalms, which he'd chosen himself. His readings revolved around forgiveness, the sins as well as the sinner; to forgive the person or persons that had wronged you. Cava caught him giving a biting gaze towards his brother, sitting beside his mother in a disheveled shirt that needed more than a few strokes of a hot iron. Sally quoted John:14, verses 1 to 4. Afterwards, she explained that her mother had helped her, and that those were the verses that had helped her when she'd lost her parents. Janjak read his verses in a strong voice, unwavering, like Malcom after Mecca. Even though his message was forgiveness, there was an incendiary undertone that Cava picked up on; an unspoken promise of divine retribution from an uncompromising Archangel. Sally trembled at the microphone, nervous, and struck with sadness and the reality of having to say goodbye. She'd glanced at Luc's peaceful, well dressed corpse and began streaking her makeup as of her last, difficult word. She returned and buried her face in Cava's shoulder.

Cava was introduced, and he walked up to the pulpit in a fog. He'd heard the church's orators, actively listened to Janjak and Sally, but was consumed with the sight of his slain friend's visage in the open casket. A forest of black flowers surrounded the oaken coffin.

People always declare that casketed bodies look peaceful. Cava fought to hold onto that thought: that his best friend was taking a big sleep, leaving his mortal carapace behind. He knew Luc too well. Luc was many things—good and unnerving—but never peaceful. The look of indifference that the mortician had fashioned was such that Cava felt strange looking at it. He'd never known Luc to be a neutral, resting being. His spirit, soul, aura, and chakras were too charged, too replete with puckish energies, to allow him to look placid, even in sleep. Seeing Luc like this was depressing. Sure, seeing any dead body would drain optimism from almost anyone; but seeing his mate lying there cold of life *and* spirit was crushing.

As Cava stopped to genuflect and perform the sign of the cross, he saw a little smirk crease Luc's face that he hadn't seen previously. Like the Mona Lisa, Cava could've sworn that he saw a flash of mischief in Luc's face. He thought that maybe Luc had popped in to listen, probably rolling a blunt, getting ready to hear about his legacy.

"There will never be someone who I'll ever be as frustrated with or have more fun with as long as I live."

The temptation to cry disappeared as Cava looked at the audience; he saw his family members tearing up, and Sally's eye makeup running with no shame. He heard sobbing, but he also heard a lot of laughter, genuine laughter, that made people's tears taste sweet.

"Luc could've been anything in the world that he wanted to be, besides a good student. But, I don't think he ever wanted that. Some people are book smart, but my friend was a street genius. He got me into more trouble than I ever dreamed of, but allowed me to have some of the best times… that made the trouble seem insignificant. If Luc was from anywhere else but Fury, he would've been the richest, most successful 17-year-old on the planet. But, he never wanted to leave. He loved this city with all of his heart. He used all of his heart for everything he loved."

He stayed focused on Sally, feeling his eyes threaten to betray his sturdy voice.

"You'd hate it when he made you mad or angry, but still made you smile against your will. That was his charm, as any teacher or parent could tell you. He'd stand up for anyone at any time, had unlimited courage, and was a man without fear. A daredevil. It didn't matter how big the bully was or who he was threatening, Luc with the C had your back. Maybe that's why you couldn't ever stay mad at him. He was too real, too genuine, and all authentic. He told you what the thought and what he felt. He wasn't afraid of showing emotion, even when that can be dangerous in a city like this. People felt his spirit and his lively soul.

They knew that however much mischief he got into, it was never with bad intentions, just from a body with so much energy, it'd explode if it didn't get out. I don't know how his accent never faded after all his time in the West, but it added to his friendliness, and his non-threatening and loveable persona."

"Possessions were nothing to Luc if they didn't bring happiness to other people. He lived to give, and gave everything he had to put a smile on his friend's faces. I remember there was a kid who came to school in Grade 2 and the kids made fun of his glasses. Luc *borrowed* glasses from the church lost and found so that the students would stop making fun of the kid now that two kids had to wear them. They gave him a headache, but no one made fun of the kid anymore. We all have stories of Luc going out of his way to make us feel better, to make us all feel special."

"I have hundreds of stories about Luc, if not more. Maybe a dozen or so... I can tell." Cava told the story about his grandfather's passing and Luc following him to the docks. "He told me that when I saw him next, I'd have the most incredible stories to tell him. I guess... I'll have two people to tell, now."

Cava saw his mother crying into his father's shoulder.

"Never will a day go by that I won't miss my best friend. I'm just honoured to have had a best friend like him. I have to thank Luc for helping me discover what friendship is. True friendship. If I never find that again, it'll only be because he set the bar so high." Cava felt his eyes itch. "There isn't a profound experience that I didn't share with Luc. Everything... everywhere I look in our city, the reflections that I see, are memories that I have with him. I know everybody will have their moments, some songs or an activity, when they know that Luc wit da C would've made it better. Luc and I did everything together. He could make a regular, boring day into something that you'd cherish for a lifetime. It will be hard to do almost anything knowing that my friend should still be here walking this journey with me. Luc was an emotional, sentimental, and forgiving man... I felt his love when I was with him—we all did, and he let us know. He forgave and loved to the point that it hurt him. But, it hurt him more not to. He was selfless and compassionate. He'd give you the shirt from his back or the food from his plate. To suggest that this is any type of weakness, only goes to show how strong he was in character. Luc died a hero, and he's leaving behind memories that I'll cling to forever, until I see him again."

Cava hugged Luc's mother and returned to his seat, where Sally put her arms around him. Janjak reached over and rubbed his thigh with his bear-like paw. Fabi simply nodded, trails of moisture running from his half-dead eyes.

The funeral had come to an end. The reception would be in the Catholic school's gymnasium, though the congregation was warned that it might not be able to accommodate everybody at once. Some people rose to view the body again, others flocked to the reception area or the bathroom.

"I'll catch up with you," Cava said to Sally.

"Are you okay?" she asked, smudging the liquefied streams of makeup on her face.

"Yeah, yeah, I'm good. Just want to avoid the crowd."

"Okay," she said, touching his shoulder. "I should go fix whatever's probably going on with my face. I probably look like a melting zombie."

"You look beautiful." Cava smiled at her.

* * *

The room had finally emptied. Well-wishers who'd come to pray at the casket thanked Cava for his words. He glibly responded at first, permitting only stiff-lipped nods towards the end.

He sat alone in the pews, with the exception of Fabienne to his right. Fabi was swaying back and forth. He began to scratch himself and look around impatiently, almost nervously.

A jarring sound of footsteps purposefully approached the altar.

"Fabienne. Say goodbye to *maman*, and get into the black SUV parked in the lot," Janjak said as he placed his hand on his brother's shoulder.

"Where am I...?" Fabi began to mutter.

"Don't worry about it. I'll meet you in the vestibule. That's where *maman* is now."

Fabi pulled himself up from the bench and rubbed his eyes groggily, then walked down the aisle. Janjak took a seat next to Cava.

"That was a touching eulogy, young brother. Luc would've been more than stirred with the kind truths you spoke. It came from the heart, and was nourishment for the soul. My brother was in good hands when I went away. He died protecting you, after all the years you protected him. It's unfortunate... it's heartbreaking that the life of that beautiful, young boy had to end the way it did. He loved you. He really did. He always wrote about you and spoke about you on the phone. He spoke about you as much as himself, if you can believe that. He's in you, he'll always be with you." Janjak put his arm around Cava and let his head rest against him.

"Are you angry?" Cava asked.

"No, Quinn... I'm sad. Anger does so little to the human condition but blind and sting. I wish I got to see my baby brother, at least once more, but I know that we all raised him well. Yes, of course, he wasn't without his troubles, but considering the lives of my two brothers, he surmounted incredible odds in his short time. No one really dies as long as they're loved and remembered. You tell people you love them. You remind them of how special they are to you. You adore those who you love. You make sure that they know. You leave nothing unspoken and nothing to regret."

"I wish—"

"Wishing is nothing but selfish prayer, young man. Don't wish, simply act, simply do, simply be the best Quinn Cavanaugh that you can be. Honour my brother whenever you can. Use the gift of his spirit to prevail and conquer your fears. Honour him with your own happiness."

"Did you find God, JJ?"

"Man is the true and living; builder and creator of his own destiny; destroyer and plunderer of his own kingdom. I wouldn't say that I found anything. I simply came to the realization that we all manufacture our own successes and our own nightmares."

"I'm just going to miss him so much. Everything reminds me of him."

"Of course. You two have done everything together. You and Luc had a friendship that most will never know in their entire lives." Here, he paused. "Can I tell you a story? One day, when I was locked up, I stuck up for this guy in the shower. Usually, I just went about and did me,

minded my business, and kept my hands clean. I was respected. I had
clout. I had fought so I didn't have to fight. I didn't want anything to
extend my sentence. I wanted out. I felt reformed. I read, I studied, I did
all the bullshit classes and sessions to get myself ready for parole. But, I
was still angry and resentful."

"Luc always said you were innocent."

"Innocent of the crime I was tried and sent away for, yes. Innocent?
No one is."

"Oh..."

"So, the kid that I protected... he was a no one. I don't know why I
helped him out. Maybe it was my anger choosing that moment to release
itself. Maybe I was itching for an unsanctioned tilt, something to prove
my power again. So, I protected him, and he went in PC after. Never saw
him again. Later, one of the guys who'd been trying to attack him came
into my cell with a shiv and tried to plug me. The blade wasn't burnt into
the handle securely enough, and it broke off. It gave me a scrape on the
stomach, but didn't go inside. No worse than a finger nail scratch. Me
and this cat both watched the ox hit the floor. I didn't think anyone had
the gall to step into the arena. I was made. I had back up. Some other
cats saw it and started chanting: 'Kill em, Kalou,' over and over again.
Just like when I was in the ring. It was getting me juiced."

"So, you mashed him out?"

"A CO came in and asked what all the noise was about. I'd covered the
blade with my foot, so I said that the cat must've been looking for some
bristles because his toothbrush was broken. The CO grabbed the busted-ass
toothbrush handle and vacated. The crowd left, but kept an eye on us. You
see, there ain't much to do there, and watching a brawl is about as good as
it gets. I disappointed them. I picked the blade up, my homeboys grabbed
the cat, and I flushed it. They were still restraining him, in disbelief, and I
told them to let him go. I told him that this, I, wasn't worth the trouble."

"And...?"

"Well, he got jumped and beaten, thrown in PC, and I'm unaware
what became of him. That's the life in there. I had a lot of friends, and you
can't control what your friends do on your behalf. I'm sure you know that
to be true. It wouldn't surprise me if he just jumped the wrong cat, either."

"Of course."

"When the blade snapped and hit the concrete, I wasn't mad... I was... something between terrified and relieved. Either I was meant for this earth and saved, or, crazy shit just happens."

"Which one do you think it is?"

"Little bit of both... I think we have to make our own meaning out of this infinite craziness."

Janjak sat silently for a moment. Cava wondered what he was thinking.

"Gibran said, 'If you would indeed behold the spirit of death, open your heart wide unto the body of life. For life and death are one, even as the river and sea are one.' He was something of a heretic, so I thought it a little gauche to use that passage in a church." Janjak shrugged.

"It's nice, though," Cava hummed.

"It is. I read a lot during my incarceration. Best way to pass the time." Janjak looked behind him and saw Joe waiting patiently in the aisle. "I have to make sure that Fabi doesn't run off... Quinn, please, if you ever need anything, let me know."

Cava thanked Janjak and watched his father shake hands with the eldest Kalou. He made Joe look compact, like a featherweight.

Joe slid into the pew, with his eyes forward as he mumbled a prayer in Latin, performed the sign of the cross and sighed.

"Son. Son... this is real pain."

"I know, Dad."

"I'm sorry for your loss. It's everyone's loss, but maybe you and his mother's the most. I'm sorry you lost Luc."

"Me too, Dad."

Joe kissed his son's head and walked backwards down the aisle, dipping his fingers into the holy water and making the sign as the big church doors creaked close. Cava remained. He sat alone. He sighed.

Eventually, he turned his head to examine the stale forbearance of the church. He and Luc were dismissed as altar boys after one day; Luc had snuck the chalice containing the blood of Christ and gotten tipsy. Cava hadn't done anything wrong, but they'd always been a package deal. Cava smiled. He saw Sally sitting a few pews back. He gestured her over.

She walked slowly and sat beside him. They stared at the casket.

They held hands and sighed. Nothing needed to be said. Sally wanted to thank him for his words, his stories, and sharing his memories. But, she felt that he knew what she was thinking.

"Quinn?"

"Yes, Sal."

"…Nothing."

She laid her head on his shoulder. He smelled her hair, kissed her head, and caressed it.

"Sal?"

"Yes, Quinn?"

"I love you."

"I love you, too."

BEAUTY IN THE THORNS

SHE SAW CLIFF drive his trailer down the road with Thunder and Lightning. Her little arm waved them goodbye, limply, like a moribund plant's wilted leaves given counterfeit life by an eastern wind. Courageous streams of morning light were breaking through the muscovite blanket above, enough to bring awareness to the visibly multiplying fits of shaking that were strumming the tendons beneath her cellophane skin.

She squinted and felt something escape from her eye and roll down her face. She dabbed her cheek with the back of her wrist and began to rub her arms. She shivered, feeling the tremors attack from somewhere deeper in her body. Looking at her moist knuckles, her bony wrists, and frail arms, she rubbed them, trying to thwart the shaking that was creeping up her spine. She felt the quaking in her stomach and in her throat, as well as each protruding, blue vein beneath her jellyfish pigment.

She smoothed her hand over her bumpy network of vessels and randomly plotted ulcers. She couldn't look at them for long. The snow, like bullet casings on the beach in Normandy, bounced the miscreant sunrays into her eyes, forcing more unintended droplets down her face.

"No more," she whispered. It'd been two days since she'd been released. She worried about her friends, as well as what his reactions and instability could impose. That concern was far less imperative than her own well-being. Her own life.

He'd probably come looking for her. She was certain. She was *his*, and he'd made that abundantly clear. Her previous attempts to escape were always met with the same conclusion. He finds her, does whatever violent or soul-punishing thing he has to do, gives her some medicine, and keeps her.

She began to walk. She'd never been so cold in her life. She'd never been so hot, either, both at the same time. It was like being entombed in dry ice, a stinging burn that made walking and even holding a thought nearly impossible. Her joints were stiff and snapped with each step. The rigours of the journey forced her to sit on a random stoop.

Mutants who'd once begged her for darts and coins passed by her without notice. She felt a force lift her, help her to her feet, walk her in a straight line, and turn her left. She hadn't opened her eyes; the searing pain was making them throb.

"I'll give you a rock if you suck my dick," came a leathery voice as she felt her jeans, already hanging below her hip bones, being pulled down. Her back was against a hard surface.

She opened her eyes. It was dark: an alleyway. She couldn't make out the face in front of her, but saw her tattered underwear being pulled to the side. She hiccupped spittle, which repulsed the stranger. Pulling up her jeans, she stumbled away as fast as she could, trying to scream, but only capable of a crackling wheeze.

* * *

X and O. One way was her home, or rather, her house: The Orch, the home of a mother and father who hadn't once tried to locate her. Had they even noticed that she hadn't been home in months? That she hadn't been to school in just as long?

The other was medicine. Something to make her feel better. To regain the cancerous homeostasis that would take the sharp things out of her body.

But, him.

He'd start the cycle over again. He'd take her world and squeeze it into sand.

The itching set in. Amidst the burning, freezing, and aching in her bones and organs came the tingling of her skin, which made chickenpox feel like a fawning caress. She dug her nails into her elbow pit, using all her might to refrain from peeling her skin back like a Christmas orange. Her face itched like maggots were hatching from beneath, trying to burrow their way out with limbs made of shrapnel.

She heard shrill horns blearing as she stumbled across the intersection. The gusts from the motorists were enough to swing her body. Her gait was no more than a kite with incremental tethering: bobbing, shooting forward, moving parallel, a step back, five paces forward, rocking on her heels, a pivot backwards, left and left again, forward. She could barely see; it was so bright. Moving cheek-to-jowl, she scraped along the juxtaposed houses. A sliding door opened automatically.

"Get in, get in. Knew you'd come crawling back, bitch."

She groped her way to the couch. It hurt to sit; the soft cushions were no more forgiving that the closing jaws of an iron maiden. Thick sweat pumped alongside the gasping of painful breaths. She thought to herself that she'd died and come back as a bruise.

"Look at you, fucking bitch. Fucking coward. What have you done to yourself? You don't think I'd forget? Huh? Like I should forgive you? Cunt!

"But, I hurt," she croaked.

"You will, but I want you to feel it."

She tilted her head and saw him working a plastic card vigorously against the coffee table, hearing the sounds of rummaging through plastic packages. She opened her eyes to see him about to warm the underside of a spoon with a lighter.

"Smoke…"

"Whatever."

The frantic sound of more hunting around concluded with

something pressed in her lips. She inhaled, but not enough to fill her lungs. He hit the pipe with a chamber-filling cloud. She took another. She felt the pain begin to siphon out of her. The prickling, the itching, the hot and cold. She was drowsy. He pressed it to her lips again.

"No, I'll puke," she whimpered.

"Fucking dumb bitch," he said before taking a loud pull.

She felt the pain trill from her skin, into her organs, and then, numbness. She heard him cursing to himself, pacing around the carpet and laminate floors. The sound of curtains being pulled. More swearing. Oven knobs being flicked on and off, over and over.

She felt him sit near her. He was breathing hard. He was tapping his calf with his hand at a staggering pace. She heard him grab the cordless phone, start punching in numbers, and then, turn it off. Again, the curtains. Again, the oven knobs. Again, the phone.

"You stay fucking put," he ordered, dropping the phone on the table. "I have to check on something. Don't you fucking move."

Lying on the couch, with her head in her hands, she opened her eyes. Her vision returned to something akin to what a hollow-tip sees while readied in the barrel. She grabbed the phone and pressed three numbers as quietly as she could.

"9-1-1, what's your emergency?"

"Please save me. He's going to kill me," she cried.

"Who is, ma'am?"

"Please, just come soon. He has a gun, and drugs and…" she heard him coming up the stairs. She quickly tried to get the address out. He reached the penultimate step as she hung up, putting the phone on the table and shutting her eyes.

"Who were you talking to?" he barked.

She felt the brain-melt kicking in.

"I asked you a question."

"… you… I asked… how you are."

"Well, aside from my bitch staying with that fuck-head, I got big problems." He went back to the kitchen window and pulled the blinds again.

She could only lie on her side. It gave her a fuzzy memory of something when she was a child. Laying on her back, just waiting, with her eyes closed. She used to close her lids so hard that it created a dull pain on her eyeballs, generating little sparks in the darkness. She tried to focus on the pain of her eyes.

She could only wait, and hope that her call made it through. He was pacing. He would only stop occasionally, to look at the phone and then, look at her.

"You use the phone?" he said with alarm. "I didn't leave it like that!"

She didn't answer. She feigned snoring, which made her drowsier. She felt like succumbing to sleep. At least she wouldn't feel anything when his rage finally rose enough to force his hand.

"Answer me! What the fuck's going on? They found out about… Wait. You! Did you call the cops, you fucking slut?" He pulled her by the hair to a seated position.

"We can see you though the window. Come out with your hands on your head!" a man's voice ordered from outside.

"Fuck them, and fuck you. I ain't going easy."

He emptied a bag of crystal shards onto the coffee table as the girl watched in horror. He took a gun from his waistband and began smashing all of it under the handle, grinding the big chunks into smaller ones.

"That's like seven grams," she said gravely.

"Then, this is a seven-point smash." He moved the granules with his gun-palm into an open hand and put the hand to his muzzle. A big sniff left his nose and mouth covered with crystalline splinters. His eyes were red. He gurgled and screamed hoarsely.

"Let's go," he said maniacally as he grabbed her by the hair.

He pressed the nozzle to her cheek and walked her out the front door, using her as a shield. "You bitch. You fucking traitor. I'm glad we stabbed your friend."

She had no clue what he was talking about. She felt the gun touch her teeth through her cheek. She saw the police brandishing their pistols. She felt him navigate her towards the edge of his lot. She felt the incredible, tense strength in his arm that was choking her. She could barely make out what the cops were saying, or what he was screaming back at them.

"Let her go," a cop said authoritatively.

"Fuck you, pig!"

She felt a moment of calm, like when a storm finally breaks.

"It's not loaded," she squirmed her neck loose for long enough to drain her energies and purge her lungs and voice-box for a harpooning shriek.

"Bitch," he muttered as his long, spidery limb hooved her in the back. He turned and ran with inhuman speed. Two cops pursued him, while one cop hit the radio in his car. The third rushed to the girl who skidded along the wet, dirty-cold pavement, scraping her chin and chest.

"My name is Shawn. Are you okay, young girl?" the officer asked as he cradled her head.

She couldn't make out his face with the hazy light jutting in from behind. She began to cry.

"It's okay, it's okay… What's your name, young girl?"

"Rosee."

"Alright, Rosee… That's a pretty name. You're going to be okay."

KICK ROCKS

THE WARM SPRING corroborated with what was looking to be an early summer. Making good on his promise, Cava hadn't passed a day without thinking about Luc; missing him and loving him in memory. It hurt. It was a hurt that ran deep, and buckets of wellspring were pulled up by any nostalgia that his memory used to quench itself.

"One day," his mother told him, "you'll look back at the memories, and there will be less sadness. Only a kind of happiness."

Cava doubted this. How could he ever not feel sorrow when he thought of his friend's life, taken and unable to be reclaimed?

"You listening?" Fink asked.

"No, sorry... What'd you say?"

"Ugh... I said that two discs are better than one, obviously."

"I dunno, yo. 36 Chambers is beyond a classic. It's gonna be like Mozart or Beethoven for our grandkids," Cava reasoned.

"*Forever* has *two discs*. And one of them, you can play on the computer and shit."

"I don't even have a computer."

Fink shook his head and the two kept walking. Cava sorely missed Luc in times like these; the simple and mundane chores of killing time. The walk to and from school, the alleviation of ruining boredom, the ability to broach a random topic and actually broaden each other's perspectives.

"Maybe, because it's new…" Cava said as he dropped back a step to kick a crushed soda can he'd been dribbling. "Maybe, I'll end up loving it more."

He kicked the can in front of Fink, who stepped over it. He went back and kicked it in front of Fink again, who again, walked past the can.

"Why the fuck do you always do that?"

"Kick the can?" Cava said, innocently. "Just something we've always done."

"It's stupid."

"What?! Is not! One time me and Luc kicked a can from the Ox to goddamn Vincennes. You know how long that is?"

"No, and I don't really give a shit. I ain't Luc."

"Yeah. *I know.*"

They walked silently for a while, Cava still kicking the can.

"You ever junk your bammer?" he asked.

"Yeah. Took a boat from Fig to the island with my folks and let her go off the ferry. Almost had second thoughts."

"You might learn how to fight better this way," Cava laughed.

Fink stewed.

With only a block remaining, Fink seemed to be obsessing over Cava's simple game.

"Seriously man, that's fucking annoying. It's like nails on a chalkboard."

"Check me," Cava said, squaring his shoulders and turning towards Fink.

"I told you, I ain't Luc!"

Fink went to kick the can away, but he whiffed. He kicked a thick stone that hopped over Cava's foot and skipped down the soft shoulder. They watched hopelessly as it bounced towards a parked vehicle. The rock danced along the gravel, kicked up, banking off a divot, and finally, colliding with a license plate. The license plate of the black SUV read "Singh."

"Oh, fu…" Cava began, turning to see Fink hot-stepping, holding his falling jeans by the waist and running the other way as fast as he could.

"Fuck. What a fucking pussy."

He approached the driver's side, slowly. He heard the illegally tinted automatic window being rolled down. For a flash, he saw the pained expression on his own face. It disappeared, and the unsmiling mug of his ex-girlfriend's cousin appeared.

"Get in." The sound of automatic locks clicked.

* * *

Cava obeyed, unaware of any other option.

He crept into the backseat and saw Janjak's smirking face looking at him. Almost smug.

"The look on your face, young Quinn. Want a ride home?"

"Uh… I live that way," he said, pointing behind him as Joti drove in the opposite direction.

"Scenic route," Joti said quietly.

Cava had been seeing JJ semi-regularly. He and Sally were invited for dinner at the Kalous once every couple of weeks, and they always attended. He liked Luc's oldest brother; he was smart, wise, and serious. He was a great man to consult regarding any questions, and they could reminisce over Luc, *my god*.

"How's the lady?" Janjak asked, a small smile on his face.

"Uh…"

"Ah," JJ said knowingly. "You were never expected to marry his cousin, young brother. You're allowed to do what you wish, Quinn."

"Still."

"Look, kid…" Joti said, looking at him through the rear-view, "I love my cousin, but she was never cut out for life here. It's too… Well, it's different. You're a good one out of all these… people. She enjoyed her time with you, and you treated her well. You were caught up, J told me, in some heavy shit. Pretty brutal. I'm proud that Anjuli kept her focus on herself and her studies. I'm protective, but I'm… new school. I don't have any grudge with you. You don't have to worry. You're the friend of a friend, which is a pretty good position to be in. Just, you know, keep your nose clean."

"Easy," Cava said. "Sal is good. I got her to accept a scholarship from New Am U."

"I'll have to congratulate her," Janjak said. "And, the two of you?"

"Doesn't matter where she is or I am. We'll always be together."

"What will you do?" Janjak asked.

"I'll work towards getting out. Need to upgrade my classes in college if I hope to join her. So maybe one or two years of that, then..." Cava trailed off.

"Good. You hold onto her as hard as you can," Janjak said.

"Yeah, she's great," Cava said, warmly.

He was amazed that, much like Anj, Sally was intelligent, beautiful, and too good for him. She was different, however, because she had the virtue of coming from the same place as Cava. She wasn't hood; she was too intelligent. She was smart enough to preserve her innocence and too smart to be naïve. She understood the mistakes that Cava had made, and why he'd been noosed into some of his adventures. She'd lived through the times of his life that'd mortified her, that'd caused disbelief; instead of anger, she'd sought solutions. Most importantly, she accepted him for exactly what he was and what *he* wanted to be. She had loyalty, the kind that one can't hope to learn, only to socialize and enculturate. She made him *better*.

"Sorry, what?" Cava asked.

"I said, did you read the Khalil book yet?" Janjak asked.

"Yeah, I can grab it for you if you want."

"Nah, it's yours now. Keep it... with my Liquid Swords tape."

"The cover says 'Dear Julius,' inside. Who's that?"

"Beats me, got it from the prison library. Originally, I wanted to use it as a vest."

"A vest... Oh, jeez."

"Phone books work best. That's why you stay out of trouble."

"Of course, of course..."

They pulled into the Ox and Joti put the car into park.

"We should have one more dinner before *maman* and I move."

"You guys are moving?"

Janjak nodded. Cava didn't need to ask why.

"Aww, I don't want new neighbours," Cava joked.

"Hopefully you won't have any, Quinn," JJ responded. "You go with her. Getting out is the best thing you can do."

"What happened to Fabi?" Cava blurted.

Joti and Janjak looked at each other.

"He was taken far away to get the help that he needs," JJ said coldly.

"You need anything. Ever. You come to me, Quinn," Joti said with his hand out.

"Thanks... but aside from maybe keeping an eye on Hank, I'm gonna go it on my own."

"Good man," Joti nodded at Janjak.

"I told you," JJ replied.

"I owe this man," Joti pointed at Janjak. "My life... His family is my family. His needs are my duty. You remember that."

"I will. Thank you, Amajot."

Cava said goodbye and thanked them for the ride. He hopped out of the car and saw Sally waving from the window. She made a funny face and stuck her tongue out.

He leaned in and said to Janjak: "To return home at eventide, with gratitude."

"Ah, your lovely Almitra awaits." Janjak smiled. "Take care, and see you soon."

Cava walked over to Sally in the window.

"Do you want to come over for dinner? Mom's making goulash!" She yelled with a bursting smile, radiant and authentically silly.

What a perfect woman.

"Tell him to bring bread. We need more bread for that Irish belly!" he heard Ivan hollering from elsewhere in the house.

"Stop yelling! You'll upset the tomatoes," Danuta yelled.

"Quinn, can you come in for a second and talk to your aunt Kathy in St. John?" his mother bellowed out their window. "They're going for dinner, and she wants to hear from you."

Cava took Sally's invitation before walking over to his door. He had an unshakable smile on his face. He held his hand out at the window to receive the phone. Sally ran up, smacked a kiss on his cheek, and hugged him.

"Want to come to the store with me?"

* * *

Sally and Cava walked to the little Polish market to get a morning fresh loaf. They sidestepped the mutants and fiends as they walked down Eckersley with linked fingers. The present was becoming a long-awaited past. The giant middle finger drifted towards the sky in the backdrop. Cava glanced up as Sally spoke about getting him into New Am University. It called out to him. *"Quinn Cavanaugh, get the fuck out of here."* The height of the tower swallowed the sun and brought dusk earlier than nature had intended.

The city was changing at a swift pace. Trap houses and crack shacks were being foreclosed by city planners, scurrying the rats from the crumbling foundations with all the copper wire that they could carry. Soon, slick, glass-faced condos and chain stores would be built from the River City Centre, spreading outwards, inviting a new brand of citizen with no memory and no fear. The homeless protested outside city hall. Where would the slings and slurs of the other Fingers be aimed? Where could the most vulnerable seek refuge from the steamrollers and contractors that saw this damaged city as something to raze and raise anew?

People were already beginning to take the train *to* Fury to work from the other boroughs, something unprecedented in the city's history, as if a rope of miners with bulb-helmets were queuing at the entrance with pick axes. Money was being injected into its veins like steroids, and Fury was swelling with structures and transplants. The underbelly was already being forced to coagulate in smaller, more desperate pockets; unlike Vincennes, however, there would likely always be stretch marks and scars. Fury was learning how to dress to conceal the ugliness.

Fury became a city the way a piece of floating debris becomes a life raft; it was a blue-collar refuge in an area where escalating costs drove poor folk to avoid drowning and survive as long as possible. The Furians, *Furies*, were survivors. They were a tough breed. But, what would happen